Praise for Lynn Michaels and *Mother of the Bride*

"Throw the rice and cut the cake!
Mother of the Bride is a winner."
—Julie Garwood

"This humorous romantic comedy warms the heart with its zany yet believable characters and snappy dialogue.... Michael's keen sense of comic timing and oddball characters never fail to entertain."
—*Publishers Weekly*

Return Engagement

Lynn Michaels

IVY BOOKS • NEW YORK

Return Engagement is a work of fiction. Names, places, and incidents either are a product of the author's imagination or are used fictitiously.

An Ivy Book
Published by the Random House Publishing Group

www.ballantinebooks.com

ISBN 0-8041-1961-9

Manufactured in the United States of America

First edition: October 2003

OPM 10 9 8 7 6 5 4 3 2 1

In memory of Frances Lee Maxon

Our dear friend has gone away,
But we'll see her again some sweet day.
She'll be here to greet us with the door open wide,
She'll reach out a hand and draw us inside.

Someday when life's full course has been run,
She'll open her arms and say, "Welcome home, hon."
But until we cast off this mortal shell,
We shall miss you, dear heart, more than words can tell.

—Betty Nicoletti

Chapter 1

NOAH PATRICK sat on the beach. He'd slept here last night, under the pier with a couple other bums. They'd built a fire, illegal as hell, but only if you got caught, and offered him rotgut wine. He'd declined. He told them his name when they asked. They'd grinned and asked for his autograph. Neither of them had pencil or paper so he'd written his name with his finger in the sand and watched the surf wash it away.

That's what gave him the idea.

He hadn't had the brains to quit drinking till it was too late, till he had nothing left. No career, no money, no place to live. Hopefully, he had guts enough to simply sit here and let the tide take him.

The sun was almost gone, just a thin orange smear on the horizon. He heard the murmur of the surf, could see the tidal surge beginning to lift toward shore. Wouldn't be long now. Wouldn't be easy, either. He was California–born and bred, raised on a surfboard, swam like a dolphin.

His instinct was to fight.

Noah closed his eyes and focused on how he'd do it. Just lie down. Pretend he was floating on his board like he used to when he was just another sunburned, bleached blond kid on the beach. Before Hollywood came knocking and made him a TV star.

He did fine till the breakers started booming and slapped spray in his face. He kept his eyes shut but he panicked. He was doing this wrong. He should've swiped a board from the idiots surfing in wet suits and paddled out past the breakers. It was December. Hypothermia would kill him before he drowned.

He had to force himself to lie down, shivering on the wet

sand, his teeth clacking like the one and only time he'd had the DT's. He'd really fucked that up. If he hadn't checked himself into detox, he'd be dead already instead of lying here freezing to death.

He drew a breath, bracing himself for the next wave. No one would miss him. He'd fucked that up, too. Hadn't bothered to make himself likable when he'd had looks and money. Nobody bothered when they were on top—only when they hit bottom.

Maybe he'd wash up someplace snazzy like Malibu, where paparazzi were as thick as starlets sunbathing without their bikini tops. If the fish didn't chew him up too bad, somebody might snap his picture, run it in the tabloids.

Dead, he might attract enough attention for a movie of the week. Four-hankie dramas about tormented celebs doomed to die young were hot. They wouldn't be hot forever, though, so the next breaker had better gets its ass moving and get up here and get him.

Noah opened one eye, saw the surf roiling and curling back on itself for another crack at him, shut his eye and thought about his movie. His former network might snap it up for old times' sake. The rights belonged to his parents. He'd signed them over in his will.

His will. Fuck. Noah opened his eyes and blinked at the first stars popping out in the sky. Where was it? And where the hell was that goddamn breaker? He was freezing his balls off here waiting to drown.

If his mother had any say, they'd cast Brad Pitt to play him. Not his first choice, but he could live with it so long as they made him shave that scraggly, sorry-ass beard. They wouldn't need a leading lady. He'd never gotten around to marriage. He'd been too busy drinking himself half to death.

If the fucking tide didn't hurry, he'd have time to finish the job. What the hell did a guy have to do around here to drown? Noah pushed up on one hand, swung his head toward the water, and took the six-foot breaker that came crashing ashore full in the face.

It knocked him flat, drenched him in cold seawater and rolled him like a ball up the beach. Body-slammed him onto the sand and slid away with a sigh. He gagged saltwater, and over the pounding in his ears heard the building roar of the next breaker coming and a scream in his head.

Get up and run, you dickhead!

What if they couldn't find his will? Or refused to make Pitt shave? The network would screw his parents and every Nielsen family in America would think he couldn't grow facial hair. That wasn't the way he wanted to be remembered.

And this wasn't the way he wanted to die.

Noah struggled up on his hands, his feet dug into the sand like a runner taking his blocks. He'd lost his left shoe, flung his head over his shoulder to look for it and saw the next breaker rushing toward him, white capped and thundering ashore. Fuck the shoe. Noah pushed off, stumbling and falling, racing the breaker up the beach.

He beat it by inches, felt icy water curl around his ankles, slide harmlessly past him as he fell on his hands in a pool of hissing foam, exhausted and breathless, black spots swimming in his vision. When he could, he reared back on his knees and sucked air into his lungs. His eyes and his throat burned with salt, but he was alive. Alive, by God.

Now what?

Find the winos, build a roaring bonfire, and get arrested. Spend a warm, dry night in jail and get shipped to a shelter in the morning. They'd give him clothes and shoes, a hot meal and a few bucks if they had it to spare. He'd scout a place to flop and get a job. Not that he could do anything but look good for a camera, but he'd figure something out.

He already knew he wouldn't try this again. Next time he'd fling himself off an overpass. A nice, *dry* overpass. *If* he tried this again. Maybe he'd give sobriety a shot first. The guys at AA said if he could make it five years he had a chance. He was going on two. Jesus. No wonder he'd wanted to kill himself.

Noah staggered to his feet and up the beach, bruised and aching from being slapped around by the surf. His soaked clothes weighed a ton and goose bumps the size of boulders popped on his skin.

It wasn't dark yet but it was getting there, the orange in the sky fading to violet. There was twilight enough to see the low wall edging the beach and the strip of shoulder beyond it that ran along this stretch of highway between L.A. and Malibu. A car, a Mercedes he thought, was parked there and a woman smoking a cigarette sat on the wall.

A woman he knew but hadn't seen in . . . shit. A lotta years. It took him a minute to recognize her. She was older and she'd cut her hair. Changed the color, too, he thought, but the memory was vague.

"Oh Christ," he said. "*You.*"

"You were expecting your fairy godmother?"

Noah wheeled away and wobbled back toward the water.

"Where are you going?" she asked.

He swung around to make sure it was *her*. Fuck. It was.

"Seeing you makes me think I do have the guts for this after all."

She laughed and got up, flipped her cigarette in the sand and went to the car. Came back with a blanket she tossed on the wall as she sat down and unscrewed the cap of a stainless steel thermos.

"Come have some coffee."

"I'd rather get arrested."

"Say the word and I'll call 911 on the car phone."

She would in a heartbeat, but she had coffee and a blanket and he was so cold his bones were chattering. On the set of *Betwixt and Be Teen*, the TV series that made him a star, he used to say if you looked up the words *stone cold bitch* you'd see Vivienne Varner's picture next to the definition. A number of the crew said you could find Noah Patrick's autographed publicity shot below the description of *soulless bastard*.

"I had a car phone once." Noah snatched up the blanket. Three-inch thick merino wool with a silk-stitched hem that made him shiver as he wrapped it around him. "I had a car, too."

"At one time, as I recall, you had six."

Noah dropped onto the wall beside her. "Thanks for reminding me."

Vivienne filled the thermos cap and passed it to him. He raised it to his mouth with both hands and drank. Straight from Rodeo Drive, blended, freshly ground, and scalding. Just the way he liked it.

"What are you doing here, Vivienne?"

"I've been looking for you. Not personally, of course. The detectives I hired. Had to turn over a lot of rocks to find you."

"If I owe you money you'll have to see my accountant. This time of day he's usually passed out under the pier."

She smiled, leaning forward on the wall with the heels of her hands on the edge, her narrow face turned toward him, her head cocked to one side. "I see you haven't lost your sense of humor."

"But you can see I've lost everything else. What do you want?"

"A better question is what do *you* want, Noah?"

A drink, he almost said, because he did. He always would, they'd told him at AA, but he didn't claw the walls for tequila anymore.

"The coffee will do me fine, thanks," he said and took another slug.

"You were never a great actor, Noah, but you're a natural in front of a camera. You play guitar and you have a pretty good voice. You're no Gregory Hines, but you can hoof it if you have to and not fall over your feet. Those are your good qualities. On the negative side, you're a miserable excuse for a human being."

He snorted into his coffee. "Takes one to know one, Vivienne."

"That's why I'm here."

Noah shifted on the wall to face her. She looked good for an old broad. At least one facelift, but that was drill in L.A. She had on dark leggings and ankle boots, a burgundy turtleneck and a white cashmere jacket. Gold on her wrists, diamonds in her ears and a glint in her eyes that Noah might have mistaken for tears if he didn't know her so well.

"You aren't dying, I can only hope?"

"Not yet. Not by a long shot." She laughed, took a gold cigarette case out of her pocket, opened it, and offered it to him.

"I quit," Noah said. "I think."

Then he shrugged and took a cigarette. She lit another one for herself and slipped the case and her gold lighter back in her pocket.

"If you had a phone," she said, blowing smoke through her nose, "you'd probably be the only person in L.A. who would take my calls."

"I've been out of touch, but let me see if I can guess why." Noah dragged on his cigarette, waited till the nicotine rush passed and said, "Your mean-as-cat-shit disposition and your piranhalike charm."

"My best qualities ten years ago," she said with a wistful sigh. "Nowadays Hollywood is so politically correct you can't say *shit* even if you have a mouthful. My clients are bailing like rats off a sinking ship. I need an image overhaul and Christ knows you do."

"I've killed a lot of brain cells, Viv. Where are you going with this?"

"Everybody in this town knows you're a drunk and I'm a ball breaker." She swung around on the wall to face him. "They know you hate my guts as much as I hate yours, that for the entire six-year run of *Betwixt and Be Teen*, when you and Lindsay weren't fighting—"

"Lindsay?" Noah interrupted. "Lindsay who?"

"Lindsay Varner. My daughter. Your costar on *BBT*."

"Oh, Lindsay. I thought you said Leslie." Noah smacked the side of his head. "Must have water in my ears."

"As I was saying. When you and Lindsay weren't fighting, you and I were. I bad-mouthed you all over town. You lost jobs because of me."

"Goddamn it, Vivienne!" Noah leaped to his feet, sloshing hot coffee over his hand. He was so chilled it felt good. "Thanks a lot!"

"Oh, stop it." She grabbed the blanket and yanked him down beside her. "You knew all this before you pickled your brain."

"I did? Oh. Well, sorry then," he muttered into the thermos cap.

"You quit boozing two years ago." She edged closer, hands raised and gesturing, her cigarette swirling excited smoke rings into the near darkness. "So all we have to do is clean up your act and put the word out that you're starting to get parts again, that you're doing good work—"

"Parts?" Noah's ears pricked. "I'm getting parts? Where?"

"In a minute. You're getting parts, you're doing good work. You're responsible and you've lost the attitude."

"If no one will take your calls, Viv, how do we get the word out?"

"We give them a story they can't ignore. You and Lindsay teamed up again. *BBT* was the hottest show on TV. You two were on the cover of every teen mag in the world. The Justin Timberlake and Britney Spears of the eighties."

"We were?" Noah asked uncertainly. "Did we like, date?"

"Hardly," she snorted. "I wouldn't allow it. You were half-lit most of the time and you went through women like you went through tequila. Studios are screaming for remakes. Networks want reunion shows. The timing is perfect."

Noah remembered the tequila, every golden drop of it. He wished he could remember the women and Vivienne's daughter. He remembered her Jessie to his Sam, the boy and girl next door who grew up together and fell in and out of love. A few pawnshops on Hollywood Boulevard still stuck TVs in the window and turned them on. He knew from the reruns of *BBT* episodes he caught while he panhandled that Lindsay Varner had been blond and slim and pretty, but that's all he knew.

"I thought tear-jerker biopics were hot," Noah said.

"Five minutes ago. Now it's Return to, Back to, whatever."

Noah stared at the tide whooshing up on the beach. If he hadn't chickened out, he would've drowned himself for nothing.

"A reunion show, huh?" he asked. "TV or theatrical release?"

"A play, for starters. I have it all arranged."

"I'll just bet you do. What do you get out of this?"

"The credit for salvaging the wreck of Noah Patrick." She rocked back on her tailbone and smiled, her fingers laced around one knee. "I'll be the Mother Teresa of Hollywood agents. I'll have to beat clients off with a stick."

"I suppose you and I will have to make nice."

"Kiss-kiss for interviews absolutely. You'll be the son I never had."

"What do I get? Besides a second chance?"

"My guest house to live in till rehearsals for the play

start. A car. A wardrobe. A grand a week salary. And providing you *do* clean up your act, behave responsibly, and lose the attitude, complete the six-week run of the play and the option time if it's a smash—and I'm sure it will be—a cash settlement of one hundred thousand dollars."

Noah thought about it for a nanosecond, then looped his arm around her shoulders and jostled her against him. "You know, Viv. Deep down inside I always liked you."

"Oh God you *reek*!" She shoved him away but she laughed, then clapped her hands on either side of his head, flattened his uncut-for-Christ-knew-how-long hair against his skull and peered into his face.

"What are you doing?"

"Trying to see how much of that heartthrob face is left under this Sasquatch-lives beard of yours."

"Gimme a razor and a couple facials and I'll bet you ten I can still get picked up in a juice bar."

"Juice bars are long gone." She let go of his head. "It's tofu now."

"You'll want me to sign a contract."

"Drawn up by my attorney and waiting at the house. Along with a bathtub and a razor." She passed him the thermos, stood up, and took her keys out of her pocket. "You ready to blow this pop stand?"

"You betcha." Noah clutched the thermos and the blanket in one hand, the cap in the other, and followed her to the car.

"You don't mind if I open the sunroof," she said as she started the engine. "I don't want to pass out from fumes."

"Open 'er up," Noah said cheerfully, hunkering down in the blanket with his second cup of coffee as Vivienne pulled onto the highway. "So where's the play being staged?"

"It's opening out of town." She glanced at him as she wheeled the Mercedes toward Malibu. "I don't have to tell you that in L.A. at the moment a marquee with your name on it wouldn't draw flies."

Damn right she didn't have to tell him. "Chicago or Philadelphia?"

"Belle Coeur, Missouri. My daughter runs the theater."

Noah sipped his coffee. "So Lindsay's still in the business."

"Lindsay owns a bookstore in Belle Coeur. She has a fifteen-year-old son, so she won't go on the road. My daughter Jolie runs the theater."

"Lindsay's married, then?"

"Widowed." Vivienne glanced at him, then back at the road. "You don't remember her at all, do you?"

Noah couldn't explain why he remembered Vivienne and not Lindsay. Just one of the tricks his booze-riddled brain played on him.

"Don't take it personally, Viv. For a long damn time I couldn't remember five minutes ago." Noah turned his head and looked at her. "What's the play?"

"Jolie wrote it." Vivienne smiled at him. "The title is *Return Engagement.*"

Chapter 2

LINDSAY VARNER WEST hated television. Long before she costarred in *Betwixt and Be Teen*, she thought TV was the surest, deadliest killer of intellect ever devised. Unfortunately, her fifteen-year-old son Trey loved TV. It was the greatest disappointment of Lindsay's life.

Her second greatest disappointment was Noah Patrick.

She read about her *BBT* costar's fall from grace in *Entertainment Weekly* and *Us*. She saw clips of his arrests in L.A. for driving drunk and showing up late or not at all on movie and TV shoots as she passed by the family room where Trey, despite her best efforts, always seemed to be surgically attached to the big screen TV.

It was thinking about Noah that made Lindsay say yes when her sister Jolie asked if she'd please-please-pretty-please-with-sugar-on-it take the role of the female lead in the new play she'd written. How could she bemoan the waste of Noah's talents if she refused to exercise her own?

Feeble as they were, in Lindsay's opinion, but she said yes to Jolie, anyway. And then promptly forgot about it.

Until the morning her sister swept into The Bookshelf. It was Tuesday, April first, and it was raining, the sky gray and low-slung with clouds, the sidewalk outside the store littered with maple buds blown off the trees lining Main Street by the blustery wind.

Pyewacket the cat slept in a ball of ebony fur on the glass display case above the counter. Lindsay had just unlocked the door and stepped into the cash wrap when Jolie burst in, tossed a water-spotted clear plastic folder on the counter, and spun out again before the door had a chance to close.

"Sign on the dotted line," she called over her shoulder. "I'll come by the house tonight and pick it up."

The door fell shut, the sleigh bells hung against it clanging, before Lindsay could open her mouth. Pyewacket cracked one emerald eye, rubbed a raindrop off his nose with a paw, and went back to sleep.

"Was that Jolie?" Emma Harrington, the eldest of Lindsay and Jolie's Fairchild cousins, leaned around the doorway at the back of the store that led to the offices. "Or the rain blowing the door open?"

"It looked like Jolie." Lindsay wiped water spots off the plastic cover and read aloud to Emma as she walked up the center aisle to the front of the store. "But according to this, it was Jolene Varner, CEO and Creative Director of Belle Coeur Entertainment Group."

"Was this person wearing a raincoat? Or carrying an umbrella?"

"No raincoat. No umbrella."

"Then it was Jolie. Let me see that." Emma pushed through the hinged half gate behind the sales counter and took the folder from Lindsay. "Yikes. This is an honest to goodness contract."

"Let me see that." Lindsay took back the folder and opened it. "My gosh. It *is* a contract. I didn't think Jolie could spell the word."

"Hmmm." Emma let her glasses fall against the breast of her red sweater by the gold beaded chain looped over the earpieces. "Do you suppose she's still dating that slick-haired lawyer from St. Louis?"

"I don't care if she's dating the Antichrist if he can drum some business sense into her." Lindsay skimmed the first few pages clipped inside the folder. "It's a contract, all right. Between the party of the first part, Belle Coeur Entertainment Group, and the party of the second part, me. It asks for a commitment of six weeks, from May twenty-fourth to July fifth, at the Belle Coeur Theatre, with an option for six more."

"Whoa," Emma said. "What are you going to do with it?"

"Sign it." Lindsay flipped to the last page and wiggled her fingers at Emma. "Hand me a pen before Jolie comes back and yells April Fool."

Emma gave her a Bic ballpoint and a frown. Pyewacket woke up and took a swipe at the pen in Lindsay's fingers.

"Group implies more than one person," Emma said. "Who do you suppose Jolie has hooked up with to form Belle Coeur Entertainment?"

"Jack the Ripper and Attila the Hun for all I care," Lindsay said.

She signed the contract in all three places that asked for her signature and wiped water spots off the plastic cover with a Kleenex. Then she tucked the folder in the middle drawer of the small oak desk she'd had built into the back wall of the cash wrap.

The drawers and pigeonholes under the rolltop lid were as perfectly ordered and precisely compartmentalized as Lindsay's life. If you could put your hand out and know exactly where to find a paperclip—or your fifteen-year-old son—you had a fighting chance against the Chaos waiting to trip you when you weren't looking. When you were careless and not vigilant. When you let someone you love out of your sight.

Or outta your clutches, Ma, as Trey frequently grumbled. More often these days with his sixteenth birthday looming in August. The only thing scarier than the thought of Trey behind the wheel of her Honda Civic was the thought of

Trey with a pilot's license. Lindsay had put the kibosh on flying lessons the one and only time Trey had mentioned them a year ago. *Not in my lifetime,* she'd told him with fire in her eyes. *When I'm dead and buried and not one second before.*

Lindsay shut the drawer, turned around, and saw Emma looking at her like she was Jolie. Like she'd just come in out of the rain with no coat and no umbrella. "What?" she said.

"That's the first impulsive thing I've seen you do since . . ." Emma pressed her lips shut. "Well. Let's just say in a long time."

"Since the night Mark and I eloped," Lindsay finished for her.

The day after he'd graduated from the University of Missouri at Rolla and three months shy of the church wedding they'd been planning for four years. Since Mark was a freshman and *BBT* was in its third season as the number one comedy-drama series on network television.

"It's all right, Em," Lindsay told her. "I won't swoon if you say Mark's name in my presence."

"I know that." Emma shrugged. "I just don't like to upset you."

Oh, come on, Em, take a shot. Upset me. Please, Lindsay opened her mouth to say, but the numbness inside her, deep down, that had been there since Mark died, welled up in her throat and wouldn't let her. Every once in a while a spark flared—like just now with Emma—but the numbness always rose up and squelched it.

"Mark's been gone eight years, Em. I'm not grieving anymore."

"If you say so," Emma replied and turned out of the cash wrap.

At least that's what Lindsay thought she said over the squeak the gate made as Emma pushed through it. "Wait a minute," Lindsay said.

"I have invoices to finish." Emma tossed her a backward wave. "And you have special orders to unpack."

"I do?" Lindsay eyed the empty wire stock cart pushed up against the half-wall of the cash wrap. "Where?"

"UPS," Emma called and disappeared through her office doorway.

Five seconds later, Lindsay heard a horn honk and gears grind and looked out the front window at the big brown step van spinning mud off its tires as it stopped at the curb. Lindsay frowned and rubbed the chill on her arms. She hated when her cousin did that. Sometimes Emma couldn't help herself—she was Dovey Fairchild Harrington's daughter, after all. Still, it creeped Lindsay out.

Trey thought Emma was ultra cool. He bugged her constantly for lucky lottery numbers. "Ask me when you're eighteen and old enough to buy a ticket," she told him, but he kept at her. He knew better than to ask Great Aunt Dovey.

By 12:45 Lindsay had scanned the UPS shipment into the PC and phoned all the customers on the special order list. She'd rearranged the Easter display of children's books in the front window and alphabetized the Cooking section. When Emma came back from lunch, she lifted her sage green trench coat off a hook in her office and tucked the contract in its plastic folder in her briefcase shoulder bag.

The rain had stopped and watery sun seeped through the clouds. The wind was still brisk enough to ripple the puddles on the sidewalk. Lindsay tied the scarf she usually wore around her neck over her head and struck off on foot for the Belle Coeur Theatre.

Downhill to the river, then up the flights of wooden steps and landings known in Belle Coeur as the Staircase. It climbed the limestone bluffs rising from the boardwalk on the riverfront, past shelves of rock dripping with rain, pine trees deep blue all year round, and hardwoods a tender shade of early spring green.

The Staircase had nearly killed Lindsay the first time she'd hiked it after she left L.A. for good and came home to marry Mark. Though she could make the almost one hundred foot climb keeping pace with Trey, she took her time today. At the top, where the bluffs flattened out above the Missouri River in a wooded ridge that ran for miles, all the way to the southernmost city limits, sat the Belle Coeur Theatre.

It looked like a barn because that's what it was. A gigantic, three-story red barn with a limestone foundation built into the bluff on its east and south sides. The west-facing, cross-planked steel doors were tall enough and wide enough to admit a tractor-trailer with room to spare. Everyone in the family, on both the Varner and the Fairchild side, and most everyone else in Belle Coeur, simply called it the barn.

Lindsay came off the Staircase on the north side, in the crumbling blacktop parking lot, the spaces so faded you could barely make them out when the pavement was dry. A red canvas canopy scrolled with BELLE COEUR THEATRE in white stitching stretched over the box office window and the entrance. Its scalloped edges snapped in the wind, which pasted Lindsay's coat to her legs and pushed her across the lot.

The bricks in the courtyard built around the sycamore trees planted by Lindsay and Jolie's grandfather bulged over the roots. In summer, the black iron tables and chairs Jolie set out under the trees wobbled on the uneven surface. Tourists thought it was charming. Lindsay thought it was a lawsuit waiting to happen.

The front entrance, two sets of double glass doors, was unlocked. The strip of duct tape Lindsay had seen on her last trip to the barn was still slapped over a fracture in the left-hand door. She'd offered to buy new doors, but Jolie had declined. She'd said no to paint and new carpet for the lobby, too. She said no to everything Lindsay offered. Taking the part in the new play was the only thing Jolie had ever asked of her.

Lindsay pushed through the doors, expecting to smell musty rug and dingy paint. Instead, her nose filled with something pungent enough to make her eyes sting. Paint remover or stripper, she thought, as she stepped through the tiled foyer into the lobby and saw Jolie, in her usual uniform of denim overalls, T-shirt, and ball cap turned backwards on her head, standing on a scaffold between two ladders. Cans with open lids and a heap of rags sat at her feet. She held a strip of wet wallpaper.

"Nice pattern," Lindsay called, nodding at the light robin's egg blue background wound with pale green leaves. "I like it."

Jolie jumped and looked at her over her shoulder. "Lindsay," she said, her voice sharp. "What are you doing here?"

Lindsay took the contract out of her bag and waved it. "Signed, sealed, and delivered."

Jolie frowned, pressed the strip of paper to the wall, and smoothed it down. "I told you I'd pick it up later," she said, a why-can't-you-do-what-you're-told snap in her voice.

For a second Lindsay felt like she was sixteen again, not thirty-four, and still under their mother's thumb. Jolie sounded so much like Viv*enne* Call-Me-Vivian-and-Die Varner, and looked enough like her—same red gold hair and whiskey brown eyes, same small nose and pointed chin—that Lindsay suddenly wanted to slug her baby sister.

Her heart pounded and her fist clenched. Then the numbness welled up and Lindsay sighed. Her fingers opened and she took off her scarf, unbelted her coat, and sat down on a worn-slick velvet bench.

"I was out anyway," she fibbed, wondering how Jolie had come up with the money for the wallpaper. "So I thought I'd drop the contract by and save you a trip out to the house."

"Gee, thanks." Jolie put the lids on the cans and turned around on the scaffold. "I planned to arrive at dinnertime so you'd have to feed me."

"Come anyway," Lindsay said. "You're always welcome."

I've told you a million times, she didn't say. *You don't have to make up excuses,* but Jolie always did. Some were logical enough to qualify as reasons. Most were so feeble they made Lindsay's heart wrench.

"So." Jolie tipped her head to one side. "You signed the contract?"

"Yes. I told you I'd do the play. I won't break my promise."

Jolie's head tipped the other way. "Did you read it?"

"Yes," Lindsay lied. "I read every word."

"And it's okay? You don't have a problem with anything?"

"The contract is just fine. I agree to all terms."

"Great." Jolie grinned. "What's for dinner?"

"Pork chops. Who wrote the contract?"

"Bill Rich." Jolie grinned. "The slick-haired lawyer from St. Louis."

"Ah." Lindsay nodded and rose. "Dinner's at seven. See you then."

She left the contract on the bench and headed back to The Bookshelf, smiling because Jolie was coming to dinner, happy because she'd kept her promise. Vivienne had broken every promise she'd ever made to Jolie. Lindsay had vowed she'd never break a promise to her sister. Not ever, no matter what.

Her attorney, Susan Fairchild, daughter of Uncle Frank, Vivienne's brother, would have a cow when she found out Lindsay signed the contract without allowing her to review it. *If she found out,* Lindsay thought, deciding not to tell her. She'd forgotten more about entertainment law than Susan knew, anyway. And besides, she trusted Jolie.

"The only problem with that," Emma said when Lindsay got back to the store, "is that Jolie doesn't trust you."

"I'm not Vivienne, Em. Eventually, Jolie will learn to trust me."

"You've been telling me that for sixteen years, Lindsay. Hell will freeze before Jolie learns to trust anybody. Especially you."

Pyewacket sat on the floor between them. He looked first at Emma, then at Lindsay. If he had eyebrows, Lindsay thought, he would've cocked one at her as if to say, "*Well?*"

"Thanks, Em," she snapped. "Do you enjoy being a wet blanket?"

Emma blinked at her. Lindsay turned away and went back to her office. Shut the door and sat down at her desk. She shouldn't have said that to Emma, but Emma shouldn't have said, "Jolie doesn't trust you." What Emma should have said was, "Jolie doesn't like you."

The cordless phone resting on its base at her right elbow rang. It rang again and her name flashed on the caller ID screen above her home phone number. Lindsay smiled, picked up the phone, and said, "The Bookshelf," because it ticked Trey off when she said, "Hi, honey."

"I'm home," he said. "I didn't get mugged at school and the bus didn't crash on the way home. I managed to walk up the driveway all by myself, unlock the door, pick up the phone, and use speed dial to call you. And I'm only fifteen. Isn't that amazing?"

"Stunning. Any homework?"

"Geometry," Trey said and made a gagging sound.

"I'll check it when I get home. Jolie's coming to dinner."

"Cool. Want me to do anything?"

"Check the pork chops. If they're still frozen, give them a minute or two on defrost in the microwave and put them back in the fridge."

"Will do, Ma. See you at six."

A little after four Lindsay went up front. Emma was straightening the magazine rack. She saw Lindsay coming, turned, and walked past her without a word, heading for the storage room between their two offices.

Lindsay pushed through the gate into the cash wrap. Pye stretched on the PC monitor, his eyes slits and his tail sweeping over the screen.

"I didn't have to call her a wet blanket," she said to the cat as she lifted his tail out of the way. "I could have called her the Voice of Doom like the rest of the Fairchilds."

Lindsay pulled up the traffic report that Emma's sister Darcy, an MIT grad, wrote to track the number of customers and the amount of each sale in four-hour increments. Emma herself was a CPA with an MBA from MU in Columbia and a tax and bookkeeping service on the side. Damn clever people, those Fairchilds.

Only fourteen customers. Rainy days were usually busy, but it was tax time and business would be slow till Uncle Sam got his due. Lindsay left the cash wrap and found Emma organizing the overstock magazines.

"I can handle the store till five if you'd like to leave early, Em."

"I'll stay." She lifted a thick stack of *Glamour* off a shelf and wiped it with a rag. "I've been meaning to dust these shelves."

"Yesterday you were up to your armpits in 1040s. I thought you could use the extra time."

"I think you just want me to leave." Emma tossed the rag aside and turned to face Lindsay. "So you can brood about Jolie."

"I was perfectly fine until you said she doesn't trust me."

"So now you're trying to think up a way to prove I'm wrong."

"I really *hate* when you do that, Em." Lindsay chafed the rush of gooseflesh that sprang up on her arms. "I wish you wouldn't."

"*If* I could read minds I wouldn't have to bother with yours," Emma retorted. "I've had a ringside seat watching you bend over backwards trying to make up to Jolie for all the rotten stuff Vivian did to her. And I've watched Jolie let you."

"Jolie hasn't let me do a thing for her. Not one thing."

"Fixing Jolie's life isn't your job, Lindsay. It's Vivian's, since she screwed it up when she took you to Hollywood and made you a star and left Jolie in Belle Coeur. Not that Vivian's likely to come back and take responsibility. Any more than Joe Varner is apt to put down his guitar and his Jim Beam long enough to remember he has two daughters."

The heat in her cousin's voice surprised Lindsay. Emma couldn't stand Vivienne. Few members of the Fairchild clan could, truth be told, but Emma adored Joe Varner. She owned all five of the CDs Lindsay and Jolie's father had managed to stay sober long enough to record.

"What happened to you don't like to upset me, Em?"

"Jolie is not a powerless child anymore, Lindsay. She's twenty-eight years old. If she wants Hollywood or New York so damn bad, why doesn't she pack up and go?"

"L.A. is a huge step, Em. I've tried to encourage Jolie." Lindsay had offered to bankroll her sister, too. "She's afraid and I don't blame her."

"Oh Lindsay." Emma shook her head. "Jolie is lazy and vindictive. You got the Hollywood career and Vivian's attention. She got left behind with my mother and Aunt Sassy when Joe Varner lit out for Nashville. In Jolie's jealous little brain you stole what should have been hers. This play has Time to Pay Up stamped all over it."

You don't know that, Lindsay wanted to say. *You can't see that,* but Emma could. A lot of the Fairchild women saw things and knew things. Some of them heard things. Lindsay had, but only once. The day Mark died. Fifty miles away from the cornfield where it crashed, she'd heard his single-engine Beechcraft splutter and stall.

"Humor me. Get that contract back. The State of Missouri gives you three days to change your mind. Let Susan get you out of it."

"I promised Jolie I'd do the play, Em. I won't renege on her."

"Fine. Then I will leave early." Emma swiped up her dust rag and wheeled toward her office.

The sleigh bells on the front door jangled. Lindsay sighed, went up front, and met Wilburta Allen, one of their best customers. She was halfway through ringing the latest Oprah title for Wilburta when the back door slammed, loud enough to echo through the store. Lindsay's fingers jumped on the keys and the register gave her a you-dummy beep.

"Sorry, Wilburta." Lindsay voided the sale. "Let's start over."

The chubby gray-haired woman, wife of Chub Allen, the sheriff of Belle Coeur, wore jeans and a sweatshirt that said GRANDMAS ARE BETTER THAN CHOCOLATE CHIP COOKIES. She slid two twenties across the display case and cocked her head toward the bang.

"That Emma leaving?" she asked.

"Yes." Lindsay gave Wilburta her change and the register receipt. "The store is slow today but Emma's tax business is booming."

"Figured it was Emma." Wilburta tucked the coins and bills in her wallet and snapped it shut. "Nobody throws a hissy fit like a Fairchild."

Lindsay slipped the book into a blue plastic sack with the store name printed above a graphic of books jumbled on a shelf. If Wilburta stopped at the Country Mart food store or McGruff's Hardware on her way home, everyone in Belle Coeur would know by suppertime that she and Emma had argued. The price of living in a small town.

"Enjoy your book, Wilburta." Lindsay handed it to her with a smile. "I'll see you next month."

"If this one's as depressing as the last you won't," she said tartly.

As soon as Wilburta shut the door behind her, a gust of wind ripped up Main Street, strong enough to strip maple buds and rattle the front window. The door blew open and the sleigh bells jangled. Lindsay crossed the store to shut it, her nerves jumping. Pyewacket went with her. She grasped the knob and looked at the cat, sitting beside her on the floor swishing his tail.

"I could slam this door," she said to him. "I could slam it and have a hissy fit but I won't. Not this time. But next time I'll slam it for sure."

Lindsay shut the door and locked it, turned the sign in the window and sighed, feeling calmer. Pye wound around her ankles and purred, followed her to the cash wrap and sat on the display case while she closed the register and made out the bank deposit. He chased the vacuum cleaner cord while she swept the floor, went with her when she carried the trash out to the Dumpster behind the store, and jumped on the hood of her blue four-door Civic.

Lindsay went back inside for her coat and her purse. She killed the lights and locked up on her way out, pressed unlock on her keypad and let Pye into the car, slid behind the wheel and started the engine.

"Next time Emma throws a hissy fit," she said to the cat, "I'll throw one right back at her."

He blinked at her as if to say, *"Right,"* and went to sleep.

"Smart aleck cat." Lindsay smiled and scratched his ears.

Pyewacket knew she'd no more throw a hissy fit than Wilburta would fail to buy Oprah's next pick. But it was comforting to know that *next time*, the mantra that had saved her sanity in L.A., still worked.

Next time, Mama, I'll know my lines. Next time I'll smile for the camera. Next time, Mama, I promise. Just don't be mad at me. Please.

That's how it had started, when she was thirteen and timid and Vivienne's approval mattered. By the time she was fifteen and locked into *BBT* by an unbreakable five-year contract, the mantra was *Next time she yells at me I'll yell back. Not this time, but next time.*

She never yelled at Vivienne—though she'd sworn she would, next time for sure—and she'd only slugged Noah once for putting moves on her that weren't in the script. Until her eighteenth birthday. Vivienne threw her a lavish celebration, her first adult party. It was the second most awful night of Lindsay's life. The first was the night Mark died.

The next day she called Emma and sobbed long distance to her cousin. A day later Lindsay was in Belle Coeur, the only place she'd ever wanted to be, and married to Mark. The network threatened to sue but chose not to, to avoid negative press. Vivienne disowned her. Jolie spoke to their mother a couple times a week by phone. Lindsay hadn't seen or spoken to her in nearly sixteen years.

Lindsay drove to Belle Coeur Bank and Trust and slipped the bank bag in the night depository, then followed Main Street the rest of the way to Business Alternate 152. She turned left and followed it to Ridge Road, which meandered east away from Belle Coeur in big loops and lazy curves, around tilled fields of wet, black earth, past budding, butter-yellow forsythia hedges and windbreaks of barely green trees.

A quarter mile shy of the split rail fence that marked the front property line of the farm Lindsay bought Mark as a wedding gift, Pye jumped into the backseat, then up on the rear window ledge. Sometimes he went home with Emma, sometimes he stayed at the store. On the nights he went home with Lindsay this was his ritual; to jump in the back window and watch behind the car. Strange cat.

Lindsay turned into her driveway, a wide blacktop ribbon gleaming with puddles and lined with sprouting daffodils. She drove past the front of the house, built of red brick and dove gray siding with a long, wide front porch tucked under the shake shingled roof.

Jolie's dented, rust red Ford pickup sat in the driveway. Lindsay smiled, pushed the remote clipped to her visor to lift the overhead door, and drove into the attached three-car garage. Pye leaped out of the Civic and shot through the cat door into the house. Lindsay followed, pressing the wall switch to shut the garage as she stepped into the kitchen.

A Dominos pizza box sat on the counter. She sniffed it and smelled pepperoni, her favorite. A two-liter bottle with the cap off fizzed on the counter in a pool of Coke. Her foot stuck in a spill on the blue tile floor. Lindsay frowned. Trey was allowed pizza only on weekends and Jolie knew it. She hung her purse and her coat over the back of a chair and stepped into the polished hallway that shot like an arrow up the middle of the house to the family room where the big screen TV blared.

Trey and Jolie sat on the gray leather couch, a half-eaten sausage and black olive pizza in a box in front of them, their blue pebbled glasses making rings on her oak coffee table. Jolie swung away from the TV and grinned at Lindsay when she stepped into the doorway.

"Surprise," she said. "I bought pizza so you wouldn't have to cook."

"Thanks." *First wallpaper,* Lindsay thought, *now Dominos.*

"Hey, Ma. Grab some pepperoni." Trey bounced up on one knee on the couch, the corners of his mouth red with tomato sauce, his thick bang of wheat-blond hair swinging over Mark's almost navy blue eyes. "Nick at Night's doing a back to back of *Betwixt and Be Teen.*"

"Yeck," Lindsay said and feigned sticking a finger down her throat.

"Aw, c'mon, Ma," Trey cajoled. "They're showing the episode where Jessie decks Sam for kissing her after he wins the football game."

The kiss was written into the script. Noah sticking his tongue down her throat and the belt in the mouth she gave him wasn't, but the director had liked the energy it gave the scene and ordered a rewrite to accommodate it.

"Oh good." Lindsay smiled. *Oh well,* she thought. *It's only one pizza on a Tuesday night.* "That's my favorite episode."

Chapter 3

EVERY YEAR the Belle Coeur Theatre began its season on Easter weekend. Saturday afternoon at four o'clock they opened with a production of *Chick the Chocolate Bunny*, a children's play written by Jolie.

It was an all-kid extravaganza, cast from the ranks of the junior high and elementary school and students from Aunt Sassy's Belle Coeur Academy of Performing Arts. When Lindsay and Jolie were students there, the Academy was called The Sassy Steppers Dance Studio. Things change when an alumna makes it big in Hollywood.

There weren't that many Varners left, but every one of them helped out on opening weekend. It was tradition. The Fairchilds pitched in, too. On the whole, the families got along well. Both could trace their roots in Belle Coeur back three generations, to the 1880s when Lindsay and Jolie's great-great-grandparents, Seth and JoEllen Varner were the town's cultural leaders. The fact that the Fairchilds despised Vivienne almost as much as the Varners didn't hurt anything, either.

Since Emma was buried in filing extensions for late taxpayers, Trey went to work with Lindsay Saturday morning. They closed The Bookshelf at noon and made a pass through Burger Chef for milkshakes and cheeseburgers. When she turned out of the drive-thru, Lindsay punched the gas. The tires squealed and the Civic shot down Spring Street.

"Whoa, Ma." Trey unwrapped a burger and broke it into pieces for Pyewacket, perched like a vulture on the edge of the backseat. "It only takes fifteen minutes to get to the barn from here."

"Uphill and down, uphill and down." Lindsay took her foot off the gas. "There's no flat, straight way *to* any place *from* any place in this town."

She loved Belle Coeur, but not today. Today the bluffs carved out of the native limestone by ancient glaciers, where the city founders for some cockamamie reason had chosen to build the town, made her jaw clench. Lindsay didn't have time to wind all the way around Robin Hood's barn—as Aunt Dovey would say—just to get to the theater. She didn't have time for the jumpy, jittery unease that had gotten out of bed with her, either, but it had been with her all day.

"We've got plenty of time to get there," Trey said. "Jolie said not to come until one."

"*Aunt* Jolie, please," Lindsay corrected him.

Trey rolled his eyes. She saw him, but let it slide in favor of wondering what had possessed Jolie to put Trey in charge of running the state-of-the-art light and sound boards she'd worked three jobs for two years to pay for. Vast computerized consoles with more lights, switches, and weird noises than a science fiction movie. When Lindsay worried that Trey might break something, Jolie had laughed.

"When he isn't watching TV, Trey is plugged into his PlayStation," she'd said. "He can make those boards sit up and sing."

So claimed Jolie, but she was single and childless. Lindsay, on the other hand, had watched Trey feed a grilled cheese sandwich to the VCR when he was seven.

"Earth to Ma," Trey said. "You're gonna miss the turn."

"What?" Lindsay blinked and put on the brake, just in time not to run the stop sign at Spring Street and Alternate 152.

"You okay?" Trey tipped his head at her, his hair falling over his eyes. "You've been like weirded out all day."

"I'm fine." Lindsay made a right turn. "Just a headache."

A dull what-next pulse behind her eyes. Maybe it was the weather screwing up her sinuses and making her edgy. This was the eleventh overcast day in a row. Enough to make anyone run for a tanning bed.

When Lindsay turned the Civic into the theater parking lot, the gray sky started spitting sleet. Tiny powdery pellets that skittered across the windshield as she drove to the back of the lot to park by Jolie's beat-up truck, Aunt

Sassy's brand new, red VW Beetle, and Aunt Dovey's turquoise, twenty-year-old, big as an aircraft carrier Lincoln Town Car.

"Heads up, Ma." Trey nodded at a black pickup gleaming with chrome, its dual pipes rumbling as it swung into the lot and nosed into a parking spot up front. "Uncle Ezra."

Aunt Sassy's husband. Lindsay turned on the wipers and peered over the dashboard to get a better look at the back window of the cab.

"The glass is fogged," she said to Trey. "Can you see the gun rack?"

He swept his hair back, leaned forward, and squinted through the windshield. "Yeah, I can see it. Looks like it's empty."

Lindsay turned off the wipers. "Thank you, fairy godmother."

Trey laughed and grinned at her. Pyewacket hopped onto his lap and meowed. Trey zipped him inside his jacket, Lindsay collected her purse, and they hurried across the parking lot, the wind whipping the fine, dry sleet across the toes of their shoes.

Tall, lanky Uncle Ezra waited for them under the canopy in his overcoat and "Russkie helmet," he called it, a tall black fur hat with earflaps. "Hey there young 'un," he said to Trey. "Afternoon, Lindsay."

"Hello, Uncle Ez." She smiled and slipped off her scarf.

He opened the door, the one with the fracture and duct tape. Gone now, Lindsay saw as she slid past it, replaced by a sparkling new pane of glass. The foyer walls were freshly painted. The beige tile floor and all weather mat underfoot were new since Lindsay's visit on April Fool's Day. This was the nineteenth. Jolie had been busy.

"Wow," Trey said as he stepped ahead of her into the lobby and unzipped his jacket.

Pyewacket sprang free and dashed across a long, plush stretch of new royal blue carpet. Lindsay watched him skim up the stairs on the far wall that led to the second floor offices and frowned. New oak paneling gleamed on the front of the staircase, a new ebony banister railed the steps and the wide gallery landing overlooking the lobby.

"Looks good, don't it?" Uncle Ezra swept off his hat and combed his thinning hair with his fingers. "Me and Frank replaced the glass yesterday. Lonnie and Donnie laid the tile and the new rug in here."

Wallpaper and pizza were peanuts compared to tile and almost two thousand yards of carpet. How had Jolie come by this kind of money?

"Looks wonderful, Uncle Ez," she said. "You did a great job."

He beamed and shed his overcoat. Underneath it he wore his tweed shooting jacket with its suede leather pad on the shoulder. It gave Lindsay a start till she remembered the empty gun rack. She took his overcoat, Trey's jacket, and her trench coat to the hat check room and hung them up. When she turned away from the rack, she saw Jolie standing in the doorway, her hands on the hips of her coveralls.

"You're twenty minutes early," she snapped.

This was another thing Lindsay didn't have time for today, Jolie's snippy, I'm-Vivienne-Varner's-daughter-and-don't-you-forget-it attitude.

"So I'm early," she snapped back. "What's the problem?"

"I'm busy. Go to the wardrobe room and stay there." Jolie spun away to leave. "I don't need people who can't tell time underfoot."

"Jolie," Lindsay said. The edge in her voice sharp enough to turn her sister around in the doorway. "Did somebody die?"

Jolie blinked. "What?"

"Some long-lost Varner or Fairchild?" Lindsay waved her hand at the new coat racks and hangers. "Did they leave you a bundle? Is that how you got the money to pay for all this?"

"I didn't get it from you. That's what pisses you off, isn't it?"

"I'm not pissed." *Though I could be any time now,* Lindsay thought. "I'm concerned that you're overextending yourself. If you need money—"

"You'll give it to me. I know," Jolie cut her off. "What

you can't seem to get through your head is I don't want your money. I want to earn my own money and buy whatever I need myself."

What you can't seem to get through your head, Lindsay wanted to fire back, *is that I'm not Vivienne. You're punishing the wrong person.* The words popped into her brain but not out of her mouth. The numbness welled up and stuck them tight in the back of her throat.

"All right, Jolie." Lindsay sighed. "Let's try this. When do I get to read the play? You've been promising me a script for two weeks."

"Monday morning," Jolie snapped and spun through the door.

Lindsay let her go. This wasn't the time to have it out with Jolie and if she listened to Emma, it wasn't her place. Perhaps Jolie had taken a loan to afford the improvements, or found an angel, the theatrical term for a silent financial partner. If she had, why didn't she just say so?

A peal of excited squeals drew Lindsay out of the hat check. A pack of about twenty kindergartners hopped around the lobby in their coats and hats and scarves while a handful of mothers tried to corral them.

"Hi, bunnies!" Lindsay called to the children. "Come with me and we'll put on our costumes."

The five-year-olds squealed again and took off for the wardrobe room. Lindsay and their mothers followed, picking up the caps and mittens the children shed as they ran. In the wardrobe room doorway Lindsay stopped and frowned. Same old ratty costumes on the racks but fresh yellow paint and new beige and buttercup tile on the floor.

Within half an hour the entire cast and all the Fairchilds and Varners had arrived. There were kids everywhere, in the wardrobe room and the makeup room, hopping and wiggling and running and shrieking all over the place. It was bedlam and Lindsay loved it.

She spent an hour fluffing cotton tails and bobby-pinning rabbit-ear headbands in baby-fine hair. The kindergartners' bright eyes made her smile and remember how much fun she'd had being on stage when she was their age. Before Vivienne realized that Lindsay, in her pink tutu and ballet slippers, was her ticket out of Belle Coeur and a bad marriage.

When she finished tails and ears, Lindsay passed the bunnies to Emma and Susan. They made sure tights and leotards were on straight and tap shoes buckled. Emma's sister Darcy flew in from Denver to be the red-nosed mother hen to a flock of preschool chicks.

"Damn Jolie." She sneezed when Lindsay came to give her a hand. "She knows I'm allergic to feathers. Why did she give me the chicks?"

"That's our Jolie," Emma said in a singsong, over the *clatta-clat* of tap shoes as she and Susan led the bunnies out of the wardrobe room.

"I'll take the chicks, Darce," Lindsay said, frowning at Emma's back as she went through the door. "You go take an allergy tab."

"And let Jolie win?" Her computer-whiz cousin plucked a Kleenex out of the pocket of her navy Armani pantsuit and glared at Lindsay. "Not a chance. C'mon, chicks. Let me hear you peep."

"Peep, peep, peep!" the children piped, flapping the cardboard, feather-covered wings looped to their arms by elastic straps.

"Wonderful!" Darcy applauded, blew her nose, and shooed her arms at her flock. "C'mon, now. Let's go find our mark."

The chicks hopped away in a flurry of yellow-dyed chicken feathers with Darcy sneezing her head off in their midst. If Darcy caught up with Jolie there'd be hell to pay, but Lindsay wasn't worried. Jolie had a knack for dodging trouble.

Lindsay checked her watch: fifteen minutes till show time. She'd collect Aunt Dovey from the makeup room and collar Uncle Ezra to keep him out of Aunt Sassy's hair. Lindsay stepped around a backdrop being rolled into place for the second-act scene change and smack into the middle of a flock of ducks and chickens.

Uncle Lonnie and Uncle Donnie, her father's twin brothers, were in charge of making sure the second and third grade boys under the feathers, red felt coxcombs, and Daffy Duck tails didn't poke each other's eyes out with their beaks and bills. She waved to her tall, bespectacled uncles, waded out of the flock, and turned into the hall that ran behind the proscenium wall. Twenty feet ahead stood a pair of chrome posts with a velvet loop and a NO ADMITTANCE sign strung between them.

What's this? Lindsay wondered, moving toward the rope. She intended to step past it and snoop, until she heard a noise in the makeup room, stuck her head past the doorway, and saw Aunt Dovey.

She wore a blue paisley dress with a bow collar, a beige sweater, and tan SAS oxfords. Emma called them her corrective shoes, but Aunt Dovey loved them. She stood with her right ear pressed to the wall dividing the makeup room from the private dressing rooms. A very old, very thin wall. Pyewacket rubbed back and forth against the baseboard.

"Aunt Dov—" Her aunt cut her off with a hush-up flap of her hand, listened a moment, then waved Lindsay toward her.

She tiptoed across the creaky floor, eased up beside Dovey, and leaned an ear to the wall. She heard the murmur of voices, a man's and a woman's, then a bray of Aunt Sassy's raucous laughter. Lindsay's eyes flew open. Dovey grabbed her arm and pulled her across the room.

"Who's in there with Aunt Sassy?" Lindsay whispered.

"Don't know. Didn't see him. Have you seen Ezra?"

"Yes. And he's unarmed, thankfully. No sign of Lucille."

"Poor man spends more time sleeping with that dang shotgun than he does my half-witted sister."

Primarily because Aunt Sassy spent more time sleeping with other men than she did her husband. And had for the last forty-five years.

"Let's find Uncle Ez," Lindsay said, "before he wanders back here."

"Reckon we best. Much as I'd like to see Sassy get caught just once and have the p-waddin' scared out of her, there's children present."

On her way out of the makeup room, Lindsay glanced back at Pye, sitting by the wall with his head cocked and his ears pricked like he was listening. She and Dovey hurried up the hall, rounded the proscenium wall, and nearly smacked into Uncle Ezra.

"Dovey. Lindsay," he said, craning his neck to look past them. "Y'all seen my sweet bride Sassy?"

"No, Ez. Haven't seen Sassy all day." Dovey hooked her brother-in-law's left elbow and gave Lindsay the high sign.

She nodded, took his right arm, and turned him around. "The show's about to start, Uncle Ez. Let's take our seats."

There wasn't much to Ezra. He was mostly bone but they were big, determined bones. Lindsay was five-seven but he towered over her and stood a full head taller than Dovey, who was six feet even without her SAS oxfords. Effortlessly, he lifted his arms out of their grasp, turned, and nodded at the NO ADMITTANCE sign.

"What's goin' on back yonder?" he asked.

"Don't know, Ez." Dovey pulled at his sleeve. "Where's Lucille?"

"Right here where she oughta be, so's I can protect my Sassy."

Ezra opened his tweed shooting jacket and Lindsay gulped. His shotgun Lucille, a short, single barrel, snuggled against his ribs, the stock tucked into an elasticized pocket sewn into the lining. Stout leather straps with snaps held the muzzle in place. Ezra wore his gun permit like a dog tag, in a plastic sleeve on a chain around his neck. It saved time when Sheriff Chub Allen, Wilburta's husband, pulled Ezra over or stopped him on the street to have a word about Lucille.

"Good Lord Agnes, Ezra! There's children everywhere!" Dovey yanked his lapels shut. "Lucille isn't loaded, is she?"

" 'Course she ain't. But that good-lookin' young blond feller lured my Sassy away don't know that."

Ezra started past them. Lindsay and Dovey grabbed him, but he stopped when the door of the closest dressing room opened and petite Aunt Sassy slipped past it. She waggled her fingers at someone in the room and shut the door, turned up the hall patting her bright red hair, saw Ezra and stopped with her hands on her hips.

"What'er you doing here, Ez? Checking up on me, I s'pose."

"Why no, Sassy darlin'." Big Uncle Ezra cowered like a puppy caught chewing slippers. "I was just, uh—"

"Jealous old fool. You go sit down now with Dovey and Lindsay, you hear me? I've got to help Jolie get these youngsters on stage."

"Yes, darlin'. I'll do that. Right now." Uncle Ezra slumped in Lindsay's grasp and went meekly when she and Dovey steered him toward the front of the house. "Ain't she the purtiest thing? And the fire in them eyes. Makes a man go wild. Ain't her fault she's irresistible. I know that and I know she can't help herself. But if I catch that blond feller I seen her go off with, him and Lucille's gonna have a chat."

"Oh for pity's sake, Ezra," Dovey said disgustedly. "Wake up and smell the coffee. Sassy's a floozy and—"

"Aunt Dovey," Lindsay said loudly. "Where's your purse?"

"Well dang." She stopped and raised her empty right arm. Dovey always carried her satchel-size purse in the crook of her elbow. "Must've left it in the makeup room."

"I'll get it," Lindsay said and hurried back down the hall.

No way was she letting Uncle Ez or Dovey anywhere near the dressing rooms. She should put Pyewacket up, too. Last season he'd wandered on stage in *Death of a Salesman* and jumped into Willie Loman's lap during his big scene with his son Biff. The audience hadn't laughed, but they'd chuckled. For two weeks Lindsay and Emma took turns hiding Pyewacket from Jolie.

She found Aunt Dovey's purse, but she couldn't find Pyewacket. She'd just given up and turned to leave when she heard someone come out of the dressing room. Lindsay ducked away from the door, peered around the frame and saw Jolie, wearing a mint-green corduroy jumper and white turtleneck, pass by the makeup room with a man in well-cut trousers and a tweed jacket.

"Thanks, Bill," she heard Jolie say. "I appreciate the advice."

Bill Rich, Lindsay thought, *the slick-haired lawyer from St. Louis.* She peeked around the doorjamb again and saw him standing at the top of the hall with Jolie. Nice-looking, dark hair. Lindsay drew back into the makeup room and frowned. She could've sworn Uncle Ez said the man who'd lured Aunt Sassy was a good-lookin' blond feller.

Lindsay gave Jolie and Bill Rich a minute to go their separate ways, peeked into the hall to make sure they had, then hot-footed it out of the backstage area to the lobby, from the lobby to the back of the house and into her seat next to Uncle Ezra. Dovey sat on his other side. Lindsay passed her aunt her purse just as the house lights blinked to let the audience know the show was about to start.

Paying customers sat up front, the family in three reserved rows at the back. It was a full house and Lindsay was pleased for Jolie. She smiled as her sister parted the closed curtain and stepped into the center of the stage, bowing to a nice round of applause.

"Welcome to the opening of the Belle Coeur Theatre's eighty-second season," Jolie called to the audience. "The show we have for you today features all the wonderful little stars of our community, our children." Everyone applauded, then Jolie continued. "We have a sensational lineup of shows for the rest of the season, too. Dates and ticket prices are listed on the back of your program, along with our telephone reservation line and Web site address. Following today's show, we'll have a song and dance program performed by the Belle Coeur Junior High Glee Club and students from the Belle Coeur Academy of Performing Arts. Last but not least, I invite you all backstage to share punch and cookies with our cast. I'll have a special announcement to make then, too, so stick around for it. And now—*Chick the Chocolate Bunny!*"

With a sweep of her arm Jolie backed off stage, the curtain parting with her and the house lights dimming.

Lindsay had seen *Chick* four times. It was a delightful story, the tale of Chick, a hollow chocolate rabbit who didn't want eggs or jelly beans for Easter, he just wanted to be marshmallow-filled so all the little children would love him. Lindsay's bunnies wiggled their tails and flopped their ears on cue and none of the chickens got their eyes poked. Trey never missed a light or sound cue.

At the end of the show, when Chick waddled offstage, fat and happy and filled with marshmallow, everyone applauded. The chicks and bunnies and ducks came out for their curtain call, then hopped away with their mothers to get a head start on the punch and cookies. The glee club came onstage and sang *Peter Cotton Tail* and *Easter Parade*. A dozen girls and boys tapped along in pink and blue satin tuxedos, top hats, and canes, the girls' hair and made-up faces sparkling with silver glitter.

Lindsay's toes tapped along with them, in steps she thought she'd forgotten. She couldn't remember the last time she'd felt the urge to get up and dance. When the number ended she sprang to her feet clapping. So did Dovey and Uncle Ez, shouting in Lindsay's ear so she could hear him, "Them's my Sassy's students! Ain't they wonnerful?" When the applause started to die down, Trey flipped a switch on his board backstage and *The Bunny Hop*—"Da-de-da-de-da-de, Da-da-da, Da-de-da-de-da-da, HOP-HOP-HOP"—blared out of the speakers on the walls.

The Bunny Hop was another opening weekend tradition. Lindsay cheered with the rest of the audience as dancers costumed like 1950s bobby-soxers twirled onto the stage. They performed the steps so everyone could see them, then formed a line that danced offstage into the audience. The seats emptied as everyone joined in, Lindsay included, laughing and hopping between Aunt Dovey and Uncle Ezra.

The line threaded its way up the aisles and into the lobby where it ended in a crescendo of taped music, whistles, and applause. Jolie popped up the stairs onto the gallery overlooking the lobby. Her face shining and her eyes bright, she stood at the railing applauding.

"Wonderful, wonderful!" she called. "I'll have to find places for all of you in the chorus of *The Music Man* next summer!"

Everyone laughed. When the applause began to wane, Jolie spread her hands on the railing and leaned toward her audience.

"Time now for the really big announcement I promised you. I'm so happy to tell you that my sister Lindsay, the delightful Jessie we all remember from *Betwixt and Be Teen*, has agreed to grace the boards of the Belle Coeur Theatre this summer in a new play I've written. Ladies and gentlemen: *Lind-s-a-a-y Var-n-e-e-r!*"

Jolie sang her name out like a ring announcer at a boxing match and pointed at her, flushed and buried in the crowd of bunny hoppers. Heads turned toward her, grins flashed, and everyone applauded. Everyone but Lindsay. Jolie should have warned her about this.

"Go on, child." Aunt Dovey gave her a good hard poke that knocked her forward. "Get up there and take a bow."

Lindsay went, pasting a big, bright smile on her face. She caught a glimpse of Trey in the crush, waved to him, and blew him a kiss. He blew one back to her as she climbed the steps to the landing and stood next to Jolie, waving at the crowd.

"I'm going to kill you for this," Lindsay said between her teeth without a twitch or a flicker in her smile.

"You gotta catch me first." Jolie slid away from her, batting her hands at the air to quiet the audience. "I can think of only one thing better than having Lindsay on stage again," she said. "And that's having her *Betwixt and Be Teen* costar on stage with her. Ladies and gentlemen, please welcome to the Belle Coeur Theatre"—Jolie paused for effect and swept her arm toward the top of the staircase—*"Noah Patrick!"*

Hoots and whistles and thunderous applause erupted. An ice cold wave of shock rushed to the top of Lindsay's head then plunged to her toes. She hadn't seen Noah since her eighteenth birthday party. She'd never expected to see him again. And she'd hoped—oh God, how she'd hoped—that she never would.

The crowd shifted, lifting their heads and their cheers toward the stairs on Lindsay's right. She could feel her smile, frozen in place on her face, her hands like ice, her fingers icicles stuck to the gallery railing. *Look at him,* she told herself. *Just look at him and get it over with.*

The image stuck in Lindsay's head was Noah as she'd known him on *Betwixt and Be Teen*, blond, brash, and beautiful. She turned her head and saw him coming down the stairs, a smile on his face as he waved to the crowd, and felt a head-spinning clash of memory and reality.

His blond hair was darker, cut to just brush the collar of the blue shirt he wore with two buttons open at the throat. His face was tanned, the Hollywood smile crinkling lines at his eyes and the corners of his mouth. He'd been slim and lean as Sam, Jessie's beloved. Now he carried more weight in his upper body. His chest and shoulders seemed a lot wider than Lindsay remembered, but he wasn't any taller. She'd always been able to look him in the eye.

He came off the last step onto the gallery, still smiling and waving. Jolie sidled up to him and slid her arm behind his waist. Noah scooped her against him with an arm around her shoulders and touched his lips to her forehead. His gaze lifted past the top of her head and settled on Lindsay. He blinked, pulled away from Jolie, and mouthed the word *whoa.*

"Hold it right there, young feller!" Uncle Ezra bellowed furiously from the lobby floor. "Lucille would like a word with you about Sassy!"

Chapter 4

"OH *SHIT*. Uncle Ezra," Jolie said to Noah out of the side of her mouth. "Get out of here. Quick."

She gave him a push, a none-too-gentle one, toward the stairs he'd just come down. It didn't budge Noah and he wasn't about to let it. After being out of the limelight for so many years, the applause swelling up from the lobby was heady stuff. So was looking at a beautiful woman. One who actually looked back at him. It had been a long damn time since that had happened.

Holy God, Lindsay Varner was gorgeous. Tall, willowy, elegantly beautiful. The pretty little teenager he barely remembered from *BBT* had grown up to be Grace Kelly in *To Catch a Thief*.

She was frowning at him, which meant she remembered

him, all right, but he could work on that. Starting right now, Noah decided, as he stepped around Jolie and headed toward Lindsay.

"You hang on to him, Jolene!" An angry voice roared out of the crowd. "That's the no-good feller what lured my Sassy!"

Lindsay spun away from Noah, spread her hands on the railing, and peered over it. Noah followed her gaze and saw a tall, bony old fart pushing his way through the crowd toward the stairs with a doughy, white-haired woman wearing gold, round-rimmed glasses—Robin Williams as *Mrs. Doubtfire*—pulling on his arm.

"Is that Lucille?" Noah asked Jolie.

"No," she replied. "That's Aunt Dovey."

"Where's Lucille?" Noah scanned the crowd. "And who's Sassy?"

"My other aunt. The one who showed you upstairs."

"The scrawny little redhead who propositioned me?"

"That's Aunt Sassy. She's Uncle Ezra's wife."

Jolie clamped her hands on Noah's arm and yanked. He held his ground and she bounced off his shoulder, rubbed her nose, and glared.

"I mean it, Noah. You don't want to tangle with Uncle Ezra."

"What's he gonna do?" Noah snorted. "Shoot me?"

The old fart gave Mrs. Doubtfire a shove, reached the stairs, and sprang up them, the angry glare on his face fixed on Noah. Lindsay wheeled off the landing to intercept him. Noah went after her, Jolie dragging at him like an anchor until he shrugged her off.

"Lind-say!" Jolie shouted.

Lindsay whipped around and saw Noah, glanced at Uncle Ezra, then at Noah again and came up two steps to meet him.

"I'll handle this," she said, looking him in the chest, not the eye.

"Handle what?" Noah asked her.

Over the top of Lindsay's head, he saw the old fart open his tweed coat and reach for—a *shotgun*. Jesus Christ. The crazy sonofabitch had a shotgun in his coat. He pulled it out and kept coming up the stairs.

"Meet Lucille," Jolie said behind him.

The crowd was still clapping. Did they think this was part of the show? Or had Vivienne arranged all this just to get him shot?

Uncle Ezra stopped a few steps shy of the landing, raised Lucille to his shoulder, and pointed her single barrel straight at Noah—and at Lindsay as she turned around to face him. Noah flung himself at her, swept his arms around her, and dragged her to the floor.

They hit the gallery with a thump. Nose to nose and out of breath with Lindsay partially on top of him. A happy accident that gave him a pulse-thudding feel of her curved-in-all-the-right-places body. Her eyes were a wonderful shade of blue, like the Pacific on a calm day. Wide-open and startled like her mouth.

What a mouth. Pink and lush. The most kissable mouth he'd been this close to in years, so he kissed her. Nothing fancy. Just a hi-there-long-time-no-remember brush of his lips. He expected her to recoil, but all she did was blink. Once, slowly. As if she shut her eyes and opened them again he'd be gone, like a bad dream.

"Noah," she said, her voice stunned. "What are you doing here?"

"Saving you from being shot by your lunatic Uncle Ezra."

"Lucille isn't loaded." Lindsay's luscious pink mouth firmed into a frown. "She's never loaded."

"So much for being a hero." Noah flashed his TV heartthrob smile. "Then I guess I stopped by to see if you'd care to pick up where we left off."

Lindsay's Pacific blue eyes darkened like a storm at sea. "Did you?" she said and then she punched him.

She barely had room to make a fist, let alone cock her arm—they were too close together, wound like lovers on the floor—still she managed to clip him a pretty good one. A four-knuckle cuff on the side of his nose that stung more than it hurt and made his eyes water.

"Quick thinkin', young feller." Uncle Ezra leaned Lucille

against the railing and bent over them. "Admire a man who thinks fast on his feet."

He offered Noah a hand. He took it, pulled himself up, and reached to help Lindsay. She pushed his hand away and stood up on her own, still glaring at him with her fist doubled.

"Smile." Jolie pushed between them and poked them both in the ribs. "You have an audience and they think this is part of the script."

Lindsay wheeled toward the railing and flashed a smile. So did Noah, his nose smarting like a stubbed toe. What had he done to Lindsay to make her punch him that he couldn't remember?

"Thank you all, thank you!" Jolie grinned and waved. "And thanks to our Uncle Ezra for playing his part to the hilt!"

The audience cheered and whistled. The crazy old fart blushed and ducked his head, gave an aw-shucks waggle of his fingers, and tried to sidle away. Jolie reached behind Lindsay and grabbed his coat.

"Punch and cookies backstage!" Jolie called. "Help yourselves!"

The crowd broke up with a smatter of applause. Jolie pushed Lindsay aside, clamped her fists on Ezra's lapels, and yanked him down to her eye level.

"Don't you *ever* bring Lucille into *my* theater again," she hissed in his face. "You do and I'll toss you out on your ear. Got it?"

"Don't know why you're takin' on so, Jolene." Ezra cowered in her grasp. "Ever'body knows Lucille ain't never loaded."

"Noah didn't know and the tourists I expect to pack the house every night this summer to see him and Lindsay perform won't know it, either." Jolie tightened her grip on Ezra's lapels and yanked him closer. "I mean it, Uncle Ez. Out on your ear. Don't cross me."

"I won't bring Lucille here no more, Jolene. I give m'word."

"Fine." Jolie let go of Ezra and smoothed his lapels. "Now let me introduce you, so you can apologize. Uncle

Ezra, Noah Patrick. Noah, this is our uncle, Ezra Pantz. He's very protective of our Aunt Sassy."

A second before his brain made the connection—Sassy Pantz, oh Jesus—Noah caught a flash of the wicked I-dare-you-to-laugh gleam in Jolie's brown eyes.

"I don't know what you saw, Mr. Pantz," Noah said, to prove he could with a straight face, "but all your wife did was show me upstairs to Jolie's office. I apologize for any misunderstanding."

Noah offered his hand. Uncle Ezra shook it.

"Reckon I 'pologize, too. Thought you had your eye on my Sassy."

"No sir, not me. I respect the bonds of matrimony."

Lindsay made a noise that sounded like a yeah-right snort. When Noah glanced at her, her hands were cupped over her nose like she'd caught a sneeze.

"Sorry." She sniffed. "New carpet. Lots of lint."

"Get Lucille out of here, Uncle Ez." Jolie picked up the shotgun and shoved it into Ezra's hands. "Or no punch and cookies for you."

"Right this second, Jolene. I'll just go lock 'er in m'truck."

Ezra turned toward the stairs as Mrs. Doubtfire came up behind them, a blond-haired, blue-eyed kid in jeans and a sweater behind her. A purse the size of a suitcase hung over her left arm. She swung it at Ezra and caught him in the chest. He staggered back a step and said, "Oof."

"Next time you shove me, Ezra Pantz, I'll snatch you bald-headed."

"I'm sorry, Dovey. Real sorry. You ain't hurt, are you?"

"No, lucky for you and what little hair you got left." Mrs. Doubtfire hung her purse over her arm and glared at Ezra. "Now you get that damn shotgun outta my sight 'fore I use it to put another crack in your head."

"Yes, Dovey. I was just doin' that."

Ezra tucked Lucille in his coat, made a wide berth around Mrs. Doubtfire, and scooted down the stairs. The kid standing behind her stepped forward and stuck out his hand. He looked exactly like Lindsay, only his eyes were a deeper shade of blue. Noah couldn't remember how old Vivienne said her grandson was, but he looked about fifteen.

"Hi, Mr. Patrick. I'm Trey." He shook Noah's hand, then plucked a pen and a program out of his pocket. "Could I have your autograph?"

What a great kid. "Sure." Noah scrawled his name on the program and handed it back to Trey. "Call me Noah."

"Cool." The kid grinned. "Thanks, Noah."

"Thanks, *Mr. Patrick,*" Lindsay said.

The squall he'd seen in her eyes when she'd clocked him was gone. Now she was looking him in the chest again. He thought he remembered her doing that a lot, looking anywhere but at his face, but wasn't sure he could trust the memory. He wished he could remember what he'd done to make her punch him. Maybe if he loaded up on that gingko stuff Vivienne crammed down his throat he'd remember.

"Come along, kiddies," Jolie said cheerfully. "Time to schmooze."

Noah let her hook his arm and pull him down the stairs. He looked over his shoulder, saw the kid sulking against the railing, Lindsay's palms pressed to her face and Mrs. Doubtfire's hand on her arm.

"What's with Lindsay?" he asked Jolie.

"What's ever with Lindsay? She's moodier than Trey."

Noah couldn't remember Lindsay being moody anymore than he could remember fighting with her on the *BBT* set. He'd taken Vivienne's word for that, but something about the way Jolie said, "She's moodier than Trey," made Noah wonder.

He glanced up the stairs, saw Lindsay pat Mrs. Doubtfire's hand and smile, toss back her wondrously blond, shoulder length hair, and lift her chin. It didn't look to Noah like Lindsay was in a mood. It looked to him like she was trying to pull herself together.

"Wait a second." Noah tugged Jolie to a stop on the lobby floor and turned her toward him. "Did you tell Lindsay I'd be here today?"

"Hell no." She grinned. "It would've ruined the surprise."

"How about the play? Did you tell her I was in the play?"

Jolie's hands went to her hips. "What are you implying?"

"I'm asking if you told Lindsay we'd be doing the play together."

"Both your names are in the contract. You know. The contract, Noah? The one you signed?"

The one you can't get out of, said the don't-cross-me snap in Jolie's voice, the same one she'd used on crazy old Uncle Ezra.

"I know I signed it." But he hadn't read it. Details hadn't seemed important at the time. He would've signed away his soul for this chance to salvage his career. "So did Lindsay, but I don't think she read it. She asked me what I was doing here."

"When I asked her if she'd read the contract she said yes."

"Did you talk to her about it? Stand with her like this, face to face, and say, 'Your old *BBT* bud Noah is in the play, too'?"

"No. Why the hell should I? If Lindsay didn't read the contract, that's her problem. I have a theater to run and an audience full of ticket-buying customers to charm so they'll buy more tickets. And so do you." Jolie stabbed a finger in his chest. "I quote clause twelve: 'Signee agrees to cooperate with and fully participate in all publicity events and opportunities.' So I suggest you hie your butt backstage and make nice."

Jolie's sharp-nailed finger burned through Noah's shirt. He'd decked an assistant director on *Cheers* for poking a finger at him. If he popped Jolie he'd lose more than a guest shot. He'd lose his hundred thousand dollar bonus and the only chance anyone, anywhere had been willing to give him to restart his career.

"I'll cooperate." Noah pushed Jolie's finger aside. "Just so I know for future discussions, who's the boss? You or Vivienne?"

"I'm the boss. My mother just writes the checks."

"Got it." Noah saluted. "By the way, boss, you do the best Vivienne Varner impersonation I've ever seen."

"It's not an impersonation. I'm my mother's daughter."

"That's no joke."

Jolie's eyes narrowed. Noah flashed her an I'm-a-shit-but-you're-a-bigger-shit grin and a smile spread across her face.

"I think we understand each other."

"Perfectly." He offered his arm. "Shall we?"

Jolie tucked her hand in the curve of his elbow and Noah led her backstage. Several tables were set up in the wings on both sides of the stage, covered with Easter motif paper tablecloths, big plastic bowls filled with red punch, and trays of pastel-iced cookies. Grownups stood in small groups chatting, while the kids from the show, most of them still in costume, ran and shrieked and raced each other across the stage.

Noah wasn't crazy about kids. Somewhere he had a sister named Phyllis who had two of them. They'd been infants, a boy and a girl, the one time Noah had seen them. He'd distinguished himself by being the only uncle to ever barf on little What's-His-Name. He'd been hung over at the time and little Whosits started it by puking on his shoulder, but Phyl went nuts and swore he'd never touch her precious darlings again.

At the closest table, Aunt Sassy stood handing out cookies and dipping punch. She saw Noah, winked, and mouthed him a kiss. A tall, broad-beamed man with gray hair, wearing a blue suit, a crisp white shirt, and a red tie, glanced over his shoulder at Noah and Jolie. He took a second cup of punch from Sassy and headed toward them.

"Here comes Uncle Frank," Jolie said. "Make sure he introduces you around. I'd better help Aunt Sassy."

She headed for the table, patting her uncle on the arm as she passed him. He nodded to Noah and gave him a cup of punch.

"Nice to meet you, Noah." He offered his hand. "Frank Fairchild. I'm Dovey and Vivian and Sassy's brother."

"Pleasure, sir." Noah shook his hand, noting the way he pronounced Vivienne's name. "Thanks for this."

Noah raised the cup and sipped. The punch was mostly cherry Kool-Aid with a 7-Up chaser. Far cry from tequila but it wasn't bad.

"You're a heck of an actor, son. By the look on your face, I'd have sworn you thought Lucille was loaded."

"Thanks. Truth is, I hadn't a clue the gun was empty."

"That wasn't part of the show?"

"Not so far as I know."

Frank turned toward the table where Jolie stood with

Sassy, a bright, welcoming smile on her face as she doled out cups of punch. "I'm surprised Jolie didn't clue you in about Lucille."

Noah wasn't. "A good director," he said, "will use whatever he or she can to get the best performance out of you."

Which was true, but Noah didn't think it had a damn thing to do with the scene on the gallery. The whole thing was a setup, he thought, engineered by Jolie. She hadn't told Lindsay he was here, she hadn't told him Lucille wasn't loaded and she'd palmed him off on Sassy. Jolie herself had probably told crazy old Ezra he'd gone upstairs with his wife.

"Then I correct my statement," Frank said. "You're a brave man to throw yourself in front of a shotgun you thought was loaded."

"No, I'm not brave. I owe Lindsay. She saved my butt more than once on *BBT*. She knew her part, my part, everybody's part. If I dropped a line she was right there to feed it to me."

And she was, Noah recalled with sudden clarity. He could hear Lindsay's voice. "Gee whiz, Patrick. The line is . . . ," could almost feel her breath in his ear as she whispered it to him. He remembered offering to teach her real profanity. At his place at the beach. "Bring your toothbrush," he'd told her. "You'll need it in the morning."

The memory made Noah squirm. So did seeing Lindsay, smiling and weaving her way through the crowd on the other side of the stage. He'd been about twenty-one or so when he'd made the toothbrush crack to her, Lindsay maybe seventeen. No wonder she'd punched him.

During one of his bouts in rehab, Noah had griped to a psychiatrist about his memory gaps. The shrink advised him not to look a gift horse in the mouth. His memories, he'd suggested, might not be all that happy. No shit. And if this was the best his memory could do, no more gingko.

Noah glanced toward the table and saw Jolie staring at him. She frowned and gave him a get-moving jerk of her head. He fisted a hand to his chest like a Roman foot soldier taking orders from a centurion.

"Nice talking to you, Frank," he said. "But the boss wants me to work the room, so I'd better get moving."

"That's Jolie. Our little huckster." Frank said it fondly,

but there was a glint in the look he slid his niece. Then he smiled and laid a hand on Noah's shoulder. "Come on. We'll circulate together."

Everyone knew Frank and most everyone he introduced Noah to seemed pleased to meet him. And a little star-struck. *BBT* was ancient history, but this wasn't L.A., where you were judged on what you'd done five minutes ago. This was Nowhereville and Lindsay's hometown. She was still a star here and so, Noah supposed by association, was he. He wasn't a big fish in an Olympic-size, marble pool, he was a guppy in a muddy, backwater pond, but he was a fish again, by God.

A fish out of water, but he'd adjust once he got used to the slow country drawls and he'd slept off the flight from L.A. He'd landed in St. Louis at five A.M. Pacific Time that morning, found a car and a driver arranged by Vivienne waiting for him, and dozed through the two-hour drive to Belle Coeur. He hadn't flown in so long he'd forgotten that the best way to rebound from jetlag was to stay awake as long as possible. He could feel his brain fuzzing over, the faces and names of the people Frank introduced him to blurring in his head.

At every table they passed Noah refilled his cup, hoping the sugar-loaded punch would take the edge off. He kept scanning the crowd, saw a blond working a punch bowl at another table and felt his pulse quicken until she looked up at him. She was lovely, but she wasn't Lindsay.

"You need a refill. And here's just the girl to give you one. My daughter Susan." Frank led him up to the blonde at the table. "Susie is an attorney. The best in town."

"Since you retired, Dad, I'm the only one in town." Susan smiled as she filled Noah's cup. She wasn't as tall as Lindsay and she was rounder of figure like Frank, but she had a great smile. "Nice to meet you, Noah."

"Same here," he said and drank his punch in one swallow.

"This is Emma Harrington." Frank nodded at the brunette working the table with Susan. "Dovey's daughter and Lindsay's partner in The Bookshelf."

Emma had her head bowed over the cookie tray. She

looked up as Frank said her name and looked right at Noah. His head started to hum and his ears rang. He hadn't felt a buzz like this since his last shot of tequila. It had to be the punch, the sugar rush he'd been striving for shooting at last to his jet-lagged brain. Yeah, that was it. It was the punch. Couldn't possibly be Emma Harrington's laser-beam dark eyes.

"Noah Patrick," she said. No pleased to meet you, no offer of her hand. She just said his name and stood next to Susan looking at him.

Emma was as tall as Lindsay, which meant she was nearly as tall as he was, but Noah liked tall women. Her hair was as dark as her eyes and had a white streak in front. Flawless skin the color of milk and a whoa-mama figure in black slacks and a turtleneck pinned with a white bunny face that had a blinking red nose.

"Hello, Emma," he said. "Love your pin."

She glanced at her breast, then back at his face, her head tipped to one side. "I thought you might. Cookie?"

She tucked one shaped like a rabbit with pink icing ears and black licorice whiskers in a cocktail napkin and offered it to him.

"Thanks." Noah bit off an ear, chewed, and smiled at her. "Yum."

Emma smiled back at him. "Forty-two," she said, turning away to hand out napkin-wrapped cookies to three boys dressed as ducks.

"Forty-two?" Noah echoed, biting off the second ear.

"You were wondering." She glanced at him. "How old I am."

Noah choked and slapped the napkin over his mouth. Frank took one arm, somebody else took the other and led him away, coughing on cookie crumbs, his eyes streaming tears, and leaned him against a wall.

"Stay with him, Trey," Frank said. "I'll get some water."

When he stopped hacking and could breathe again, Noah wiped his eyes and saw Lindsay's kid standing in front of him grinning.

"Em loves doing that to people," he said.

"What is she? The family psychic or the family psycho?"

"She says she can't read minds. She says she's just good at guessing stuff. Her white hair stumps people so saying you were wondering how old she is was a pretty safe guess. 'Bout fifty-fifty, I figure."

"Somebody ought to buy her a bottle of Miss Clairol."

Lindsay's kid grinned wider. Noah coughed one last time to clear his throat and sat down on a gray metal folding chair. The kid grabbed a second one, straddled it backward, and folded his arms on the back.

"Do you know my grandmother, Vivian?"

"Yeah, I know her, but I call her Vivienne."

"My mother calls her Vivienne, too. Ma says she changed the way she spells her name when they moved to L.A. so it would sound French."

"That's ninety percent of everybody in Tinseltown. They all want a name that'll look good in lights. I was lucky. I was born with one."

"Are you and Vivian friends? What's she like?"

The kid's questions and the eager way he hunched over his arms on the back of the chair threw Noah. "Why are you asking me?"

"I've never met Vivian, never talked to her. She sends me presents at Christmas and money on my birthday. Ma lets me keep the presents and the cards but she puts the checks in my savings account. Vivian called our house when my dad died. I heard Ma tell her never to call again. Then she hung up on her."

What the hell was this? Vivienne hadn't said a word about an estrangement. How had she come by the framed pictures of this kid she had displayed all over her Malibu beach house?

"Jolie," Noah said. "Jolie reminds me a lot of Vivienne."

"That's what Em says." The corners of the kid's mouth dipped with disappointment. "She calls Jolie Vivian Junior."

"I'd say that's a pretty apt nickname. Where's your mother? I'd like to say hello to her."

"She has a headache so she left. She would've dragged me with her, but Em said she'd drive me home. Ma made her promise she'd watch me." Trey slid his eyes toward the refreshment table and snorted. "See?"

Noah turned in his chair and saw Emma looking at them over her shoulder. She waved and turned back to the cookie tray. Noah held up his index fingers and made a cross. Trey grinned.

"Aren't you a little big to need a baby-sitter?"

"I'm a lot too big." Trey made a face. "Ma says I'll be lucky if she lets me out of the backyard when I'm eighteen."

There was some heat in his voice; not as much as Noah expected. He was a good-looking kid. Not much of a beard yet. Only a couple real whiskers in the wannabe fuzz on his chin. *Give it a year,* Noah thought, *and he'll bust out of the backyard on his own.*

Frank reappeared with a bottle of Evian he handed to Noah. He said, "Thanks," unscrewed the cap, and drank half the bottle.

"Looks like the party's breaking up." Frank nodded at the people tossing their cups and napkins in trash cans as they moved toward the lobby. "Enjoyed talking to you, Noah. I'm sure we'll see each other again."

"Hope so." He stood up and shook Frank's hand. "Thanks for introducing me around."

"Can I drop you someplace? Where are you staying?"

"Here, I'm told. There's a couple rooms upstairs, Jolie said."

"Must be Joe's old apartment. That's Joe Varner," Frank explained. "Jolie and Lindsay's father. Hope Jolie cleaned the place up."

Trey started folding chairs. Frank shed his suit coat and pitched in. So did Noah, capping his bottle of Evian and setting it aside.

Trey and Frank carried the chairs into a big, well-lit utility closet. Noah took them from there and stacked them against the back wall. He was nearly finished when he heard the door shut behind him, turned and saw Aunt Sassy leaning against it with one hand on the knob.

"Noah." She breathed his name in a husky, you-want-me-I-know-you-want-me voice. "At last we're alone."

He jumped back a step and reached for a chair, just in case crazy old Ezra came looking for his wife. She wore a baggy green sweater with a nappy weave, a cowl neck, and a long hem that didn't quite hide the apple-dumpling poof of her stomach, black tights, and pointy black pumps. Her red hair spiked around her head like a neon flame.

"Open the door," Noah said. "I've met your husband once today. I'd just as soon not make it twice."

"Don't you fret, honey," Sassy cooed. "Ezra is helping Dovey pass out coats in the hat check room."

She let go of the knob and came toward him, rolling her hips in a slinky sashay. The door sprang open behind her, whacked her between the shoulder blades, and nearly knocked her off her three-inch heels. She spun around and glared at Jolie, who popped her head into the closet.

"Oh—Aunt Sassy," she said with a bright smile. "And Noah. I've been looking for you. Could I have a word with you?"

"You bet." He slid past Sassy, her lip pushed out in a frustrated pout, and shut the door on her. "Does this closet lock?"

"Nope." Jolie grinned. "But there's a deadbolt and a chain on your apartment. Come on. I'll show you."

Chapter 5

TO ESCAPE Sassy, Noah would've followed Jolie into Hell. Crazy Ezra didn't scare him, but Lucille did. One of these days she might be loaded.

Jolie led him past the makeup, wardrobe, and prop rooms down a hallway that twisted into the back reaches of the theater. This place was a barn. Literally. Before she'd jumped his bones in Jolie's office, Sassy told him it had been built by a Varner ancestor in eighteen something or other.

Just when Noah thought he'd have to leave a trail of bread crumbs to find his way, the corridor came to an end in a vast space that looked like it was part warehouse and part workshop. The bare rafter ceiling soared overhead. The floor was paint-spattered concrete.

"What is this place?" he asked Jolie.

"We call it the workroom," she said, leading him across it.

A pair of steel doors big enough to admit a semi ate up most of one wall. A tow chain and a thick lock sort of held them together, but Noah could see cracks and daylight. A gust of wind hit the doors, rattled the chain, and raised a nasty-ass chill that chased gooseflesh up his arms and prickled his chest hair.

Flats of scenery stood everywhere. Sheets of plywood and one-by-twos were stacked on metal racks. A cutting table held three bolted-down saws. Hand tools hung from a pegboard above a long bench where two men dressed in gray coveralls sat on tall stools, two green mugs in front of them and a stained coffeemaker on a shelf.

"Hey Uncle Donnie, Uncle Lonnie," Jolie called. "Here we are."

The two men turned on their stools. Noah closed, then opened his eyes to make sure he wasn't seeing double. Jolie's uncles were twins, so eerily identical they looked like clones. Both had blond hair, neatly combed and turning gray, and both wore wire frame glasses.

"Noah, this is Donnie and Lonnie Varner. They build sets for me and help take care of the barn."

"How do. I'm Donnie." The twin on the left rose and shook Noah's hand. "This here's my brother Lonnie."

Lonnie didn't say anything, just nodded and shook Noah's hand.

"We're right pleased to have your help," Donnie said.

"My help?" Noah asked.

"Your keys." Jolie pulled a king-size ring out of her jumper pocket. "The barn has three furnaces, five hot water heaters, and about a dozen breaker boxes. The uncles will show you where everything is. The trash Dumpster, which key goes to which door, and how to lock up at night."

Jolie dropped the ring in Noah's hand.

"Have fun." She grinned and turned away, almost skipping.

" 'Scuse me," Noah said to the uncles. He wheeled after Jolie, caught her halfway across the workroom and turned her around. "I'm not a janitor, babe. I'm the talent."

"I'm the boss, *babe*." Jolie notched up her pointy chin.

"So long as my mother's paying you a grand a week, you're whatever I say you are."

Noah drew a breath to suck in his temper. "I was hired to perform."

"Oh you'll perform," Jolie replied, the don't-cross-me snap in her voice. "Every stinking, crappy little job I can think of. That should keep you out of the tavern."

"What the hell's this? A sobriety clause?"

"Why don't you read the contract and find out? I'll slip a copy under your door. Better yet, why don't you hook up with Lindsay and read it together? It'll be good practice for learning your lines."

"I'll memorize the goddamn contract. You'd better do the same and you'd better stick to it." Noah jangled the keys an inch from Jolie's nose. "Misquote so much as a word to me and you'll eat these one by one."

Jolie grinned. "We do understand each other."

"You bet your ass we do, Vivienne Junior."

"Thank you. I'll take that as a compliment."

"I wouldn't." Noah walked back to the uncles and tossed the keys on the bench. "Okay, fellas. Where do we start?"

Donnie craned his neck to look over the top of Noah's head. He glanced behind him and saw Jolie striding away across the workroom. When she disappeared into the corridor, Donnie sighed.

"Sure do hate it," he said, "when she carries on like Vivian."

"I kind of enjoy it." Noah grinned. It was grin or bite the keys in two with his teeth. "Reminds me of the good old days on *BBT*."

Donnie's pale blue eyes twinkled behind his glasses. "Lindsay sure looked surprised to see you today."

"She sure did." Surprised wasn't the word Noah would use. The more he thought about it, the more he thought the word was *horrified*.

Lonnie offered him a pair of coveralls. Gray like theirs with NOAH stitched in red on a white oval above the breast pocket. Goddamn Jolie. He sucked another breath to calm the furious pounding in his ears.

He could walk out and go back to being a bum, or suit up and sweep up. If the play bombed he'd at least have a job skill to fall back on. Not to mention that he'd rather throw himself in front of Ezra and Lucille with one in the chamber than let Jolie win. He stepped into the coveralls, snapped them up the front, rolled one shoulder, and curled his lip.

"All righty, gents," he said in his best Memphis drawl. "Let's rock."

"Well lookie here." Donnie grinned. "We got the King with us."

"That's right, boys." Noah looped an arm around each of them. At the shoulder blades since the twins were six-three if they were an inch. "Elvis is in the building. Hi ho, hi ho," he sang. "It's off to work we go."

Donnie roared with laughter. Lonnie grinned from ear to ear.

Noah kept up the Elvis routine, sneaking in other impressions he'd learned on the beach to entertain his surfer buds. The uncles loved it. So did Noah. He thought he'd forgotten these old bits, but Jimmy Cagney and Jimmy Stewart were right there in the front of his brain when he reached for them. It gave him hope that he might start remembering more than random snatches of Lindsay. Like why she'd punched him.

At least a dozen psychiatrists had told him that displaced anger was the root of his drinking problem. Noah thought he just plain loved the taste of tequila, but he'd learned to meditate to keep the shrinks happy. It hadn't done shit to keep his temper in check, but clowning for the uncles while they cleaned the auditorium eased the knot of blind-eyed fury in his chest.

Noticing the shabby, worn-out fabric on the seats and the threadbare patches on the aisle runners gave him something to think about rather than how he was gonna kill Jolie. By the time they finished bagging the trash in the lobby, he just wanted to smack her, not choke her.

"That's it," Donnie said. " 'Cept for the Ladies and the Gents."

"The what?" Noah asked.

Lonnie touched his arm and pointed at the rest room doors.

"I'm afraid to ask what we have to do in there."

"Since it's your first time, Your Kingness," Donnie grinned, "why don't you take out the trash while me and Lonnie finish up here."

"Great. Just point me."

"I'd best show you. You see to the Gents, Lonnie. I'll tend to the Ladies when I get back."

Lonnie nodded and headed for the men's john.

"I always do the Ladies anyway," Donnie said to Noah as they pushed the trash cart on wheels down the corridor toward the workroom. "Lonnie's a mite shy. But he ain't dumb, in case you were wondering."

"I did notice he doesn't talk much."

"Well, he can. Talks just fine when he's got something to say."

Noah and Donnie pushed the trash cart past the big steel doors. The wind was still blowing and rattling the chain. Noah shivered in his coveralls and helped steer the cart toward a regular-size steel door in the alcove at the back of the workroom.

"Too many keys to keep straight around here." Donnie lifted a key from a nail in the wall above a numerical alarm pad. "So we just hang 'em up by the door. There's a master set in a cabinet above the workbench. Each key's labeled to which door it fits. Don't know why Jolene strung that big wad for you."

To rub my nose in it and remind me who's boss, Noah thought, but he just smiled and said, "It'll make a nice paperweight."

Donnie grinned and turned the key in the lock, pushed the door open, and kicked a chunk of broken cinder block in front of it. Cold air whooshed inside and shot straight to Noah's bones.

"This here's a fire door so mind the bar." Donnie tapped it with his fist. "Push it in and the fire alarm goes off. Dumpster's to your left. Trash cart stays here against the wall. Lock the door and put the key back. Me and Lonnie'll set the alarm."

"I can handle that." Noah took the quilted nylon jacket Donnie tossed him, shrugged into it, and bumped the cart over the threshold.

"Mind your feet," Donnie called after him. "It's still spittin'."

"Spitting what?" Noah asked, but Donnie was gone.

Some kind of powdery white shit, Noah discovered, when he pushed the cart outside into the frigid, gray afternoon. It looked like rice scattered on the concrete apron between the door and the Dumpster, but it was wet enough to stick to his lashes and blur his vision when he cocked an eye at the sky.

And it was slick as greased snot, Noah found out, once he and the trash cart cleared the overhang of the barn. The wheels went crazy and so did his feet. He clutched the handle and hung on, his weight dragging the cart through a purely-by-dumb-luck skid straight at the dented green metal Dumpster. The lid was open on one side. Noah grabbed the edge and clung to it, one hand on the Dumpster, the other on the cart, his feet trying to shoot out from under him.

If he let go of the Dumpster he and the trash cart would slide away. If he let go of the cart he'd fall on his ass. He could've stayed in California and drowned, but no. He had to come to Missouri and freeze to death stuck like a Popsicle to the side of a Dumpster.

"Stinking little white shit!" he howled at the sky.

"It's sleet," someone said from the doorway.

Noah peered through his ice-blurred lashes at the man walking carefully toward him. He wore gray coveralls, a navy pea coat, and a red stocking cap pulled over his face with slits for his eyes and mouth. He carried a plastic bag in the crook of his arm, scooped some white stuff out of it, and tossed it on the ground.

"At last," Noah said. "Lonnie speaks."

"I'm Ron." He tossed two more handfuls of the stuff around Noah's feet, put the bag down, and tugged off his ski mask. He pulled off the wire frame glasses he wore underneath, too, nearly fell when he bent to pick them up, straightened and put them on. "I'm Lonnie and Donnie and Joe's baby brother."

Noah blinked to clear his eyes and took a good look at Ron Varner. There were some speckles of white shit in his blond hair but no gray and no bifocal in his glasses. He looked to be in his mid-thirties, and though it was hard to tell hanging off the side of a Dumpster, about his height.

"What's this stinking white shit again?"

"Sleet. Ice pellets that form when rain falls through a layer of below freezing air. Sleet also forms if snow falls through a layer of warm air. It melts, but if it hits colder air again on its way down, it'll refreeze and hit the ground as a mix of rain and snow, which is basically what sleet is."

"I knew that," Noah deadpanned.

"Sorry." Ron grinned. "I'm a meteorologist."

"A weatherman." Next to drunks, the most despised people on the planet. "Tough gig."

"Only when I blow a forecast, like I did today." He squinted sourly at the sky. "I'm in a real slump. Have been since Thanksgiving. If I don't get a forecast right pretty soon, I'm gonna be run out of town on a rail. Hence my clever disguise." Ron stuck his hand inside his cap and wiggled his first two fingers through the eye slits. "You must be Noah."

"I must be. Who else would be dumb enough to come out here and get his ass frozen to a Dumpster?"

"You can let go. The potassium chloride's done the trick by now. I mean, the Ice Melt." Ron poked his toe at the brand name on the bag. "It also contains calcium chloride and magnesium chloride. Sucks the moisture right out of the ice."

"I knew that, too."

Ron laughed and offered his hand. Noah took it and levered himself off the Dumpster, teeth chattering and ass numb.

"Go on inside," Ron said. "I'll take care of the trash."

"No, I'll do it." Noah blew out a breath that turned to white vapor in the cold air. "Just hold the cart."

Ron did and Noah pitched the green plastic trash bags into the Dumpster. The two of them flipped the lid shut and pushed the cart inside. Ron locked the door and hung up the key, waved a hand in front of his face to defog his glasses, and tugged off his stocking cap.

"You look like you could use a hot toddy," he said.

"No thanks on the toddy. How 'bout a cup of coffee?"

"You're staying in Joe's apartment, aren't you?"

"So I'm told, though I've yet to see the place."

"Come on, I'll show it to you."

Frank said he hoped Jolie had cleaned the place up. If she hadn't, it wasn't the end of the world. Living in Vivienne's guesthouse for four months had spoiled Noah, but fleabag hotels and dumps in general weren't unknown to him. Good thing. Knowing Jolie—or Satan's Handmaiden as he'd decided to call her—the apartment would be a real rattrap.

He scooped up the giant ring of keys and followed Ron down the corridor, through a right turn into another hallway he hadn't noticed before, up a steep, uncarpeted staircase into another carpeted hall. Noah recognized the ugly, red and green and gold–striped runner and the cheap paneling on the walls.

"I was up here earlier." The hallway turned a corner at both ends. Noah cocked his thumb to the right. "Jolie's office is this way."

"It's that way." Ron pointed left. "Joe's apartment is this way."

He led Noah to the right. Around the corner, the hallway ended at a door with the deadbolt Jolie promised. A mat covered the ugly runner. In shoe-worn white letters it warned, PREMISES PROTECTED BY SMITH & WESSON. Ron peeled it back and picked up a key. He unlocked the deadbolt, pushed the door open, and gave Noah the key.

Then he stepped over the threshold and put a foot down smack in the middle of the contract Jolie said she'd slip under the door. Paper crunched and Ron jumped, turned around, and blinked at the print of his cleated boot stamped on the sheaf of stapled pages.

"Oh man." He picked up the contract and dangled it between his fingers, wrinkled and wet enough to drip. "Sorry."

"No problem." Noah grinned and tossed the contract on a small table that sat against the wall next to a wing chair.

He'd expected the worst, but the apartment was nice. Good-size living room with beige berber carpet, a brown leather sofa with a striped afghan and cushions on it against the windows, an overstuffed blue fabric chair, and an ottoman. Tables and lamps, the wing chair by the door, a stone fireplace with shelves and cabinets built on both sides.

The kitchen had two windows, the dining room one big one. There was a cutout in the wall between the two rooms. A small sideboard sat beneath it on the dining room side. In the kitchen a counter with stools and a built-in electric stove. On the opposite counter sat a microwave and the sink. A wooden door with a window led outside. The fridge sat at the far end of the room.

Through the window over the sink Noah saw pale grass speckled with stinking white shit and the trunks of two trees at eye level. He thought he was seeing things until Ron opened the wooden door and pushed open an aluminum storm door.

"Looks like a window well out here 'cause that's basically what it is," he said. "The back side of the barn is built into the side of the bluff. Smart move on my great-great-grandfather's part or the wind up here would've blown the whole thing down in his lifetime."

The walkway outside the door was built in a trench about five feet deep, six feet wide, and twelve feet long, floored and walled in cinder blocks with a wooden rail around the top. Steps in the middle led up to the grass. Noah leaned outside into the misty, gray damp and looked up. He had to tip his head way back to see the bare tops of the two big trees.

"When it rains hard the well fills up with water. And frogs." Ron shut both doors and grinned. "Great eating if you can catch 'em."

Noah shuddered. "I'll take your word for it."

"Bathroom and the bedroom are through there." Ron waved at a door standing ajar on Noah's left. "Feel free to look around."

The bathroom was small with white fixtures, a shower in the tub, and two doors. One adjoined the kitchen, the other led into the bedroom. The king-size bed fit below the window on the back wall. The mist was thicker on this side of the barn and creeping up the hill so Noah couldn't see much, just that the ground fell away sharply so the windows were above ground like in the living room.

His luggage, the six matching suitcases Vivienne had bought him to hold his new wardrobe, sat in a row at the foot of the bed. Someone had carried them up here. And someone had left a black cat sound asleep on the pillows tossed on top of the quilted forest green comforter.

"Whose cat is this?" Noah called.

"Cat?" Ron came through the bathroom and looked over Noah's shoulder. "Pyewacket," he said, puzzled. "How'd you get in here?"

The cat cracked a *piss-off* eye at Ron and went back to sleep.

"Pyewacket," Noah said. "That's the cat in *Bell, Book, and Candle.*"

"That's the play our town company, the Belle Coeur Players, were performing when he showed up, so that's what Jolie named him."

The black cat in the play belonged to a witch. How fitting, Noah thought, that Satan's Handmaiden had a familiar, too.

"If he bugs you, chase him out," Ron said and turned away, the bathroom floor creaking as he walked back to the kitchen.

Pyewacket sat up and yawned, looked at Noah and blinked his deep green eyes as if to say, *"Well, sport. What'll it be?"*

"Don't expect me to let you out at three in the morning," Noah said.

The cat sneezed and jumped off the bed. Noah followed him through the doorway that led into the living room. Ron loitered by the door, but Pyewacket had disappeared. Noah smelled coffee and sighed.

"Started a pot for you," Ron said. "Everything okay?"

"Fine. Thanks." Noah drifted into the dining room, looked out the big window, blinked, and said, "Whoa."

He felt a wash of vertigo as he gazed at the steep, wooded fall beyond the glass. It looked to Noah—once a rowdy, half-smashed teen who'd raced his old man's Cadillac DeVille up and down Mulholland Drive—more like a cliff in a canyon than a bluff tumbling down, down, *way* down to a big winding loop of silver water.

"What am I looking at?" Noah asked.

"The Missouri River," Ron said beside him. "The headwaters are in Montana. Comes out of the ground a little trickle in a clump of rocks you can step over. Here at Belle Coeur it's about half a mile wide."

"That's a big damn river."

Ron grinned. "Wait'll you see the Mississippi."

"My plane landed in St. Louis. The pilot was a real card. He sang a couple bars of *Old Man River* on the intercom, but I didn't see the Mississippi." Noah stifled a yawn. "I was mostly asleep."

"Looks like you still are." Ron headed to the door and opened it. "There's food in the fridge courtesy of Lonnie. Get some rest."

Just in case Sassy was hanging around, Noah hooked the chain behind Ron and flipped the deadbolt. The one on the kitchen door, too. He drank a glass of milk and poured a mug of coffee, carried it into the bedroom and unpacked clean socks and underwear and a pair of sweats. He took them into the bathroom, shut both doors, and ran a hot bath.

He soaked till the water cooled, scrubbed himself, and got out. The cabinet built into the wall by the john held two folded stacks of big white towels. Brand new by their feel and freshly washed by the smell of fabric softener. He dried and dressed, hung a towel over his head, and went to the bedroom for the hair dryer in his luggage. He could've shaved but didn't, poured another cup of coffee and took it into the living room.

It had been almost ten years since he'd lit a fire, but he managed to get one going in the fireplace, even remembered to check the flue and make sure it was open. The beach house he'd lost to back taxes had six fireplaces. Noah sat on the raised stone hearth drinking coffee and watching the fire. Seeing himself in the flames, weaving around his teak-beamed, white carpeted living room in L.A., barefoot and half-naked, with a bottle of tequila swinging from one hand.

"Schmuck," he muttered, and shook his head, finished his

coffee, and got up to explore, which sounded better than snoop.

On the living room shelves he found a 25-inch color TV hooked up to cable. A DVD/VCR player and a stereo system. CD, tape deck, and a turntable for the vinyl albums stacked like books.

There was a closet on the same wall as the fireplace and another door. Noah opened it. He flipped a switch and looked into a small room. Paint cans sat on a plastic sheet that covered the bare floor, which explained the faint, what-is-that smell he'd noticed. A roll of the beige Berber carpet and one of padding lay against a baseboard.

He remembered Lindsay's fake sneeze and lame excuse about carpet lint. The brush of her mouth against his—so fleeting he hadn't even gotten a taste—her go-away-you're-a-bad-dream blink. And the punch. What was that about? Seemed a little extreme for smarting off about a toothbrush. Noah touched his nose. Wasn't even sore anymore.

He wandered around the apartment, ran a hand over the living room paneling. Quality stuff, no cheap shit like in the hall. The carpet was new, probably the electronics, too. Was any of this stuff Joe Varner's or was it all fresh out of the box?

A pine table and chairs sat in the middle of the dining room, a wall-unit style desk on the wall opposite the sideboard. Noah crossed the room and looked out the window. He couldn't see squat. It was almost dark and the fog was too thick. His shoulders felt sore, his hamstrings tight, his brain as fogged up as the view. Most of it was fatigue, some of it a restless, edgy anxiety. In his drinking days, he'd called it The Prowl.

Noah shrugged it off, went into the kitchen, and opened the fridge. Like a mirage, Pyewacket materialized in front of him, standing on his hind legs with his front paws on the crisper.

"What do you recommend?" Noah asked.

The cat sniffed at a glass casserole dish. Noah took it out of the fridge, put it on the counter, and lifted the lid.

"Tuna something," he said to the cat. "Leave it to you."

He nuked a plateful in the microwave, scraped some onto

a saucer, and headed for the dining room. When he pulled out a chair, Pyewacket jumped into it, put his paws on the table, and looked at Noah.

"Has anyone ever told you that you're a cat?" he asked.

He set the saucer in front of Pyewacket and pulled out another chair. Noah ate with a fork, the cat in neat bites, dropping onto the chair seat and all fours to chew. The casserole was great. Noodles and tuna in some kind of soup with hard-boiled eggs, peas, and cheese and crushed potato chips on top. Noah had seconds and so did Pyewacket, with a glass of milk the cat helped himself to once he'd licked his saucer.

When Noah got up to rinse the dishes, he found a bowl, filled it with water, and put it on the floor. The cat came and drank, went to the door, and meowed. Noah let him out, watched him disappear into the chilly, foggy darkness, and shut the door.

And now—drum roll—the contract.

It had dried on the table where he'd left it, the last few pages crunched and curled around the imprint of Ron's boot. Noah tossed it on the desk and went for the reading glasses Vivienne had paid for. She'd taken him to the ophthalmologist, to the dentist for the crowns and fillings he'd needed, paid to have his teeth whitened, and hauled him to an internist for a physical that included blood work, X rays, an EKG, and a treadmill test he'd flunked. "Severely de-conditioned," the M.D. said. *No shit, buddy,* Noah had thought. *You live on the street and stay in shape.*

The next day a personal trainer arrived with an exercise program. Laps in Vivienne's pool and runs on the beach, weightlifting, a stationary bike, and another goddamn treadmill. Hot on the trainer's heels came the nutritionist with the gingko, other supplements, and a diet designed to detoxify and nourish his beat-up and depleted body.

Vivienne played deaf when he swore it would kill him. To his own amazement, he'd thrived. He lost the flab on his gut. No six-pack but he was inching up on four and he could actually see his biceps when he flexed. His ass wasn't tight but it was firm. He'd never love tofu, but the casserole, great as it was, laid like a rock in his stomach.

He doubted Belle Coeur had a health food store, but he'd ask Ron. He'd ask Jolie if there was a spa anywhere close. No. He'd ask Lindsay. It would be an excuse to talk to her. After the punch he was pretty sure he'd need a damn good reason. He didn't need body wraps. The L.A. spa Vivienne had taken him to had leached all the bloat and toxins out of his tissues, but she'd insisted he stick to his manicures and pedicures and biweekly facials. She'd written him a check to cover it and warned him he might have to go as far as St. Louis to find a decent hair stylist.

"This is an investment in my future," she'd told him when he balked at the expense. "Yours, too, so stick to the regimen."

Noah thought *reclamation project* was a better phrase than *investment* but Vivienne had a point so he hadn't argued. He'd said, "Thank you," and taken the check. Would Donnie and Lonnie think he was gay if he wore rubber gloves when he helped them around the barn?

At last he found his glasses, zipped into a pocket of the garment bag where he could've sworn he hadn't put them. If this memory shit kept up he'd have to start writing himself notes.

He wanted another cup of coffee but turned off the pot—too many stimulants were a no-no for a recovering drunk—and poured a glass of milk. He turned a chair away from the dining room table and sat down at the desk with the contract.

He found the sobriety clause, which basically said one whiff of tequila and the agreement was void, the bonus forfeit, and he was out on his ass. Noah didn't blame Vivienne. Nor did it surprise him that this was the final clause. She always saved her best gotcha for last.

The clause above it, the one that Jolie thought made her God, was the most interesting. It was ambiguous as hell, deliberately so, Noah guessed. He read it five times. He might ask Susan Fairchild, but he was pretty sure he had it figured right. He took off his glasses, tossed the giant ring of keys on top of the contract, and leaned back in the chair, his arms and his ankles crossed.

"Vivienne, Vivienne." He tsked, grinning until he yawned. He got up then, went into the kitchen, and washed the dishes. He'd just finished and started to turn away from the sink when he saw Pyewacket sitting on the ledge outside the window. He let him in and killed the lights, brushed his teeth to protect Vivienne's investment, and went to bed. The sheets were cool enough that Noah shivered till Pyewacket jumped on his stomach and started to purr. He started to warm up then, and he started to drowse.

"Remember," he muttered half-asleep to the cat. "No three A.M. shit."

Chapter 6

NOAH HOPED he'd dream about Lindsay—maybe his subconscious knew why she'd punched him—but he dreamed about Jolie and his half-assed attempt to drown himself. The breaker he'd outrun, the one that would have finished him had it caught him, *did* catch him in his dream. It lassoed him and dragged him, kicking and screaming and clawing, toward a towering, foaming whitecap with Jolie Varner's face.

He thought he was still dreaming when he woke up and saw her sitting across the room in a wooden chair next to the closet. Until she moved and Noah realized Jolie was actually in the room.

"Jesus Christ!" He shot straight up, launching Pyewacket dead ass asleep off his chest and whacking his head against the window behind the bed. "What the hell are you doing here?"

"Morning, Noah." She smiled cheerfully. "Happy Easter."

Jolie placed an Easter basket wrapped in cellophane tied with a curly red bow on the foot of the bed. She wore a pink sweater, black slacks, and gold barrettes in her hair.

Noah rubbed the stinging back of his head and squinted over his shoulder at the window. The glass wasn't cracked, but his head felt like it was. He swung around and glared at Jolie. "Are you bipolar?"

"I'm trying to apologize." She leaned forward earnestly, the heels of her hand on the chair seat. "I'm always a bitch on opening day."

"Oh, well." Noah kicked back the sheet and comforter. Thank God he'd slept in his sweats. "I thought you were just always a bitch."

Jolie grinned. "You've been talking to Emma and Uncle Ron."

"I said five words to Emma, then she tried to strangle me with a cookie." Noah peered out the window. "Ron and I talked about stinking little white shit. Only he called it sleet."

Most of it had melted off the grass, but wisps of fog still clung to the trees. The sky looked gray and drippy. Jolie woke him up for this?

"What are you doing here?" he asked her again.

"It's almost eleven o'clock." She sat back in the chair, let Pyewacket onto her lap, and stroked his ears. "We're supposed to be at Aunt Dovey's at two for Easter dinner, so I thought I'd better wake you."

"Okay. I'm awake." Noah scrubbed his face with his hands, yawned, and blinked his eyes till they opened all the way. "Now scram and take your cat with you. He got me up twice to let him out."

"Good boy, Pyewacket." Jolie rubbed the cat's chin. Noah shot her a scowl and she grinned. "I'll take him but he's not my cat."

"Ron said you named him."

"So I named him." Jolie shrugged. "That doesn't make him mine."

Pyewacket hopped off her lap and padded through the bathroom toward the kitchen. Jolie got up and followed him.

"Whose cat is he?"

Jolie turned in the doorway. "He hangs out at The Bookshelf a lot. That's Lindsay and Emma's store. Sometimes he goes home with Emma, sometimes Lindsay. The rest of the time Pyewacket pretty much belongs to Pyewacket."

She shrugged again and went into the kitchen. Noah got out of bed and shivered. The cold that had swept through him yesterday when Donnie opened the workroom door had settled in his bones. He needed the sun, a hot-sand beach, and a cup of the coffee he could smell.

He went into the bathroom, shut and locked both doors, peed and splashed his face with warm water, dried off with a towel he hung around his neck, and opened the kitchen door. Pyewacket crouched on the floor over a saucer of bacon and scrambled eggs.

The dishes he'd washed last night were still in the drainer. There was a frying pan in the sink caked with dried egg, a plate and a glass, a knife and fork, a glob of grease, and a bunch of eggshells.

"Coffee's ready," Jolie said from the dining room. "I saved you some eggs and bacon in the microwave."

She sat at the table with a newspaper spread in front of her and a cup of coffee beside her. She didn't even look up.

"You could've at least soaked the dishes," Noah said.

Jolie glanced over her shoulder. "Not my dishes," she said, and turned back to the paper.

Noah ran hot water in the pan, slid the plate and silverware into it, and squirted the mess with Ivory liquid. Then he walked through the dining room to check the door in the living room, clenching the ends of the towel to keep from winding it around Jolie's neck and choking her till her eyes popped. The chain was still fastened. He went back to the dining room and sat down across the table from Jolie.

"Hadn't you better eat and get dressed?" She looked up at him from the paper. "I told you. We're due at Aunt Dovey's at two."

"I'm guessing you've got a key to the deadbolt," Noah said, "and that you used it to come in through the kitchen door."

"Yes I've got a key. I'm your boss and your landlord." She nodded at the desk behind Noah. "You read the contract. Got it memorized?"

"The high points." He reached across the table and picked up Jolie's coffee. It was loaded with milk and sugar but he drank it anyway. Every drop. "How much is Vivienne paying you to put up with me?"

"You waded through all the legal bullshit in the contract and figured that out?" Jolie faked a shiver and wiggled her shoulders. "Ooh. I'm im-*pressed*."

"How much?"

"Twenty-five hundred a week."

"Ten grand a month." He gave an approving nod and held up her empty cup. "More coffee?"

"Love some. Thanks."

Noah poured himself a mug and refilled Jolie's. Instead of the sugar bowl he picked up the salt shaker, upended it, and stirred, and carried the mugs into the dining room. He put Jolie's down, in front of her but far enough away that she wouldn't reach for it just yet.

"Are you miffed that I'm making more money than you?"

"Not at all," Noah said. "You'll earn every penny."

Jolie smiled. A sly, I'm-holding-all-the-cards smile. "Vivian said you'd be a royal pain in my ass."

"Takes one to know one."

"So tell me, Noah." Jolie hunched forward on her elbows. "What else did you divine from all the legal mumbo jumbo in the contract?"

"I didn't divine anything. I put two and two together, added it to what I know of Vivienne, and came up with a pretty fair scenario for how this deal went together. I know how Viv conned you into this, what you think you're gonna get out of it, and how much you stand to lose."

"Lose? Me?" Jolie laughed. "I can't lose."

"Sure you can. Watch." Noah reached across the table and shook her right hand. "Nice to meet you. I'll be going now."

He pushed to his feet and started toward the bedroom.

"If you leave," Jolie said, "you get nothing."

"That's not the point." Noah walked back to his chair and sat down. "The point is what do *you* get if I walk out?"

"I get twenty-five hundred a week no matter what."

"Did you read the force majeur clause?"

Jolie snorted. "There is no force majeur clause in the contract."

"Yes, there is. Every contract has one. A clause that defines a set of conditions or circumstances that absolves all parties from obligation."

"My boyfriend's an attorney. I know what force majeur means," Jolie snapped. "An act of God, a natural disaster—"

"Or me saying fuck you and slamming the door on my way out."

"Vivian promised I'd get my money no matter what. Bill read the contract and he assured me I would."

"I got bad news, babe. Vivienne lied and Bill is a lousy attorney."

"You're not an attorney *period*."

"My parents are, both of them. I spoke lawyer before I spoke English. The last time I talked to my father before he disowned me, he'd just been appointed to the California State Supreme Court."

Jolie reached for her coffee. Noah caught her hand.

"I wouldn't drink that. It's got salt in it."

She flipped his hand away and picked up the mug. Took a sip and made a face, spat the coffee back in the cup, and looked at him.

"Shit. Which clause is it?"

"Nineteen. Next to last." Noah turned in his chair, plucked the contract off the desk, and offered it to Jolie. She snatched it out of his hand and flipped to the end. "Doesn't say force majeur anywhere in the wording, but that's what it is. Go slow and think like Vivienne. I had to read it five times to get it."

Since she already thought like Vivienne, Jolie got it on the second read. Noah watched the color drain from her face and the corners of her mouth pinch. She threw the contract to the far end of the table, tipped her head to one side, and narrowed her eyes.

"How much of my cut do you want to stay?"

"This isn't about money for me. For *you* it's about money."

"Everything is about money."

"Yes and no. See, I thought Lindsay was an only child. I hadn't a clue Vivienne had another daughter till she hit me up to do this play. I kept wondering about that, why I never met you in L.A."

Noah didn't tell Jolie he wouldn't remember even if he had.

"I finally decided the reason I didn't meet you is because you weren't there. You were here in Belle Coeur, probably with Aunt Dovey. Now I'm guessing, but I'd say you figure that sixty grand—which is the minimum Vivienne will pay you if the play is a hit and you extend the run—is the least your mother owes you for leaving you behind."

Jolie's face flamed from the neck up. Emma Harrington wasn't the only person good at guessing stuff.

"I will *kill*," Jolie said between gritted teeth, "Donnie and Lonnie."

"Leave them alone. I figured this out all by myself."

"Right." Jolie snorted. "A drunk."

"I was only stupid when I drank, kid."

"I'm not a *kid*," she said hotly.

"You're an infant, a babe in the woods, and if I walk out that door—or if Lindsay walks, for that matter—I think you're bankrupt. You could be Wilhelmina Fucking Shakespeare but it won't matter if you can't fill seats. You need names on that stage to draw people out here to the backwater of nowhere. If you don't get them, sooner or later this place is going down the tubes. I'm betting sooner. I'm betting this is about the last shot you've got."

Jolie jammed her arms together and turned her head toward the window. "I can't believe Vivian screwed me on the contract." She didn't say, *"Again."* The tears clinging to her ginger lashes said it for her.

"Vivienne has screwed, pissed off, and generally annoyed damn near everybody in Hollywood," Noah replied. "That's why her agency is in the toilet, why she's losing clients left, right, and sideways."

Jolie's head snapped around like a rubber band. "What?"

"Do you think she scraped me off the street out of the kindness of her heart? Vivienne doesn't have a heart. The autopsy will prove it. Here's the way she figures it. If she can put my career and me back on the fast track, all will be forgiven. People will take her calls and she'll end up with more clients than Meryl Streep has accents."

"Vivian said she felt sorry for you."

"If you believe that I feel sorry for *you.*"

"She also said you'd killed one too many brain cells."

Noah smiled and sipped his coffee. "Surprise."

Jolie got up, went to the kitchen, and poured herself a fresh cup of coffee. She brought it back to the table and sat down.

"If you don't want money what do you want?"

"Let's start with a little respect."

"For what?" Jolie smirked. "Your staggering talent?"

"For restraint. I haven't killed you yet."

"I suppose you want out of helping Donnie and Lonnie."

"I don't mind giving them a hand. They're nice guys and I like having something to do for a change. I don't know what you pay them, but my guess is nothing or next to it."

"The Belle Coeur Theatre is a Varner family enterprise," Jolie said indignantly. "We all donate our time and our skills."

"Great. How much of Vivienne's sixty grand are you donating to your uncles?"

"Donnie and Lonnie own a farm. They do okay."

"I'll bet it's the family farm. The uncles inherited the Ponderosa, didn't they? And you inherited the family white elephant."

Jolie opened her mouth, blinked, and shut it, stood up and shoved her chair into the table with a whack. "I don't like you."

"I don't like waking up to find a woman I didn't invite in my bedroom." Noah got up, spread his hands on the table, and leaned toward Jolie. "Next time I find you in here without an invitation I will bodily throw you out. Landlord or no landlord. Boss or no boss. Got it?"

"I'll pick you up out back. There's a road just beyond the two big hickory trees. Be ready by one o'clock."

"I'll pass on the invitation. I don't do family."

"Suit yourself," Jolie snapped and wheeled away.

She stalked across the dining room and through the kitchen, out the back door, slamming it behind her. Pyewacket appeared in the doorway, sat with his tail curled around his paws, and looked at Noah.

"I think that went well, don't you?" he said to the cat. "I know why I signed the contract and I know why Jolie signed the contract. Now all I have to do is figure out why Lindsay signed the contract."

Chapter 7

LINDSAY COULDN'T FIND Pyewacket anywhere. He didn't come home with Trey and he hadn't gone home with Emma. The phone at the farm was out—if it rained hard the phone at the farm went out—so she couldn't call Uncle Donnie, and Uncle Ron's cell phone was turned off.

No surprise since he'd blown another forecast. The sleet killed her daffodils, so there'd be no bouquet for Aunt Dovey, but overnight the temperature had risen, so at least the roads were clear. Trey groaned when Lindsay woke him and said they could make it to church.

She was sure Sassy or Dovey would've phoned if Pye had gone home with them, but she asked anyway after the service. Her aunts hadn't seen him. Neither had Uncle Frank or Susan. She tried the farm again when she and Trey got home and talked to Uncle Donnie.

"Didn't see Pye when we cleaned up yesterday," he said. "But I 'spect he's locked in the barn havin' a high time chasing mice. Ron's gone to work but how 'bout Jolie? Maybe she seen him."

"I haven't talked to Jolie," Lindsay said. She refused to call Jolie, but she was thinking about calling Susan.

"Me and Lonnie'll stop by the barn if you want. We're gonna be late, anyhow. Just rung Dovey to let her know Lonnie's fussin' with his crème brûlée. He ain't at all happy how the glaze come out."

"Thanks, Uncle Donnie, but no. I'm sure you're right. Pyewacket is just shut up in the barn."

Lindsay put the phone down, sat at the built-in desk in her kitchen, and thought about joining Pyewacket. No. She'd done that yesterday. Jumped in the car torn between fright and fury and ran home to hide. She was still disgusted with herself. What could Noah do to her that he hadn't already done? Nothing. What could Jolie say that would make everything all better? Nothing.

She expected Emma to make both points when she called to see if Pyewacket had shown up, but Em was sympathetic. And livid with Jolie.

"What a rotten trick to spring Noah on you. Soooo Jolie, but it was a stinking thing to do. I don't blame you for walking out."

"If she'd told me he was going to be there. Or if I'd listened to you and read the contract before I signed it. Now I'm stuck doing this play."

"I think Jolie knew damn good and well you wouldn't read the contract. I think she was counting on it."

"I should've stayed, Em. I should've stayed and had it out with Jolie. And Noah, too."

"You don't think he'll say anything, do you?"

"I don't know. Right now I'm so angry at Jolie I don't even care."

"If I were you, I wouldn't bring up my eighteenth birthday party. If Noah does I'd laugh and say, 'Gosh. We did *what*? Are you sure? It was such a long time ago.' "

"Oooh, that's good. Can I use it?"

"With my blessing. See you at Mother's."

All the Fairchilds and Varners would be there. Lindsay promised she'd be there at one to help, glanced at the microwave and saw that it was 12:45.

"Trey!" She stepped into the hall, hollering over the blare of the big screen TV in the family room. "Time to leave!"

"Coming!" he yelled back.

Lindsay stood in the hallway, timing Trey on her watch. He had the volume so high—typical teen, the pediatrician said when she'd asked if Trey needed his hearing checked—that it took her a minute to tune into the voices on the soundtrack and realize Trey was watching yet another episode of *Betwixt and Be Teen.*

"How could you, Sam!" Lindsay heard her voice as Jessie throb with tears. "You said you loved me but you went out with Abby!"

"It was Sadie Hawkins, Jess," Noah replied as Sam. "You weren't here to ask me to the dance. You were at your grandmother's funeral."

Oh God. Lindsay remembered that awful episode. Shedding the gallons of tears Jessie always seemed to be weeping over Sam had never been a problem for her until Jessie's grandmother died. Then her tear ducts dried up like the Sahara. The director tried everything but onions. "Think how you'd feel if Vivienne died," he'd suggested and Lindsay, to her horror, smiled. The crew cracked up. The director called for glycerin.

"Phil broke up with Abby the day before the dance, Jess," Sam pleaded. "I felt sorry for her so I said yes. It was only one date."

"And one *kiss*, Sam!" Jessie wailed, her heart broken for about the eighth episode in a row. "You kissed Abby in the middle of the dance floor in front of the whole school! Everybody saw it! I'm so embarrassed I can't even go to cheerleading practice!"

"She kissed *me*, Jess! Abby kissed *me*! I'd *never* kiss another girl!"

"Liar," Lindsay muttered, then hollered, "*Today,* Trey!"

The TV snapped off and Trey came tearing out of the family room, shrugging into his camel wool blazer and skidding on the hardwood floor in his dress loafers. He slid to a stop in front of Lindsay, leaving a big black heel mark down the middle of the hallway she'd waxed in the middle of the night because she was too wound-up to sleep.

"Yo, Ma. I just noticed that you bawled your eyes out on *BBT* at least once an episode. Was it hard to cry like that all the time?"

"No, not really." All she'd had to do was look at Noah. "I was a method actress."

Trey blinked. "Huh?"

"Never mind." Lindsay lifted her coat from the back of

the desk chair and smiled, surprised, when Trey took it and held it for her.

"Thank you, kind sir." She slid her arms into the sleeves.

Trey picked up the insulated carrier that held a casserole of au gratin potatoes without being asked. Lindsay's Mother Radar went up.

"So, Ma. Can I drive to Aunt Dovey's?"

He jiggled on one foot in front of her, his hair combed for a change, an excited maybe-she'll-say-yes-this-time flush on his face. He'd grown again. Lindsay hadn't noticed the extra inch of red sock between his loafers and his navy dress slacks when he'd put them on this morning.

First he'd get a driver's license, then he'd get a girlfriend, and then he'd go to college. He kept talking about Berkeley. So far away, Lindsay thought, and felt her heart seize. Too far away to keep him safe.

"You can drive to the end of the driveway," she said.

"I've been driving to the end of the driveway for six months! How'm I gonna learn to drive in traffic if I never get out of the driveway?"

"There could still be slick spots."

"Oh, come on, Ma!"

"Take it or leave it." Lindsay dangled the keys.

"I'll take it," Trey grumbled and snatched the keys.

The au gratin potatoes went in the backseat, Lindsay in the front passenger seat with her belt fastened and Trey behind the wheel. He snapped his seat belt, started the engine, and pushed the remote on the visor. He waited till the door cranked all the way up and stopped before he put his foot on the brake, shifted into reverse, and looked at her.

"Can I back out now? The chain didn't break. The door didn't come crashing down and smash the roof of the car."

"It *happens*, Trey, but yes, you can back out now."

And he did, smoothly, cutting the wheels perfectly to point the Civic down the driveway. He pushed the remote to bring down the door, braked before he shifted into drive, gripped the wheel at two and ten, and barely tapped the gas. The Civic crawled down the drive like Aunt Dovey was behind the wheel. His drawn together eyebrows and pursed lips gave Lindsay a stab of guilt. He was trying so hard to please her and drive defensively like she'd taught him.

What idiot decreed that sixteen-year-olds were mature enough to drive? Sixteen was a baby, *her* baby. Half the time Trey couldn't find his shoes. How was he going to find his way home? But if she never gave him the chance, how would he learn?

It was Sunday. There was never much traffic on Ridge Road on Sunday. She'd lied about the slick spots. Aunt Dovey only lived fifteen miles away. If she didn't let him drive one of his friends might.

"Okay," Lindsay said when Trey braked at the end of the driveway. "Put on the right turn signal and drive us to Aunt Dovey's."

"Thanks, Ma!" Trey flashed her a blinding grin, flipped on the blinker, and made a jaunty right turn.

Aunt Dovey lived on what was left of the old Fairchild farm fifteen miles east of Lindsay's place. Three minutes overland from her back door but a twenty-minute drive along Ridge Road with all its loops and curves.

This side of town, the east side, was Fairchild country. The west side, where the barn stood and the uncles' farm spread across the ridge atop the bluffs, was Varner turf. Belle Coeur had always been sort of a no man's land between the two families until Vivienne Fairchild married Joe Varner and became the force that united them.

At family dinners there was always a toast to Vivienne, wishing her well and wishing her well away from Belle Coeur. Uncle Frank was usually the one who said, "Amen." Everyone would laugh, even Jolie. Lindsay was the only one who didn't think it was funny. She thought it was cruel. The kind of thing Vivienne would do.

Like putting Noah Patrick on the stage of the Belle Coeur Theatre. That was the kind of thing Vivienne would do, too.

"Oh my God," Lindsay blurted, stunned.

"Relax, Ma. It was just a wobble. I wasn't that close to the ditch."

"What?" Lindsay blinked at Trey.

He shot her a nervous glance, his fingers flexing on the steering wheel. Obviously she'd missed something—thank

God. She glanced at the speedometer—30 MPH—and saw the first stretch of white board fence that marked Aunt Dovey's property line slide by her window.

"You're doing fine. We're almost there. Watch the gateposts."

Two tall limestone pillars flanked Aunt Dovey's wide-mouthed driveway. Lindsay had clipped one in Mark's pick-up when she was sixteen, home on hiatus from *BBT*, and he'd taught her to drive, but Trey guided the Civic between them with room to spare.

Uncle Ezra and Aunt Sassy and Emma were already there. Trey parked the Civic on the grass between Uncle Ez's big black pickup and Emma's red Mustang convertible, put on the brake, switched off the engine, and handed Lindsay the keys.

"How'd I do?" he asked.

"Great," she said, wondering just how close he'd come to the ditch.

Two dogwood trees budded and about to bloom grew on either side of the walk that led up to the porch steps. Every Easter Aunt Dovey hung pastel eggs from their branches. The wind gusted and the eggs swung on their wires. One bonked Trey on the head. He faked a swoon and a stagger and grinned at Lindsay. She laughed as they climbed the porch steps. He could be so funny when he wasn't being almost sixteen.

Emma pushed open the glass storm door, the oval pattern in its center etched in frosted glass, and grinned at Trey. "He walks, he talks, he *drives*. Way to go, sprout."

Trey beamed, so proud of himself he forgot to sulk because Emma called him sprout. "When do I get to drive the Mustang?"

"I'll tell you when," Emma said jovially. "Same day pigs fly."

Trey gave her the raspberry. Emma gave it right back to him. She'd been calling him sprout and they'd been giving each other the raspberry since Trey was three and a half. He caught the door and held it for Lindsay. She stepped inside, took off her scarf, and sighed.

The house smelled like ham baking and potpourri. A big

glass bowl of it sat on a doily tatted by Aunt Dovey on a claw-footed drum table in the middle of the foyer. She'd made the potpourri, too, and the needlepoint rug beneath the table. The rest of the floor was polished hardwood. Oak like the banister on the staircase curving up the wall on Lindsay's right above stair-stepped bookcases with glass doors.

She loved this house, the Fairchild home place. Fifteen rooms with high ceilings and tongue and groove floors, two and a half stories sided in white clapboard that needed scraping and painting every three years, its wonderful wraparound porch, the gingerbread trim inside and out.

Jolie resented Lindsay for being raised in L.A. Lindsay envied Jolie for being raised in Aunt Dovey's house. Lindsay took off her coat, tucked her scarf in her sleeve, and thought for the umpteenth time that Vivienne had taken the wrong one of them to Hollywood.

"The Tetris tournament is rejoined." Emma took the casserole in its carrier from Trey. "Uncle Ez is whipping the pants off Mama."

A howl echoed from the family room at the back of the house. "I hate this dadgum game!" Aunt Dovey screeched.

Trey laid a hand on Lindsay's shoulder. "I am called to battle."

"Go forth my son," she replied solemnly. "Live long and prosper."

"That's *Star Trek*, Ma."

Trey loped off, through the gingerbread archway into the living room and across the dining room. When he disappeared through the kitchen doorway at the far end of the house, Lindsay turned to Emma.

"Who does Jolie know in L.A., Em?"

"Well, nobody but—" Her dark eyes shot wide open. *"Vivian."*

"The last I heard of Noah he'd been arrested for loitering and he was trying to stop drinking. That was two years ago. I haven't read a thing since. How do you suppose Jolie found him?"

"Vivian," Emma said grimly. "But Jolie called her last season when the receipts were so dismal. She begged Vivian to find somebody, anybody with a name she could put on stage. Vivian told her tough cookies, kid. Sink or swim on your own."

"That's what Jolie *said* Vivienne said. Now I'm not so sure."

"It makes sense that Vivian found Noah. Jolie sure couldn't have, not on her own," Emma said, puzzled. "What am I missing?"

"Did Jolie ask her to find him? If so, why? When Vivian said sink or swim I told Jolie I'd do the play. She already had a name."

"That's what I missed." Emma blinked. So did the red nose on the bunny face pinned to her sweater, a pale blue turtleneck. "Well, that cinches it. No more Cadbury eggs for breakfast."

"How dare you blame chocolate. It's this thing." Lindsay switched the pin off. "It's sucking all the electrical impulses out of your brain."

Emma had worn the bunny pin all week long. Lindsay kept praying the battery would die but the damn thing just kept going and going.

"Not to insult you, Linz, but you aren't exactly a household name anymore." Emma flicked the pin on with her thumbnail. "Maybe Jolie felt she needed two names, which makes Noah the obvious perfect choice."

"Absolutely, but Vivienne had already told Jolie tough cookies. Why did she change her mind? What made her decide to help Jolie?"

"Self-interest. What does Jolie have that Vivian wants?"

"I can't think of a single thing."

"Neither can I. Boy am I off today." Emma shook her head and eyed Lindsay. "Are you *sure* it's not the chocolate?"

"Positive. I'm telling you, it's that pin."

"Hands off my bunny." Emma slapped her hand over it.

A bang and a crash and a startled whoop rang out of the kitchen.

"Aunt Sassy." Emma wheeled toward the kitchen. "I told Darcy to keep her away from the food."

Lindsay headed for Aunt Dovey's bedroom, next to the bathroom at the end of the short hall adjacent to the dining room. She tossed her coat and her purse on the bed and gazed at herself in the dresser mirror. She looked pale, tense. Frightened.

How ridiculous. How *infuriating*. So what if Noah was in Belle Coeur? Vivienne was still two thousand miles away. She couldn't hurt her anymore and neither could Noah. Oh, he could be annoying and obnoxious—like kissing her yesterday—but when wasn't he?

She'd read the contract and she'd talk to Susan, but Lindsay was positive she was stuck doing the play. She'd have to read lines with Noah, rehearse with him, perform with him, but beyond that, she didn't have to see him. She'd be pleasant and professional. She was an actress, after all. Hardly the world's best, but she wasn't an eighteen-year-old nitwit totally infatuated with Noah Patrick anymore, either.

She was a grown, mature, and very wealthy woman. She owned a thriving business with Emma, she had a terrific son, she loved her family, and she loved Belle Coeur. She was secure and stable and totally in charge of her life. She'd show Vivienne that she couldn't control her anymore. She'd show Noah that she was immune to him.

And she'd show Jolie . . . Lindsay didn't know what she'd show Jolie. Certainly not the tears she could see filling her eyes in the mirror. Jolie would turn them into a weapon. Lindsay wiped her lashes, made sure her mascara hadn't smeared, and carried the casserole into the kitchen.

Emma was wiping a greasy brown splat off the floor with a rag.

"What's that?" Lindsay asked.

"Ham drippings. There'd better be enough left for gravy."

God help Aunt Sassy if there wasn't, said the glint in her eyes. Lindsay stepped around the spill to the long, wide counter with shelves and drawers in the base that separated the kitchen from the family room. The French doors at the far end of the room stood ajar. Aunt Sassy and Darcy were out on the porch smoking cigarettes. Banished there by Emma, Queen of the Ham Gravy, Lindsay guessed.

The wind was strong enough to whip Darcy's hair, trail sparks off Aunt Sassy's cigarette, and finally tear a hole in the overcast. Sunshine spilled into the kitchen, sparkling on the china and silver already set for dinner on the round oak table in the curve of the bay window on the other side of the counter. The floor glowed where it wasn't covered with couches and chairs and big oval rugs hooked by Aunt Dovey.

She and Uncle Ezra, still in their Easter best, hunched side by side on the sofa nearest the fireplace. Brows furrowed and thumbs clicking on their game controllers, the Tetris screen blinking and bleeping on the TV. Trey slouched on the overstuffed arm at Dovey's elbow coaching her.

Lindsay put her casserole in the microwave and smiled. The sun was shining, the floor was clean, and Emma hadn't throttled Aunt Sassy. So far, so good. Uncle Frank and Susan and Aunt Muriel in her wheelchair would be along soon. So would the Fairchild and Varner cousins with their spouses and kids. Uncle Donnie and Uncle Lonnie and the crème brûlée would be late, but not as late as Jolie. She was always last to arrive so she could make an entrance.

She came in as they were sitting down to dinner—all forty of them—on the heels of Uncle Frank's well away toast to Vivienne and Uncle Donnie saying grace. The adults were spread between the mahogany trestle table in the dining room and four metal banquet tables covered with white linen cloths in the living room.

Lindsay was in the kitchen with Susan, cutting meat for the little kids arranged around card tables. She didn't see Jolie come in, but she heard her slam Aunt Dovey's expensive glass storm door. She always did when she came through it.

"The day you bust that door, Jolene—" Dovey's stern voice floated into the kitchen "—you best be prepared to pay for it."

"Well, Aunt Dovey," Jolie said. "Happy Easter to you, too."

She laughed, but no one else did.

Lindsay finished cutting five-year-old Tiffany May's ham and moved to the counter where Susan stood, lifting two plates off a stack that sat beside the ham and a twenty-pound turkey smoked by Uncle Frank. She handed one to Lindsay and cocked an eyebrow at her.

"I had no idea you'd signed to do a play for Jolie until she announced it yesterday. Why didn't you bring me the contract?"

"Because I'm an idiot," Lindsay said forthrightly.

"You're not an idiot. You did it for Jolie."

"I think that makes me an idiot. Do you have time to see me in the office tomorrow?"

"Doubt it, but we both have to eat lunch. Call me about eleven."

Lindsay filled her plate and turned with Susan toward the dining room, heard Jolie's trilling laugh, and stopped in the doorway, her heart beating hard and fast. How many times had Emma told her she was a fool to try to make up to Jolie for all the hurt Vivienne caused? A zillion, and look where not listening had landed her. Lindsay couldn't remember the last time she'd felt so angry and betrayed. Oh wait. Yes she could. The morning after her eighteenth birthday party. How ironic was that?

Much as she'd love to dump her plate on Jolie's head, she wouldn't make a scene in Dovey's house. And she wouldn't hide in the kitchen. Linday stuck a smile on her face and stepped into the dining room.

Jolie sat at one of the tables in the living room, talking to Tiffany's mother, Jo Beth May, a single mother and a third cousin on the Varner side. Jolie looked up as Lindsay came through the doorway and waved toward the empty chair beside her.

Lindsay smiled, waggled her fingers at Jo Beth, and turned her back on Jolie. She caught just a flash of her sister's startled blink as she sat down next to Aunt Muriel's wheelchair at the dining room table. Uncle Frank sat on his wife's other side with his arm around her.

"Happy Easter, Lindsay," they said together.

"Happy Easter." Lindsay lifted Aunt Muriel's hand from the padded arm of her wheelchair. Her joints, knotted by rheumatoid arthritis, felt hot and puffier than usual. It was the damp weather, Lindsay knew, and gently cupped her aunt's hand in both of hers. "So, Aunt Muriel. Was the Easter Bunny good to you?"

"The Bunny was very good to me." Aunt Muriel smiled at Uncle Frank and wiggled a little in her chair. "A magnetic seat cushion. It's wonderful. My back doesn't hurt at all. And look what Emma gave me."

It took Aunt Muriel a minute with her stiff, swollen fingers to pluck a bunny pin with furry white ears and a blinking red nose out of the quilted tote bag in her lap and hold it up to Lindsay.

"I hid it," she said. "So the children couldn't weasel it out of me."

All through dinner, Lindsay was aware of Jolie watching her from the corner of her eye. As much as she hated the silent treatment, Lindsay was good at it. She'd been raised by the Queen of the Cold Shoulder, Vivienne's favorite tactic for controlling her. Her mother once went ten days without saying a single word to her. Only when Lindsay broke out in hives and couldn't breathe did Vivienne break down and speak to her.

Since the sun was shining, it was decided after dinner that the Egg Hunt could be held outside. The little kids cheered, pulled on sweaters, and headed for the backyard with Uncle Donnie and Uncle Lonnie. Aunt Sassy and Uncle Ez and Aunt Dovey, wrapped in a bulky beige cardigan, followed. Uncle Frank brought up the rear, pushing Aunt Muriel in her wheelchair. Little towheaded Tiffany sat on Aunt Muriel's lap, the bunny pin from Emma blinking on her yellow sweater.

Darcy and Emma, Jo Beth, and a handful of female cousins cleared the tables. Lindsay rinsed dishes, setting Aunt Dovey's china aside to be hand washed, and passed the dishwasher-safe pieces to Susan.

"Where's Jolie?" Darcy demanded, coming into the kitchen with a bowl of silverware. "Why does she disappear when there's work to do?"

"She always does, Darce," Susan said. "She has a knack for it."

"I'm sick of Jolie and her *knack*." Darcy banged the bowl of dirty silverware on the counter next to Lindsay. "I've got a plane to catch in St. Louis at nine o'clock tonight and I'm out here pitching in."

"Oh come on, Darce," Susan cajoled. "You're just miffed about the chickens yesterday."

"Damn right I'm miffed. I flew in from Denver to give Jolie a hand on her big opening weekend and she buries me in feathers."

"I'm sorry, Darcy." Lindsay wiped her hands on a dish-towel and faced her. "If I had any idea Jolie was going to assign you the chicks—"

"Stop it, Lindsay," Darcy said. "Stop apologizing for Jolie. How can you defend her after she threw Noah Patrick in your face?"

Lindsay blinked, so startled that Darcy knew anything about Noah that her mouth fell open. Susan scowled and hollered, "*Emma!*"

Jo Beth and the other cousins looked at each other and fled the kitchen. Lindsay felt her face flame and swept a hand over her eyes.

"Don't you pin this on Em, Susan. I saw Lindsay's face when Jolie introduced Noah. She looked like she'd been punched in the stomach." Darcy tugged Lindsay's hand away from her eyes. "You didn't know he was going to be there, did you? And I'll bet you didn't know he was going to be in the play with you, either."

"Well, no—" Lindsay stammered. "But I—"

"What's going on?" Emma popped through the doorway, took one look at Lindsay, then Susan, and swung a glare on Darcy. "What did you say that you weren't supposed to?"

"Not a damn thing that wasn't obvious to everyone standing in the lobby yesterday," Darcy replied. "I said Lindsay looked like she'd been punched in the stomach when Jolie introduced Noah Patrick."

"Well, she wouldn't have," Jolie said from the family room, "if she'd bothered to read the contract."

Chapter 8

THE FLIP, so-what tone in Jolie's voice spun Lindsay away from the sink. Her baby sister, the skinny, freckled little brat she'd missed the most next to Mark during her years in L.A., stood by the French doors in the family room, her face flushed and her red-gold hair tousled. She'd been outside, obviously. Too bad she hadn't stayed there.

"Really, Jolie? It's all *my* fault because I didn't read the contract?"

"Well, yeah, it's your fault. If you'd read the damn thing you would've known Noah was in the play."

"You knew I wouldn't read it." Lindsay quoted Emma because it sounded the way she felt, angry and accusatory. "You counted on it."

"That's crazy. Why would I do that?"

"Why didn't you just *tell* me, Jolie?"

"Why the hell should I?"

"Because," Darcy said, "she's your *sister*, you changeling."

"You know, Darce." Jolie tipped her head to one side. "I like you better with puffy eyes and a red nose."

"C'mere, you little pill," Darcy snarled, and started toward her.

Jolie grinned but didn't budge. She knew, because they always had, that Lindsay and Emma would keep Darcy off her. And they did. Lindsay caught her left arm, Emma her right, and hauled her back.

"C'mon, Em," Darcy said. "Let me hit her just once."

"No, Darce. It's Easter and we're in Mama's house."

"There's always my place," Susan said. Lindsay shot her a don't-help frown and she shrugged. "Just a thought."

"This is a gift from the Easter Bunny, Jolie," Darcy warned. "Just remember. One of these days Lindsay and Emma won't be around."

"Gosh this is *fun*," Jolie gushed. "I can't tell you how much I've enjoyed all of you jumping me at once. I'd love to stay and play some more, but I've got a date in St. Louis. With somebody who likes me."

"Oh, stuff it, Jolie," Lindsay snapped. "Why didn't you tell me Noah was going to be at the barn yesterday?"

"I wanted to surprise you. I thought you'd get a kick out of it."

"I don't like surprises. You know that."

"You know what, Lindsay? I don't think you like much of anything. You float around, so perfect and serene, a loopy, I'm-happy-oh-so-happy smile on your face. So maybe you can act, but I don't think so. I think you're just too damn dumb to realize you're miserable."

"The only thing I've been dumb about," Lindsay shot back, "is *you*."

"Don't think you can beat me in court." Jolie yanked the door open and glared at her. "I've got the money to fight and I will *not* let you out of the contract. Come hell or high water you're gonna be on stage with Noah Patrick on May twenty-fourth."

She banged out of the house, slamming the French door so hard it bounced open again. Through the tall family room windows Lindsay saw her stalk across the porch and disappear around the corner of the house.

"Where did Jolie get the money to fight a lawsuit?" she wondered out loud. "Not that I plan to file one."

Emma looked at Darcy. Darcy looked at Susan. Susan looked at Emma and all three of them looked away from Lindsay.

"I'll tell you what I think," she said. "I think she got the money from Vivienne. I think Vivienne has paid for the improvements Jolie has made to the barn. What do you think?"

"Makes as much sense as anything else," Susan said.

" 'Bout time Vivian behaved like a mother," Darcy smirked.

"Stranger things have happened." Emma shrugged.

"You're lying. All three of you." Lindsay put her hands on her hips. "Vivienne hates the barn. Technically it still belongs to my father, the man she despises above all others.

She tried to burn it down on our way out of town the night we left Belle Coeur."

"Oh yeah." Emma snapped her fingers. "Forgot about that."

"I can see how it would slip your mind. It only woke everyone in town when the fire truck hit the sheriff's car on Main Street."

It was hardly more than a fender bender, really. By the time the two vehicles were pulled apart and the fire truck arrived at the barn, Uncle Donnie had hooked up the garden hose and doused the fire.

"All right, you three." Lindsay frowned at her cousins. "How much did you contribute to the Jolie Varner Defense Fund?"

"We aren't telling," Susan said. "You'll just write us checks."

"You bet I'll write you checks, so you better tell me."

"I know what I can afford and what I can't, Lindsay," Darcy said. "Corporations pay me megabucks to write software for them because I can think like Bill Gates. I don't need to be paid back."

"Same here," Emma added.

"We know how much you want to help Jolie," Susan said. "We think she's nuts to refuse your help, but God knows she needs it. If we can make it easier for her, so she only has to work two jobs instead of three in the off-season to keep the barn going, then we're glad to help."

"The barn belongs to the Varners," Lindsay argued. "It's our responsibility to keep it afloat, not the Fairchilds'."

"You're a Fairchild, too, and so is Jolie," Emma said. "We love that old place and we love Jolie. Even when we want to wring her neck."

"She's a pain in the ass," Darcy agreed, "but she's *our* pain in the ass. We aren't about to stand by and watch her sink with the ship."

"Even when she sticks you with the chicks, Darce?"

"I will get her for that one," Darcy warned. "You hide and watch."

This was more like it, Darcy threatening Jolie with bodily harm. Lindsay laughed. So did Emma and Susan. Darcy grinned and headed for the dining room to finish clearing the table. Emma went with her. Susan went back to the dishwasher, Lindsay to the sink.

"What did Jolie borrow the money for, Suze? Did she tell you?"

"First of all, she didn't ask. Emma and Darcy and I offered her a twenty-thousand-dollar loan so she could replace the lobby carpet, do the painting and papering, and fix up the wardrobe and the makeup room."

Twenty grand minus the repairs wouldn't leave Jolie much of a legal defense fund. It might pay to file a counter petition and afford a few hours of Bill Rich's time, but not a heck of a lot more.

"Thanks, Suze." Lindsay cranked on the hot water and reached for the sink sprayer. "I appreciate you telling me."

"Did you make that up about Vivian giving Jolie money?"

"Of course I made it up." Lindsay rinsed a platter and passed it to Susan. "Vivienne give money to her own child?"

Susan laughed. Lindsay smiled. She was kidding when she'd said it, but now she was beginning to wonder. It wasn't like Jolie to claim what she didn't have or make a threat she couldn't back up. If she said she had the money to fight a lawsuit, then she did. The question was how she'd come by it and how Lindsay was going to find out.

The Egg Hunters came in, red-cheeked and wind-blown and ready for dessert. Pecan pie, cherry pie, carrot cake, and Uncle Lonnie's crème brûlée. Lindsay pronounced it perfect, glaze and all. Uncle Lonnie grinned, so pleased he blushed.

"Hey, Ma." Trey bounced down beside Lindsay, where she sat on one of the family room couches drinking tea with Aunt Dovey and Aunt Sassy. His shirttails were hanging out, his tie long gone. "Can I sleep over at Denny's? Jo Beth says it's okay."

Lindsay looked past Trey at Jo Beth, standing with her oldest, fifteen-year-old Denny, beside her and her youngest, Tiffany, asleep on her shoulder. The bunny pin still blinked on Tiff's yellow sweater and Trey's tie made a big red silk bow around the waist of her blue jeans.

"Last day of spring vacation tomorrow," Jo Beth said.

"The kids have dentist appointments at one, but the boys will have the morning to play video games."

"Thanks, Jo. Tell you what, mister." Lindsay gave Trey an evil smile. "Jo can drop you at the store at noon and you can clean the stockroom like you've been promising for two weeks."

Trey groaned and let his head fall.

"Take it or leave it," Lindsay said.

Trey raised his head. "I'll take it."

"Got your key?" Lindsay asked and Trey nodded. "Then stop by the house for your toothbrush and clean clothes. Do you mind, Jo?"

"Not a bit," she said, shifting Tiffany on her shoulder.

Uncle Lonnie got up from his chair by the fire, smiled at Jo Beth, and held out his hands. "Oh, thank you, Uncle Lonnie." Jo sighed and passed Tiffany to him. She mewed a little, till Uncle Lonnie laid his cheek against her hair. Then she smiled and snuggled and went back to sleep.

" 'Kay, Ma. We're outta here. Love you." Trey swooped kisses on Lindsay, Aunt Dovey, and Aunt Sassy, bounced off the couch, and blinked at his red socks. "Oh, *man*. Where are my shoes?"

It took five minutes to find them under a chair in the living room and another ten to find his blazer, flung over the deck rail outside where he'd thrown it during the Easter Egg Hunt.

"Some days," Aunt Dovcy said once Jo Beth and the kids were gone, "that boy can't find his head."

She and Aunt Sassy settled on the flowered couch, Lindsay in a plaid armchair to finish their tea. English Breakfast with who-knew-what-else tossed in. Aunt Dovey blended her own tea and used only loose leaves. The china pot in its cozy and three cups and saucers in an English Rose pattern sat on the square oak table between them.

"Give Trey two years," Aunt Sassy said, winking at Lindsay, "and he'll be breakin' hearts all over the county."

Only if I let him out of the backyard, Lindsay thought, but smiled at Aunt Sassy. In two years Trey would be eighteen and almost a man. Ready for college and ready to leave home. This morning she'd noticed he'd grown an inch when she wasn't looking. If she blinked her eyes in the next two years, would she open them to find Trey walking out the door with his bags packed and a BERKELEY OR BUST sticker on his back?

"Sure feels good to sit down." Aunt Dovey slipped off her SAS oxfords and put her feet up on a needlepoint stool. "I'm pooped."

"Well, here then. Read my leaves." Sassy picked up her teacup and handed it to Dovey. "It'll perk you right up."

"Good night nurse, Sassy. I read your damn tea leaves every time you set foot in my house."

"Why do you think I come? Sure as hell ain't for your green bean casserole. Wouldn't be half bad if you'd fix it like I told you."

"I'm not gonna shred half a carrot in my green bean casserole."

"Why not? Makes it better."

"Coming from you, Sassy, that ain't much of a recommendation."

"Least I'm willing to try new things in the kitchen."

"I heard about that." Dovey looked around for Ezra and lowered her voice. "You and Leroy damn near got caught."

"Well, we didn't. And what's it to you, I'd like to know, or that nosy biddy next door, Mary Lou Hanley?"

"I warned you to be careful in the kitchen," Dovey said severely. "If you ain't gonna heed what I say you can read your own damn tea leaves."

Which Aunt Sassy could no more do than Vivienne. The Fairchild gift had skipped the middle and youngest sisters. If Jolie or Darcy or Susan ever saw or heard things, Lindsay didn't know about it and didn't want to. Her brush with it the night Mark died was her only experience, thank God. So far it was just Emma who exhibited any talent.

"Oh, all right." Sassy rolled her eyes. "I'll hang on your every word."

"You'd best," Dovey warned, and sat up straight on the couch.

She placed the saucer on her left palm, held the cup by its

delicately curved handle with her right thumb and forefinger, swirled it three times clockwise, and set the saucer down in front of Sassy.

Usually Lindsay could sit through one of these, but a chill crawled through her watching the tea settle in the cup. Good time to leave, she decided, before the leaves stilled and Aunt Dovey leaned forward to read them. She started to rise, but Aunt Sassy shot her a don't-break-the-mood frown. Lindsay sighed and sat down.

"All right, Sassy." Dovey leaned toward the cup, her elbows on her knees and her palms pressed together. "Let's see what we got."

"I'm all ears," Sassy said, hunching forward with her.

The sun was starting down, the light in the room fading. Aunt Dovey took off her glasses but still had to squint to see the bottom of Sassy's cup. Uncle Lonnie, who had slipped silently back into his chair by the fire after he'd carried Tiffany out to Jo Beth's car, turned on a lamp that chased the shadows in the room straight up Lindsay's spine.

"I see a house, an hourglass, and a flag. A threat to your comfort and your security." Dovey shot Sassy a stern look and dropped her voice. "I suggest you and Leroy cool it for a spell."

"Oh, you always say that." Sassy waved impatiently. "Move on."

"Well, now. Here's a surprise—a rose for love."

"At my age I hardly think so." Sassy scooted forward to peer into the cup. "Where the hell you see that?"

"Right there." Dovey traced the pattern with her finger above the cup. "A perfect little rose."

Sassy snorted. "I don't see any rose."

"Quit looking for the fish," Dovey snapped. The fish was a symbol of sexuality. Aunt Sassy usually had a Great White Shark in the bottom of her cup. "See? The rose is right there next to the knife."

"Good. I can use it to cut down that damn rose."

"The knife means a misunderstanding, Sassy. Or duplicity."

"That's a two-faced person, ain't it? Like Mary Lou Hanley?"

"Look how the knife is pointing. Right straight at—"

Aunt Dovey blinked. Her lips parted and she shot straight up on the couch. She blinked again and put on her glasses, looked down at the table and frowned. "That ain't your cup, Sassy. This is your cup."

She picked up the one next to it and shoved it under Sassy's nose. The blazing red lipstick on the rim shot a chill through Lindsay. The numbness welled up inside her and closed a fist around her throat.

"Kiss-Me-You-Fool Red. Sassy, you goose. You gave me Lindsay's cup."

"So what?" Aunt Sassy pushed Dovey's hand away. "Keep reading. I want to know what the knife's pointing at."

Lindsay pulled the cup away. The quick jerk she gave the saucer stirred the leaves out of their pattern and eased the clamp on her throat.

"Why, Lindsay Evelyn," Sassy said. "How rude."

"Sorry, Aunt Sassy. My cup, my tea leaves."

"Don't you want to know where the knife's pointing?"

At my back, Lindsay thought, *and it's in Jolie's hand.* "No," she said and carried the cup to the sink.

She turned on the water, poured the tea and the leaves down the drain, and rinsed the cup. Her hands were shaking. Dovey came up beside her and took it and the saucer away from her.

"There's only signs and portents in tea leaves, child," she said gently. "Nothing that can't be changed and nothing to fear."

"Thank you for dinner, Aunt Dovey." Lindsay kissed her cheek.

She sped through her good-byes, the fist tightening around her throat. As she grabbed her coat and purse off Aunt Dovey's bed, the dresser mirror whispered at her to take a peek, but Lindsay ignored it. She rushed into the foyer, tossing a wave over her shoulder as she slid into her coat and shot through Aunt Dovey's glass storm door. It banged shut behind her—just like Jolie—and she winced.

Lindsay raced to the Civic, slammed the door, and gripped the wheel. She drew a breath, felt the numbness ebb and the vise on her throat ease, and drew her lungs full of air.

"Nothing but tea leaves," she muttered. "Nothing to be afraid of."

Just signs and portents. Swirls of tea leaves in the bottom of a cup to Aunt Dovey, but Chaos to Lindsay, the thing that terrified her the most. She knew what the numbness was, panic attacks. They'd started in L.A. when she was thirteen and Vivienne wouldn't speak to her. She'd had six months of therapy to learn how to control her bouts of panic, slipping into her appointments in a wig so she wouldn't be recognized.

The attacks stopped when she came home to Belle Coeur, fired up again when Mark died, and eased off around the six-month anniversary of his death. Now they were back. They'd started again last fall, when she told Jolie she'd do the play. And they were getting worse. She couldn't remember her lungs ever seizing up and refusing to breathe.

Lindsay knew what the attacks meant. As if Emma weren't enough, now her psyche was trying to tell her this play was a *really* bad idea.

"You're right, Self, but we signed a contract we can't get out of. Not this time," Lindsay said to her reflection as she adjusted the rearview mirror. "But next time we will for sure. I promise. No more plays."

The last clutch of panic let go in her chest. Lindsay sighed, backed the Civic out of its spot between Uncle Ezra's truck and Emma's Mustang, and turned toward home. She still felt jumpy and now she had a headache. A dull thud right in the middle of her forehead.

What a stupid place for a headache. Lindsay rubbed it and made a left into her driveway. She'd soak in the tub and make a cup of tea—nice, normal tea in a bag with LIPTON stamped on the tab at the end of the string—and curl up in a chair with a book and Pyewacket. It was impossible to be tense with a purring cat in your lap.

Only Pyewacket was locked in the barn.

Well, damn. Lindsay stepped on the brake. Well, *duh*. All she had to do was go get him. She wheeled the car around and turned left, heading west toward Belle Coeur, the barn, and the mass of silver-edged storm clouds spreading across the horizon.

Looked like a thunderstorm. Sleet yesterday, rain today. Good old Missouri weather. Lindsay flipped on the radio but there was only static where Uncle Ron's station should be. When the sun went down, MOJO went with it. Had to do with the curve of the earth and how the AM signal bounced off the ionosphere. Uncle Ron could explain it, but only Uncle Ron could understand it. Poor man. The weather wasn't his fault.

Lindsay turned off the radio and dug in her purse to make sure she had the key Uncle Donnie had given her, the key Jolie didn't know about. "Our daddy left the barn to Joe," Donnie told Lindsay. "So far as me and Lonnie is concerned, that gives you as much right to come and go as the rest of us. Let's just don't tell You-Know-Who."

She'd better check, Lindsay decided, better make sure You-Know-Who really had gone to St. Louis before she let herself into the barn. She'd had enough Chaos for one day, and she'd promised Uncle Donnie she'd be careful how she used the key. Stouthearted as her uncles were, Donnie and Lonnie both quailed at the mere thought of Jolie's temper.

She lived rent-free in the house where Lindsay had spent the first eight years of her life listening to Vivienne scream and throw things at Joe. The white bungalow with dormer windows in its blue roof sat at the edge of the apple orchard. About a mile past the barn at the end of the farm road Donnie had paved so Jolie could get out when it snowed. She'd moved in when she was nineteen and couldn't stand being under Aunt Dovey's roof another second.

Lindsay hadn't set foot in the place since the night Vivienne woke her once Joe was passed out drunk in the living room and hustled her into the car. Jolie wakened, too. She'd stood in the open front door, the porch light making a halo around her frizzy little red head, crying hysterically as her mother and her sister sped away.

The memory washed through Lindsay as she steered the Civic around the curve in the short stretch of private road, stopped next to a split rail fence under a gnarled hedge apple tree, and stared at the front door. Painted blue behind an aluminum storm door, a white and blue awning hung above the concrete stoop. In her head she heard Jolie scream

"Mama! Don't leave! Mama! Take me, too! Mama! Please!", felt her heart start to pound and her breath hitch.

Lindsay shoved the gearshift into park and pushed a button to bring down the window. The outside air was damp and cool, but there wasn't enough of it. Spots were swimming at the edges of her vision.

She fell out of the car, half-fainting, and grabbed the door, pulled herself up, and managed a shallow breath. Okay. This was good. She could breathe standing up. Lindsay hung on to the car, closed her eyes, and focused on breathing, in and out, slow and deep, till the fist in her chest unclenched. Then she opened her eyes and looked at the house.

It would be dark soon, good and dark back here at the end of the road under the hedge apple and the other hardwoods and pines edging the orchard. Yet the porch light wasn't on and all the windows were dark. How many times had she told Jolie to leave a light on when she went out at night? She'd bought her a timer, but Jolie wouldn't use it.

Why? It wasn't safe here at night. It had never been safe. This was an awful place, a terrible place. How could Jolie live here?

Lindsay offered to buy her a house, build her a house, anything to get her away from here, but Jolie refused. She said no to everything Lindsay offered. She wanted to make it on her own, she said, a million times she'd said it, yet she'd accepted a twenty-thousand-dollar loan from her cousins.

Lindsay obviously had more money than sense or she would've given up on Jolie long ago. Why did she keep hanging in, keep getting kicked in the heart? What was wrong with her? What was wrong with Jolie that she wouldn't accept a lousy $4.99 timer from Wal-Mart?

Lindsay sucked in a breath and felt her chest start to seize. Oh no. She was not going to have another panic attack. She'd had them in L.A. because she was miserable and depressed. Depressed because she was angry and too timid because she was a child to stand up to her mother.

Well. She wasn't a kid anymore. She wasn't timid anymore, either. She'd punched Noah in the nose yesterday, hadn't she? How dare he grin at her and wisecrack, "Then I guess I stopped by to see if you'd like to pick up where we left off."

And she was livid with Jolie for springing Noah on her without warning, so furious her heart pounded in her ears.

She needed to hit something to release the anger pent up inside her, the anger that was choking off her breath. No Hollywood smart-ass handy and no plastic baseball bat like the one she'd used in L.A. to whack the hell out of her bed when she got mad at Vivienne.

What could she use? Lindsay looked around for a stick, a branch. Anything. Her gaze fell on the hedge apples littering the ground along the edge of the road. Green sponge balls about the size of small grapefruit. Last year's crop, but hedge apples had the same half-life as uranium.

Lindsay snatched one up. It was brown and mottled in spots but still mostly green and pretty firm. Now she needed a target. Not her car, she'd just washed it. The trunk of the hedge apple was too small—her gaze swung around and locked on the house.

"Perfect," she said grimly. "The Amityville Horror."

Lindsay drew back her arm and threw. The hedge apple sailed about ten feet and plopped to the ground. She was too far way and she'd thrown like a girl, limp-wristed and overhand. Lindsay pushed her door shut and hurried around the car, her breath coming in shallow pants. She snatched up another hedge apple, wound up, and threw underhand like she was pitching softball.

It hit the step and bounced into the flowerbed next to the stoop. Better, but she was still too far away. Lindsay snatched up a few more hedge apples, moved closer, and hurled one at the house.

Smack! It hit just beside the living room window, split, and oozed bits of scaly green skin on the glass.

"That's for the timer!" Lindsay shouted and threw another one—*Splat!* It hit between the window and the front door, burst, and spewed a glop of seeds and the milky white goo inside all over the mailbox.

"That's for saying I can't act!" she hollered, and lobbed another one.

Thwack! It exploded, spraying skin and seeds everywhere.

"And that's for Noah!" she shouted. "Too bad it wasn't his head!"

Lindsay fired hedge apples till the front of the house dripped with lumps of green skin, globs of seeds, and slimy white gunk. Until her arms ached and her body shook from the adrenaline burning out of her. She leaned forward with her hands on her knees, out of breath from exertion, not panic. She was out of hedge apples, too. She could gather more, but Lindsay figured she'd done enough. She straightened, drew a deep, unrestricted breath, looked at the house, winced, and said, "*Ooh.*"

Jolie would be livid when she saw the mess, but it wouldn't scare her. Nothing scared her, which was too bad. If Jolie were frightened enough it might get her out of here, might break the hold this place and its old hurts and sorrows had on her.

This house was an emotional and spiritual sinkhole. Lindsay knew it but couldn't convince Jolie. It was so maddening, so frustrating. Lately she'd started praying the house would be struck by lightning some night when Jolie wasn't home. Lindsay heard a far-off rumble of thunder and thought *tonight, maybe tonight*. It was an awful thing to wish, but if the house burned, if Jolie didn't have it to cling to . . .

"Oh my God." Lindsay's breath caught and the hair on the back of her neck stood as she stared at the house and remembered.

Vivienne throwing her in the beat-up station wagon and jumping in beside her. Jolie's screams as the car shot away up the road to the barn. Vivienne's clamped jaw and hands like claws on the wheel. Bumping her head on the dashboard when Vivienne slammed on the brakes in front of the barn and switched off the engine. "You stay here," she'd said to Lindsay. "Don't you move. I'll be right back."

The gleam in her mother's eyes terrified her. Now, Lindsay realized, because she'd never seen Vivienne cry before. She'd watched her hurry toward the barn with a newspaper, drop to her knees, and spring the flame of her cigarette lighter between her cupped palms.

The barn had stood on top of its bluff for almost a century against wind, rain, hail, and tornadoes. It had been hit by lightning dozens of times and survived. A Bic and a rolled up copy of *The Belle Coeur Beacon* wouldn't bring it down.

But Vivienne had tried, out of sheer anger and frustration. Not to burn it down, but to get Joe Varner's attention. God knew she'd tried everything else to make him realize that every time he tossed a Jim Beam bottle in the trash he threw away a little piece of his life and his family with it. Lindsay could see that now, standing here still shaking with anger and frustration from lobbing hedge apples at Jolie's house.

The Varners and the Fairchilds saw it as sheer spite and meanness. Joe wrote a song about it, a broken-hearted country ballad that got him noticed in Nashville. He left Jolie with Dovey and went off to cut a record and go on tour. Then another record and another tour, till he finally just didn't come back to Belle Coeur anymore. He sent money and presents to Jolie and called her at least once a month. He'd tried to call Lindsay, but Vivienne always hung up on him.

He showed up when Trey was born but he didn't stay long. He'd drift back occasionally, sleep at the barn or with the uncles at the farm, then drift away again, his gentle spirit broken by drink and Vivienne.

Lindsay sighed and turned toward the car, saw a hedge apple lying on the edge of the road, in the grass by the right front tire, and smiled.

"Well, what do you know." She picked it up and turned it in her hand. "This one has Vivienne's name on it."

Lindsay spun around and fired the hedge apple. It smashed into the house like a pistol shot and blew apart in chunks.

"That's for you, Vivienne! For abandoning my baby sister!"

For breaking her heart, for leaving her behind feeling unloved. So frightened and angry all Jolie knew how to do was lash out and hurt.

"Lindsay?" Noah said behind her. "What the hell are you doing?"

Chapter 9

NOAH SOUNDED WINDED, as short of breath as Lindsay suddenly felt. *Again,* but odds were he wasn't having a panic attack. Neither was she, by God. No way was she going to fall apart in front of Noah Patrick.

"Lindsay?" he repeated. "What are you doing?"

Wondering where the heck you came from, she thought, as she drew a deep breath and turned around. Noah stood next to her car in red sweats and a L.A. Dodgers ball cap. He had whiskers on his chin, his hands on his hips, and sweat circles under his arms. The road was the only way in or out of here, except for the tractor path that wound through the orchard. By the mud and leaves stuck to his white running shoes, Lindsay figured Noah must've come from there.

"I'm getting caught red-handed," she said, "throwing hedge apples at Jolie's house."

"What's a hedge apple?" he asked.

"That's one." Lindsay nodded. "By your left foot."

"This thing?" Noah picked up the splotched and yellowed hedge apple and turned it in his hand. "Looks like a Nerf ball with acne."

"It's a fruit, inedible unless you're a squirrel. They don't eat the skin, just the seeds inside if they can get at them."

"Where's it come from?" Noah looked around at the woods enclosing the road on one side and the orchard on the other.

"That tree." She pointed at the stooped and thorny mother tree. "It's an Osage orange. The settlers planted them in hedges as corrals and windbreaks. That's where the name hedge apple comes from."

Noah stepped away from the car and came toward her. Lindsay's pulse jumped but she held her ground. This was her turf. He was the outsider here and that's where she intended to keep him—*way* outside and *way* away from her. She wasn't angry anymore; she'd spent all her fury on the hedge apples. She actually wanted to smile seeing him like this, sweaty, unshaven, and unkempt. The Noah Patrick she'd known couldn't pass a mirror, a window, or any reflective surface without admiring his appearance. And it didn't hurt to see him. Well, a little, but it was just a dull, God-you-were-a-jerk ache.

"So this is it." Noah swung wider into the road so he could see around her. "This is where Jolie lives."

"Yes. We both lived here when we were children."

"Huh." Noah shook his head. "I expected it to be made of gingerbread. The front yard strewn with the bones of unwary children she caught and ate for breakfast."

Lindsay laughed, a startled, I-shouldn't-but-it's-funny laugh. Noah grinned. She smiled, cool and poised. There wasn't a single trace left of the anger—and it had to be anger, gut-deep and screaming to get out—that had driven Lindsay to wreak hedge-apple havoc on Jolie's house. Noah knew a thing or two about that kind of anger. It was weird, almost eerie, not to see so much as a flicker of it in her eyes.

He turned away from her, working his index and middle fingers around the hedge apple in a split-fingered grip. The thing was twice the size of a hardball but it was soft so he managed it, drew back his arm, and fired a perfect strike. The hedge apple smashed into the house and exploded, spewing seeds and gooey white shit all over the steps.

"There." Noah faced Lindsay. "Now we've both been caught throwing hedge apples at Jolie's house. I won't tell if you don't."

She blinked at him. Twice. "When'd you get to be a nice guy?"

Noah laughed. "When'd you get to be gorgeous?"

She smiled. Vaguely, like she hadn't quite heard him, and nodded at the house. "Are you staying with Jolie?"

"Hell no. I hear she turns into a bat at night and sucks blood. I've come up with the perfect nickname for her. Satan's Handmaiden. What d'you think?"

"I think she'd like it."

Okay. This was officially bizarre. Twice he'd insulted her sister and twice she'd smiled at him. Either Lindsay despised Jolie as much as Jolie despised her or the Stepford Wives had come to Belle Coeur, Missouri.

"Is pelting houses with hedge apples some weird Easter ritual?"

"No." He half expected her to drop her eyes and look him in the chest like she had yesterday, but she held his gaze. "I guess you could say I was having a temper tantrum."

"I've had a few of those. Usually with a bottle of tequila in my hand." Noah picked up another hedge apple. "I like this better. No hangover."

"Please don't throw that. I've got a big enough mess to clean up."

"You're light years ahead of me." Noah pitched the hedge apple over the split-rail fence sagging along the edge of the road. "Took me a long time to learn how to clean up after myself. Can I give you a hand?"

"No," she said sharply, then added quickly, "I mean, no thank you. I don't want to keep you."

In other words, take a hike, Ike. At last he was getting to her, but not in a good way. She'd shouted something, as he'd come jogging out of the trees, but he hadn't heard the words. He'd been too lost and too worried that the bears he just knew were lurking in these so-goddamn-thick-you-can't-see-the-bears-hiding-in-them woods would find *him* before he found his way back to the barn.

"The only thing you're keeping me from is a shower," Noah said. "If Jolie has a hose, I can kill two birds with one stone."

"When Jolie needs a hose she borrows one from our Uncle Donnie and Uncle Lonnie." Lindsay drew a key ring from the pocket of her green trench coat. "I'm on my way up to the barn to get one."

"I know where Donnie keeps the hoses." Noah backed up to the car, opened the driver's door, and made a ladies-first sweep of his arm.

He hadn't the foggiest idea where Donnie kept the hoses, but the lie sounded way more macho than "For the love of

God, take me with you! Don't leave me here to be eaten by bears!"

"How do you know Uncle Donnie and where he keeps the hoses?"

"I'm staying at the barn, in your father's old pad. I got the grand tour yesterday." Noah walked around the car and opened the rear door. "I smell like dead sweat socks, but I'll be glad to sit in back."

Lindsay cocked her head at him. "You're lost, aren't you?"

"Yeah, I am," Noah admitted. "Totally."

"Get in." She smiled and came toward the car. "I'll drive you."

She didn't say he could ride in front, so he scraped the worst of the gunk off his shoes and got in back. When Lindsay started the engine he pushed the button and lowered the window. He wanted to knock her off her feet but not with B.O.

"If it weren't for all the trees," she said, as she turned the car away from Jolie's house, "you could see the barn from here."

"If it weren't for all the trees I could see the bears, too."

"Bears?" Lindsay laughed at him in the rearview mirror. "There aren't any bears in Missouri."

"How 'bout lions and tigers?"

"None of those, either."

"Good. Then maybe I'll stay."

Noah had no idea why he'd said that until Lindsay's gaze flew to the rearview mirror. "You're leaving?"

"Thinking about it. I'm not sure I can deal with your sister."

She looked back at the road. Noah counted to eleven before she said, "Did you sign a contract?"

"Sure. A real piece of crap, not that it matters. I would've signed whatever Vivienne put in front of me."

"What does Vivienne have to do with you being here?"

"She cooked this whole deal. In a cauldron in the dead of night, I'm sure. She pulled me off the streets, she hired me, she's paying my salary and she's paying Jolie to put up with me."

"Lucky me. I get to do it for free," Lindsay said, then

winced at him in the mirror. "I'm sorry. I didn't mean that the way it sounded."

"Oh, I think you did. I'm sure you've got a reason, but I won't ask. I probably wouldn't remember and I don't want to know. I just want to say I'm sorry for whatever I did that made you punch me yesterday."

Lindsay steered the car through a right hand curve and up a rise through still more goddamn trees. Then she glanced at him in the mirror.

"What exactly don't you remember?"

"I don't *exactly* remember much of anything. Booze kills a lot of brain cells. I remember Jessie, for instance, better than I remember you. Vivienne said you and I fought all the time."

"Oh, we did," Lindsay said quickly. "I didn't like you and you didn't like me. Not one bit. We didn't get along at *all*."

"We seem to be getting along now."

"Well, we're adults." Her right shoulder lifted in a shrug. "We're not silly, immature children. *BBT* and all that I'm-a-star foolishness was a long time ago. I should hope we've moved past that."

Oh, they had. Noah was sure of it. He was also sure they'd moved past the reason she'd punched him at the speed of light.

"I'm sorry you're leaving." Lindsay reached up and adjusted the rearview mirror. "I was looking forward to the play. I haven't done any acting since *BBT*. It would've been fun."

She dropped the mirror enough that Noah could see the smile lighting her face. A sorry-my-ass, I'm-so-happy-you're-leaving-I-can-hardly-goddamn-stand-it smile.

"I said I was *thinking* about leaving."

"Oh." Lindsay's gaze flashed back to the road. "Sorry."

"Nobody in L.A. will hire me, Lindsay. Not that I blame them. I wouldn't hire a rude, arrogant drunk who didn't show up half the time and didn't know his lines when he did. I need this job to prove to the big boys that I've quit drinking and cleaned up my act."

"I'm glad you have," she said, but it was a platitude, a cool, polite little platitude she no more meant than she'd meant anything else she'd said to him. "But I doubt anyone in L.A. will notice. The Belle Coeur Theatre isn't exactly in the theatrical mainstream."

"That's where you come in. My name won't draw flies, but hooked up with yours, performing together like we did on *BBT*, Vivienne seems to think I'll get noticed. If the play is a hit and I keep my nose clean."

She arched an eyebrow at him. "*You* will get noticed?"

"And Vivienne. She'll get the credit for salvaging the wreck of Noah Patrick and his career. She'll be the Mother Teresa of Hollywood agents. That's how she phrased it to me."

"*Vivienne?*" Lindsay laughed but it had a bitter edge.

"She and I are in the same boat. Her shitty reputation has caught up with her. It's about to sink her agency. She needs an image overhaul and she figures if she can resurrect my career it'll resurrect hers, too."

"I had no idea Vivienne's agency was in trouble."

"Neither did Jolie till I told her this morning. Just before I told her I'd throw her out if I ever woke up and found her in my apartment again. Does she make a habit of letting herself into men's bedrooms?"

"Not that I'm aware of." Lindsay tipped the mirror again and looked him square in the eye. "Why are you telling me this, Noah?"

"I think you deserve to know that you're being used. I had no idea till you almost fainted when I came down the stairs yesterday that you hadn't a clue what's going on."

The car emerged from the trees. On the same stretch of road Noah had jauntily taken off on two hours ago to do his daily run. There was the barn, big, huge, bright fucking red and right smack in front of him. Noah twisted around, looked behind the car, and saw the path he'd followed, a graveled track veering to the left away from the road.

"That's the way I went," he said, pointing out the rear window.

Lindsay glanced in the mirror. "Well no wonder you got lost. That's a tractor path. It winds all over the farm."

"This is part of the farm? Donnie and Lonnie's farm?"

"My grandparents left the barn to my father, but the rest

of it, all thirty-five hundred acres, belong to Donnie and Lonnie and Uncle Ron."

Lindsay drove past the back door to Joe Varner's apartment, down the hill past the barn and made a left into the theater parking lot. Noah turned around, saw the sky dead ahead, and said, "Whoa."

It was dark as the mouth of hell and it was *moving*, rolling toward the barn like a big black wave. Noah heard a rumble of thunder and felt a cold slap of wind through his rolled down window.

"Just a guess," he said, "but I think it's gonna rain."

"It's going to pour." Lindsay parked the car parallel to the entrance, as close to the canopy over the walkway as she could. "Any second," she said as a handful of big fat raindrops splattered the windshield.

"I don't have a key to this door," Noah said, yanking his hat down around his ears as he pushed up the window.

"I do," Lindsay replied and shoved her door open.

They bailed out of the car and dashed under the canopy. For all the good it did them when a huge crack of thunder boomed and the sky opened in sheets of rain that lashed sideways across the parking lot. Lindsay stuck a key in the double glass doors, squinting so she could see through the rain blowing under the canopy.

"This should take care of hosing off Jolie's house," Noah said, raising his voice so she could hear him above the drum of the rain.

"The worst of it, anyway." Lindsay pulled her key out of the lock and reached to open the left-hand door.

So did Noah. He felt her hand jerk as his fingers wrapped over hers but she didn't pull away. She slid around the door and caught the inside bar, hanging on to keep the door from blowing back on its hinges as Noah ducked into the foyer and helped her pull it shut.

"Is the weather around here always this much fun?" He swept his hat off and raked back his hair. The ends were wet and dripping down his neck. "Sleet yesterday, today a monsoon."

"Spring is the most volatile season." Lindsay flicked rain off her fingers. "And the summers can get pretty hot."

"I'm from California. I like hot. I thrive on hot."

"Then you'll love July." Lindsay slipped out of her coat and shook the rain off it. She wore tailored navy trousers and a sweater banded in cream and navy. No wedding ring, only a watch.

He looked like a bag of trash left out in the rain for about a week, Lindsay like a dew-kissed rose. The damp on her cheeks and lashes glistened in the stormy half-light coming through the glass doors.

"When you talked to Jolie," she asked, combing her hair back with her fingers, "did you tell her you were thinking about leaving?"

"I told her that if I walk out she won't get any more money from Vivienne. She didn't believe me until she read the contract again."

"If you leave you won't get any more money, either."

"This isn't about money for me. For Jolie this is about money. What about you? What's in this for you, Lindsay?"

"No motive and no agenda here." She turned away, flipping a wall switch to turn on the lights as she stepped into the lobby. "I'm just keeping the promise I made Jolie."

Noah toed off his shoes, picked them up, and followed Lindsay across the lobby. She tossed her coat over the hat check counter and slipped her key in the pocket.

"Where's your kid?" Noah asked her.

"Trey is spending the night with his cousin Denny." She tucked the flap over her pocket and turned toward him. "Have you seen a cat wandering around? He's black and his name is Pyewacket."

"When I left to go running he was snoring on my pillow."

"Oh." She blinked. "I'd like to take him home, if you don't mind."

"Sure. He's not my cat." Noah shrugged. He hoped it looked indifferent rather than disappointed. "Right this way."

"I'll wait here. Pyewacket will go anywhere with anyone. Just say 'Come Pye' and he'll follow you downstairs."

"I could give you a glass of milk."

"Thank you but I just finished dinner." Lindsay held her hand up to her throat. "I'm full up to here."

So was Noah with her keep-away attitude. He was more

than willing to let bygones be bygones, but clearly she wasn't. Maybe he shouldn't have told her he remembered Jessie better than he remembered her. Or maybe he really did smell like dead sweat socks.

"Fine. Be right back."

Noah crossed the lobby, bounded up the stairs to the second floor and down the hall to Joe Varner's apartment. Pyewacket was still asleep on the bed. He cracked an eye when Noah dropped his shoes on the floor and pointed his thumb over his shoulder.

"Somebody here to see you," he said. "She's down in the lobby."

Pyewacket sat up and stretched. He licked a paw and ran it over his whiskers, winked one emerald eye as if to say, *"See you around, sport,"* and jumped off the bed. He padded out of the bedroom, across the living room, and out the door Noah had left open.

He locked the apartment with the key Ron had given him and followed Pyewacket. When he came down the steps to the landing he saw the cat in Lindsay's arms—the place Noah had concluded he was never gonna be—rubbing noses with her and purring so loudly he could hear it clear across the lobby. Furry little shitbag.

"Your cat's a real pain in the ass." Noah came down the last flight of steps and crossed the lobby in his stocking feet. "He woke me up twice last night to let him out."

"Cats are nocturnal." Lindsay looked at him over Pyewacket's pointy black ears. "They prowl all night."

"So do drunks, but I don't drink anymore. I gave it up. Not just for Lent, either. For good."

"I'm not one of the big boys, Noah." Lindsay opened her arms and let Pyewacket jump to the floor. "You don't have to convince me."

"Just thought I'd let you know you can count on me to show up and know my lines."

"If you stay, you mean." Lindsay smiled and reached for her coat.

Noah beat her to it, shook it open and held it for her. The water-repellent fabric was damp and smelled like flowers. Spicy flowers.

"Thank you." Lindsay slipped her arms into the sleeves and turned to face him. Celebrity magazines raved about Jennifer Aniston's hair because they hadn't seen Lindsay Varner's lately. She swept it free of her coat collar and it fell into a perfect golden swing around her shoulders.

"I didn't read the contract before I signed it," she said. "I didn't know till Jolie announced it that we were doing this play together."

"I figured that when you asked me what I was doing here. Nice of Jolie to let you know I was coming."

"She said she wanted to surprise me."

"You don't like surprises."

Noah said it with such certainty it surprised him. Lindsay, too, by the swift lift of her chin and the startled blink she gave him.

"Well, what do you know. I guess I do remember you."

"I don't allow myself to be used, Noah." Lindsay drew her shoulders straight and looked him in the eye. "If you stay and the play is a hit, if your career takes off, it won't be because of me. It'll be because you made the commitment, because you chose to show up and know your lines."

"That's what they say half of life is, don't they? Just showing up? 'Course I've learned that it helps if you show up sober."

"It's worked for me so far," Lindsay said and he laughed. It was the first glimmer of humor he'd seen in her.

She smiled and turned toward the foyer. Pyewacket padded along beside her. Like a dog, the dopey cat. Noah stepped ahead of Lindsay, pushed the door open, and swung outside to hold it for her.

Rain dripped off the canopy, pooling into puddles on the pitted walkway. He stepped in one, naturally, and soaked his socks. The cloudburst had passed. The sun or what was left of it—Noah figured it had to be pushing six o'clock—had come out. Patches of pale gold light shimmered on the wet surface of the parking lot.

"Thank you." Lindsay drew her car keys out of her pocket. "Jolie told me she'll have the script ready tomorrow."

"I'll read it," Noah said, then remembered to add, "If I stay."

"Oh, I think you'll stay," Lindsay replied, and turned away.

No good-bye, no see you later. Noah thought about whistling at her just to see what she'd do, but he didn't. He held the door and watched her walk to her car, open it, and get in and drive away with Pyewacket curled in the back window. Couple of cool customers, Lindsay Varner and her cat. On the surface, anyway.

Noah went inside and locked the door, peeled off his wet socks, and took himself upstairs. He showered and washed his hair, shaved and drank a glass of milk, put on jeans and a white T-shirt, and flopped on the couch. He meant to watch *Sportscenter* on ESPN but there was nothing on TV but snow and static. The weather, he guessed, and tossed the remote aside, went into the kitchen, and opened the back door. Water stood on the cement block floor of the stairwell but there were no frogs.

Noah shut the door, locked it, and put on the chain, opened the fridge, and poked through the dishes on the shelves. The tuna casserole, chicken and dumplings, a cake with white frosting, a pie he thought was apple, a dish with cheese and shredded lettuce he thought was Mexican.

Nothing looked good to him. Lindsay's rain-kissed mouth . . . now that would've been delicious, licking her lips dry with his tongue. Holding her, caressing her, finding out what, besides a whole boatload of anger, seethed beneath her cool, serene façade.

A telephone rang somewhere in the apartment. Noah didn't even know he had one. He shut the fridge, went looking, and found a 900 MHz cordless phone on its base on a shelf behind the doors of the hutch-top desk. He punched TALK and said, "Hello?"

"I called earlier," Vivienne said. "Where were you?"

"Out running, warden."

"Has Jolie given you a script yet?"

"No. She said she'll have it ready tomorrow."

"Remind her to FedEx me a copy. I've only seen a draft."

"Remind her yourself. The less I have to talk to Jolie the better."

"Problem?"

"Let's just say she reminds me an awful lot of you."

"Stick around tomorrow. I'm having a car delivered for you."

"I don't need a car. Doesn't look like there's much of anyplace to go around here, anyway. Except maybe the feed store."

"That reminds me. Don't let my sisters cook for you. All they know is red meat and starch and sugar. Your arteries will explode in a week."

Vivienne didn't say good-bye—she never did. She just hung up. So did Noah. He looked at the base sitting on the shelf inside the top of the desk, slammed the phone on it, and smacked the doors shut.

If Vivienne was the only person who ever called, he'd just as soon the damn thing never rang again.

Chapter 10

EMMA BEAT LINDSAY to the store Monday morning. For the first time since they'd bought The Bookshelf from Aunt Muriel. Ten years ago, when her arthritis got so bad she couldn't stand for eight hours. Emma had coffee and four Krispy Kreme raspberry-filled donuts ready in the breakroom. Lindsay had circles under her eyes.

"I haven't seen that face since you got off the plane from L.A.," Emma said. "That face has Noah Patrick written all over it."

"If this face has to talk," Lindsay warned, "before it inhales those donuts and sucks up that coffee, this face will crack."

"Eek," Emma said, and pushed the Krispy Kreme box toward her.

Aunt Dovey called jelly donuts Bismarcks. Lindsay called them Nirvana. Pyewacket was partial to blueberry crullers. Emma broke one into pieces for him. Lindsay wondered how she'd known that Pye, MIA this time yesterday, would be with her. Probably the same way Fairchild women always knew things, which meant Lindsay was not going to ask.

"I went by the barn yesterday to find Pye," she said when she finished eating. "But I found Noah instead. Or rather, he found me."

She told Emma she'd driven by Jolie's to make sure she'd gone to St. Louis and about the panic attack, which made Emma frown. When she started on the hedge apples, Emma grinned. When she finished, Emma was laughing so hard she had tears in her eyes.

"It isn't funny, Em. It was an awful thing to do."

"It was the perfect thing to do. You're the last person Jolie would suspect of a drive-by hedge apple pelting. It'll make her crazy trying to figure out who did it." Emma stopped laughing. "Unless you tell her. And if you do, so help me I'll say you're lying and tell her I did it."

"I thought a lot about Jolie last night." A lot about Noah, too. "I've decided it's time to fight fire with fire. I'm going to confess. I want to see the look on her face when I tell her I threw the hedge apples and she realizes I can be just as sneaky and stinky as she can."

"Sounds like fun. Hope I get to watch." Emma shut the donut box. "If we're going to change the window displays, we'd better get a move on."

"I thought gardening in one window and Mother's Day in the other."

"Perfect. Let's do it."

Emma headed up front, Lindsay to the stock room. Pyewacket followed her. He jumped up on the stock cart, white-painted stainless steel with six shelves, three on each side, and let Lindsay push him up the center aisle to the front of the store. Emma had the east window, the one closest to the cash wrap, half-emptied. Lindsay parked the cart and Pyewacket between them and started stripping the west window.

"If you change your mind about confessing," Emma said, "you could always blame the hedge apples on Noah. He did throw one."

"He offered to help me clean up the mess, too."

"He did? That doesn't sound like the Noah Patrick of old."

"I know. He was so . . . un-Noah-like. It was weird."

Weird enough to keep Lindsay awake half the night wondering if Noah had grown up when he sobered up or if aliens had landed in L.A. and taken over the population. Not that anyone would notice.

"Did he make a pass at you?" Emma asked.

"Not exactly. He just asked me when I got to be gorgeous."

"Then he doesn't remember you. You've always been gorgeous."

"Please, Em." Lindsay made a face. "I just ate."

"Well, you have. That's two of the reasons Jolie hates you. Number one because you were born with a face made for TV, and number two because she wasn't."

"I refuse to believe Jolie hates me." Lindsay carried an armful of books to the cart and nudged Pyewacket out of the way. "Yes, she resents me. Yes, she blames me for everything that's ever gone wrong in her life, but that's transference. She takes her anger out on me because she can't take it out on Vivienne."

"Believe what you want about Jolie." Emma plucked an Easter basket out of the window and faced Lindsay. "Just please don't tell me you believe Noah remembers Jessie better than he remembers you."

"The only thing he remembers is I don't like surprises. He said he was sorry for whatever he did that made me punch him on Saturday."

Emma dropped the basket. It hit the floor and bounced, rolling striped plastic Easter eggs all over the carpet. Pyewacket leaped off the cart and pounced on one.

"On *Saturday*?" Emma gaped at her. "He doesn't remember you coming to his house the day after your birthday party, ready to dump Mark and run away with him? You mean he's forgotten you belted him when he opened the door wrapped in a naked, big-breasted blond?"

"That's what I mean." Lindsay gave Emma a can-you-believe-it smile. Her stomach twisted a little, but it was just a twinge compared to the heart-ripping wrench she'd felt when Noah opened the door to her that long-ago morning. "He thought he was apologizing because he lipped off when he tackled me and I cuffed him one."

"I'll kill him," Emma said, then blinked. "No I won't.

This is good news that he can't remember. So why do you look like hell?"

"I always look like hell when I don't sleep."

"Oh, that's right. Trey spent the night with Denny." Emma dropped to the floor and picked up the Easter eggs. Pyewacket latched onto the last one and clung to it by his claws. "Why else couldn't you sleep?"

"I got caught in a tea leaf reading." Lindsay sighed as she walked back to the west window. "If I hadn't been so angry with Jolie I don't think it would've fazed me."

"Mama ad libs when she reads for Aunt Sassy, you know."

Lindsay had always thought so, but Dovey wasn't faking it. There'd been no need since she'd been reading *her* cup, but Lindsay didn't say so. On a need-to-know basis, she figured Emma didn't need to know.

"So long as she has fish in her cup, Sassy's happy." Emma pried the egg away from Pye and tossed it toward the cash wrap. He sprang after it and she stood up, put the basket and the rest of the eggs on the cart. "Sassy doesn't know Mama's fibbing to her, but I think you do. I think that's why the tea leaves freak you out."

"I don't *know* anything," Lindsay said sharply. "Not the way you do and I really wish you wouldn't say so."

"You are a Fairchild."

"Not *that* kind of Fairchild."

"Okay, okay." Emma put her hands up. "Sorry."

"No, I'm sorry." Lindsay rubbed her forehead. The smack in the middle headache was still there, but it had faded to a dull now and then pulse. "I'm just tired."

"Let's finish this," Emma said, "and have another cup of coffee."

They did, while Emma counted the base fund into the register and Lindsay checked Saturday's sales totals on the PC, courtesy of the whiz-bang program designed by Darcy. At 9:57 she unlocked the front door, stepped into the cash wrap, and slipped the key in a desk drawer.

"Uh-oh. Here comes Jolie," Emma said.

Like Radar O'Reilly on *M.A.S.H.*, about five seconds before her rust bucket red pickup stopped at the curb in front of the store. Jolie hopped out of the cab in her ball cap, coveralls, and a red plaid shirt and came stalking around the nose of the truck clutching a manila envelope.

"Want me to lock the door?" Emma asked.

"No. You wanted to watch. Let her come in."

Jolie did, like the low pressure cell Uncle Ron likened her to, a storm looking for a place to happen. She shoved the door open, banging the sleigh bells that hung against the glass, marched up to the cash wrap, and slapped the envelope on the top of the display case.

"As promised, here's the play," she said. "Happy?"

"No. I'm still furious with you."

"Get over it. The read-through is tomorrow night at seven."

"If I decide to do the play."

"So." Jolie jammed her hands on her hips. "You're gonna sue me."

"I haven't decided yet. I'm meeting Susan for lunch."

"You don't have a leg to stand on."

"I have two size-eight double-A feet to stand on." Lindsay leaned over the display case into Jolie's face. "If you don't want the imprint of one of them on your fanny you'll turn around and walk out of my store."

Jolie didn't budge. "I'll fight you in court. I mean it. I've got money."

"So do I. A lot more than you have. Now go away. You're annoying me. You'll hear from Susan later today."

Jolie spun toward the door. "Emma," she said, grabbing the knob and flinging herself around. "Tell Darcy I expected a classier response from her than busting hedge apples all over my house."

"Darcy didn't do it," Lindsay shot back. "I did."

"Oh right, Miss Perfect." Jolie sneered. "I *s-o-o-o* don't believe you."

She wheeled out the door, slamming it so hard the sleigh bells leaped off their nail and hit the floor with a clunk. Jolie sprang into her truck and gunned the engine, ground the gears, and shot away.

"How do you like that?" Lindsay smacked the counter and wheeled on Emma. "She doesn't believe me!"

"I told you. I said you'd be the last person Jolie would suspect."

"But *I* did it!" Lindsay slapped her hand to her chest. "Me! Miss Perfect! And by God, I want credit for it!"

"Ain't gonna happen. You went against type." Emma grinned. "But I loved hearing you threaten to kick Jolie's butt. 'Bout time."

"I'm through being Jolie's punching bag."

"Good for you. Oops. There's the magazine vendor. I'll let him in."

Emma pushed through the gate about ten seconds ahead of the buzzer on the back door. Pyewacket jumped up on the display case, curled his tail around his front paws, and cocked his head at Lindsay.

"Vivienne isn't the only one who needs an image overhaul," she said to him. "So do I."

Noah gave her the idea. Jolie refusing to believe she'd thrown the hedge apples cinched it. If Vivienne thought she could convince Hollywood she was Mother Teresa, how hard could it be to convince Jolie she deserved the title of Satan's Handmaiden just as much as she did?

She was an actress—well, sort of—and she'd been raised by the Bitch Queen of the Universe.

"All I have to do," she told Pye, "is behave like Vivienne."

This was the first time she'd spoken her plan out loud. Lindsay expected her lungs to seize, but she was able to draw a deep breath. She hoped it meant her subconscious agreed that this was about her last chance to get through to Jolie. If payback in kind didn't make her realize it was time to stop being mad at the world because she was mad at Vivienne and get on with her life, nothing would.

"Let's see what's in here," Lindsay said to Pyewacket and upended the unsealed manila envelope on the counter.

The play, bound inside an eight and a half by eleven beige cardstock cover, tumbled out facedown on the counter. So did a blue business-size envelope, glued shut with EMMA written on the front and underlined in Jolie's bold hand. Lindsay held it up to the display case and saw a long, rectangular shadow inside—just as Emma came up the middle aisle pushing a dolly stacked with three plastic magazine crates.

"What's that?" she asked.

"An envelope from Jolie with your name on it."

Emma parked the dolly next to the wire cart. "Is it ticking?"

"No." Lindsay plucked a letter opener out of the pencil cup and handed it to her with the envelope. "Looks like a check inside."

"You snooped. I'm so proud of you," Emma said, and slit the flap.

It was a check, all right, imprinted with the name Belle Coeur Entertainment Group and signed by Jolene Varner, CEO. Drawn on Belle Coeur Bank and Trust, payable to Emma Harrington in the amount of five thousand dollars. On the memo line it said LOAN/PAID IN FULL.

Emma raised an eyebrow at Lindsay. "I thought you were kidding when you said Vivienne was giving Jolie money."

"I *was* kidding, but Noah said Vivienne is paying his salary and paying Jolie to put up with him."

"If she can afford to repay the loan with the threat of you suing her hanging over her head, Vivienne must be paying her a bundle." Emma put the check back in the envelope. "Did Noah tell you how much?"

"I'm not sure he knows but I'll ask next time I see him."

"You have plans to see him?"

"Plans? No." A sinking feeling in the pit of her stomach that she would, whether she wanted to or not, yes. "But I will tomorrow night at the read-through, if not before."

"You aren't going to sue Jolie." A slow, the-dawn-breaks smile spread across Emma's face. "You're just gonna make her sweat."

"It sounds awful out loud." Lindsay made a face. "Is it too mean?"

"Hell no." Emma laughed. "It's even better than the hedge apples."

Susan said the same thing when Lindsay met her for lunch. After she got through laughing about the hedge apples and the fact that Jolie didn't believe she'd thrown them.

"Maybe I don't need an image overhaul," Lindsay said glumly. "Maybe I need an image transplant."

Susan cocked an eyebrow at her. "What are you talking about?"

Lindsay repeated what Noah had said and told her about her plan to snap Jolie out of her lifelong snit by behaving like Vivienne.

"I think you'd have more luck transforming Jolie with voodoo. Or shock therapy. Maybe a lobotomy," Susan said, stirring Sweet 'N Low into her coffee. "She stopped by the office this morning, by the way. She gave me a check to repay my portion of the twenty-thousand-dollar loan."

"She repaid Emma, too. With Vivienne's money," Lindsay said and told Susan what Noah had told her.

"Well. That explains how she's able to pay back the loan."

"It explains everything. I couldn't figure out why Jolie went looking for Noah. It didn't make sense—she already had my promise to do this play. But if Vivienne came to her and offered her money to take Noah on so she could overhaul both their images, then it all fits."

"The circumstances fit," Susan said. "What I have trouble with is the motive. I can't see a man—any man—admitting that a woman had to pay another woman to put up with him. Talk about a hit to the ego."

That was it, Lindsay realized. That's what she hadn't seen a single trace of in Noah—his soaring, colossal ego.

"I believe him, Susan. It amazes me to admit it, but I do."

"I didn't say he was making it up, Lindsay. I just think it's odd that he was so forthright."

"This isn't the Noah Patrick I knew in L.A.," she said, the suspicion she'd had since yesterday crystallizing in her head. "He was rarely sober and he never told the truth about anything."

The old Noah, the disingenuous drunk, would be easy to blow off—a sober, forthright, and still mightily attractive Noah, a lot tougher. Not that *she* was attracted to him. She'd outgrown her idiotic infatuation, but Lindsay was sure he could still turn heads. Just not hers, not anymore.

"So how far do you want to take this with Jolie?" Susan asked.

"How far can I take it?"

"Let me have a look at the contract."

Lindsay passed it to her over the table. While Susan read it, she picked at the potato chips she hadn't eaten with her

BLT. Because it was Monday and the day after a holiday, the midday traffic on Main Street was sparse and sluggish. Even the yellow Corvette she saw, so vivid a shade of canary that it made her wince, seemed to be crawling past the Belle Coeur Café where she and Susan sat in a blue vinyl booth smack in the middle of the front window.

She looked at her watch—12:20—and tucked it under the cuff of her peach sweater. Trey would be at the store by now, inhaling the pizza she'd ordered and feeling bummed because she'd left him with Emma. She'd make sure he worked more than he goofed off. Lindsay sipped her Coke and smiled. It was good to be the Mommy.

"Someone who knows a lot more about entertainment law than I do wrote this." Susan closed the clear plastic cover and laid the contract aside. "That someone is not Bill Rich. I talked to him on Saturday. His specialty is corporate law. Some L.A. hotshot wrote this. If you'd shown it to me I could've told you a month ago that Vivian had her fingers in it."

"How many fingers," Lindsay asked, "and where exactly are they?"

"I can't tell from this. I'd say there's an addendum, probably attached to Jolie's copy, that spells out the financial arrangements."

"Aren't I entitled to know that information?"

"Nope. You're just the talent. All you're entitled to know is how much you're being paid." Susan snatched a potato chip off Lindsay's plate and munched. "Since you waived a salary, that's nothing, and that's clearly stated in your contract."

"Then how did Noah discover Vivienne's involvement? I got the impression it was from the contract, but obviously not. Unless his contract is different from mine."

"I imagine it is. His salary would be spelled out, probably travel expenses. I can't see Vivian disclosing her arrangement with Jolie to Noah or anybody else. Especially on paper. I think Jolie told him."

"No. She didn't tell him." Lindsay shook her head emphatically. "If it isn't in the contract, then he wheedled it out of her. Noah's very good at wheedling things out of people."

Or wheedling people out of things. Like their clothes. She didn't want to bash herself over the head with something heavy anymore when she remembered how easily Noah had wheedled her out of her midnight blue Valentino, her first grown-up designer gown. She'd wanted him to—stupid, idiot, naïve twit—so it hadn't taken much.

"Noah's name is all over the contract, so Jolie's right. If you'd read it you'd have known he was in the play." Susan shrugged and folded her arms on the edge of the table. " 'Course, you're right, too. You've always been such a lamb to the slaughter, Jolie figured you wouldn't read it."

"I don't like it that Vivienne has her fingers in this," Lindsay said.

"Dad won't like it either," Susan said, "so I'm not going to tell him."

"No, don't. And don't tell Dovey or Sassy. Emma knows, but so long as she doesn't tell Darcy we should be able to keep it quiet."

The yellow Corvette cruised by again, slowing as it passed the café. Like the driver was lost or looking for an address. Susan glanced at the window and blinked at it, hovering near the curb like a neon banana.

"Whoa," she said. "Do you think that car is yellow enough?"

"I think it's hideous." Lindsay clasped her hands in her lap and leaned toward Susan. There was plenty of background noise, laughter and conversation and dishes rattling, but she kept her voice low. "Is there any way I can find out how involved Vivienne is in all this?"

"Sure." Susan sipped her coffee. "Ask Jolie."

"Legally. I doubt Jolie would tell me what time it is just now."

"You mean file a petition that would force her to disclose the source of her financing?" Lindsay nodded; Susan shook her head. "It would be thrown out of court so fast it'd make our heads spin."

"Damn." Lindsay bent an elbow on the table and rubbed her brow.

The headache was back. Big surprise. Vivienne was enough to give anybody a rip-snorting headache. It flared suddenly, a sharp stab between her eyes as she glanced out the window and the Corvette went by again, this time heading west up Main Street.

"I think that guy is lost." Susan looked over her shoulder, watched the car disappear down the street, then turned around and plucked another chip off Lindsay's plate. "Why don't you ask Noah how he found out? As forthcoming as he was yesterday, I'll bet he'd tell you."

"I could," Lindsay said. "But then I'd have to talk to him."

"Well, yeah." Susan laughed. "Like you've never done that before."

"We weren't friends in L.A., Suze. We worked together. Noah was older. Wild as a March hare and Vivienne kept me on a very short leash."

A choke chain, Noah called it. He'd teased her about it. Tantalized her with it, whispered to her between takes the things he could do to her. He'd touched her in ways she burned for Mark to touch her, but Mark wasn't there—Noah was on her eighteenth birthday, the night she'd chosen to snap her leash. Going to bed with him was as much an act of defiance as it was of desire.

"That was then, Lindsay, this is now," Susan said. "You didn't have a problem talking to Noah yesterday."

"I didn't have a choice. He was lost and—"

He was still lost. Lindsay realized it as the Corvette went past the window, slowed, and the brake lights flashed. She pushed up on her hands, leaned toward the window, and peered at the back bumper.

"He's lost again," she said. "That's Noah in the Corvette."

"How can you tell?" Susan twisted around. "The glass is tinted."

"California license plate." Lindsay snatched up her purse and slid out of the booth. "Be right back."

"I'm coming with you." Susan grabbed her bag and the check.

She raced for the counter and the cashier. Lindsay dashed out the door, out from under the blue and white striped awning over the café window and hurried up the sidewalk.

"Noah!" She shouted and waved, but the Corvette was a good half a block ahead, creeping along Main Street with the brake lights winking on and off. Lindsay hung her purse over her shoulder, jumped up and down, waved both arms like flags, and bellowed, "NOAH!"

Susan came up beside her, hooked her elbow and pulled her forward, stuck her thumb and middle finger in her mouth, and gave an ear-splitting whistle. The Corvette's brake lights flashed on, then the right turn signal as it nosed up to the curb and parked. Smack dab between the two maple trees in front of The Bookshelf.

When the driver's door opened and Noah stretched out of the low-slung sports job, Lindsay's stomach jumped. He wasn't a sweaty, unshaven mess today. He wore faded jeans, blue-tinted rock star shades, and white Nikes. An appreciative little *mmm* hummed through her.

Lindsay pressed a hand to her cheek and felt the flush in her skin. What was *wrong* with her? What was she *doing*? Why had she flagged Noah down? She should've let him keep going, let him get hopelessly lost. Hopefully far, far away from Belle Coeur. But no, she'd had to stop him, had to keep him here. Why?

Noah shut the car door and stepped up on the sidewalk to meet her and Susan. The polo shirt he wore with the collar flipped up was the same butt ugly yellow as the Corvette. It was Trey's favorite expression, butt ugly, his dream car a Corvette. And here came her car crazy son bolting out of The Bookshelf with Pyewacket on his heels.

"Wow!" Trey shot off the sidewalk and into the street, circling and all but drooling over the car. "W-a-a-a-y cool wheels, man."

"You don't think it's too yellow?" Noah turned to watch Trey ogle the Corvette. "If it glows in the dark I'm gonna paint it."

"No way. This is a kick-ass color." Trey shot a grin over the roof of the car at Noah, saw Lindsay coming toward him with Susan, and gulped. "Uh—I mean it's an awesome color."

Lindsay stopped next to the Corvette, put on her Mother Face and pointed at the sidewalk. "Out of the street, please."

"Jeez, Ma! I'm not a baby!" Trey flared back at her, but

he stepped out of the street, head down and turning red around the ears.

Oh no, she'd done it again. Put another dent in his fragile teenage psyche. Lindsay bit her lip. When was she going to get the hang of this adolescent male ego stuff?

"Well hi, Noah," Susan said brightly. "Looks like you're lost again."

"Again?" He pivoted on one foot, hooked his shades over the collar of his shirt, and smiled at her. "I think *still* would be a better word."

Susan laughed. Noah smiled at Lindsay. "At least there aren't any bears around today."

"Bears?" Susan said. "There aren't any bears in Missouri."

But there was a small crowd gathering. Lindsay looked from Trey, sulking with his head down and his hands in his pockets, to the handful of diners who'd trailed her and Susan out of the café. A couple of passersby were stopping to look. And across the street, Mary Lou Hanley, Aunt Sassy's nosy neighbor here on Main Street as well as on Sycamore Lane, turned away from the wire cart full of potted daffodils and tulips she was arranging on the sidewalk in front of her flower shop, La Fleur.

Two doors down stood The Belle Coeur Academy of Performing Arts. The front door flew open and out popped Aunt Sassy in a lime green leotard and a flowered scarf tied Apache-style around her forehead.

"Ahoy," Lindsay said. "Thar she blows."

Susan turned around. So did Noah. "Oh boy," he said as Aunt Sassy shot into the street, a gleam in her eyes and a swing in her hips.

"I'll head her off." Susan stepped off the curb. "See you, Noah."

"Ahoy?" Noah cocked an eyebrow at Lindsay. "Thar she blows?"

"We call Aunt Sassy Fish Woman," Lindsay said, keeping an eye on the front of the flower shop. "I'll explain why some other time."

Mary Lou, a rail thin little woman with wren brown hair, turned away from the wire cart to watch Susan cross Main Street. Aunt Sassy tried to duck around her but Susan cut her off and they stopped, squared off and glaring at each other in the middle of the street. Aunt Sassy with her hands on her hips, Susan with her feet spread blocking her path. Mary Lou picked up the cordless phone she'd brought outside with her from the window ledge.

Everybody in Belle Coeur knew where Uncle Ezra was this time of day. At McGruff's Hardware, playing dominoes on his lunch break. That was the only thought in Lindsay's head as she watched Mary Lou turn to go inside with the phone to her ear. She didn't see Pyewacket perched on the green wheelbarrow full of petunias next to the door. Neither did Mary Lou till he sprang off the wheel and tripped her.

She yelped and dropped the phone on the doormat. It didn't break, but it bounced out of reach and slowed Mary Lou down. She aimed a kick at Pyewacket as she snatched up the phone and went on inside, but he was already gone, darting across the street to safety.

"Thank you, Pye," Lindsay murmured with a grin.

She didn't think about yesterday, about the jolt she'd felt when Noah touched her. Until she took his arm to turn him toward the car and the same flash of heat she'd felt when he'd closed his fingers over hers on the door handle raced through her like a scald.

"I don't mean to be rude," she said, willing herself not to jerk her hand back, "but I think you should go."

"Before Ezra gets here with Lucille?" Noah glanced over his shoulder. Lindsay looked with him and saw Sassy and Susan still dodging and feinting in the middle of Main Street. "Good idea."

He let her steer him around the back end of the Corvette and up to the driver's door. He took the key out of his pocket and glanced at Susan and Sassy again.

"On the other hand," he said. "Might be kinda fun to stick around."

Lindsay caught a glimpse of Chaos in the devilish, what-the-hell gleam in his eyes. Her stomach sank, but it was just a flash of the old Noah, only a flicker that vanished the instant he looked at her face.

"Relax, princess." He gave her a one-sided smile. "I'm going."

He pressed the keypad and Lindsay jumped. Not at the pop of the door locks but at hearing Noah call her princess. That's what he'd called her on the *BBT* set. Never Lindsay, always princess.

"Later, sport." Noah opened the door and nodded at Trey over the vivid yellow roof of the Corvette. "Take you for a spin sometime."

"Yeah, great," Trey said glumly. "Thanks."

He tossed Noah a sure-you-will wave and shot a fat-chance-you'd-let-me-go glare at Lindsay that made her heart twist. There wasn't enough sausage and black olive pizza in the world to fix this, but there was a Corvette. A butt ugly yellow one.

For Trey, Lindsay put her hand on Noah's arm. "He has time now," she said with a smile. "If you do."

"Sure." Noah crooked a come-on finger. "Load up, sport."

Trey's mouth fell open. "I can go?" He blinked at Lindsay as she stepped out of the street. "Really?"

"You can go." Lindsay swept an arm toward the car. "Really."

"Thanks, Ma!" He flung his arms around her, then leaped into the Corvette as Noah leaned across the console and pushed the door open. Trey shut it, leaned his bent elbow out the open window, and grinned at her, his face shining. "You're the best, Ma."

Oh son, I wish I were, Lindsay thought. "Have fun," she said and waggled her fingers at him.

"Seat belt," she heard Noah say, which gave her hope that she might actually get her child back in one piece.

Until Trey snapped on his safety harness and Noah turned the key in the ignition. The engine sprang to life with a big cat snarl that sent a jolt of panic through Lindsay. "Stop! I changed my mind!" she wanted to shout, but the Corvette was already pulling away from the curb.

Lindsay bit her lip and watched it go. So did Mary Lou, peering through the front window of La Fleur to keep the Corvette in view as it disappeared down the hill. Barely ten seconds ahead of Uncle Ezra's black pickup, swinging around the corner off Third Street onto Main.

The truck screeched to a halt and Uncle Ezra hopped out

of the cab, leaving the door open and the engine running. Aunt Sassy wheeled on him, punching a finger in his chest. Uncle Ezra waved his arms. Over the rumble of the truck's gleaming chrome side pipes, Lindsay couldn't hear a single word they shouted at each other.

Susan escaped onto the sidewalk, flipped a wave at Lindsay, and turned toward her office a block over on Maple. The passersby went on their way, the café patrons filed back inside. Only Mary Lou had any interest in the scene everyone else in Belle Coeur had witnessed a million times. She twisted and turned her head to get a better view. Lindsay thought for sure she'd fall into the flower-filled window, but she didn't. Darn it. She managed to right herself, looked across the street as she straightened, and finally noticed Lindsay, standing between the two fully leafed-out, fifteen-foot-tall maple trees in front of The Bookshelf.

Lindsay smiled and gave Mary Lou a toodle-loo wave. She frowned and wheeled out of the window.

Behind her, Lindsay heard The Bookshelf door click shut and looked over her shoulder at Emma, popping a pizza crust in her mouth and dusting crumbs off her fingers. She glanced toward Aunt Sassy and Uncle Ezra, now locked in a passionate embrace, rolled her eyes, and came up beside Lindsay.

"Do you think that was smart?" Emma gazed down Main Street, the light breeze off the river fluttering the white streak in her hair. "To let Trey go with Noah?"

"Smart? No." Lindsay sighed. "But I think it was wise."

Chapter 11

WITHOUT LINDSAY'S KID in the car, Noah never would've found the Country Mart food store. Main Street was the only straight stretch of road he'd run across in Belle Coeur. Every other damn street twisted uphill or down, around corners and hairpin curves. It was crazy, nuts. Kind of like the L.A. freeways in a fun house mirror.

"It's the geography," Trey said. "My mom says there's no straight way *to* anyplace *from* anyplace in Belle Coeur."

Maybe to the loony bin, Noah thought, but didn't say so. He drove down Main Street following Trey's directions. Way down a long, swooping hill, made a right at the bottom and cruised along the river past clusters of shops and small eateries closed up behind wooden shutters.

"Stuff down here opens on Memorial Day weekend," Trey said when he asked about it. "That's when the riverboats start running."

"Riverboats?" Noah asked. "You mean like Mark Twain?"

"Yeah. Old time paddle-wheelers. They run tourists up and down river all summer. My mom and Emma and a whole bunch of people formed this committee. They petitioned the city council to build up the Riverfront—that's what they call it down here—to attract the boats and tourists. A trolley runs up to Main Street to all the stores. And there's a fireworks display, a great big huge one, on Memorial Day."

"Sounds fun. Think we'll find the damn grocery store by then?"

Trey grinned and bounced in his seat. "Take the next right."

Noah did, changed gears, and climbed the Corvette up Spring Street, back up the same big-ass hill they'd just come down. At Third Street, Spring Street died. Just vanished. He stopped at a stop sign and looked at a red brick building staring at him across Third Street through dusty plate glass windows. A sign on the front said McGruff's Hardware.

"Turn left," Trey said. "Spring Street picks up two blocks north."

Noah found Spring Street again and turned right. The Country Mart food store was at the far end of the block, and what looked like the far end of town, across from Burger Chef. A dead cow on a bun joint with a drive-thru window and carhop slots under a green aluminum canopy. He thought Lindsay's kid was gonna break his neck twisting it to watch a twig-thin little brunette with a ponytail pulled through a green ball cap hang a tray full of burgers on the window of a black Ford Escort.

"I haven't had lunch," Noah said. "How 'bout I park at Burger Chef and you order me the special while I grab what I need from the store?"

Trey shrugged. "Whatever."

Noah swung the Corvette into Burger Chef and nosed it into a slot under the canopy. Mr. I-Could-Care-Less scooted down in his seat so he could see himself in the right side mirror and took a swipe at his hair.

Noah got out of the car, shut the door, and leaned down to hand Trey a twenty through the open window.

"Order yourself something if you want. And feel free to play with the buttons." Maybe the kid could figure out the in-dash CD player. He sure as hell couldn't. "Just don't take off."

"I wouldn't do that," Trey said. Noah believed him in spite of the oh-man-would-I-love-to gleam in his eyes.

"Back in a few." He rapped his knuckles on the sunroof, crossed the street to Country Mart, opened the door, and stepped inside.

Into an episode of *Happy Days* by the look of the place. Shiny black and green linoleum floor. White enamel fixtures straight out of the fifties. One counter and one cash register. He lifted a plastic basket with metal handles off a stack and started down the aisles, following the sweet, fruity smell in the air to the produce section.

He bagged a couple apples and oranges, three bananas, and a bunch of grapes. No avocados, but he found kiwi fruit; milk and yogurt, but no tofu. Couldn't find it anywhere, but he found a skinny, redheaded kid with spiked hair, on his knees shoving cans of green beans on a shelf.

" 'Scuse me," Noah said. "Where's the tofu?"

The kid gave him a blank look. "The what?"

"Tofu. T-o-f-u," Noah said. "Where is it?"

The kid stood up. He wore jeans, a red apron tied over a white shirt, and an honest to God Mr. Whipple don't-squeeze-the-Charmin bow tie.

"We don't carry martial arts stuff. This is a food store. F-o-o-d."

"Right." Noah sighed and lifted his basket. "Can you ring me up?"

"S-u-r-e." The kid grinned and headed up front.

"S-n-o-t," Noah muttered and followed him.

He paid for his fruit, let Ralph Malph bag it in a white plastic sack, pushed through the plate glass door and looked across the street. A cluster of teenage girls—the brunette carhop among them—hovered around the Corvette and Lindsay's kid. He leaned against the left front fender in their midst, like a sheik in his harem, a blasé, I'm-cool expression on his face. Noah grinned and slipped on his shades.

Ah, to be fifteen and a babe magnet again. Not. The way Vivienne told it, he'd enjoyed the hell out of it the first time. Too bad he couldn't remember. And too bad testosterone was wasted on the young. He wasn't ancient—he wouldn't turn thirty-eight till July—but some mornings he felt like he was sliding into the grave. No more than he deserved, he supposed, for pissing a decade of his life into a tequila bottle. Noah sighed and took his time crossing the street. Let the kid enjoy himself. God knew fame was fleeting.

When he approached the Corvette the swarm around Trey broke and veered in his direction, circling him in a ring of bright faces and sassy eyes. Noah was so surprised he almost whacked the brunette carhop in the knees with the sack swinging from his fingers.

"Mr. Patrick. Hi! Could I have your autograph?"

She had an upturned nose and Julia Roberts's teeth, took her order pad and a pen out of her apron pocket and shoved them at him.

"Sure. Happy to." Noah took the pad and pen and squinted at the white plastic nametag on her green polo shirt. "Meggie?"

"Oh it's not for me. It's for my Mom," she said brightly. "She like still goes crazy when they run your old TV show. She has all these pictures of you in her high school scrapbook she cut out of *Seventeen* and *Tiger Beat*. Her name is Pat." She went up on the toes of her white Keds and pointed a lime green fingernail at her pad. "That's spelled P-a-t."

Noah raised just his eyes from the order pad. Miss Perky

blinked and dropped back on her heels. "I think I can spell Pat."

"I was just trying to help. Trey said you're like brain-dead."

Noah raised his gaze another notch. Lindsay's kid winced and wiped an oh-man-I'm-gonna-get-killed hand over his face.

"What's your mother's name? Patricia? P-a-t-r-i-c-i-a?"

Meggie nodded. *For Pat, your kid's a brat,* he wanted to write, but didn't. *Patricia,* he wrote, *Catch a wave with me, babe,* the catch phrase he'd scrawled on everything from boobs to butts to bikinis when he ruled TV as Sam, surfer dude and coolest guy in school. Why he remembered that stupid line and couldn't remember Lindsay was really starting to piss him off. Noah signed his name and handed Meggie her pad.

"Tell your mom to come see the play. I enjoy meeting my fans."

Like he enjoyed a root canal, but he was trying. When he wasn't thinking about the shape and shimmer of Lindsay's mouth, he was thinking about what she'd said. If his career took off it would be because he'd chosen to show up and know his lines. In other words, quit dicking around, apply yourself, and play by the rules.

"She'll be there, I'm sure," Meggie said. "Like in the front row."

"I'll look for her. We'll take our order to go, please."

"Sure thing." Meggie spun away toward the pickup window, on her way passing her pad and her pen to the other girls.

They converged on him for autographs. They didn't say, "For my mom," but Noah suspected. He obliged, smiling till his teeth hurt.

Lindsay had looked so good, so gorgeous standing on the sidewalk in front of the bookstore with the sun in her hair. All he'd wanted was to stay there and look at her. All she'd wanted was him gone, outta there. Once upon a time the only flesh he'd been interested in was nubile. Now it depressed the hell out of him that it was the best he could do.

Meggie came back, handed Lindsay's kid a cardboard tray that held a white paper sack and two tall plastic cups and took back her pad and pen. The girls said thanks and drifted away, glancing back at Trey clutching the cardboard tray to his chest.

Noah leveled a finger at him. "In the car."

Trey scrambled around the Corvette and into the passenger seat. Noah got in and started the engine, clamped his hands on the wheel just in case the urge to clamp them around the kid's throat overcame him.

"Brain-dead?" he said to Trey. "Do I *look* brain-dead to you?"

"I didn't say you were brain-dead. Jolie did."

"But you repeated it to your little fan club so you'd look cool. If I'm brain-dead what's that make you? Custodian of the retard?"

"I said I was helping you find your way around."

"Right. 'Cause I'm brain-dead."

Trey turned his head and looked out the side window. Noah backed the Corvette out of its slot and drove to the exit.

"Okay, slick. How do I get to the theater from here?"

Trey swung toward him. "You aren't taking me back?"

"This stuff's gotta go in the fridge. Which way?"

"Left to One-fifty-two then make a right." Trey balanced the cardboard tray on his knees and opened the sack. "I got you the special. Barbecued pork tenderloin, onion rings, and a blueberry shake."Noah's gorge rose. "Sounds a little heavy. Toss me an apple."

Trey fished him one out of the Country Mart sack, then unwrapped a giant sandwich that reeked of tomato and onions.

"Well hey, buddy," he said.

Noah thought the kid was talking to the sandwich—damn thing looked big enough to have a name—till he saw a flash of black, turned his head, and saw Pyewacket sitting between Trey's feet on the floor.

"Where'd he come from?"

"Under the seat." Trey grinned. "He loves barbecued tenderloin."

"How'd he get here?"

"He must've followed me out of The Bookshelf and jumped through the window when we weren't looking."

"That's the last time I lock the doors and leave the windows down."

The shitbag cat ignored him. Noah ignored the shitbag cat, followed Spring Street to Business Alternate 152, and made a right. Two hills and a dip later he made another right where Trey told him, a left, and then another right, zigzaging the Corvette across town toward the bluff above the river, where the barn loomed out of its surrounding ring of trees, its bright red roof glaring like a beacon in the sun.

Somehow they ended up on the same road Lindsay had taken yesterday to deliver him from the bears. They came on to it from the opposite direction where it looped off a larger road. It passed the theater parking lot in a wide, paved strip, then narrowed and veered through the trees to the back door of Joe Varner's apartment.

Trey and the cat went inside with him. Noah put the milk, the yogurt, the kiwi, and the grapes in the fridge. Trey parked on a kitchen stool, finished the second sandwich, and let the cat lick blueberry milkshake off the cup lids while Noah rolled the oranges into a basket. He put the bananas on top and caught Trey eyeing the place through the cutout. "Any of the stuff in here look familiar to you?"

Trey shook his head. "I haven't been up here since the last time Grampa Joe blew through town, but no. It all looks new to me. Why?"

"Just wondered." Noah leaned back against the fridge. "Do you have your driver's license?"

"Not till August when I turn sixteen. I have a learner's permit. Means I can drive with a licensed driver in the car." He swiped his hair out of his eyes and smirked. "Not that my mom lets me."

"Can you drive a five-speed?"

"No. Emma's afraid I'll burn the clutch out of her Mustang."

"Girls dig a stick shift." Noah wagged his eyebrows and tossed him the Corvette keys. "C'mon. I'll teach you."

"You mean it?" Trey's eyes lit up. "What about the clutch?"

"It's not my clutch." Noah moved to the back door and opened it. "Not my car, either. It's Vivienne's."

"Cool." A grin spread across Trey's face. "I'm her favorite grandson."

He was her only grandson, her only grandchild. Vivienne had pictures of him all over her house, yet she'd never talked to him, never met him. Next time Vivienne called he'd ask her about that.

"Let's hit it," Noah said and waved Trey through the door. He started to shut it, glanced behind him, and saw the cat sitting on the counter by the cutout looking at him. "If you're coming, let's go."

Pyewacket leaped onto the floor and sprang past him. Noah shut the door, used the key to turn the deadbolt, and followed Trey and the cat across the grass toward the Corvette, so obscenely yellow it hurt to look at it without his shades. Jesus Christ, what an ugly car. Wouldn't break his heart if Trey ripped out the clutch. The college kid who'd driven the Bananamobile to Belle Coeur from L.A. had given him an envelope with a gas company credit card inside and a note from Vivienne: *"If you look the part, you'll feel the part."* It was almost—gag, puke—sweet.

Noah kept the Corvette on the farm roads where there was no traffic. Trey knew the basics of driving a stick, the brake from the clutch and what the clutch did. Noah ran him through the H-shaped gear pattern, told him to watch the RPMs and listen to the engine to know when to shift and cut him loose.

You could only teach a kid so much, then you had to let 'em go. Why Lindsay didn't know that, Noah couldn't fathom. Ordering Trey out of the street like a five-year-old only made him feel like one. Not that he was Dr. Spock. Or Sir Galahad, either, using the kid like this to make points with Lindsay. On the other hand, he *was* doing him a favor by teaching him how to drive a five-speed.

Trey did pretty well at first, but the Corvette was a lotta car for a kid. It scared the hell out of him the first time it leaped out of third into fourth ready to run. He slammed his foot on the clutch instead of the brake and killed the engine.

Then he got flustered and red-faced and couldn't get it out of first to save his ass.

"You're doing fine," Noah said to encourage him.

"I'm *not*!" Trey shook the wheel like he wanted to rip it off. "I *suck*!"

"So get mad and pissed off. That'll make it easier."

The kid shot him a dirty look from under his thick bang of hair, started the engine, and off they went, lurching forward a foot or two at a time, till the engine stalled. The Corvette yanked to a stop, a scorched stink like burnt rubber filling Noah's nose.

"What's that smell?" Trey asked. "Is it the clutch?"

What smell? Noah wanted to say, but the worried look on the kid's face gave him the guilts. "It's the clutch."

"Oh man." Trey thudded his forehead against the steering wheel. "Emma was right! I burned out the clutch!"

"You didn't burn out the clutch. It's just overheated." So was Noah. Even with the sunroof open, the inside of the car was like an oven with the sun beating through the windshield. He popped his door and pushed it wide open on its hinges. "It'll cool off in a while and be fine."

Trey raised his head from the wheel. "You sure?"

"I'm brain-dead, kid, not a liar."

"I'm really sorry. I didn't mean to say that. It just popped out."

"Don't sweat it. We all say things we shouldn't."

Like what he'd said to Lindsay about picking up where they'd left off and *bam*—she'd punched him. Didn't make sense that his smart-ass toothbrush comment would provoke her after so many years. He must've said or done something else. All he had to do was remember what.

"Why would Jolie say you're brain-dead if you aren't?"

'Cause she's a bitch, Noah thought, but said, "I made a comment about booze killing a lot of brain cells. I think she elaborated."

"You don't drink anymore, do you?"

"Haven't touched tequila in two years." Two years, eight months, three weeks, five days, twelve hours, forty-seven minutes, and—Noah glanced at his watch—eighteen seconds. But who was counting?

"My Grampa Joe is an alcoholic. My mom won't talk to me about it, but I've heard her tell Emma that Vivian drove him to drink."

If anybody could, Vivienne could, but Noah didn't say so. He didn't want to talk about this, but the kid did. Maybe because Lindsay wouldn't. He sat looking at Noah expectantly, waiting for an answer.

"I don't know why your grandfather drinks. I only know why I drank. I love the taste of tequila and the way it makes me feel, like I'm king of the world. I was drunk all the time but it was always somebody else's fault. Drunks are good at that, blaming other people for the fact that they're drunks. Maybe that's why your Grampa Joe told your mother that Vivienne drove him to drink."

"He's never said that. He only says he likes Jim Beam."

Ah, a kindred spirit. A bead of sweat trickled down Noah's temple. He flicked it off and squinted at the road, a paved, narrow strip shimmering out of sight in a sandy haze. Gazing at it made him dizzy. He couldn't see the barn roof in the rearview mirror but he saw a line of trees about twenty yards off the road, the pool of shade, and a crumbling rock wall beneath their low-spreading branches.

"Looks cooler over there," he said. "What d'you say?"

"Whatever." Trey shrugged.

The cat sprang ahead of them through the shin-high grass; a dull dry beige greening at the roots that cracked and snapped underfoot. The cat hopped up on the wall, licked a paw, and cleaned his whiskers. When Noah sat down beside him, he turned his back and flicked his tail.

"If I didn't know better," he said, "I'd swear this cat was a dog."

Pyewacket shot him a drop-dead look, jumped off the wall, and slithered away into the grass. "Where's he going?" Noah asked.

Trey glanced over his shoulder. "Probably to get a drink. There's a creek down there."

"A creek?" A creek meant water, Noah's favorite element. "Great," he said, pushing off the wall. "Let's go."

Chapter 12

Noah followed Pyewacket down the hill, veering toward the vivid bright green tree line that marked the banks of the creek. Behind him he heard Trey's footsteps crunching through the grass to catch up.

"If I were you," Lindsay's kid said, "I wouldn't drink the water."

"I don't want to drink it. I want to wash off the sweat." Noah could feel it stinging the back of his neck. "Saturday I froze my ass off, yesterday I got drenched. Today it's hot enough to be a damn sauna."

Noah's head ached, his throat hurt, and he felt half-sick to his stomach. If he didn't know better, he'd swear he was hungover.

It was a good ten degrees cooler beneath the trees overhanging the creek. Noah went down on one knee beside Pyewacket, crouched on the edge of a pool on a flat slab of rock.

The first handful of water he splashed on the back of his neck made him shiver; the second made him sigh. He rinsed his hands, let them hang damp and dripping off his knees, and watched Trey wander up the middle of the creek. The streambed was mostly loose stone and gravel with a thin trickle of water wandering between deep pools. A couple times Trey stopped, picked up a rock, examined it, and tossed it back.

"You looking for something?" Noah asked.

"Yeah. Geodes." Trey showed him a lopsided rock. "They're rounder than this, almost round as a ball. When you crack 'em open they look like little caves of quartz crystal inside. Uncle Ron used to bring me here to look for 'em." Trey pitched the rock away and looked around. "I think it was here. Might have been farther downstream."

He turned and headed off down the creek, making his way up the middle from rock to rock. Noah pushed to his feet and followed. Why not? It would take the 'Vette a while to cool off and it was nice down here.

This wasn't the kind of water he was used to; no surf, no salt, no tidal pools as blue as Lindsay's eyes. The water here was brown as strong tea. The stream slipping down the channel reeked of mud and wet stone, but still Noah smiled. He'd always been happiest around water.

He saw fish in the pools, silver flickers gliding around submerged tree roots. Trey said they washed into the creek from the farm ponds. The cat snapped at dragonflies and goofy-looking, half-spider, half-moth bugs that skated across the surface. Water skippers, Trey called them.

"You ever find any of those geode things?" Noah asked.

"They're not common but Uncle Ron's found a couple. He cracked them and polished them and gave them to me."

Trey tossed the rock in his hand and kept going. The cat tagged along beside him, ranging between the banks and the creek bed, jumping nimbly around the pools to keep his feet dry.

The first time the creek forked and Trey followed it to the left Noah didn't say anything. When it forked again and Trey followed it to the right, he said, "You know where you're going. Right, slick?"

"Don't you know anything?" Trey frowned at him over his shoulder. "As long as you follow a stream you can't get lost."

"Hey, pal. *I* can drive a five speed." Something rustled in the depths of the trees along the bank. Noah swung toward it. "What was that?"

"Deer, probably. They sleep in thickets and come out at dusk."

"What about bears?"

"There aren't any bears in Missouri."

"So people keep telling me." Whatever it was in the trees moved again, snapping branches. Noah jerked his thumb toward the sound. "Then I hear something like that and I have to wonder."

"If you're scared, wait here and I'll come back for you."

"Not on your life, Natty Bumppo. Lead on."

The air didn't feel cool anymore; it felt dank and clammy on Noah's skin. His Nikes were wet and slipped on the stones. The next time Trey stopped to pick up a rock, Noah grabbed a tree branch and pulled himself up the bank for a look around.

A flat, plowed field planted with something pale green and ankle high stretched away from the creek. From a bare patch in the center of the field soared a single, huge tree. About a dozen big, fat feathered brown things with long, flat tails parked on its thinly leafed branches.

"Hey kid," Noah said. "Come here and tell me what I'm looking at."

Trey scrambled up the bank beside him. "That's a tree."

"Very funny. What are those things sitting in it?"

"Birds."

"Look, Mr. Sulu. I'm sorry I questioned your navigational skills, okay? What kind of birds?"

"Quail."

"Whoa. A family of four could eat for a week on one of those."

"We grow 'em big in Missouri," Trey said, and slid down the bank.

So did Noah, still hanging onto the branch. It broke on him halfway down and sent him sliding the rest of the way on his ass. He landed feet first in a shallow pool that splashed cold muddy water on his chest.

"You okay?" Trey asked, the corners of his mouth twitching.

"I'm fine." Noah gritted his teeth, pushed off the bank, and lifted his feet, dripping mud and water, one at a time out of the pool. "Just fine."

"Well, no geodes." Trey shrugged. "Guess we oughta head back."

He led the way, the cat trotting along beside him with his tail in the air. Noah followed, his soaked, slimy feet squishing inside his ruined Nikes. The mud on his jeans had dried and caked his Jockeys to his ass by the time Trey climbed out of the creek and up a grassy, dull beige slope. At the top there was a rock wall, a line of trees, and a strip of paved road, but no glow-in-the-dark yellow Corvette.

Trey blinked. "Where's the car?"

"Where we left it," Noah said. "This isn't where we left it."

"Is, too." Trey pointed at the wall. "That's where we were sitting."

"Then where's the car?"

Trey looked around, bewildered. "I don't know."

"Gimme the keys. It's got an alarm. Maybe we can hear it."

"Uh." Trey ducked his head. "I left them in the ignition."

"You *what*? You left the keys in a forty-thousand-dollar car?"

"Who's gonna take it out here in the middle of the farm?"

"Well somebody did—or we're in the wrong place."

"Okay, okay. Let me think." Trey ran a hand through his hair. He was turning red around the ears. "We must be in the wrong place."

"No shit, Sherlock. I say we go back to the fork and hang a left."

"*Fine,*" Trey gritted between his teeth and stomped down the hill.

Noah followed, but the cat didn't. He turned around and saw Pyewacket sitting on the rock wall.

"If you want the rest of the tuna casserole in my fridge," Noah said, "I suggest you hie your furry little butt down here."

The cat sprang off the wall and trailed him back into the creek. At the fork where they'd turned right, they made a left, then a right at the fork where they'd gone left. Trey went about twenty yards and frowned.

"This doesn't look right."

"It's gotta be right," Noah said, coming up beside him.

"Why? 'Cause you say so?"

"No," Noah replied, ignoring the you're-old-and-brain-dead sneer in Trey's voice. "It's got to be right because we haven't found the car yet."

"How'er we gonna find it if we're down here in the creek?"

"Beats me. You're the one who said we can't get lost so long as we follow the stream."

"All right *fine*," Trey snapped. "We'll keep going."

They did, with the kid striding out front in a stiff-legged snit and the old brain-dead guy scrambling to keep up. He could run like a gazelle on a sandy beach, but this hopping from rock to rock shit was for frogs. He was sweating again by the time Trey called the next halt.

The creek banks looked farther apart than Noah remembered. The channel deeper, the water swifter. An arrow-shaped ripple of current shot across the surface and curled whitecaps around the rocks.

"This doesn't look right," Noah said.

"No shit, Sherlock."

The kid wasn't being snide. Well, maybe a little. The corners of his mouth looked white and pinched in his heat-flushed face. Noah thought he was mostly freaked. He'd lost the Corvette and now he'd lost them.

"So where the hell are we?" he asked.

"I don't know, exactly. I only know my Mom's gonna kill me." Trey pointed at a break in the trees. "Look at the sun."

Noah turned and squinted. He'd put his shades on to keep the sweat out of his eyes. Through the mud-spattered lenses the sun looked like a silver smear, so he bent his wrist and peered at his watch. Blinked, ripped off his shades, and looked again. The digital face read 5:37.

"She's not gonna kill you. She's gonna kill me."

"Oh no, she's gonna kill me for losing your car."

"*I* get to kill you for that. She's gonna kill me for losing you."

Pyewacket arched against Trey's muddy jeans and meowed. The kid dropped to his heels and ran a hand down his back.

"Hey buddy. You know where we are? Can you get us outta here?"

"What d'you think he's gonna do?" Noah asked. "Run up to the barn barking like Lassie and fetch Donnie back here? He's a cat."

"Ignore him. He's brain-dead," Trey said to Pyewacket. "We gotta get home, buddy. C'mon. Show us the way."

The cat sprang away. Up the bank and slithered out of sight into a tangle of bushes sprouting along the edge of the creek. Trey gave Noah a so-there smirk and climbed the muddy bank. Noah sighed and put on his shades, grabbed a tree branch, and pulled himself out of the creek.

He didn't see Trey or the cat at the top, just a shade-speckled clearing ringed by trees. The bushes drooping over the lip of the creek looked harmless and half-dead—until Noah tried to wade through them. Then they whipped their puny arms around him, sank wicked little thorns into him that ripped his shirt and drew blood.

"Ow!" Noah howled. "Fuck!"

"Hold still." Trey appeared, wrapped the tail of his T-shirt around his hand, and pulled the bushes apart.

Pyewacket sat a foot or two away looking at him. If he had lips he'd be grinning, Noah thought. He gritted his teeth and scraped himself free of the thorns, rubbing the stinging, bloody chevrons on his arms, and glared at the bushes. "What the hell are those things?"

"They're raspberries," Ron Varner said.

From the far side of the clearing, where thirty seconds ago Noah would've sworn there wasn't a damn thing but trees. He spun around with Trey and still didn't see anything but trees and leaves.

Until the wind stirred, the branches broke, and a horse with Ron on its back stepped into the clearing. The weirdest looking horse Noah had ever seen, with a white-speckled black coat that blended into the trees.

"We're saved, kid," Noah said. "It's the cavalry."

"I left my bugle at the barracks." Ron grinned, slid off the horse, and took a couple of stiff steps toward them. "You guys all right?"

"We're fine. Lost, but fine," Noah said. "What're you doing here?"

"I found your car abandoned on the road on my way to work. I couldn't get hold of Jolie so I called Lindsay. She told me Trey was with you and asked Donnie and Lonnie and me to help her look for you two."

"Uh-oh." Trey groaned. "If Ma's here, I'm dead."

"You're not dead, nephew. Your mother was just worried."

"Yeah, right. That's what she always says—*I was worried*—just before she grounds me."

Trey's shoulders sagged and he shoved his hands in his pockets. The horse took a step and bumped him in the chest with its nose. Trey smiled and rubbed its spotted neck.

"Nice nag," Noah said. "Where'd you get it?"

"That's Lucky." Ron nodded at the horse. "He belongs to Jolie, actually, but he keeps running away."

"Running away?" Noah asked. "From what?"

Ron grinned. "From Jolie."

Well, no wonder she was so damn crabby. Abandoned by both her parents and dumped by a horse. It was sad, but it was funny, too, and Noah couldn't help laughing.

"Why are you just wandering around out here?" Ron asked Trey. "When you got lost, why didn't you follow the road back to the barn?"

"*See?* I told you that's what we should've done." Trey shot Noah a dirty look. "We should've stayed on the road."

"Oh, bite me, kid," Noah snarled. Trey stuck his tongue out.

"Your mother's waiting for you with the car," Ron said. "The road isn't far from here, just through there. Lucky will show you."

The horse wheeled toward a gap in the trees Ron pointed out, swiveled its head around, and snorted. When Pyewacket sprang onto its back, it turned and started off into the woods. Trey walked alongside. The cat rode on its spotted rump, looking back at Noah.

"Are you okay, Noah?" Ron asked. "You don't look too good."

He felt his forehead. Jesus Christ. He was burning up.

"I'm fine. If you need a lift to work I'll be glad to drive you."

"Thanks, but I'm not going in," Ron said glumly. "When I called to say I'd be late, the station manager suggested I take the day off. They've had death threats."

"You're shitting me." Noah laughed. "Over the weather?"

"Yeah, over the weather. Belle Coeur's economy is based on agriculture. My forecasts are as important as the price of soybean futures. I've been getting anonymous mail for weeks. Copies of *The Old Farmer's Almanac* with notes that say, 'Read this. It might help.' "

"That's a tough audience," Noah said. "Care to join me in drowning myself in the creek? I figure it'll be a quicker, less painful death than the one Lindsay has planned for me for losing her kid."

"Honestly, Noah, she's not angry. She really was just worried."

"Pardon me, but bullshit. Lindsay puts a whole new spin on the term *overprotective mother*. She damn near had a stroke when Trey stepped into a street totally devoid of traffic to take a look at my car."

"Now there's a thought." Ron grinned. "The next time you decide to abandon that ugly yellow heap with the keys in it, park it in downtown St. Louis. That should get rid of it in a heartbeat."

I didn't leave the keys in it, Noah started to say, then caught himself. Hmmm. Perhaps this was another opportunity to make points. "Great idea, Willard Scott," he said to Ron. "I'll keep it in mind."

Trey and Lucky and Pyewacket were waiting for them on the other side of the trees. At the top of a hill that swooped down to a small ditch and up on the other side to the road.

The Corvette sat there and Lindsay leaned against it on the driver's side. One arm bent to prop her chin, the other on the roof. A beam of late afternoon sun winked on her sunglasses and gleamed on the hood of the car. Noah couldn't see his hand in front of his face but his distance vision was sharp as a hawk's.

The wind fluttered Lindsay's hair, catching a strand of it in her shades. When Trey ventured a nervous, hi-Mom wave, she raised her hand to tug her hair free and waved back to him, a wide and—even from forty yards away—clearly amused smile spreading across her face.

"I told you Lindsay wasn't angry," Ron said.

No, she wasn't angry. She was doing her best not to laugh. *She thinks this is funny,* Noah realized. *A real laugh riot that she had to form a search party to come and rescue us from the woods.*

He glanced at Ron. He'd swung himself onto the horse and sat grinning at him with Pyewacket draped around his shoulders.

"This is a trap, isn't it?" he said.

"No, it's not a trap." Ron waved at Lindsay and gave the horse a nudge with his heels. "C'mon, Lucky. Let's take you home and see if you'll stay this time."

Ron and the horse and the cat turned away into the trees. Noah looked at Trey, hanging at his side with his head down.

"Why are we just standing here?" Noah asked him.

"I'm savoring my last moments of freedom," Trey said in a doomed voice. "I figure I'll be grounded all summer for losing your car."

"You didn't lose the car. Your mother drove it off."

"That's 'cause she can drive a five-speed." *And I never will,* said the end-of-the-world look on Trey's face as he gazed at the Corvette. It was hell to be fifteen and want something so bad you could taste it.

"She won't know you left the key in the car unless you tell her."

Trey goggled at him. "You mean I should *lie* to my mother?"

"No. I mean I should lie to your mother." Noah hooked Trey's arm and drew him down the slope. "I'll tell her I left the key in the car and got us lost. She'll buy that. She had to rescue me yesterday."

"You're gonna lie to my mom to keep me out of trouble?"

"This isn't your fault. I'm the guy who wanted to go down to the creek. And you'll never learn a five-speed if you're under house arrest."

"You're still gonna teach me?"

"Keep moving." Noah felt the kid's stride falter and caught his arm again. "Keep your head and your voice down."

"She can't hear us. She's too far away."

"Yeah? What if she can read lips?"

"She can't read lips."

"Wanna bet your summer she can't? Mothers have powers beyond those of mere mortals, kid. Never underestimate them."

They'd drawn within twenty yards of the ditch. Lindsay still leaned against the Corvette, her chin on her hand, a smile on her face.

"Look like you're glad to see her," Noah whispered to Trey.

He pasted a grin on his face and waved like an idiot. "Hi, Ma!"

"Hi, son!" Lindsay called, and waved back.

Noah jumped the ditch and climbed up the other side. Lindsay came around the Corvette to meet him, slid her hands in the pockets of her khaki slacks and her eyes up and down the filthy, muddy length of him. Noah stepped onto the road, his ruined Nikes squeaking.

"Boy am I glad I left the keys in the ignition." He heaved a weary sigh. "I don't think I could've walked much farther."

"You two had quite a hike. You're almost six miles from the barn."

"Wow! Really?" Trey hopped the ditch, the idiot grin still on his face. "We had the coolest time looking for geodes."

"Way cool." Noah gave Lindsay a my-bad grin. "Till I got us lost."

"See any bears?" she asked, smiling just a little.

"Don't tease him, Ma." Trey bounced up next to her and leaned against the Corvette. "Noah's gonna teach me to drive a five-speed."

"Oh *is* he?" Lindsay hissed the *s*. "Well. How *nice*."

She hissed the *nice*, too. *That's it,* Noah thought. *I'm dead.* Lindsay's eyes narrowed. Then a horn honked and she turned away from him on one foot.

Noah followed her gaze and saw a big, dark-blue pickup with a double rear axle coming over the small rise in the road toward the Corvette. Donnie was behind the wheel.

"Glad you turned up, Noah!" Donnie hollered from his rolled-down window. "Thought me and Lonnie was gonna have to start knocking down trees to find you and the boy, here!"

The boy grinned at him. So did Donnie. Lindsay tried not to, but lost the battle. Noah wished he'd thrown himself in the creek.

"I'm gonna ride back with Uncle Donnie, Ma," Trey said, and trotted toward the pickup.

Lindsay turned toward Noah and offered him the key to the Corvette. He shook his head. "I'm bushed," he said. "You drive."

She'd have to keep one hand on the steering wheel and the other on the gearshift, Noah reasoned as he steered Lindsay around the car and opened the driver's door. She wouldn't have one free to choke him.

Donnie's pickup led the way back to the barn. Noah and Lindsay followed in the Corvette. Lindsay had put on her sunglasses, so Noah couldn't see her eyes—just the beautifully curved line of her jaw and the pucker over her eyes in the rearview mirror. She was focused on driving, not him.

"I'm really sorry," he said. "I didn't intend for us to get lost, and I sure didn't mean to keep Trey out all day. I'll bet you were worried."

"I was until Uncle Ron called," Lindsay said, shifting from second to first. "He was on his way to work when he found your car. He looked around for you, waited as long as he could, then called the uncles and started them looking. They were out in the fields, but all the tractors have walkie-talkies and Ron carries one. He didn't know Trey was with you until he called me, which he did when he couldn't find Jolie."

Donnie's pickup crested another rise in the road and swept around a left-hand curve that Noah didn't remember at all. Over the trees crowding the shoulder soared the flank of the barn, its bright red roof glowing like neon in the just-beginning-to-set sun.

"Am I the only person," Noah asked, exasperated, covered in mud, and itching like hell in places he couldn't scratch in front of Lindsay, "who can't find that goddamn huge, fire-fucking-engine-red barn?"

"No, you're not," she laughed. "Some days Trey can't find his feet, let alone his shoes, so this isn't entirely your fault."

"Does that mean you aren't going to kill me for losing your kid?"

Lindsay slid him a sideways smile. "Not today," she said, and made a left into the theater parking lot behind the pickup.

She swung the Corvette into the space next to her Civic and turned off the engine, shifted toward him, and took off her sunglasses. "Would you like to come to dinner, Noah? It's nothing fancy. Just spaghetti."

"I'd love to come to dinner. I'm so hungry I could eat a

dozen of those big fat quail Trey and I saw down by the creek."

"Big fat quail?" Lindsay blinked. "Where did you see big fat quail?"

"In a tree. I'm so hungry I could eat every stinking one of them."

"Quail are small, Noah." Lindsay cupped her palms. "They nest on the ground. Big fat birds in a tree were probably wild turkeys."

Noah looked in the mirror at Trey jumping down from the pickup's cab. *Little shit,* he thought, but he wanted to laugh.

"I'd like to clean up first," he said to Lindsay.

"Fine. I'll go on and get dinner started, but I'll leave Trey with you. Believe me, he can find his way home from here."

"Great," Noah said, smiling and already thinking of a way to get even for the quail.

Chapter 13

THE SPAGHETTI wasn't fancy but it was tasty. Lindsay served a salad first with an antipasto tray and garlic bread with the pasta.

"I cheat," she confessed when Noah told her it was delicious. "I start with Ragu spaghetti sauce and add things to it."

Her house wasn't fancy either if you compared it to Vivienne's Malibu spread, but it was crapping huge. Several million dollars' worth of square footage in L.A. Trey gave him the tour while Lindsay cleared the table and fixed dessert. She suggested it, which surprised Noah, since she'd sat him out on the covered back deck with a glass of ice tea while she'd put dinner on the table and Trey cleaned himself up.

On their way out here, he'd shown Noah how to operate the CD player in the Corvette. Now he showed him a living room with a stone fireplace and bookshelves, a bay window with a padded seat and lots of furniture arranged on a blue-green carpet. Couches and chairs tossed with cushions and afghans and lap-size quilts. Tables held lamps and flowers, some real and some fake, and about a billion family photos.

Most of the faces were unknown to Noah, but he recognized Frank and Susan, Ezra and Sassy, Donnie and Lonnie and Ron, Emma Fairchild and her mother, Mrs. Doubtfire. And Jolie, who looked crabby, or maybe it was constipated, in every single photo. Noah wished he had a grease pencil so could draw devil horns on her pointed little head. He didn't see a single picture of Vivienne or a fourth Varner brother who would be Joe, Lindsay and Jolie's father.

The books in the room outnumbered the photos two to one. They were everywhere. Fanned on tables, stacked on the ledge of the window seat between bookends, tucked in chair cushions.

"In case you can't tell," Trey said, "my mom has a thing for books."

Now that Trey said it, Noah remembered it. His brain slipped him a snapshot of Lindsay between takes on the *BBT* set; sitting on a reel full of sound cable between takes with her nose buried in a book.

"C'mon," Trey said. "I'll show you the geodes Uncle Ron found."

He led Noah past the double front doors and the stone-floored foyer up the hardwood hallway that ran past the dining room and the kitchen all the way to the family room. A second hallway ran the length of the house from a room with a stone floor and big sinks. The mudroom, Trey called it. Noah had come in this way with Trey, straight into the kitchen from the three-car garage. At the far end of this hallway, past four bedrooms and bathrooms, one of them Trey's, was Lindsay's suite. That's what Trey called it, "My mom's suite."

"Hold it, sport," Noah said. "Closed doors mean private."

"She said show you the house. This is part of the house," Trey replied. "She's got even more books in there."

"I'll take your word for it." Noah turned his back to the doors. He had zero interest in seeing the bedroom Lindsay had shared with her husband. "Show me the geodes."

Trey's room wasn't quite the size of an airplane hangar. It held a set of triple bunk beds with built-in shelves. A holdover from his younger days, Noah guessed, eyeing the dozen or so Corvette posters on the walls. A black futon with red cushions sat on the beige carpet. A long pine table held a computer and printer. A telescope on a tripod sat on the wooden seat in one of the four windows. There was no TV. No TV in the living room, either, only the big screen in the family room.

Noah fell into a black leather chair by one of the windows and stared at his hands wrapped on the arms. Lindsay owned more books than the L.A. public library, more furniture than Ethan Allen. Outside her back door she had a pool built around the covered deck. He had a back door at the moment but it belonged to somebody else.

They'd both made a bloody-ass fortune on *BBT*. Lindsay had been smart with her money. He'd been stupid with his. So fucking stupid it made his limbs feel like lead just thinking about it.

"Here you go." Trey tossed him something. "That's a geode."

A gray lump of rounded rock, cut in half and banded blue on the inside like a tree stump. The hollow in the middle glittered with quartz.

"Ron found this in the creek?"

"He figured a glacier dumped it there a couple million years ago."

"Make a great paper weight." Noah hefted it in his hand. "Or a murder weapon."

One good whack between the eyes ought to do it. He could use it on Jolie if she gave him any more shit. Or himself if this play flopped.

Trey switched on a lamp, dragged an ottoman that matched the black chair next to it, sat down, and laid a big red album in Noah's lap. The cover was padded leather with gold capped edges.

"Vivian sent me this," he said.

It was a scrapbook filled with pictures of Lindsay. No cutesy snapshots of her first bath, no locks of baby hair tied in a ribbon and taped to a page. No Kodak moments of adoring parents and beautiful baby girl, either, though Lindsay had been a stunner even as a toddler. These were publicity shots, color 5x7s of Lindsay in dozens of dance costumes. Tap, ballet, and jazz from age three and up, her face painted with eye shadow and mascara, vivid red lipstick and blushed pink cheeks, her golden hair teased up and sprayed in elaborate, adult styles.

She smiled and held graceful, grown-up poses for the camera. A princess ballerina, a Yankee Doodle Dandy in red white and blue and black patent tap shoes, a Spanish dancer in black lace and heeled tap shoes, castanets curled in her fingers above the mantilla draped over her hair. A woman in a little girl's body.

Noah glanced at Trey. He'd bent one elbow to prop his chin; the other hand dangled off his knee. Noah didn't see anybody's genes but Lindsay's in Trey's face. Except for his eyes, which were a darker shade of blue, he was the image of his mother.

Noah turned back to the album, flipping past group shots of dance recitals. Lindsay was always out front, always the star. He saw Sassy in a bunch of these, kneeling among the chorus line. A shapely, saucy redhead in black spandex. He saw Jolie, too, her costume always crooked or her headdress askew, her face tight and frowning, even in the photos of the chorus line where Sassy had her arms around her.

From dance recitals to school plays, write-ups in local papers to national magazines, the album covered Lindsay's whole career. Stills from TV commercials and modeling jobs, her gorgeous publicity head shot for *Betwixt and Be Teen*. In the photo she looked about eighteen, which is how old he was when the show started. By the dates Vivienne had carefully lettered on each page, Lindsay was barely fourteen.

Jessie and Sam were fifteen and starting high school in the first episode of *BBT*. Lindsay had played older, but then, these photos said, she always had. She had the bone structure and the poise learned during a lifetime on stage to pull it off. Noah had a baby face, a what-the-fuck-let's-party attitude honed on the beach along with his surfing skills.

Plastic overlays protected the photos and interviews Noah didn't have time to read. He turned a page and saw himself with Lindsay on the cover of *TV Guide*. She sat on a bleacher in Jessie's blue and gold cheerleader uniform, leaning forward with her pom-poms cupped around her chin. Noah lounged behind her, leaning past her on one hand.

There they were—Jessie and Sam, the perfectly blond, perfectly beautiful California teen couple. Noah didn't remember this shoot, but he remembered that he and Lindsay were often photographed sitting down so she didn't look taller. Which she was till he grew four inches during the third season—late growth spurts ran in his father's family—and he finally topped her by three inches. The network gave him a raise.

There were dozens of pictures of the two of them. Stills from the show, publicity appearances, magazine features. Noah looked through them, turning pages, something stirring in the back of his mind. Not memories, not quite, but something . . .

"This is me and my dad," Trey said.

He laid a picture frame over the album in Noah's lap. An 8x10 with three photos showing through ovals cut in the pale green mat. A nice looking blond guy with a much younger Trey in goofy hats stuck with lures. In ski parkas wearing snow goggles and knit caps tugged over their ears. In swim trunks and T-shirts, a lake glittering in the background and water skis slung over the man's shoulders.

Trey laid a finger on the first photo, the one where he had no front teeth and held a string of trout. "These," he said, "are fish."

Noah raised just his eyes. Trey grinned at him.

"Your dad's name was Mark, right?" Noah asked.

"Yeah. Mark Richard West the second. I'm the third. That's why they call me Trey. For three, get it?"

"Yeah, I get it. How'd he die?"

"His plane crashed. My Gramma and Grampa West were down at the lake. This is our cabin on Table Rock Lake." Trey pointed at the water-skiing shot. "It's in the Ozarks. That's southern Missouri. My dad was flying them home to Belle Coeur. I was seven."

"Sorry, sport," Noah said gently and laid his finger on the snow skiing photo. "Where was this taken?"

"At our condo in Telluride. That's in Colorado."

"I know where Telluride is."

Three houses. Jesus Christ. *Gimme the geode,* Noah thought.

"Hey, fellas!" Lindsay's voice rang up the hall. "Dessert!"

" 'Kay, Ma!" Trey hollered, and bounced off the ottoman to put the picture frame back on a shelf above the computer.

Noah stood up with the album. When Trey turned around he asked, "Can I borrow this? I'd like to have more time to look through it."

"Sure." Trey shrugged. "Go ahead. I'll be there in a second."

"Thanks." Noah put the album on the table and headed for the dining room, which adjoined the kitchen and was probably large enough to qualify as an Elizabethan banquet hall.

A massive breakfront fit into a niche cut into one long wall to hold it. A walnut chair rail ran around the room. The table sat on a blue and mauve Oriental rug. Lindsay glanced up at him, spoons in her hand.

"Did you lose Trey again?" she asked. "So soon?"

The half-beat pause between the questions and the eyebrow she raised made Noah grin. He glanced behind him, then back at Lindsay.

"Trey who?" he said.

She thought about laughing. He saw it in her eyes, but she settled for a smile. She seemed less on her guard than she had yesterday when she'd driven him back to the barn. And why not? This was her house, her turf. She'd changed before he and Trey arrived, into jeans and a blue pullover with pushed up sleeves.

"Hope you like tiramisu." She swept a hand toward the chair he'd sat in at dinner. "I buy it frozen but it's pretty good. Coffee?"

Noah glanced at his watch. It was nine-twenty. "I'd rather have milk. I try to avoid stimulants after eight."

"Milk. Sure. Coming up." She went past him into the kitchen.

Did her eyes slide away from him at the word *stimulants* or was it his guilty conscience? Telling lies, even itty-bitty ones, were not part of the Twelve Steps. This wasn't the first time he'd stubbed his toe on the truth step, but this time it was eating at him like the spaghetti.

He should've passed on the meatballs. Should've let the kid take his own heat, too, but he'd felt guilty for using him to make points with Lindsay. What the hell was he thinking there? He was two years away from rock bottom, six months off the street by the grace of Vivienne Varner, of all people. What did he have to offer Lindsay? Friendship, maybe—providing she'd still talk to him once he came clean about the car keys. If he'd learned nothing else from Hollywood and tequila, he'd learned that anything based on a lie had the life span of a tsetse fly. Kind of like his career.

When Lindsay came back with a glass of milk and a cup of coffee for herself, he held her chair. She said "Thank you," and sat down. So did Noah, eyeing the tiramisu scooped in a footed dish on a white plate.

"It's non-alcoholic. No Marsala, but it's loaded with espresso," Lindsay said. "I won't be offended if you pass."

Noah's stomach clenched. She was being kind and sympathetic. He was sitting at her table, eating her food, and lying to her. He put down the spoon he'd picked up and looked Lindsay in the eye.

"I need to tell you something."

"I'd like to talk to you, too," she replied.

A door slammed, feet thumped, and Trey burst into the room and flung himself in his chair.

"I put that book you want to borrow in your car," he said.

Lindsay glanced at him. "What book?"

A bell rang. A doorbell, Noah guessed, when Lindsay dabbed her napkin to her mouth and said, "Excuse me."

Trey leaned across the table toward Noah. "Don't tell her which book," he said in an urgent whisper.

"Why not?" Noah asked, lowering his voice.

" 'Cause Vivian didn't send it to me. She sent it to my mom at the bookstore. She threw it away in the Dumpster out in the alley. I fished it out and smuggled it home."

"Aw shit, kid. Don't do this to me."

"If my Mom finds out I took that book she'll kill me. Then she'll burn it. How bad do you want to look at it?"

Bad enough that the thought of the red leather album going up in flames was almost it for the meatballs. Noah dragged a hand over his mouth to muffle a snarled *"Fuck,"* and leaned toward Trey.

"All right. I'll keep my mouth shut about the book but I'm telling her the truth about the car keys."

Trey's eyes narrowed. "That's blackmail."

"This is very sweet, Aunt Dovey," Lindsay said, her voice floating from the hallway, coming toward them from the front door, "but you didn't have to return my dish. I could've picked it up another time."

"That's the deal," Noah said to Trey. "Yes or no?"

"Go ahead. Tell her about the keys. Who gives a fuck."

"Watch your mouth," Noah snapped.

"You watch yours," Trey shot back.

Well, if this didn't bring back fond memories. He and his old man squared off over the dinner table. His mother holding her breath, his sister Phyllis smirking into her Slim-Fast.

"It's no bother," Mrs. Doubtfire answered Lindsay as they came through the archway from the hallway into the dining room. "Had to drive right past on my way home from—" Her gaze fell on Noah springing up to push in his chair. She blinked and said, "bing-*oh*."

"Aunt Dovey, Noah Patrick." Lindsay put a blue quilted thing with handles that held a white glass dish on the table. "Noah, this is my aunt, Dovey Harrington."

"Mrs. Harrington. Pleasure to meet you."

Noah offered his hand. She clasped it and gave it a firm shake.

"Well, well. Noah Patrick. You sure do look different on TV."

"*Betwixt and Be Teen* was a long time ago."

Mrs. Doubtfire didn't look anything at all like Robin Williams, but enough like Frank that he could tell they were brother and sister. Petite like Vivienne and Sassy she was not. Noah had to tip his head back to meet her brown eyes, past shoulders like Sly. Or maybe Arnold.

"Sit, Aunt Dovey. The water's still hot." Lindsay turned toward the kitchen. "I'll make you a cup of tea."

"Darjeeling for me and a cup of mullein tea for Noah." Mrs. Doubtfire moved his glass of milk away from his plate. "Sick as you're trying to get, milk's the last thing you need."

Mrs. Doubtfire hung her purse on the chair next to his. The same black suitcase she'd belted Ezra with. The chair started to keel over under the weight, but Noah caught the harp-shaped back and held it.

"I appreciate your concern," he said, "but I'm fine, really."

"That so?" She settled herself on the padded chair seat, her green flowered dress dipping between her spread knees like a rain-soaked tent. "Your hand's hotter'n a pistol and your eyes look like navy blue marbles."

Noah felt an urge to cough. *The power of suggestion,* he thought.

"Mullein tea." Trey grabbed his throat and made a choking sound.

"I put lemon in it." Lindsay set a steaming cup on a saucer in front of Noah and smiled. A better-you-than-me smile. "It helps."

The hell it did. The mullein tea tasted exactly like what it looked like—warmed-over piss. Noah took a sip and nearly gagged, held his breath, chugged the rest, and shuddered like a wet dog.

"Atta boy. Your head'll be clear as a bell come morning."

Mrs. Doubtfire clapped him on the shoulder, nearly dislodging the lump of meatballs awash in mullein tea in his stomach. Noah snatched up his water glass from dinner and drank.

"Hear you and Mr. Can't Find His Shoes over there—" she slid an amused eye at Trey "—got lost out on the farm today."

"We were *not* lost," Trey said. "We got back to where we'd parked Noah's car, but Mom had driven it off so we thought we were lost."

"It didn't seem smart to leave the car there with the key in it," Lindsay said as she slid into her chair. "I thought you couldn't find it. Otherwise," she glanced at Noah, "I would've just taken the key."

He opened his mouth to confess, then shut it. It was the perfect opening, but with Mrs. Doubtfire listening, he let it pass.

"I left the key in the car." Trey shot him a *happy-now* glare. "I told Noah you'd ground me. That's why he told you he did it."

Oh, nice one kid, Noah thought. *Just blurt it out and make me look like a bigger liar than I am.*

"I see." Lindsay turned her head and looked at Trey. The kid flushed a shade of red Noah had never seen before.

Mrs. Doubtfire reached for her purse. "I should go."

"Stay, Aunt Dovey." Lindsay rose from her chair. "I'll just see Trey off to bed then I'll fix you another cup of tea."

"No, no, it's late," she said. "I should be on my way."

Noah beat Mrs. Doubtfire to her feet and held her chair. "I can leave, too, if you want," he said to Lindsay.

"I'd like you to walk Aunt Dovey to her car, please. Thank you for returning the dish, Aunt Dovey. Good night."

Lindsay spoke to them both without taking her eyes off Trey. He pushed to his feet, mumbled, "G'night, Aunt Dovey. G'night, Noah," and turned out of the dining room ahead of his mother.

"Little rat fink," Mrs. Doubtfire said. "You told Lindsay a whopper to keep him outta trouble, then he hands you to her on a silver plate."

"I volunteered to tell Lindsay the whopper. He didn't ask."

"You must've been feverish."

"Or brain-dead. That's what Jolie says I am—brain-dead."

"Fine thing to say about the fella come to town to save your fanny." Mrs. Doubtfire tapped two fingers on his arm. "You tell Jolene that next time she gets uppity. And she will, I guarantee it."

"I'm ready for her," Noah said and offered his arm.

"Where's that car of yours? Didn't see it in the driveway."

"It's in the garage. Trey insisted. Would you like to see it?"

"I surely would." She smiled and slipped her arm through his.

Mrs. Doubtfire knew where the wall switches were. One

turned on the lights; three others cranked up the overhead doors. The Corvette sat next to Lindsay's blue Civic. Mrs. Doubtfire flipped the middle switch and the door behind the Corvette rolled up. Cool spring night air that smelled like damp grass wafted into the garage. Mrs. Doubtfire walked around the Corvette, looking it over from front bumper to back.

"Lonnie's right." She nodded. "Same color as horse piss."

"Lonnie?" Noah gave a shout of laughter. "He actually speaks?"

"Lord, yes. Man's a magpie. Talk your leg off once he knows you."

Sure, Noah thought, *and there aren't any bears in Missouri.* He'd been in the workroom drinking coffee with the uncles and Ron when the kid from L.A. showed up with the Bananamobile. Donnie and Ron laughed themselves silly trying to come up with just the right word to describe the color. That Lonnie, the Boo Radley of Belle Coeur, who had yet to utter a single word in Noah's presence, came up with the raunchy but apt yellow as horse piss made him shake his head.

A telephone rang. Faintly, like it was stuffed under a pillow. Must be in the house, Noah thought, until Mrs. Doubtfire pointed at the Bananamobile. Sounded better than the Horse Piss Mobile.

"Do believe your car's ringing, Noah."

She helped him search for the phone. They found it on the fifth ring, a palm-sized cellular, inside the console between the seats. Mrs. Doubtfire showed him how to turn it on and handed it to him.

"Where the hell are you?" Vivienne demanded.

"Where the hell are *you*?" Noah shot back.

"Jolie's been looking for you all day."

"Jolie's not my keeper," Noah said. "Jolie says she's the boss."

"The hell she is." Even long distance and on a cell phone, Noah could hear Vivienne breathing fire. "*I* am the boss."

"I just had dinner with your grandson."

"Where *are* you?"

"In the car. That's where I found this freaking little

phone." Noah was so angry he could feel the veins in his temples pulsing. "Have you got my underwear bugged?"

"I need to be able to reach you twenty-four seven."

"No, you don't. You don't need to keep tabs on me either. I've gone two years on my own without drinking. Stop breathing down my neck."

"I'm not checking up on you."

"Damn right you're not." Noah took the phone away from his ear and held it out to Mrs. Doubtfire. She switched it off and he dropped it in the console. Shut the lid and the door and leaned against the Corvette. "That was your sister Vivienne. Did you want to talk to her?"

"Lord no. I haven't talked to Vivian in twenty-five years. You think it was smart for you to talk to her like that?"

"Vivienne would like the world to think otherwise, but she doesn't respect people she can push around."

"She fixed it for you to come here and do the play, didn't she?"

"Yep. Nobody schemes and connives better than Vivienne."

"Thought it was her doing. Wonder what she's up to. No, no." She waved a hand as Noah opened his mouth to tell her. "You come see me later in the week. We'll have a cup of tea and I'll read your leaves."

Huh? Tea leaves? Then Noah remembered—Mrs. Doubtfire was Emma Harrington's mother. She of the great body, the white streak in her hair and the killer bunny cookies. Oh joy.

"My place is about fifteen miles east of here. Two big stone pillars out front. Can't miss it. Have Lindsay pack you up some mullein case you need it in the morning. 'Night now."

Mrs. Doubtfire wiggled her fingers and turned toward the open overhead door. Noah pushed off the Corvette, caught up with her, and took her arm. She smiled and let him keep it.

It was dark as the mouth of hell outside the garage, but the stars, wow—he'd never seen so many flung across a night sky. Noah felt disappointed when a motion sensitive light came on above their heads and the stars faded into the glare.

Mrs. Doubtfire pointed down the drive. "Right there's my car."

It was turquoise, roughly the size of a Hummer, and parked where the front walk intersected the drive. A 1970-something Lincoln Town Car, its wide chrome bumper grinning in the bright floodlight.

"That's an oldie but a goodie," Noah said.

"Twenty-two thousand original miles," Mrs. Doubtfire said proudly, then patted his arm. "Go back inside, Noah. Lindsay isn't gonna break your neck for telling a fib. She doesn't get that kind of angry."

The hell she doesn't, he thought, but kept his mouth shut about the hedge apples. "Never?" he asked.

"Wish she would. Do her good, but no." Mrs. Doubtfire sighed. "Lindsay just gets hurt, then she closes everything up inside."

That fit the surreal calm he'd seen on her face when she'd turned around to look at him after she'd busted hedge apples all over Jolie's house. She'd stuffed her anger back inside and clamped a cool, I'm-in-control mask over it.

"From what I've seen," he said, "Jolie's the family neck breaker."

"Vivian Junior. That's what Frank and Emma call her."

When they reached the Lincoln, Mrs. Doubtfire slipped her hand free and took her keys out of her purse, opened the driver's door, and faced Noah. The dome light that winked on shone on her white hair but threw shadows on her cheekbones.

"Mind you don't turn your back on Jolene, Noah. Love her I do. Took her in when Vivian lit outta here with Lindsay and left her behind, but she has a hard, bad spot inside for anyone Vivian seems to favor."

"Vivienne doesn't favor anyone but Vivienne."

"You and I know that but Jolene doesn't. If she ever finds out I fear it'll break her heart." Mrs. Doubtfire slid behind the Ferris wheel–size steering wheel and started the engine. Noah shut the door and leaned his hands on the rolled down window. "You come see me now."

"I will," he said, and backed away from the Lincoln.

Mrs. Doubtfire turned the Town Car around in front of

the garage and waved as it purred past him, the engine so smooth Noah could barely hear it. He waved back and stood there watching until she made a right at the end of the drive and the taillights faded into the night.

A hard, bad spot inside for anyone Vivienne seemed to favor. Like Lindsay. He'd called it right—Vivienne had left Jolie in Belle Coeur with Mrs. Doubtfire. Sometimes he was so smart he scared himself. Too bad the rest of the time he was so fucking stupid.

He hadn't seen the red album in the Corvette when he and Mrs. Doubtfire looked for the phone. He went back into the garage and opened the trunk. It was there, all right, and sitting on top of it, right smack in the middle of the red leather cover, sat the geode Trey had shown him.

Noah heard footsteps and glanced up. Lindsay stood in the doorway between the garage and the kitchen, the cool, I'm-in-control mask on her face. He put the trunk down and stepped around the side of the car.

"Trey didn't ask me to cover for him. I offered to teach him to drive the Corvette. I offered to lie about the key. It was all my idea."

"Is that what you wanted to tell me? What you started to say when I mentioned the key?"

Noah nodded. Lindsay folded her arms, leaned one shoulder against the door frame and tipped her head at him. "When did you start caring about anyone but yourself?"

Oh yeah. She remembered him, all right. Perfectly.

"When I ended up on the street and nobody gave a shit. I realized then, why should they? I was a rotten, lying, selfish, spoiled drunk."

"Why did you offer to teach Trey? Why did you lie for him?"

"This won't surprise you. So I could make points with you."

It did surprise her. Or maybe it surprised her that he admitted it. She blinked, pushed straight in the doorway, dropped her arms, and stared at him.

"Thank you for dinner, Lindsay. I can't remember the last time anyone invited me for a meal. I really enjoyed the evening. The spaghetti was delicious. You have a great house and a great kid."

A great life, too—and because he had nothing to contribute to it, a life he did not belong in. Noah fished the key—the lousy, stinking key—out of his pocket, stepped toward the door, and reached for the handle. "Wait!" Lindsay flung her hand out, her fingers spread.

He turned away from the Corvette. She sat down in the doorway. Just folded up like her legs wouldn't hold her, her feet on the step between the garage and the kitchen, her hands cupped on her knees.

"Jolie and I are arguing. I was upset that she didn't tell me you were in the play. I let her think I'm going to sue to get out of the contract. I'm not. I'm doing the play. I just want Jolie to stew for a few days."

"Did you argue with Jolie before or after the hedge apples?"

"Before. I told her this morning I did it. She didn't believe me."

"Want me to tell her I did it? I did throw one."

"No, no." She shook her head. "I don't want to involve you. I just thought you should know in case Jolie says something about a lawsuit."

"I doubt she'll say anything to me, but thanks for the heads-up." He opened the car door and smiled at her. "Good night, Lindsay."

"Good night, Noah." She didn't smile. She didn't move. She still sat in the doorway with her hands over her knees.

He got in the car and started the engine, backed into the drive and cut the wheels toward the road, glanced into the garage and saw Lindsay on her feet, reaching for the switch to bring down the door. Noah considered waving but didn't. Neither did Lindsay. She just stood looking at the Corvette, her hand on the switch but not pressing it. He didn't know if she could see him sitting behind the wheel looking at her, slim, shapely, and golden standing on the step in the doorway.

Didn't matter, either. Noah turned his head away, changed gears, and nosed the Corvette down the drive. He hoped to hell he could find his way back to the barn in the dark.

Chapter 14

Act III
SCENE IV

(Stage rear lights come up slowly on chair, floor lamp, and Murphy bed. Center spot falls on Moira. She's dressed in street clothes, slacks, a blouse, and a cardigan sweater. She lifts Sonnets from the Portuguese *from the table, presses the book to her cheek, and begins to hum, then to waltz. Cliff strides on stage, a duffel bag over his shoulder. Moira pirouettes. Cliff tosses bag aside, takes her in his arms, and they waltz. Cliff changes tempo to polka. Moira laughs. They make a circuit of the stage, then collapse, laughing, on the Murphy bed. Cliff sits up first on foot of bed.)*

CLIFF: Every time we've done that scene I've wanted to polka.

MOIRA: *(Sits beside him)* All six thousand four hundred and eight performances?

CLIFF: I could do it another six thousand four hundred and eight times. How 'bout you?

MOIRA: Define do it.

CLIFF: The play, Moira. I mean do the play.

MOIRA: Oh, the play. Sure. I was afraid you meant polka another six thousand four hundred and eight times.

CLIFF: It was a good run, wasn't it? Just like the old days.

MOIRA: Except that we were much younger in the old days.

CLIFF: You haven't aged a day, Moira.

MOIRA: I've aged five thousand four hundred and seventy-five days since we first debuted *Return Engagement*, Cliff. That's fifteen years.

CLIFF: You haven't aged a day. Not a single day. Not in my eyes.

MOIRA: *(Peers at him)* You aren't wearing your contacts, are you?

CLIFF: It was great being Martin and Lizabeth again, wasn't it? To bring them back for another run?

MOIRA: Say what you will about my father, he writes damn good plays.

CLIFF: Martin and Lizabeth still love each other, Moira.

(Moira rises, crosses stage to put book back on table. Cliff frowns.)

MOIRA: You'll miss your flight to L.A.

CLIFF: I'll miss you.

MOIRA: Then don't wait fifteen years to call me next time.

CLIFF: You called me, Moira.

MOIRA: I did not call you. I called your agent.

CLIFF: I kissed Jimmy when he told me you wanted me to do this revival of *Return Engagement* with you.

MOIRA: Who else would I call? You created Martin. You won a Tony for the play and an Oscar for the movie.

CLIFF: So did you, Moira. We won together. A Tony and an Oscar for Cliff and Moira.

MOIRA: Yes. Then it was an Emmy for Cliff and Chloe. A Screen Actor's Guild for Cliff and Caroline. For Cliff and Tawny it was—gimme a minute.

CLIFF: A cable ACE award.

MOIRA: Right. An ACE. *(Snaps fingers)* How could I forget?

CLIFF: You didn't forget. You can't forget. That's the problem.

MOIRA: No, Clifford. The problem is that you keep falling in love with your leading ladies.

CLIFF: I don't love them, Moira. I sleep with them. When you dumped me over Chloe, I figured what the hell. Why not?

MOIRA: And you wonder why it took me fifteen years to call you?

CLIFF: I didn't realize how miserable I was without you till we made love again on this old Murphy bed. It's the same one we made love on during the first run of *Return Engagement*. On our first opening night after our curtain calls.

MOIRA: This is not the same old Murphy bed.

CLIFF: Yes, it is. There's a tear in the mattress right here— *(He lifts the sheet off the bottom corner.)* Must be the other corner.

(Moira folds her arms and watches Cliff crawl up the bed tugging at the sheets. There's a loud groan. The bed flies up into the wall and the doors slam shut. Moira runs to the door and tries to wrench them open.)

MOIRA: Cliff! Cliff! Are you all right in there? *(Listens, ear pressed to the doors)* Cliff? Cliff!

(Pounds her fists, listens again. No response. Runs to center stage, then to stage left, stage right, and back to center.)

MOIRA: Help! Someone! Help me! Hank! Where are you? What good is a handyman who's never handy!

(Moira runs back to Murphy bed. Tries again to open doors. Pounds on them. Calls to Cliff and listens. No response)

MOIRA: Breathe, Cliff, breathe! Don't you dare suffocate! I'll get you out!

(Runs to center stage, looks around frantically)

MOIRA: But how? What can I do? What can I use?

(Races to floor lamp. Struggles to unplug and lift it. Behind her, doors open, Murphy bed drops soundlessly to the floor. Cliff is lying on rumpled sheets, grinning, chin propped on one hand watching Moira. She picks up the lamp and wheels toward the bed.)

MOIRA: Cliff! *(Puts lamp down and rushes to him. Cliff rises on his knees and catches her as she flings herself into his arms.)* Are you all right? *(Showers him with kisses)* Are you hurt anywhere?

CLIFF: Ouch! Right here. *(Rubs his ribs)*

MOIRA: My poor love! *(Pushes his jacket off his shoulders, rips open his shirt, kisses his chest)*

CLIFF: *(cups her head in his hands)* Oh, God. Oh, Moira.

(Drags her down on the bed. They embrace and kiss. Limbs tangle. Cliff's jacket flies off the bed, then Moira's sweater. Cliff kicks off his shoes, rolls on top of Moira. She pushes him off and jumps to her feet.)

MOIRA: All right, Clifford. How did you do that?

CLIFF: *(Rips off his shirt and throws it)* How did I do what, darling?

MOIRA: Make the bed fly up into the wall?

CLIFF: Moira, darling. Why would I do a thing like that?

MOIRA: *(Picks up his shirt and throws it at him)* To lure me onto the bed so you could seduce me.

CLIFF: I'm an actor, Moira. I have no more control over this bed than—

(Bed starts to rise again. Cliff clutches mattress. Moira jumps on the foot. Her weight drops the bed back to the floor.)

CLIFF: See? I told you. I'm not Houdini.

MOIRA: Oh, all right. You didn't do it. *(Stuffs his shirt in his hands)* Put your shirt on, Clifford.

CLIFF: I don't want to put my shirt on. I want to make love with you. Right here, right now.

MOIRA: You don't love me, Cliff. *(Pushes her hand against his bare chest.)* I'm just your current leading lady. You'll start your new movie in L.A. in two weeks. The second you lay eyes on your costar you'll forget all about me. Just like with Chloe.

CLIFF: I didn't forget about this, Moira. *(Takes his wallet out of his pocket, plucks out a ring, and lays it on her palm)* I've kept this with me for fifteen years.

MOIRA: My ring. My engagement ring. I threw it in your swimming pool!

CLIFF: I damn near drowned myself scouring the bottom for it. It caught in the filter. I got it out before it went through.

MOIRA: I can't believe this. You kept my ring. All these years.

CLIFF: I've just been waiting to give it back to you. *(Cups her face in his hands)* I love you, Moira. Will you marry me?

MOIRA: Do you love me, Cliff? Really? Only me?

CLIFF: Yes, Moira. Like Martin loves Lizabeth. I love only you. Forever.

(He slips ring on her finger. They kiss, embrace, and tumble on the bed, murmuring endearments as the stage lights dim.)

MOIRA: Oh Cliff! Oh, darling! Yes!

(A loud bang as the Murphy bed slams into the wall and blackout)

The End

Everyone seated at the fold-up banquet table in the rehearsal room of the Belle Coeur Theatre laughed. Uncle

Frank, Moira's overbearing playwright father; Emma, sitting in for Darcy, who would vamp it up as Moira's friend Roxy when she finished her consulting job in Denver; and Uncle Ron, cast as Hank the unhandy handyman.

Aunt Sassy brayed and leered at Noah. Even Uncle Ezra stopped glaring at him and chortled. Susan smiled like a good little attorney, politely and noncommittally.

Lindsay sat at the end of the table farthest away from Jolie. Her gaze glued to the snippet of stage direction: *Pushes his jacket off his shoulders, rips open his shirt, kisses his chest.*

Not on your life. She'd kissed Noah's chest once. In his bedroom, at his place at the beach. In the dark but for a gleam of moonlight off the ocean that found its way through the glass wall next to his bed. He'd cupped her head, said "Jesus, princess. At last," and dragged her down on the sheets.

She and Susan had come up with a list of things Lindsay supposedly wanted before she'd agree to do the play. An article in *Entertainment Weekly* about outrageous stars and their outrageous demands gave them the idea. Lindsay's list was guaranteed to make Jolie howl, but the list was history. She had only one demand now—rewrite the last scene. She would not kiss Noah's chest. Even for Jolie.

Noah sneezed, startling Lindsay in her chair. She glanced up at him and the wad of Kleenex clapped over his nose. He'd seemed fine at dinner last night. Bloodied by the raspberry bushes, but the scratches had scabbed over. They looked like little red zippers on his forearms.

Jolie scowled at him. "Get rid of the cold."

"Come a little closer," Noah snarled. "I'll give it to you."

Then he sneezed again, so hard his chair slid back from the table. Susan rose and turned to the drip coffee machine on the old microwave cart between her chair and Uncle Ezra's.

The coffee was putrid; Aunt Sassy made it. Susan poured a mug and took it to Noah. *I wouldn't,* Lindsay started to say, but bit her lip. The mullein tea hadn't killed him. Maybe Aunt Sassy's coffee would. Then she wouldn't have to worry about kissing his chest.

"Thanks, Suze." Noah picked up the faded green mug she'd put in front of him. "You're an angel."

Susan's smile sparkled. "Hope it helps."

Lindsay hoped it helped him to the hospital to get his stomach pumped. Maybe that would convince him Belle Coeur was no place for him. Attacked by killer bushes, felled by a nasty cold, and poisoned—all in three days. If he went back to L.A. where he belonged she wouldn't have to worry about the last scene.

"That poor man ought to be in bed, Jolene," Aunt Sassy said, sliding Noah a look that said with-me-big-boy-how-'bout-it?

"I need Noah here," Jolie said curtly. "You're just the set decorator and the costume coordinator, Aunt Sassy. You I don't need."

"I taught you how to buckle your tap shoes, young lady. You keep a civil tongue or you find some other fool to scrape costumes together from those rags you got hanging in the wardrobe room."

"Those aren't rags, Aunt Sassy. They're vintage clothing."

"I got dust cloths tore from Ezra's old shirts newer than that crap."

"All *right*." A leather portfolio lay open on the table in front of Jolie. She yanked her checkbook out of a pocket next to the lined tablet where she'd jotted notes during the read-through, tore out a check, signed it, and pushed it across the table. "Go shopping."

Sassy eyed the check, then Jolie. "You didn't fill in an amount."

"Spend whatever you need."

"Oh no, missy. We're not playing that game again." *What game,* Lindsay wondered, watching Sassy shove the check at Jolie. "You fill in an amount. An *exact* amount."

Jolie's face turned as red-orange as her hair, but she filled out the check and slid it toward Sassy. "Happy?"

"Thank you." Sassy folded the check into the V-neck of her pullover sweater. "I'll cash this in the morning and I'll bring you receipts."

"Any questions?" Jolie looked around the table at her cast.

Noah sank back in his chair, his face almost the same shade of chalky beige as the walls. Uncle Frank and Emma shook their head no.

Uncle Ron raised his hand. "Why did Moira hire Hank as the theater handyman if he can't even change a lightbulb?"

"That's why Moira hired him, Ron, because no one else will. Hank illustrates Moira's kindness toward the congenitally inept."

"He stumbles and bumbles around. He drops things, he breaks things. He looks ridiculous."

"He's supposed to look ridiculous. He's the comic relief."

"I understand that, but couldn't I do something right just once? Kind of redeem Hank?"

"I don't know, Ron. You tell me." Jolie folded her arms on the table and cocked her head. "Do you think you got tomorrow's forecast right?"

"Huh?" Ron blinked behind his glasses. "What does my job have to do with Hank's job?"

"Your forecast for last Saturday was cloudy and cold. We had a sleet storm. You haven't gotten a forecast right since Thanksgiving. Everyone in Belle Coeur knows that. When you come on stage as Hank and you can't even change a lightbulb it will be doubly hilarious."

Uncle Ron fell back in his chair. He looked like she'd just kicked him in the mouth. So did Susan, Uncle Frank, and Aunt Sassy. Uncle Ezra wiped a hand over his mouth. Emma simply gaped at Jolie.

"That's not funny," Lindsay said. "The audience won't be laughing at Hank. They'll be laughing at Uncle Ron. That's humiliating."

"It's not humiliating," Jolie insisted. "It's funny."

"No, it isn't," Emma said. "It's cruel."

"Guess what, Emma?" Jolie said. "I don't need *you* here, either."

"Lindsay's got a point. So does Ron." Noah pushed himself straight in his chair, bleary-eyed and sniffling. "Ron can't get the weather right and Hank can't change a lightbulb. Funny. But if your audience starts laughing at Ron, you'll break the spell of disbelief you've established so they can believe in your characters and care what happens to them.

"If Hank gets it right once. If he screws that bulb in straight the audience will cheer. And on the way home maybe Farmer Fred says to his wife, 'Well, Mother. If he can screw in a lightbulb, maybe he can get the weather right.' Then everybody wins."

It was the perfect triumph for the hapless Hank. Plus it saved Uncle Ron's dignity. That it came from Noah was the thing that floored Lindsay. *My God,* she thought. *He* can *see past the end of his nose.*

"Noah," Susan breathed. "That's brilliant." She gazed at him, her eyes shining like she wanted to jump across the table and kiss him.

Here Suze, Lindsay wanted to say. *You can have my part.*

That's what Jolie's narrowed eyes said she wanted to do—take Noah apart. She was insensitive, but she wasn't stupid. It took her five seconds to realize Noah's suggestion was terrific, for the fire to die in her eyes and a smile to lift her mouth.

"Not bad," she said to him. "I'll think about it."

"Swell." Noah sucked a congested breath. "You done with me?"

"Anyone have anything else?" Jolie looked around the table. When no one said anything, she nodded at Noah. "I'm done with you till tomorrow night. Blocking rehearsal at seven-thirty. Don't be late."

"I'll be there." He flattened his hands on the table and pushed to his feet. "Unless I'm dead."

Noah looked so awful Lindsay felt bad for wishing him ill. He picked up his glasses and his Kleenex box and turned toward the door. Jolie swiveled in her chair to watch him weave across the room. When he bumped the doorway going through it, she turned toward Uncle Frank.

"Follow Noah upstairs. I want to know if he's drinking."

"He's sick, Jolie," Ron said. "So sick he can hardly stand up."

"He's also a drunk, Ron. He was living on the streets in L.A."

Uncle Ron blinked, taken aback. Susan's eyebrows drew together.

"Uncle Frank," Jolie said to him. "You're still here."

"And here I'm staying," he replied. "I won't spy on Noah."

"I said Noah is a *drunk*. If he starts drinking he jeopardizes this production and this theater. If he's boozing it up, up there in Joe's apartment, I can fire him. He has a sobriety clause in his contract."

"Since you seem so eager to exercise it, Jolie." Uncle Frank put on his Circuit Court Judge face. "You go smell Noah's breath."

Jolie blinked like a gecko, then swept a scathing look around the table. "Thank you, family, for your overwhelming show of support."

"You're just as welcome as you can be, Jolene," Aunt Sassy said cheerfully. "Now I'm gonna go pick through rags in the wardrobe room."

She sashayed away from the table in her usual uniform of leotard and tights, raspberry tonight with a sweater to match, and black stiletto heels. Lindsay wanted to follow her, but crooked a finger at Susan.

"Where's the list?" Lindsay asked her. Susan slipped it out of her pocket and Lindsay tore it in half. "I will not kiss Noah's chest. If Jolie agrees to scratch that piece of business, I'll do the play."

"This isn't a ploy to make her sweat, is it? You mean this."

"I absolutely mean it. Trey does not need to see me rip the shirt off his new best friend. Even if it is only make-believe."

"Hel-*lo*, counselor. Do we have contract terms to discuss or not?" Jolie frowned impatiently at them from the other end of the table. "I have a dinner date. Bill is picking me up in an hour."

"One second." Susan glanced at Jolie, then at Lindsay and lowered her voice. "Noah is Trey's new best friend? Does this have anything to do with a horse piss yellow Corvette?"

"I mean it, Suze. That piece of business goes or I go."

"It's as good as gone. I'll call you later at home."

Susan turned away to follow Jolie up to her office. Lindsay made a beeline for the wardrobe room and Aunt Sassy. She was flipping through the costumes. Same old ratty ones hung on new chrome racks lined up against the freshly painted yellow walls.

"Need help, Aunt Sassy?" Lindsay asked.

"I need a box marked Salvation Army for this crap."

"I might have some things in my closet that would work for Moira and Roxy. Darcy and I are about the same size."

"That'd be a big help. Skinflint only gave me five hundred."

That much, Lindsay thought, but didn't say so since the smirk on Aunt Sassy's face said she thought it was peanuts.

"How am I s'posed to dress Frank like a New York swell plus design and furnish the sets on a measly five hundred? Lucky Noah don't need much gussying up. He was born looking like a movie star." Sassy said it without drooling, then sharpened her gaze at Lindsay. "He don't look to me like a drunk who was living on the streets. Does he to you?"

"No, he doesn't," Lindsay agreed. On Sunday Noah told her that Vivienne scraped him off the sidewalk but she wasn't going to tell Sassy. That bit of information was for Noah to confirm or not as he chose.

"Nice of Jolene to blurt it out," Sassy said disgustedly. "She did it, a'course, 'cause Ron spoke up for Noah. Wonder how she'd like it if I told her whole damn cast she clipped me for two hundred dollars the last time I went costume and prop shopping for her."

Aunt Sassy would give you the leotard off her back. You didn't have to ask, but she did not like to be flimflammed.

"So that's what you meant when you said you wouldn't play that game again."

"Ex-*actly*. Thinks she's owed 'cause her mama and daddy took off and left her. Can't say I blame 'em. Jolene was not a pleasant child."

"Aunt Sassy." Lindsay's instinct to protect Jolie kicked in like a reflex. "Jolie was only a baby."

"She ain't a baby now." Sassy turned away from the costume racks and scowled. "I'm sick to death of her shenanigans and I ain't alone. Why do you think Frank told her to do her own snooping?"

Lindsay's stomach clutched. "What are you trying to tell me?"

"I'm not *trying* to tell you a thing. I'm saying it bold as brass, just like Jolie popped off about Noah. She's this close—" Sassy pinched her first two fingers together "—to wearing out her welcome in this family. Only reason any of us puts up with her is because of you."

"I'm working on Jolie, Aunt Sassy. If you could just be patient."

"Ever'body's been patient, Lindsay. Jolie's whole damn life we been patient, waiting for her to grow out of her mad at Vivian. That's near thirty years. It ain't happened 'cause it ain't *gonna* happen. Me and Dovey has talked and she's spoken to Frank."

"Which means what, Aunt Sassy?"

"The way she behaved on Saturday." Sassy flipped a hand in the air. "Putting Darcy with the chicks when she's allergic. Yelling at Donnie and Lonnie like they're dogs. Throwing Noah in your face. Then she started a fuss with you in Dovey's *house*. At Easter dinner, mind."

"Jolie is always touchy on opening weekend. You know that."

"And just now she tried to humiliate Ron and would've if Noah hadn't spoke up. Don't know why the rest of us was struck dumb. Think we'd be used to Jolie sticking it to us, wouldn't you?"

"I know you love Jolie, Aunt Sassy. She's just so unhappy—"

"She ain't unhappy. She's mean. Plain damn mean as a snake."

"Aunt Sassy." Lindsay's breath caught. "You don't mean that."

"I sure as hell do. I know mean when it bites me in the butt and that niece of mine is one nasty-tempered little copperhead. I'd sure miss this old place if it closed up, but I believe it's time this family wished Jolene Varner well and wished her well away. Just like we done Vivian."

"Lindsay," Emma said, leaning into the room from the hallway. Lindsay jumped, startled, and turned toward Emma, wondering how much she'd heard. "Do you know how Noah got all scratched up?"

"He tangled with a raspberry bush. Why?"

"Uncle Ezra asked me. I thought it was odd."

"Anyway, odd is Ezra's middle name," Sassy said. "He

caught me filing a broken fingernail and quizzed me like I was a murder suspect."

"About a fingernail?" Lindsay said.

"About scratches?" Emma said.

They both looked at Sassy. She shrugged. It hit Lindsay, just as Sassy blinked like a rabbit caught out in the yard at night when you flipped on the porch light, that the scrapes on Noah's arms *could*—if you were Uncle Ezra—look like fingernail scratches.

"Lucille," they all said, and bolted out of the wardrobe room.

Straight down the back hall toward the workroom, around the corner into the side corridor. They raced up the back stairs, the old bare board steps groaning. Emma led the charge down the hallway toward Joe Varner's apartment, Sassy hard behind her, running nimbly as a deer in her stiletto pumps. Lindsay brought up the rear, winded by the steep stairs and trying to keep up.

The door was closed but unlocked. Emma burst through it and jerked to a stop. Sassy stumbled past her. Lindsay pushed last through the door into the living room. She caught herself on the back of an upholstered wing chair and her breath in a deep gasp for air.

Noah sat on the couch. The crooked shade on the lamp beside him beamed a spotlight on Lucille's single barrel planted in the middle of his chest. Uncle Ezra sat on the coffee table in front of him holding the shotgun in place.

Noah's face looked as white as the tissues crumpled around him on the couch cushions. He raised just his eyes to Lindsay. She'd told him Lucille was never loaded, so she doubted the glitter in his deep blue eyes was fear. She thought it was fever—and probably fury at having a shotgun, even an empty one, pinning him to his own couch.

"You go on, Frank," Uncle Ezra said, his back to the three of them. "Me and Noah's just having a little chat like I told you we was gonna. No need for you to be here."

"I ain't Frank, you old fool!" Sassy shrilled at him.

Uncle Ezra leaped to his feet, taking Lucille with him as he spun toward his wife. Noah sneezed into a handful of Kleenex.

"Sassy!" Uncle Ezra blurted, then narrowed his eyes. "Long as you're here." He waved her toward Noah with the shotgun. "Git your busted fingernail over here and we'll see if it matches up with these scratches on Noah's arms."

"They won't match, Uncle Ezra," Lindsay said. "Aunt Sassy did not scratch Noah. He got caught in a raspberry bramble."

"Hell he did," Uncle Ezra sneered. "S'pose you seen it happen."

"Yes, Uncle Ez. I was there."

Lindsay could feel Noah's eyes on her but she kept her gaze fixed on Uncle Ezra, her focus on catching her breath.

"Ain't no raspberries 'round the barn," he said suspiciously.

"The woods are full of berry patches, Uncle Ez. You know that. Noah and Trey were out walking the creek yesterday looking for geodes."

"Heard about that," he said, backing down some. "And you was there, Lindsay Evelyn?"

"Yes, Uncle Ez. I drove out to pick them up."

"Heard about that, too. Well, hell," Uncle Ezra said, with a sigh that let the bluster out of him. He flushed and Lucille wilted in his grasp.

Noah sneezed. Uncle Ezra turned toward him and offered his hand, thought better of it, and took it back. "I'm right sorry, Noah."

"Not a problem, Mr. Pantz." Noah raised a Kleenex-filled hand. "If you don't mind, I'd like to go to bed now and pray for death."

"Chicken soup," Uncle Ezra said. "That's what you need. Some of my sweet bride Sassy's *dee*-licious chicken soup."

He turned, slumped and cowering, toward his wife. Sassy smacked him on the back of the head and yanked Lucille out of his grasp.

"Next time I see you with this damn gun I'm gonna wrap it 'round your neck, Ezra Pantz. You'll wear it the rest of your sorry fool life and you'll be buried with Lucille, not me. You understand?"

"Yes, Sassy." Uncle Ezra cringed. "Yes, darlin'."

"Get moving." Sassy gave him a boot in the butt toward the door, paused on her way through it behind Ezra, and smiled at Noah. "I'll keep my eye on this crazy old coot. You get better."

"I'll tag along with Uncle Ez and Aunt Sassy. Make sure he doesn't talk her out of Lucille," Emma said to Lindsay. To Noah she said, "Do *not* eat anything Aunt Sassy cooks. Especially her chicken soup."

She left and shut the door. Lindsay blinked at the brass knob. It had a halo around it and dancing stars. Oh hell. She wasn't just winded by the dash up the stairs—she was starting another panic attack.

"You lied for me, princess," Noah said behind her.

"I did not." Lindsay clutched the wing chair, wheeled around, and blinked at Noah. His face swam with black spots. "I *was* there."

Noah cocked his head. "You don't look so hot."

"Neither do you." Lindsay fell into the wing chair, the room starting to tilt on her, bent forward, and stuck her head between her knees. She'd worn slacks today; green ones with a sweater set to match. The floor evened out when she closed her eyes. *Breathe,* she told herself, *breathe.*

She heard the couch cushions sigh and footsteps creak. When the tiny white sunbursts stopped exploding against her eyelids, she sat up. Noah stood beside the wing chair, offering her a paper bag. Lindsay took it and breathed into it while Noah tottered back to the couch.

He pulled the striped afghan folded over the back around him and shivered. Once she could breathe without hyperventilating, Lindsay took the bag away from her mouth.

"Asthma attack?" Noah asked.

"Panic attack." Lindsay sighed and folded the bag. "They stopped when I left L.A., came back for about six months when my husband Mark died. They started again when I told Jolie I'd do this play."

"I'd say your psyche isn't happy about that, princess."

"If Susan and Jolie can iron out my contract my psyche will have to get used to it. If they can't, where will that leave you?"

"In a hellova lot better shape than I was six months ago."

"Jolie told everyone that you'd been living on the streets."

"Let me guess." Noah smiled wryly. "She announced it to all of you at the table after I left."

Lindsay thought of Emma and felt a chill. "How did you know?"

"Your sister is so much like Vivienne she gives me nightmares."Noah turned his head away and coughed. A deep, wrenching cough that doubled him and made the veins in his temples pop, left him pale and shaking and his eyes streaming tears.

"I don't like the sound of that cough," Lindsay said with a frown.

"You should be on this side of it."

Noah laid his head against the back of the couch and shut his eyes. His hair stuck out around his ears and he didn't care. He was sick, all right. Possibly dying if he didn't give a flip what he looked like.

Lindsay got up and went to the coffee table, sat on it in front of Noah, and cupped her hand around his cheek. His eyes opened and blinked at her, bloodshot with misery. His skin felt clammy. When he turned his head away from her, she felt his whiskers scrape against her palm and a quiver in her stomach.

"Go away, princess. Whatever I've got you don't need."

"Oh, be quiet. I'm a mother. I've been through childhood diseases pediatricians haven't even named yet."

The Mother Voice worked every time. Noah stilled and laid his head back against the couch. His pulse thudded like a jackhammer in his throat, his breath rattled when he breathed. His forehead when she pressed her hand to it scorched her palm.

"You're burning up, Noah."

A gleam of devilment leaped into his fever-bright eyes. "It's you, princess. You've got your hands on me. At last my dream has come true."

Moron. Sick as he was, Lindsay wanted to smack him. *Your dream came true on my eighteenth birthday but you were too drunk to remember.*

"I don't suppose you have a thermometer?"

"Might be one in the bathroom. I don't know."

There was, in the medicine cabinet behind the mirror above the sink. There was Tylenol, Band-Aids, alcohol, Neosporin ointment, all the basics in unopened packages. The bathroom fixtures were new, the kitchen appliances, the linoleum, the carpet, and most of the furniture.

The paneling was pecan and not cheap. Lindsay noticed that while she sat on the coffee table timing the thermometer. Her father had kept this place like a pigsty. She was glad the uncles had fixed it up. Noah's arrival had clearly been planned. *But who paid for all this,* she wondered, as she plucked the thermometer out of Noah's mouth and read it.

He coughed into a Kleenex and crumpled the tissue. Quickly, but not quite quickly enough.

"That's blood." Lindsay stood up. "You're going to the hospital."

"I'm going to bed." He leered at her. "You're welcome to join me."

"You can't fluster and embarrass me with innuendo and double entendres, Noah. I'm not a silly little girl anymore. I'm a grown woman. I'm not going to blush and run away."

"You were never a silly little girl, princess. I kept trying to help you be one, but Vivienne was always there to spoil your fun."

"Not always," Lindsay said. She said it, then wanted to bite her tongue, but the comment sailed right past Noah. He mumbled "Good for you" and keeled over sideways on the couch. He'd kicked off his shoes, drew his stocking feet up, and huddled under the afghan.

"Get up, Noah. Your temperature is one-oh-four. Convulsions start at one-oh-six."

"I had DT's in detox. Convulsions can't be any worse."

He shivered, stuffed a needlepoint cushion under his head, and burrowed into it. This was not good. If she couldn't get him on his feet, she'd have to call Uncle Frank and Uncle Ron up here.

She sat down, leaned her elbows on her knees, and bent toward Noah. "Convulsions can cause brain damage."

"So what? I can't remember jack shit anyway." He opened his eyes and blinked at her blearily. "Your face is all fuzzy."

"Of course it is. Your fever is so high you're delirious."

"No, in my head, in my brain. I keep trying to remember you but you're all fuzzy. I can only remember that twerp Jesse."

"You do remember me. I was a silly little girl. You just said so."

"I said you *weren't* a silly little girl, princess. Pay attention. There's more, I know it. It's in my head somewhere. I just can't get hold of it."

"You have pneumonia, Noah. You need to go to the hospital."

"I'm going to bed. With you, I hope. Just once before I die."

Been there, done that, you dummy, Lindsay thought, but didn't say so. She stood up and put her hands on her hips.

"Don't think I can't get you off this couch. I'm taller than you."

"The hell you are." He kicked off the afghan and swung his feet to the floor. "I grew four inches in the third season and got a raise."

He managed to stand but he was weak and woozy. Lindsay caught him by the arms and steadied him. If she hadn't he would've gone headfirst over the coffee table.

"No fair," he said, weaving on his feet and peering at the tip of her nose dead even with his. "You're wearing shoes and I'm not." He pitched forward suddenly. Lindsay caught him again as his forehead thudded against her collarbone. "Oh God. I'm sick, princess."

"I know you are." Lindsay slid her shoulder under Noah's right arm. He looped his left around her neck, his body so hot with fever against hers she shivered. She didn't think she could get him down the front stairs, through the lobby, and into her Civic in the parking lot. She hoped she could get him up the back steps. "Where's your car?"

"Out back. The key's in my pocket."

The outside fixture above the back door gave Lindsay enough light to get him up the steps, across the small stretch of yard, and into the Corvette. When she slid in behind the wheel and started the engine, Noah turned his head and looked at her, his face gray and pasty in the glow of the dome light.

"I've got bad news for Trey," he said. "This goddamn car glows in the dark."

Chapter 15

NOAH HAD PNEUMONIA, all right—left lung, upper lobe—and by seven A.M. Wednesday, the RNs and LPNs who worked the day shift in the acute care wing on the second floor of the Belle Coeur Community Hospital were fighting over who was going to give him a sponge bath.

Straws were drawn. The winner was Pat Hannity, mother of Meggie, the cute little carhop at Burger Chef from Trey's geometry class. Pat emerged from Noah's room with her cheeks flushed, a dreamy smile on her face—and her lip zipped. In the nurse's lounge she was pelted with microwave popcorn. Double butter, no salt.

"Lots of unpopped kernels." Aunt Muriel sighed, disappointed. "But she wouldn't talk."

Aunt Muriel was chairwoman of the Women's Hospital Auxiliary. Plugged in to everything that happened in the small, fifty-five-bed hospital. She stopped by The Bookshelf after the Women's Auxiliary tea in her electric scooter, painted candle apple red with a pair of fuzzy dice tied on the handlebars, to tell the sponge bath story to Emma and Lindsay.

"Woohoo," Emma said, leaning over the cash wrap on her elbows to wink at Aunt Muriel in her scooter. "Noah must still be pretty hot stuff."

Wilburta Allen, wearing jeans and a T-shirt that said CAMP GRANDMA: WHERE NO IS NEVER SPOKEN, turned away from the hardcover fiction section. "Wonder how hot?"

"Buy a ticket for opening night," Emma told her. "Noah takes his shirt off in the last scene."

"Now that's worth the price of admission." Wilburta grinned, then glanced at Lindsay. "No offense."

"None taken, Wilburta." She smiled and headed for the young adult section with an armload of paperbacks to shelve.

Thank God the nurses were fighting over Noah. It meant the hum she'd felt watching him stretch out of the Corvette in front of The Bookshelf, the quiver in her stomach when his whiskers scraped her palm, was perfectly normal. It didn't mean she was attracted to Noah. Well, yes it did—yes, she was—but not because he was Noah. Because he was a man and she was a woman. It was biology. And maybe a sign that it was time to stop sighing over Mel Gibson movies and go out on a date.

But not with Noah. Lindsay suspected he was going to ask her. He'd said as much when he admitted he'd lied for Trey so he could make points with her. He knew what he'd been like when he drank and seemed committed to being a better person now that he was sober.

Admirable, but the wild child he'd once been was still lurking inside him. She'd seen a glimpse of it, of the old Noah when he'd said it might be fun to hang around and wait for Uncle Ezra and Lucille. That Noah was Chaos and that Noah Lindsay wanted no part of.

"So how sick is Noah, Lindsay?" Wilburta called to her.

"Sick enough," she replied, sticking her head around the end of the five-shelf bay to answer Wilburta. "Dehydrated on top of the pneumonia. They kept him so they could give him fluids intravenously along with antibiotics. He should be released in a couple days."

Until then, the Varners and Fairchilds were keeping a round-the-clock Jolie Watch at the hospital. Emma was first to arrive, within half an hour of Lindsay calling her from the emergency waiting room pay phone to ask her to call Trey and bring her purse, which she'd left in the rehearsal room. Emma was still at the barn, washing the coffee cups from the read-through, when Lindsay reached her on her cell phone.

"Noah flat on his back five weeks shy of opening night," Emma said with a groan. "Jolie will go ballistic."

"If Uncle Frank is still there," Lindsay replied, "let him tell her."

He could usually keep Jolie from launching herself at the moon, but Frank had already gone home and Jolie had left. To keep her date with Bill Rich, they all assumed, but just in case, Uncle Ron stayed the night with Noah. Susan was there this morning. Lindsay had the afternoon shift. When Emma closed The Bookshelf she'd sit with Noah until Uncle Donnie came to play night watchman.

The aunts and uncles and cousins putting themselves between a too-sick-to-deal-with-it Noah and Jolie's temper said everything Aunt Sassy had told her about Jolie. It was very depressing and worrying.

Lindsay could talk to Dovey. Find out if the rest of the family had truly had it with Jolie, make sure it wasn't just Sassy the spitfire popping off, but this was only the third day of her campaign to overhaul her image. If she abandoned it and went back to being Jolie's apologist, her plan would never work.

Not that it was such a roaring success so far. Jolie didn't believe she'd thrown the hedge apples and Lindsay had traded making her sweat for changing the last scene. The Image Overhaul Campaign wasn't voodoo or the lobotomy Susan suggested, it was shock therapy—Lindsay's last chance to convince Jolie that behaving like Vivienne was a poor way to live, that it was time to bury the past and get on with her life.

Time for both of them, really, Lindsay decided, once she finished shelving the new inventory and drove Noah's Corvette to the hospital to relieve Susan. Aunt Sassy's coffee hadn't killed him and pneumonia wouldn't either. He wasn't going to leave Belle Coeur. He'd been teasing her, trying to gauge her reaction when he'd said that. He needed this job to prove to the big boys in L.A. that he'd cleaned up his act.

When he'd said "There's more, I know it. It's in my head somewhere. I just can't get hold of it," her stomach had dropped like a stone. She'd still been shaky from the panic attack triggered by Aunt Sassy's threats toward Jolie, but now she was calm, in control again, and years past the guilt she'd felt for betraying Mark.

For sleeping with a jerk that didn't give a damn about her, who saw her as nothing but a sexual conquest. She'd never told Mark about Noah. When she found out she was pregnant so soon after they eloped, she'd taken it as a sign that

God had forgiven her so it was okay to forgive herself. She wouldn't let Noah scare the bejesus out of her again.

She was over the shock of him popping down the stairs from Jolie's office like a jack-in-the-box. She wouldn't run away anymore like she had on Saturday. She was a grown woman who'd done one stupendously stupid thing in her life. So what if Noah remembered? As Susan pointed out, what did then have to do with now?

He'd been drunk as a skunk the night of her birthday party and still smashed when she'd shown up at his house the next day. If Noah couldn't remember they'd slept together the morning after, what made her think he'd remember after all this time? Lindsay felt like Jesse the twerp for even worrying about it.

The Belle Coeur Community Hospital, two stories of sandstone brick, stood on Ridge Road just east of Alternate 152, in the midst of a tree-shaded park with a walking track and sand pit volleyball court. As Lindsay turned into the visitor's lot, the sun vanished beneath a bank of thick, dark clouds and it started to rain. Big fat drops that splashed on the windshield and ran across the glass.

She cruised the first six rows, peering through the wipers looking for Jolie's truck before she realized what she was doing. How paranoid was this? Checking out the lot for Jolie the Boogie Woman? Lindsay made a disgusted noise and parked in the next empty space, tucked her book and the magazines she'd brought for Noah in her bag, tied on her scarf, gathered her coat at her throat, and dashed for the door.

It wasn't far but it was pouring, a good old Missouri gully washer as Aunt Dovey would say. Lindsay ducked under the aluminum canopy, her soaked shoes squishing and cold rain dripping off her nose. She tugged off her scarf, eyed the rain driving in sheets across the lot and felt for Uncle Ron. His forecast on the radio this morning called for sunny skies, a high around sixty, and a near zero chance for precipitation.

When Lindsay stepped off the elevator on two, Pat Hannity was on the phone at the nurses' station. She looked up at the *whoosh* the doors made and raised a finger. Lindsay nodded and slipped out of her damp coat while Pat, a pretty brunette in pink scrubs and a flowered lab coat, ended the call and came up to the desk to talk to her.

"Noah enjoyed his bath this morning." She grinned. "So did I."

"Has he had any visitors?" Lindsay asked.

"You mean Jolie. Susan warned us. We'll do our best to make sure she doesn't get past us. Our patients don't need a ruckus up here."

"You're a doll, Pat. How about tickets for opening night?"

"Already got 'em, thanks. What I want to know is this. Does Noah really take his shirt off in the last scene?"

"Boy, that one got around fast." Lindsay laughed. "Yes, he does."

"I'll spread the word." Pat grinned again. "It'll be a sellout."

"From your lips to God's ears," Lindsay said and turned down the green walled corridor, her wet shoes squeaking on the beige tile floor.

Room 224 was around the corner. Noah was asleep; the head of his bed raised, a two-prong oxygen tube in his nose when she eased open his partially closed door. Susan sat in the chair beside the bed. She slid the papers in her lap into her briefcase and tiptoed into the corridor.

"All quiet," she said in a low voice. "No sign of Jolie."

"Don't worry. She'll turn up. How's Noah?"

"Out cold, thanks to Jo Beth. She brought him flowers and gave him a back rub. She had a cancellation this evening and I grabbed it."

"Lucky you," Lindsay said and meant it.

If the headache that had been plaguing her since Saturday didn't go away she'd have to beg Jo Beth for an appointment. She was a genius at massage and a hairdresser to boot. Jo Beth could slather you up with oil, spend an hour melting every muscle in your body, then shampoo your hair, do your nails, and send you out the door of her little shop looking like you'd stepped out of a bandbox.

"Lonnie was here, too," Susan said. "Noah was cold so he brought him some sleep pants and socks and undershirts. Jo Beth offered to sit if we need her. I'll try to get back after court in case Jolie shows. You shouldn't be here alone with her."

"Why? Did she throw a fit about changing the last scene?"

"No, not at all. She said the chest kissing thing was just a suggestion, that she'd leave working out the business in that scene to you and Noah." Susan frowned. "I've just got a bad feeling about this play."

"I count on you to be sensible, Suze," Lindsay said, suppressing a shiver. "Don't turn into Emma on me."

"I *am* being sensible. I want to know where Jolie is, where she took off to on a Tuesday night. That's not like her. She has a play in the infant stages of production. A play with Vivian's fingerprints all over it. She arranged all of this, Noah told you that. Vivian is paying his salary and she's paying Jolie. I keep wondering about that and I keep getting stuck on why. I don't buy Vivian's story that saving Noah will save her agency. I think there's more to it than that. But I can't figure out what."

"I can't either. Emma and I have talked about it, but we can't come up with a single thing Jolie has that Vivienne wants."

"That's what bothers me. Vivian knows and we don't. I've got this scary picture of her sitting out in L.A. pulling all our strings and I don't like it. I want to know what she has up her sleeve."

So did Lindsay. That's why she'd invited Noah to dinner Monday night. She'd intended to pick his brain but chickened out. Involving him in her affairs was not keeping him an outsider.

"I had a feeling this is where you were headed." Lindsay sighed. "You want me to ask Noah about Vivienne, don't you?"

"Yes, I do. I think it's entirely possible that he knows something he doesn't know he knows." Susan blinked. "Did that make sense?"

"No, but I get your drift. If Noah wakes up, I'll talk to him."

"Great. I'll try to get back later." Susan eyed Lindsay's wet scarf hanging limply over her arm with her coat. "Is it *raining*?"

"Pouring. And it's cold. I'll bet Uncle Ron's hiding under his desk."

"Oh swell." Susan made a face. "My umbrella's in the car."

"Here." Lindsay offered her coat. "So you don't look like a drowned rat in court."

"Thanks." Susan took it and hurried away toward the elevator.

Lindsay crept into Noah's room. The blue chair beside his bed had a high back and deep vinyl cushions; one of those chairs that wheezed like a bagpipe when you sat down. She eased into it, holding her breath as the cushions hissed, but Noah didn't stir. He stayed asleep, his head turned toward her on the pillow and his chin dipping toward his shoulder, snoring softly between his parted lips.

Lindsay grinned. In their *BBT* days this would've made headlines in teen magazines all over the planet—NOAH PATRICK SHARES THE HEARTACHE OF HIS MOST INTIMATE SECRET! HE SNORES!

In the second season, once the producers realized they had a bona fide heartthrob on their hands, the writers had crashed their hard drives coming up with ways to undress Noah. Because he surfed like a pro, Sam gave up football for the swim team. Whole shows were written around the beach. He got bonked with his board filming an episode about a surfing competition, hard enough to split his scalp. He didn't lose consciousness but he saw stars. The clip of Noah staggering out of the surf with his board and his head bloody made *Entertainment Tonight*.

An ambulance trip to the ER and six stitches closed the cut. Two Tylenol took care of the headache, but Noah spent a week in Cedars Sinai; his room was flooded with teddy bears and get well cards. Vivienne hit the roof, incensed that Noah was reaping all that publicity. She sent Lindsay to the hospital with a photographer to keep vigil at his bedside. She walked in on Noah and a nurse groping each other, surrounded by enough floral arrangements to decorate a float in the Rose Parade.

Lindsay smiled at the oh-so-Hollywood memory and Jo Beth's jar of yellow and white tulips, the only ornament in the room. She plucked the magazines out of her shoulder bag and fanned them on the bedside table. There. That looked better.

So did Noah, his face flushed from the oxygen. Two cotton blankets covered him, a hem of folded sheet between their woven beige pattern and his white undershirt. An IV needle was paper-taped to the back of his left hand. A clear plastic bag hung from a metal pole with a pump on it that beeped faintly with each drip into his bloodstream. *Even sick as a dog,* Lindsay thought, *he looked light years better than he did in his driver's license photo.*

She'd seen it last night, when Noah entrusted her with his wallet so the admissions clerk could copy his insurance card and his California license. The issue date was December twentieth of last year. He looked dull-eyed and unhealthy in the photo, his face gaunt, his smile tight-lipped.

Lindsay could see the dirty, gritty streets of L.A. in that photo, the delirium tremens Noah suffered in detox. She couldn't see them in his face now, she thought, leaning close to the raised bed rail for a better look. Near enough that the cocoon of warmth radiating from his tucked-in-snug-as-a-bug body made her shiver. Her pulse kicked, too, but that was biology. It was perfectly healthy, perfectly natural.

She could see a *little* something around his eyes. At the corners if she squinted, fine lines just beginning to show. *He'd had dermabrasion,* Lindsay thought. *Possibly some laser work.* Vivienne would consider it an investment. She'd obviously sunk a fortune, pinned all her hopes for her agency and God knew what else on Noah Patrick.

He sighed, opened his eyes, and blinked at her. Lindsay blinked, too, caught nearly nose to nose with him through the bed rail.

"If you're trying to figure out if I've quit breathing get a mirror."

His voice grated like a rusty saw. He coughed, his throat dry from the oxygen, Lindsay guessed, and reached for the cup of ice on the table pushed over the bed. She sat up straight in the blue chair.

"You must be feeling better. You're cracking jokes."

"I was dreaming about those turkeys again." Noah put

the cup down and scowled at the needle in his arm. "I don't get any real food until this thing comes out. All the years I drank I never caught so much as a cold. Then Vivienne gets hold of me, pumps me full of health food, and I end up with pneumonia."

Lindsay smiled. "Sometimes life's a bitch."

"Speaking of bitches, where's Jolie? I keep expecting her to bust in here, grab me by the hair, and drag me back to the barn so I won't miss the blocking rehearsal." Noah shivered. "I wish she'd hurry. This place is as cold as a tomb."

Gooseflesh sprang on his arms. Lindsay rose, leaned over the bed rail, and lifted the blankets. Noah huddled under them, scrunching his head into the pillow, springing his dark gold hair every which way. He looked so funny, all shivery and rumpled. Mr. Hotshot Hollywood Hunk with the world's worst case of bed head. Lindsay wanted to smooth his hair and kiss his forehead but didn't.

"Jolie had a date last night." She tucked the covers around him, being careful of the IV. "We're not sure where she is at the moment."

"That explains why you're all taking turns hovering at my bedside." Noah's teeth chattered. "You're protecting me from Satan's Handmaiden."

"Well—yes." Lindsay sat down. "After you left last night Jolie told Uncle Frank to follow you upstairs and make sure you weren't drinking. She said she can fire you if you drink."

"Oh, she can. There's a neon-lit sobriety clause in the contract." Noah plucked the oxygen prongs out of his nose. Lindsay caught his hand and frowned at him. "I don't think you should take that off."

"I can't talk with a vacuum cleaner up my nose," Noah said, and tossed the oxygen hose over the bed rail.

"You've seen Jolie's contract, haven't you?" Lindsay asked.

"Yep. She and I had a disagreement on Saturday. She gave me her copy to prove her point. Either she didn't know hers was different than mine or she was too pissed to care."

"Jolie's contract is with Vivienne's agency, isn't it?"

"Yeah. So is mine."

"Oh, Noah." Lindsay tsked. "What were you *thinking*?"

"Listen, princess." He rolled toward her on his right shoulder, cradling his left arm and the IV against his hip. "Vivienne found me half-drowned on the beach. I was trying to kill myself. I didn't have one damn thing to hang around for. Vivienne gave me a reason to stay alive and stay sober. I would've signed whatever she put in front of me."

Lindsay couldn't imagine such despair, such hopelessness. But she'd seen it, she realized, in his driver's license photo. She blinked, her throat so tight all she could say was "Oh, Noah."

"Aw, c'mon, princess. Vivienne and I are birds of a feather. I can handle her. But Jolie." Noah shook his head. "She's out of her league. Her entire agreement with Vivienne is hinged on you and me—no subs, no second stringers, no understudies—performing this play from opening night to closing, including the six-week option if it's a hit."

Lindsay stared at him, stunned. "You are *shitting* me, Patrick."

"Princess!" Noah gave a shout of laughter, started coughing, and rolled away from her. Lindsay sprang over the bed rail and yanked him back. "Ow!" He laughed, grinning up at her. "There's hair under there."

Lindsay could feel it, crisp strands of Noah's chest hair wound in her fists along with the front of his T-shirt. She could feel his heart beating, too, under the thin white cotton, and blinked. What was she *doing*? She let go and wrapped her hands on the bed rail, the metal cold as ice against her fingers after the heat in Noah's sleep-warmed skin.

"Jolie's agreement with Vivienne is tied to you and me *how*?" Lindsay demanded. "What does that mean?"

"It means if you walk out or I walk out at any time during the run Jolie won't get jack." Noah pushed himself up on the pillow and rubbed his chest. "Her boyfriend the lawyer told her she'd get sixty grand no matter what. I told her she'd better read Clause Nineteen again and think like Vivienne. She did and then she got it. I felt kind of sorry for her. She looked like I'd slugged her."

"When did you have this conversation with Jolie?"

"Sunday morning when she crashed my bedroom."

"Oh God." Lindsay dropped into the blue chair. "She

must've still been reeling when we argued at Aunt Dovey's house. I didn't say I was going to sue her, I just let her assume. I can't imagine what she's been going through, thinking I meant to sue her to get out of the play."

"She's your sister, princess. You do what you want, but let me tell you something about Jolie. She reminds me of me when I drank." Noah eyed her steadily over the bed rail. "Nothing was ever my fault. Somebody else was always to blame. It was just poor, pitiful, abused little me against the world."

"You don't like Jolie, do you?"

"No more than she likes me. You've still got my keys. Last night the contract was on the dining room table. It should still be there. If you don't believe me, go get it and let Susan have a look at it."

"I do believe you," Lindsay said, amazed to hear herself say it, amazed that it was true. "Though I never thought I'd say that to you."

"You know, princess, I wouldn't put it past Jolie to crash my place again and nose through my stuff while I'm in here. If I were you, I'd hotfoot it out to the barn and snag the contract."

"What's this? Are you trying to get rid of me?"

"Unless you want to help me into the bathroom, yes."

"No thanks." Lindsay laughed and stood up. "I'll wait in the hall."

"Rats." Noah snapped his fingers and pushed the call button.

The door burst open and Jolie swept past it, her face wind-flushed and her ball cap speckled with rain. The bowl of white hyacinths she carried trembled in her hands.

"If you break that over my head," Noah said, "you'll eat the pieces."

"You're really here." Jolie put the bowl on the table and gripped the bed rail. "Ron said you were, that you have pneumonia, but I wasn't sure I could trust him. I could kick myself for keeping you at the read-through last night. Can I do anything?"

"Yeah," Noah said suspiciously. "Get your medication checked."

"Always the kidder." Jolie laughed. "When do you get out of here?"

"Probably Friday, they tell me."

"That's terrific, but you'll still need to rest. Don't worry about a thing. If you feel like it, study your lines, but don't push yourself. Just rest and get well. Right, Lindsay?"

Jolie beamed a smile at her over the bed. "Uh—right," Lindsay agreed, wondering what she was up to. "Absolutely."

"There you go," Jolie said cheerfully. "I've got a million things, so I can't stay. Take care of yourself and call me if you need anything."

She patted Noah's shoulder and wheeled toward the door. Lindsay half-expected Jolie to turn back, say "Okay. So much for the jokes," and leap for Noah's throat. When she didn't, Lindsay frowned and looked at Noah. He was frowning at her.

"I think your sister is bipolar, princess."

"Possibly," Lindsay said. "But I believe that was a performance."

"Then quit standing around here and go get the contract."

It was tempting. Oh, it was tempting, but it was wrong. Probably not stealing, but definitely snooping.

"I can't do that, Noah. The contract belongs to Jolie. If she shows it to me, that's one thing. Until then, it's her private business."

"Okay." He shrugged. "Then sit down and answer a question for me. How come Vivienne has photos of Trey all over her house when he says he's never talked to her?"

It was sit down or fall down, so Lindsay sat down, so surprised all she could do was blink at Noah. "Pictures of Trey? All over her house?"

"School pix, snapshots in frames. Trey told me Vivienne called when his father died and you hung up on her. How long has it been since you've talked to her?"

"I haven't spoken to Vivienne since I left L.A."

Noah leveled a finger at her. "I've figured that out, too. Why you've been so standoffish with me."

"Have you?" Lindsay said, amazed she could talk with her heart in her mouth. "Why is that?"

"You think I'm pissed 'cause you split, because you dumped

out on *BBT*. You think I'm mad because your leaving killed the show."

A surge of relief washed through Lindsay, so swift and sudden her ears rang. "I wouldn't blame you. I'd understand if you were angry."

"No hard feelings, princess. My contract with the network was bulletproof. They had to pay me." Noah cocked his head at her. "Now if I could just figure out why you punched me."

"I punched you because you kissed me."

"That wasn't a kiss." Noah pushed up in bed, the muscles in his right arm flexing to take his weight. "Come here and I'll show you a kiss."

Lindsay's stomach flipped. *Biology,* she told herself, *it's just biology,* but the gleam in Noah's eyes was Chaos. Pure, weapons grade Chaos. He leaned toward her, all warm skin and hot eyes, strong arms ready to enfold her if only she had the guts to stand up and claim them. Lindsay shot to her feet, her heart racing, just as Pat Hannity and two LPNs tried to wedge their way through the door.

"Now this," Noah said, "is what I call first rate nursing care."

The LPNs, both younger girls Lindsay had seen around town, giggled and blushed. Pat shouldered her way past them into the room.

"Yes, Noah?" She came up to the bed and turned off the call light.

"I need to take a leak." He thumbed at the IV pole. "And you told me not to try to wrestle R2-D2 by myself."

"Good boy." Pat glanced at Lindsay. "You can wait in the hall."

"Thanks, but I was just leaving. Noah." She raised her eyebrows at him. "I'll be glad to bring your script so you can study your lines. I have to drive your car back to the barn, anyway. Where did you say it is?"

"On the dining room table. Maybe. You might have to look for it."

"Do you think I might need help finding it?" Lindsay prodded, just to make sure he knew where she was headed with this.

He did. His wink-wink smile said so. "Yeah, you might."

"Susan is very good at finding things. Would you mind?"

"Not a bit. Lots of papers on the table." Pat lowered the bed rail and Noah swung his legs encased in blue plaid sleep pants over the side. "You might have to look through them to find the script."

"Don't worry. We won't snoop." *Not much,* Lindsay thought. *Just till we find Jolie's contract.* She swung her purse over her shoulder, waggled her fingers at Noah, and turned toward the door. "I'll be back."

Chapter 16

VIVIENNE HAD PHOTOGRAPHS of Trey all over her house. School pictures, Noah said, snapshots in frames. No one else in the family had spoken to Vivienne since she'd left Belle Coeur, which meant the only way she could've gotten her hands on the photos was through Jolie.

Lindsay had never seen any of the pictures she'd dutifully given her sister over the years in Jolie's office. Stupid, naïve Lindsay thought Jolie had put them away in albums, but now stupid, naïve Lindsay knew better and she was furious.

So furious her hands shook on the steering wheel and the gearshift of the horse piss yellow Corvette. She'd been too tired last night to drive from the hospital to the barn to pick up her Civic. She'd make the switch this afternoon, right after she killed Jolie.

She'd read the contract, too. She'd read it, throw it in Jolie's face, and tell her she'd read it. What could she do about it? Blow her stack, but what was new about that? Let her.

All this snooping and tiptoeing around was ridiculous. So was dragging Susan into a covert reading of the contract. She was an attorney, an officer of the court, but Lindsay hadn't been thinking about Susan's ethics when she'd made the suggestion—she'd been thinking how fast could she get out of Noah's hospital room.

She was so disgusted she wanted to scream. She'd told Noah he couldn't rattle her with innuendo and double entendres. Oh, right. All he'd had to say was "Come here and I'll show you a kiss" and she'd fled like a silly little girl. He would've found another way to make her do what he wanted—which is exactly what she *was* doing, driving out to the barn to get the contract—and it just galled the crap out of her that she'd thrown him the perfect line.

"Here, Noah, make a fool of me," Lindsay said to her reflection in the rearview mirror. "I punched you because you kissed me."

She'd walked right into it, wide-eyed and naïve like she'd done a million times on *BBT*. But that was Chaos, a snake charmer's dance in the bloodstream. So alluring, so mesmerizing—and she was such a sucker for it. That's why it terrified her; that's why she ran from it. But it was always there, skipping out of sight just ahead of her, waiting to leap out and yell "Gotcha!" when she wasn't looking.

"It will always be there. *Always,*" Lindsay said out loud. "Until I grab it by the throat and yell 'Gotcha back!' "

Oh great. Now she was talking to herself. She hadn't done that in years. Emma said talking to yourself was nothing to worry about until you started answering yourself, but what did Emma know? She loved Chaos. She ate it for breakfast with milk and sugar. Lindsay hated it, despised it. She stamped out Chaos at every turn, like Smokey the Bear used to stamp out forest fires. She'd built a Chaos-free life for herself and Trey and she would not let Noah or Vivienne or anyone else—

"Oh my *God*—" Lindsay gasped and slammed on the brake.

So stricken she forgot the clutch and killed the engine ten feet shy of the three-way stop near the crest of the bluff just above the barn, the juncture of Riverfront Road, Alternate 152, and Route 10.

Vivienne wanted Trey. Why hadn't she seen it? It was right in front of her, plain as the blinking red light swinging in the wind above the intersection. It wasn't raining anymore but it was still gray and cold. As cold as the dread seeping into Lindsay's heart.

Vivienne had pictures of Trey all over her house. She sent him gifts and money, checks with at least five zeros. On Vivienne's largesse alone Trey could afford a Corvette of his own.

Oh God. This horse piss yellow monstrosity was Trey's dream car.

Lindsay shoved the gearshift into park and yanked on the brake, leaped out of the Corvette, and backed away from it, the wind ripping up the bluff from the river biting through her pink sweater and cardigan.

At least a dozen Corvette posters papered Trey's bedroom walls. Jolie had seen them a million times. For Christmas, she'd given her nephew a subscription to *Corvette* magazine. If this was coincidence, if Vivienne had just *happened* to send Noah a Corvette to tool around in while he was in Belle Coeur, then she was Julia Roberts.

The pricey gifts and big fat checks hadn't worked, so now Vivienne was trying to sneak in the back door—and Jolie was helping her.

The tea leaf reading and the knife slammed into Lindsay's head. So did the headache between her eyes, a slice of pain cutting through the middle of her face. A house, an hourglass, and a flag, threats to her comfort and security, her Chaos-free and Vivienne-free life. The knife was in Jolie's hand, all right—and it was definitely pointed at her back.

A fierce gust of wind buffeted the Corvette and snatched Lindsay's breath. Her lungs heaved for air; the wet pavement tilted beneath her feet. Black spots sprang in front of her and her ears started to ring. Oh no. Not another panic attack. Not now, not here on the side of the road.

She couldn't faint. She had to stay conscious and save Trey from Vivienne's clutches. The cold wind tore at her, streaming her hair in her eyes. She raked it away frantically, looking around for something to hit, something to throw.

No hedge apples handy and no ugly little white bungalow. She flung her hand out toward the Corvette, its yellow shape blurring out of focus, fumbled for the door she'd left hanging open, slammed it and drove her knee into it, made a fist and clobbered the sunroof. The jolt rocked her, but the vice on her chest let go and her breath came back.

"Damn you, Vivienne!" Lindsay shouted, beating her fists against the roof of the car. "Damn you, Jolie!"

She shrieked like a banshee and pummeled the Corvette. Over and over, pounding the rage and the panic out of her body till her hands stung so badly she couldn't land another blow. She wheeled, drew her right leg back soccer-style, and kicked the rock hard left front tire.

Pain flashed up her calf. Her toes crunched and she fell on her fanny in the road beside the Corvette, winded but breathing, her heart thundering. She'd probably hurt herself, but Lindsay didn't care. She sighed, in control again, leaned on her hands, and tilted her head up. Through the hair blowing in her eyes she saw Sheriff Chub Allen, his plump, kind face pulled into a frown, peering at her upside down.

"Lindsay?" he asked. "You having a problem here?"

"Uh—not anymore," she said, raking the hair out of her face.

Chub offered her a gloved hand. Lindsay took it and let him help her up. His uniform jacket, thick, navy blue nylon, was zipped to the throat. The fake fur flaps on his cap were turned down over his ears and his nose was red with cold. Lindsay shivered, as much from the adrenaline burn off as the bite in the wind.

"Car trouble?" Chub asked.

"Driver trouble." Lindsay folded her arms and huddled into them. "It's been ages since I drove a five-speed. I keep forgetting the clutch and killing the engine. I got so annoyed I kicked the tires."

"That all?" Chub raised an eyebrow at the Corvette.

"Yes," Lindsay said, and turned toward Noah's car.

The wind grabbed her hair again. She pushed it out of her face and stared, appalled, at the yellow monstrosity. Splinters ran across the roof. A spiderweb-shaped fracture split the driver's door.

"How did I do that?" Lindsay asked. "I'm not Wonder Woman."

"Don't have to be in this kind of weather." Chub laid his gloved hand on the shattered roof. "These babies is mostly plastic. Don't dent or ding, but they crack like an egg when it's cold. Cost a fortune to insure."

Lindsay's stomach sank. "Probably to repair, too."

"Be my guess." Chub patted the Corvette. Gently, as if he felt its pain. "Heard about this car. Belongs to that actor friend of yours, Noah Patrick, don't it?"

"Yes. I'm driving it back to the barn for him."

"You ain't got far to go, then," Chub said. Lindsay thought he sounded relieved about that. "You okay to drive?"

"Absolutely," she said, although her back muscles were screaming and her right ankle felt like it was the size of a grapefruit.

"You be careful." Chub held the bill of his cap against the wind and turned toward his dark blue cruiser. "And don't forget to clutch."

Lindsay hobbled into the Corvette, so cold her fingers were blue. She started the engine and kicked the heater on high, plucked a packet of tissues out of her purse, blew her nose, and shivered behind the wheel, so mortified she wanted to crawl under the seat.

Chub's cruiser pulled around the Corvette and made a left onto Route 10. Lindsay watched it, wondering what the odds were that the sheriff would just happen by the most remote intersection in Belle Coeur and catch her beating the hell out of Noah's car.

About the same, she decided, as the odds that Vivienne *wasn't* trying to worm her way into Trey's life—slim and none.

Lindsay's ankle shrieked when she pushed on the gas pedal. She bit her lip, worked the clutch and the gears, and steered the Corvette through the three-way intersection. A right onto Riverfront Road, then a left-hand jog onto the side road that ran behind the barn. She turned into the lot and frowned. Jolie usually parked her truck by the front entrance, but her Civic was the only vehicle in sight.

"Where *is* she?" Lindsay gritted between her teeth.

She'd saved enough anger to rip into Jolie and now she wasn't here. Unless she'd parked by the workroom. She did if she had stuff to unload. Lindsay made a right out of the lot onto the road, drove around the barn to the big overhead workroom doors, but there was no sign of Jolie's truck anywhere.

"Damn it." She smacked the steering wheel and parked the Corvette between the two big hickory trees behind Joe Varner's apartment.

She used Noah's key to let herself in through the kitchen and hurried into the dining room. The only thing on the table was a Post-It note with a brass key on top of it. The note said, "Here's my key. Hope you memorized the contract. I'll be holding you to EVERY WORD OF IT."

It wasn't signed, but Lindsay recognized Jolie's handwriting. She picked up the brass key and compared it to the deadbolt key on Noah's ring. They matched. Damn it. Jolie had taken the contract. Lindsay put the key on the table and limped down the hall to Jolie's office.

Her sister wasn't there, but the contract was—smack in the middle of the blotter on her desk. Jolie would never trust her again if she read it, but when had she ever? Lindsay had trusted Jolie to play fair with the contract and Trey's pictures and look where that had gotten her.

She sat down in the slatted-wooden chair behind the desk and read the contract. It didn't take long. She read fast and she was mostly interested in Clause Nineteen, which said exactly what Noah had told her—if either one of them missed a performance between opening night and closing the contract was null and void and all monies were forfeit.

Wasn't this amazing? In her wildest dreams she'd never thought she could trust Noah Patrick. In her worst nightmare she never imagined that Jolie would betray her to Vivienne.

Lindsay put the contract back on the desk, pushed to her feet, and hobbled out of the office. She winced her way along the hall and down the stairs, leaning heavily on the banister.

Jolie wasn't in the workroom but Uncle Donnie sat at the bench drawing in a pad with a mechanical pencil. Lindsay frowned at his gray coveralls. Jolie insisted he and Lonnie wear them. Lindsay hated them.

Pyewacket sat above Donnie's head on the shelf that held the coffeemaker, his tail twitching and his emerald eyes fixed on the pencil. He came down to rub noses with Lindsay when she limped up to the bench.

"Hey, Uncle Donnie. Have you seen Jolie?"

"Nope. Ain't seen her all day."

"Then why are you wearing that god-awful thing?"

"Now Lindsay." He put his pencil down. "It's just a coverall."

"It's an emblem of servitude. You are not a servant."

"Jolene says the coveralls make me and Lonnie look professional."

"They make you look like the hired help, which is exactly how Jolie treats you. I don't know why you put up with it."

"All right, Lindsay, all right. I'll have a word with Lonnie."

He always said that when she carped about the coveralls—he'd have a word with Lonnie. Lindsay sighed and glanced at the sketch of pulleys and ropes on the pad of graph paper.

"Is that the Murphy bed?" she asked.

"Yep. Wish Jolene had gave us more time. It's gonna be a bear." He turned his stool and looked at her. "You get caught in the rain?"

Lindsay had seen how filthy her hands were on the steering wheel, the black tread marks from the tire on her right foot that had likely ruined her beige leather flats. God knew what the rest of her looked like.

"Sort of," she said, easing her aching body onto Uncle Lonnie's stool. Pyewacket hopped into her lap.

"You're sitting funny." Donnie frowned. "You hurt yourself?"

"I sprained my ankle." Kicking an eighty-pound tire. *What a stupid thing to do,* Lindsay thought, raising her foot to look at it.

Donnie leaned forward and had a look, too, cupping his hand gently around her ankle. It was so swollen she couldn't see the bones and it was starting to bruise.

"Oughta get some ice on that." Donnie glanced up at her face and frowned. "You look beat up. You sick or is something wrong?"

Everything's wrong, Lindsay wanted to say. *Vivienne's*

trying to get her hands on Trey, Jolie's helping her, and I'm just as big a sucker for Noah as I ever was. That's what she wanted to say.

"I'm freezing," she said, shivering as Pyewacket curled himself into a ball and started to purr. "I loaned Susan my coat."

"You need a cup of coffee." Donnie reached a mug off the shelf, blew dust out of it, and filled it from the coffee-stained glass carafe.

Lindsay scratched Pyewacket's ears and watched him. If she could prove what Vivienne was up to and told the uncles, then what? Donnie shook like a Chihuahua at the mention of Vivienne's name. Lonnie the staunch Baptist crossed himself like a Catholic. If Sassy was telling the truth and the Fairchilds were fed up with Jolie, what would happen when Lonnie told Dovey at Monday night bingo—and he would—that Vivienne was after Trey and Jolie was helping her?

Jolie would be shunned, banished, cast out forever.

She didn't have the guts to leave Belle Coeur on her own. Maybe subconsciously she was behaving badly so she'd be kicked out. Lindsay knew what it felt like to be ripped away from your family. She couldn't imagine how it would feel to be tossed out like the garbage. As tough as Jolie thought she was, she probably thought she could survive it, but Lindsay had her doubts.

She wanted proof of what Vivienne was up to and she'd get it. She didn't know how but she would, and when she had it she wouldn't tell the uncles. Or Dovey or Frank or Sassy. If Jolie wanted to be thrown out of the family she'd have to do it without any help from Lindsay.

Donnie set a steaming green mug of coffee in front of her. She wrapped her hands around it, sipped, and sighed as the chill melted out of her. Uncle Donnie made the best darn coffee. In a drip machine he paid two dollars for at a garage sale ten years ago and hadn't cleaned since. That was the secret, he said, never wash the pot, just rinse it.

"You hunting Jolene for a reason?" Donnie asked, refilling his own cup. "Like what Dovey said to Lonnie at bingo Monday night?"

"I don't know." Lindsay sat up straight. Monday night Dovey had stopped by her house to return her casserole dish. "What did she say?"

"Same thing me and Lonnie's been saying to each other. How outta control Jolene's getting. How more'n more she's behaving like Vivian. Lonnie says Dovey's real worried about Jolene."

"I'm worried about her, too." Lindsay sighed and raised her mug in both hands. "I think Jolie's in way over her head with this play."

"I think she's out of her head. The person who tried to burn down the barn ain't about to help her save it."

The mug jumped in Lindsay's grasp and splashed coffee on her fingers. "Who told you about Vivienne?"

"Noah." Donnie put the carafe back on the base and looked at her. "I told Jolene she was a fool to trust Vivian. She told me to butt out. Fine, I said. Lonnie and me'll butt out of sweeping floors and cleaning toilets. That sweetened her up right quick."

The glint in Donnie's eyes said the Varners were as fed up with Jolie as Sassy claimed the Fairchilds were. Aunt Dovey was the bellwether for both families. Where she led, everyone else followed. She'd talked to Sassy, she'd talked to Lonnie, and Lonnie had talked to Donnie. If Noah hadn't come to dinner Monday night, Lindsay wondered, what might Aunt Dovey have said to her?

"Jolie thinks she's the only Varner busts her fanny around here. Hell." Donnie snorted into his mug. "Me and Lonnie got the farm to run besides, but according to Jolene we just sit around all day and drink coffee. Weren't for Noah I'd be out on my tractor and Jolene'd be sitting back here trying to figure out how to build this damn Murphy bed."

"Noah?" Lindsay wiped the coffee off her fingers on her ruined slacks. "What's he got to do with this?"

"He's a nice young fella. Does the best dang Elvis impersonation I've ever seen." Donnie turned his stool toward Lindsay and squared his shoulders as if he expected an argument. "All he needs is a chance to get his life right. If me and Lonnie quit on Jolene he won't get it. Man's got the gumption to quit drinking I won't quit on him."

"When do you plan to quit on Jolie?" *Your own flesh and blood,* Lindsay thought. "Noah isn't going to stay in Belle Coeur, Uncle Donnie. The second the play closes he'll be on the next plane out of here."

"Maybe Jolene'll get smart and go with him. She's beating a dead horse trying to keep this place going, Lindsay. You know it well as me and Lonnie. She needs to give this place up and get on with her life."

Lindsay couldn't argue with the truth. She could argue with Donnie about Noah, warn him not to be taken in by an Elvis impersonation, but that would make her look small and mean and petty. Which was exactly how she felt perched on Lonnie's stool doing a slow burn because her uncles were dumping Jolie for Noah. She didn't blame them. God knew Donnie and Lonnie had taken the brunt of Jolie's abuse. It just steamed her, that's all, and made her heart hurt.

Donnie frowned at her. "You ain't saying nothing, Lindsay."

"Aunt Sassy told me at the read-through that she and Aunt Dovey and Uncle Frank had talked about Jolie."

"Me and Lonnie ain't happy 'bout this. Worst thing is, Jolie ain't happy. She's miserable. And bound and determined to make ever'body else miserable right along with her. Helping her ain't helping her anymore. It's only making things worse."

"You're right." Lindsay sighed unhappily. "We aren't helping Jolie. We're only making it easier for her to behave badly."

To behave like Vivienne, Lindsay thought. All of a sudden her image overhaul didn't sound like such a hot idea. It soured her stomach and left a bad taste in her mouth. That or it was time for Uncle Donnie to wash the coffeepot. She pushed her mug away, tried to smile at him and failed. The corners of her mouth wanted to turn down, not up.

"Do me a favor, would you, Uncle Donnie? Don't tell Jolie I'm looking for her."

"Fat chance. Lil' Miss Hitler'll be lucky if I tell her the time of day."

"Thanks for the coffee. I think I'll go home now and ice my ankle."

"Lemme help you," Donnie said, and strode out of the workroom.

He came back with a wheelchair from the prop room, an antique with a wicker seat and back. Pyewacket trotted alongside the chair as Donnie pushed her through the lobby and out the front doors. A little sunshine seeped through the overcast but it was still windy and cold enough to raise gooseflesh. Lindsay glanced at her watch. It was 3:15.

Her purse was in the Corvette, her keys in her pocket with Noah's. Lindsay thanked Donnie for the lift, shivered into the Civic with Pye, and drove around to the apartment. She parked next to the Corvette, left the Civic's engine running and the heater blowing for Pye, unlocked the Corvette, and slid behind the wheel. Her purse was on the floor on the passenger side. She picked it up and turned on her cell phone so Trey could call her when he got home from school. Her book had fallen under the seat. While she groped for it a cell phone rang.

Lindsay's played *The William Tell Overture*. This one beeped out the theme from *BBT*, a god-awful '80s rip-off of the Beach Boys. Oh, how cheesy, oh how Noah. Lindsay found the palm-size phone in the console between the seats, held it up and wondered if she should answer. Noah had a phone in his room and she'd told him she was driving the Corvette back to the barn. Lindsay flipped the phone open and put it to her ear.

"Where the hell are you today?" Vivienne barked.

She never said good-bye or hello—just launched straight into ranting, railing, and deriding. Oblivious to who she hurt, who she frightened, who she browbeat. Calm, icy fury rose up in Lindsay.

"I want every photograph of my son that you have returned to me. Today. By overnight mail."

"Lindsay?" The bottom went out of Vivienne's voice. It sounded hollow, stunned. "Is that you?"

"Every school picture, every snapshot Jolie sent you."

"Trey is my grandson." Vivienne's voice came back, deep and angry and throaty from too many cigarettes. "I have every right—"

"You have no right to Trey. You never have and you never will."

"When he's eighteen he'll be old enough to decide that for himself. I understand he's interested in attending Berkeley. That's only a two-hour drive. I think he'll enjoy visiting me in Malibu."

Lindsay's heart seized. Vivienne was *sooo* good at this, sketching horrific little scenarios designed to turn your hair white. The wind switched and came around the corner of the barn, *whoosh*ed through the hickory trees and tried to suck the breath out of her. Oh no. Not again. Lindsay sprang out of the Corvette and slammed the door, wheeled her back to the wind, and raked the hair out of her eyes.

"That's three years from now," she said. "Plenty of time for me to tell Trey every rotten thing you did to Jolie and me and my father. You'll be the last person he wants to visit in California."

"What did I do that was so terrible?" Vivienne demanded. "I took you to L.A. and made you a star. I made a man out of Joe Varner. He'd still be passed out on the couch if I hadn't left him. These days at least he's drunk only half the time."

"What about Jolie?" Lindsay spun around, so enraged she paced the graveled space between the trees and the road, from the Corvette to the shoulder and back. "You left a five-year-old child, your own daughter, screaming on the doorstep for her mother."

She heard Vivienne's lighter spin. The puff of her breath on a cigarette, her own heart thundering in her ears.

"I sent her money to refurbish the theater. Fifty thousand more than I paid her to take Noah on. This play is the best thing Jolie's ever written. You were never a great actress, Lindsay. You'll need all the help you can get on that stage. With you and Noah both on the bill the play has a fighting chance to draw some attention."

"What's Noah's part in this, in your plan to appropriate my son? Be Trey's pal, praise you, smooth your way through the back door?"

"My God, you're paranoid. This is a family matter. Noah isn't family. He's a draw for the play and another sixty thousand for Jolie. Nothing more."

"I'm amazed you can say the word *family* without choking."

Vivienne laughed. Just like Sassy, a raucous bray in Lindsay's ear. Another blast of wind rattled the hickory trees. A dead branch fell at her feet as she turned in the gravel beneath them and felt her ankle wrench. Her heart, too, when she heard an engine gun, glanced at the road, and saw Jolie's old pickup rattling up the hill.

The truck stopped behind the Corvette. Jolie hopped out and came around the rusted-out front end with her ball cap on backward and a bounce in her step that faltered when she saw Lindsay's face. Her cheerful, hi-there smile vanished.

"You're such a hypocrite, Lindsay," Vivienne said in her ear. "With you everything is family. Well, I'm family, too. I'm your mother and Trey's grandmother. You can't change it and it makes you crazy, doesn't it?"

"I want Trey's pictures," Lindsay repeated, staring her sister square in the eye. "Every single photograph of my son that Jolie sent you."

Jolie took a step back and blinked. One of her lidless little gecko blinks that meant she was caught and she knew it. Lindsay slapped the phone shut and closed it in her fist.

"Who told you?" Jolie demanded. "Vivian didn't, that's for sure."

"Noah told me. He saw the pictures in Vivienne's house. Trey's school photos, the snapshots I gave you. All over Vivienne's house."

"That was stupid. Noah's a blabbermouth." Jolie stuck her chin out, belligerent and affronted, trying to shift the blame to someone else so she could slide off the hook. "Why didn't Vivian put the pictures away before she opened the door to Mr. Just Ask and I'll Tell You Everything?"

"Noah didn't do this. *You* did. You sent the pictures to Vivienne."

"You gave them to me, I gave them to Vivian." Jolie shrugged. "She is Trey's grandmother."

"She's the woman who abandoned you. The woman who drove away and left you screaming for her to come back and take you, too."

"I remember. I was there," Jolie snapped. "It's ancient history."

"Why did you tell Vivienne Trey wants to go to Berkeley?"

"She asked me. I told her. What's the harm?"

This was like talking to Vivienne. Pointless, impossible, infuriating.

"*I* am Trey's mother. *I* decide what's harmful to him, not *you*."

"What's Vivian going to do? She's two thousand miles away."

"I'll tell you what she's doing! She's looking forward to Trey attending Berkeley because *you* told her!"

"God, Lindsay! You're so stupid you make me sick!" Jolie yanked off her ball cap and slapped the Corvette. "I had to tell her! She wanted details. She wanted to know everything about Trey or I wouldn't get a dime, not one lousy penny. She made that clear, so I told her. I sent her the pictures and she wrote me a check."

Lindsay stared at Jolie. Just stared and wondered—why and how, how in hell, in spite of all of Emma's warnings—she'd never seen this vicious streak of me-me-and-screw-you selfishness in her sister.

"Congratulations. You've finally done it," Lindsay said. "You've made me hate you as much as you hate me."

She said it calmly and stepped around Jolie and the Corvette. Pye stood in the Civic's driver's seat, his paws pressed to the window.

"Let's see if I can guess where you're going," Jolie jeered behind her. "Oh, wait. I know. Home to call Susan and tell her to sue me."

The anger Lindsay had saved, the anger that her baby sister, the person she loved most in the world second to Trey, had shocked out of her, spun her away from the Civic.

"I should." Lindsay stalked Jolie, watching her eyes widen as she backpedaled away from her. "I should make you spend every cent of Vivienne's money in court but I won't. I'll do the play. I'll give you the best damn performance I've ever given anyone and when it's over and done with I will never *ever* speak to you again."

"How else was I going to save the barn?" Jolie stumbled in the gravel and fell against the side of her truck. "I didn't have a choice."

"You had a million choices. You made the wrong one when you sold Trey to Vivienne. I would have given you everything I have."

"You still don't get it, do you?" Tears welled up in Jolie's whiskey brown eyes. "I don't want anything from you. I want it from Vivian. I want every fucking cent she has. She owes it to me for ruining my life."

"You ruined your own life, Jolie. You chose to be angry and vindictive. Now you can pay for it."

Lindsay spun away, so pumped on rage she didn't even limp. Pyewacket leaped into the passenger seat, his green eyes huge, and his fur bristled when she slid behind the wheel of the Civic. She pushed down the window and looked at Jolie, staring back at her pale-faced and pinned like a fly against her truck.

"Don't come near me or Trey," Lindsay said to her. "You can leave messages about the play on my machine at home. Show up at my house or my store and I will personally and bodily throw you out."

Chapter 17

THE CORVETTE looked like an ice cube that had been dropped in a glass of warm ice tea. Cracked and splintered to the tune of fifty-five hundred dollars according to the written estimate in Noah's hand.

"The driver's side door needs to be replaced," Lindsay said. "Otherwise the damage is mostly just the paint job."

She stood about three feet away from him on the walk in front of the theater, the red canvas canopy above her head waffling in the breeze. The ends of her hair and the legs of her cream-colored trousers fluttered, too. She'd dressed carefully for this, for springing him from the hospital and breaking it to him about the car. An apricot sweater, a wink of gold at her ears and gray-tinted sunglasses. Noah had done the same thing a million times, donned his best threads and a pair of snazzy shades to hide the shakes and the bloodshot eyes.

She'd parked the Corvette just as carefully, parallel with the curb, the nose pointing downhill with the slope of the parking lot. Perfectly positioned so the bright afternoon sun hit it like a klieg light and showed every teensy little fracture in the finish. Noah tucked the estimate into his pocket, leaned against the totaled door, and folded his arms.

He felt pretty good for a guy who'd spent two days flat on his back. Restless and edgy from being confined. Sweltering in the jacket Lindsay had stuffed him into to ward off a chill. A little shaky in the knees, but that wasn't pneumonia. It was being close to Lindsay.

"Tell me again how this happened," he said to her.

"I had another panic attack. I needed to hit something. I felt like I was going to faint, so I kicked the door and punched the roof."

"No hedge apples handy, huh?"

"I wish there had been." She bit her lip and looked away. "I feel awful about this."

"It's a car, Lindsay. To hell with it. Did you hurt yourself?"

"No. Just sprained my ankle when I kicked the tire."

She lifted the hem of her right trouser leg and showed him the ugly beige elastic brace on her foot. Well, that explained the shoes. He'd wondered about her clunky, flat-heeled loafers. She tottered a little on her left foot, put her right one down on the sidewalk again and her hands in her pockets. She'd been standing with her hands in her pockets since they'd gotten out of her Civic to look at the Corvette.

"When are you due back at the store? Got time for a glass of milk?"

Lindsay took her left hand out of her pocket to check her watch. Noah pushed off the Corvette and caught her wrist. Gently, expecting the yellow and green bruises he saw when he turned her hand over in his. Lindsay swung her head away and said, "Damn."

"You had these bruises looked at, right?"

"Yes. When I had my ankle x-rayed. No broken bones."

"You know, princess." Noah brushed the inside of her wrist with his thumb. "A course in anger management would've been a whole lot cheaper than beating the hell out of this car."

A smile would've been nice. A shiver of reaction to his touch even better, but Lindsay just looked at him, a vertical crease in her forehead above her oval, alien-shaped sunglasses.

"That was a joke. You were supposed to laugh."

"Sorry. I'm not feeling very funny. Of course I'll pay for the repairs."

"Why do you want to do that? The Corvette is insured."

"In Vivienne's name. I checked the registration and the insurance papers. I'd just as soon she didn't know about this."

"If that's the way you want it." Noah shrugged. "Okay."

"Okay?" Lindsay snatched off her *E.T.* shades. Her eyes looked drawn tight at the corners and smudged like she'd rubbed off her mascara. "You aren't dying to ask me why I don't want Vivienne to know?"

"Oh, I'm dying to ask. But I'm afraid if I do you'll realize I'm still holding your hand."

She glanced down at his fingers loosely laced with hers, then back up at his face. "Why *are* you still holding my hand?"

"I'm torn between two answers. One, that I'm an opportunist and I never pass up a chance to touch a beautiful woman and two, that I'm feeling weak and I need you to hold me up. Which one do you like?"

"Oh *please*." Lindsay took her hand back, rolled her eyes, and wheeled away from him.

Not the reaction he was hoping for but at least it was a reaction. Noah hurried up the walk behind her, got ahead of her a step or two shy of the glass doors, and put himself between the lock and the key in her hand. "Gimme a minute and I'll think of another one."

Lindsay stared at him like he'd just crawled out from under a rock. "And here I thought you'd grown up when you sobered up."

"Aw, c'mon, princess." Noah gave her a lighten-up bump with his shoulder. She jerked back a step and glared at him. "You used to love it when I heckled you like this on the set."

"No, I did *not*. I despised it," she snapped, then tipped her head to one side. "I thought you said you couldn't remember."

"Things are starting to come back to me. In bits and pieces, a little here, a little there. Mostly when I'm asleep, but I'm having trouble making sense of it. I'm not used to dreaming. I'm used to passing out and not remembering jack shit when I wake up."

Noah hoped the red leather album he'd borrowed from Trey, the one Vivienne sent Lindsay and the kid fished out of the Dumpster would help him focus the images that were trying to bubble up out of the sludge in his subconscious. Which reminded him with an oh-shit clutch in his stomach. Where in hell in Joe Varner's apartment had he left the album?

"I can make this one little *bit*, this one little *piece* crystal clear for you," Lindsay said, her voice icy. "I *hate* being shagged like a dog. It's demeaning to me, and it makes you look like an adolescent idiot. I thought you'd changed, Noah. I thought you'd *finally* grown up."

Here it comes, he thought, *the fury of the hedge apples, the rage that wrecked the Corvette.* Noah saw it flood her face with red, light sparks in her eyes, and curl her hands into fists. He expected her to pop him one. She was that angry, so angry she was quivering. One minute. The next she drew a breath, a deep, shuddery one, and the fury faded from her eyes. She sighed and the rage wilted out of her shoulders.

This is where he'd come in on the hedge apples. It was the weirdest thing watching Lindsay stuff all that anger back inside and clamp a lid on it. So weird it gave Noah chills.

"If you'd like to punch the Corvette," he said, "I doubt the guys at the body shop will notice one more crack."

"I'm fine." She pushed her hair back as the wind caught it, the pulse jumping in her throat the only sign that she'd nearly come unglued. "I'm sorry I snapped at you."

"No, I'm sorry. I apologize for everything I ever did or said that made you feel uncomfortable. I swear to God I'll never heckle you again."

Noah held up three fingers, his pinkie tucked under his thumb.

"You, a Boy Scout." Lindsay smiled. "Now that's funny."

"I was never a Boy Scout. Always a Girl Scout."

"Old lame joke, Patrick." She pushed him aside, unlocked the door, and glanced at him. "I should drive you around to the back door. There are thirty-five steps between the lobby and the landing. At least as many between the landing and the second floor and you aren't supposed to exert yourself."

"I can manage a couple flights of stairs," Noah said. "I can also carry my own stuff in from the car."

"Hold it." She planted a hand in the middle of his chest as he started around her. "I'll let you do the stairs and unlock the back door for me, but *I* will move the cars and bring in your things."

Goody. You do that, Noah thought. It would give him time to find the album and hide it. "For Christ's sake, Lindsay," he said. "Come *on.*"

"Excuse me." She stuck a hand on her hip. "Are you *whining*?"

"Will it help?"

"No. In you go." Lindsay opened the door. "And *walk* up the stairs."

She stayed at the door, peering through the glass to watch him cross the lobby. Noah figured she would. He put his hand on the banister when he reached the stairs and climbed them in s-l-o-o-w m-o-o-t-i-o-o-n. Lindsay stayed at the door till he reached the landing. The second her back turned Noah grabbed the banister and hauled ass, two steps at a time, up the second flight of stairs.

He raced down the hallway, fishing the deadbolt key out of his jacket, dropped it and had to go back for it, dropped it again as he picked it up, snarled "Fuck" as he snatched it off the ugly red and green and gold runner, and ran on. At the end of the hall he overshot the corner and bounced off the wall, tripped over the PREMISES PROTECTED BY SMITH &

WESSON mat, flung his hands out, and missed by an inch smashing his nose against the door.

The deadbolt fought him but he got through it and kicked the door shut, ripped off his jacket, and tore around the living room searching for the album. It wasn't on the coffee table, on the shelves beside the fireplace, or stuck in one of the chairs. It wasn't on the couch buried under the afghan, on the desk in the dining room or on the table. Had Lindsay found it when she came to get the contract and thrown it away?

Noah wheeled into the kitchen, cut the corner too short and tripped, caught himself on the corner of the countertop and hung there, out of breath. Through the window in the back door he saw the Corvette parked in the gravel between the two big hickory trees, the Civic beside it and Lindsay walking around the back end to fetch his stuff out of the open trunk. *Shit!* How did she move so fast?

"Wheels, dickhead," Noah muttered. "She has *wheels*."

Eight of 'em if you counted both cars. He had two legs that turned to rubber when he pushed off the counter and stumbled to the door. He flipped the lock, careened through the bathroom, and smacked into the bedroom door frame. From there he could see the album on the bedside table, his glasses on top of it, the geode Trey gave him next to the lamp.

The back door scraped open. Noah spun around and slammed the door between the bathroom and the kitchen. Locked it and raced into the bedroom, snatched the album off the table, fell to his knees, and gave it a shove under the bed. It hit the far wall with a thump.

"Noah?" Lindsay tapped on the door. "Are you all right?"

Hell no, he wasn't all right. His head was spinning and pounding. He felt like he was going to pass out or puke. Or maybe puke and then pass out. He staggered into the bathroom and sucked a breath.

"I'm fine!" he called through the door, hoping Lindsay couldn't hear his heart thumping in his voice. "Out in a second!"

He pushed the bedroom door shut, collapsed on the toilet

but couldn't breathe. He felt like his lungs were stuck in his throat. He grabbed the sink and hauled himself up, cranked on the faucet and drank a handful of water. Coughed till he hacked up a wad of green stuff, gagged and splashed his face, grabbed a towel off the bar, and slid to the floor with his back against the side of the tub. Jesus Christ.

Noah sat there till his heart stopped trying to jump out of his chest like one of those things in the *Alien* movies. Then he gripped the tub and pushed to his feet, drew a breath through his nose and smelled chicken soup. He expected his stomach to roll but it growled. Good sign. He hung up the towel and opened the door to the kitchen.

A pot with a lid on it hissed chicken and celery and carrot scented steam on the stove. Next to it sat a stainless steel teakettle, the electric ring underneath it just beginning to glow red. Lindsay was in the living room hanging his jacket in the closet. She glanced at him over her shoulder as he wove toward the couch. It was made up like a bed with yellow sheets tucked over the cushions, a patchwork quilt he hadn't seen before, and two big pillows.

"You okay?" Lindsay asked.

"Fine." Noah bumped into the coffee table and collapsed on the couch, one arm thrown over his eyes. "You were right about the stairs."

She shut the closet and crossed the room. When Noah heard her footsteps come back, he cracked an eye and saw her bent over the coffee table with a paper towel wiping the spill under the glass of water he'd bumped when he whacked into the table. Her hair swung forward over her left shoulder, the V-neck of her apricot sweater gaped just enough to give him a mouth-watering peek of her creamy cleavage.

"Go ahead," he said. "Say I told you so."

Lindsay moved a Kleenex box, the two amber prescription bottles and the inhaler they'd given him in the hospital, sat down on the table with the paper towel crumpled between her hands, and smiled at him.

"That would be redundant, don't you think?"

Noah lowered his arm and turned his head toward her.

Jesus she was beautiful. So gorgeous it hurt to look at her. That she was here making him soup and a bed on the couch so he could watch TV made him wish she was his, that he had a right to kiss her. He shouldn't want to—he had nothing to offer her—but almost more than he wanted to draw his next breath Noah wanted to kiss Lindsay.

"If pneumonia is anything like one of your panic attacks," he said, "how did you have breath enough to beat the crap out of the Corvette?"

"Hitting something helps me get my breath." Lindsay plucked at the paper towel and lifted one shoulder. "I know it sounds crazy."

"Hitting a thing you can't hurt makes more sense than slugging somebody who can hurt you back." Noah toed off his shoes and slid his feet under the covers. The cool, soothing feel of the sheets through his socks made him sigh. "I lost a guest shot on *Cheers* because I was shitfaced and punched a director."

"So your advice about anger management comes from firsthand experience."

"It comes from the shrinks in rehab. *They* say I have a problem with anger. I say I like the taste of tequila."

"My father says the same thing about Jim Beam."

"Yeah, I know. Trey told me." The vertical crease came back between Lindsay's eyebrows. "Getting lost in the woods with no hope of rescue makes you say things like that. You're sitting on a TV gold mine, princess. I can see it now—*Survivor: Missouri.*"

Lindsay laughed. A real, honest to God laugh, the first he'd heard out of her. A little bit of a shine came into her eyes. Not enough to ease the tension lines drawing the corners so tight she looked like that old Mommy-my-braids-are-too-tight joke, but enough that Noah smiled.

"Why don't you want Vivienne to know about the Corvette?"

"I don't want her to know *anything* about me, not one thing." Lindsay ripped a corner off the paper towel. "I've managed to keep her out of my life until now. Until Jolie sent her the photographs of Trey you saw all over her house."

"Vivienne didn't tell me you two were estranged. She said you were a widow with a fifteen-year-old son and you own a bookstore. That's it."

"I never wanted to be a TV star, Noah." Lindsay looked at him and tore another strip off the towel. "I left *BBT* when I turned eighteen, when I was of legal age and Vivienne couldn't manipulate me anymore. She'd do the same thing to Trey if she got her hands on him. I won't allow that."

"When he told me he'd never spoken to Vivienne, that you'd hung up on her the one time she called, I wondered how the pictures got to California. I figured Jolie must've sent them."

"Oh, she did. She admitted it. I couldn't figure out what Vivienne hoped to gain by helping Jolie until you told me about the photos. That's when it hit me—Vivienne wants to be part of Trey's life." Noah listened and watched Lindsay shred the paper towel. "Jolie wants Vivienne to pay for taking me to L.A. and leaving her behind in Belle Coeur."

"Vivienne doesn't make reparations. She makes deals."

"Exactly. So Jolie sold her Trey's pictures and every detail of his life for fifty thousand dollars."

"That's it. I say we vote Jolie off the island."

The teakettle shrieked. Lindsay jumped, glanced down at the pile of confetti in her lap, and scooped it into one hand.

"I'll get your tea," she said and scurried into the kitchen.

Noah listened to Lindsay rattle cups and spoons and wondered why she was telling him all this. It was none of his business and it sure as hell didn't fit with the hands-off-buddy way she'd treated him so far.

She came back with a white mug steaming with a pale brew that smelled like grass. "Aunt Dovey suggested green tea. It's a blood purifier." She put the cup down on the table where he could reach it and sat beside it. "Jolie and I aren't speaking unless we have to about the play."

"Oh swell." Noah grinned. "Rehearsals should be a blast."

"I still know people in L.A.," Lindsay said, gazing at him intently. "I made some calls after Jolie and I had it out about Trey. Vivienne's agency isn't failing. She has so many clients she had to take on another agent to handle the workload."

"So now you're wondering," Noah said, trying to figure

out if the glint in Lindsay's eyes was accusation or I-caught-you-in-a-big-one-you-scumbag triumph. "Did Vivienne lie to me or did I lie to you?"

"I wondered, yes, so I asked Vivienne. She called the cell phone in your Corvette and I answered. She said you aren't involved in her bid for Trey. She said you're just an extra sixty thousand in Jolie's pocket."

"And you believe her? What if she hired me to come out here and sing her praises?" Noah decided it was best to point this out before Lindsay did. "You know. Tell Trey how wonderful she is, that he only needs to be careful around Grandma on the full moon."

"I thought of that. In fact I said it to Vivienne. She told me I was paranoid. You told me the truth about what's in the contract, Noah. I found Jolie's copy and read it. You told me the truth about the photos. If you were Vivienne's front man you wouldn't have been so honest."

"I might. If I were playing both ends against the middle."

"Why would you do that?"

"Because I'm just like Vivienne. We're birds of a feather."

"You don't know how badly I want to believe that." Lindsay sighed. "But I can't. When I asked why you lied for Trey you said so you could make points with me. That's too blunt to be anything but the truth."

"Well, don't abandon all hope. I did lie to you about the car keys."

"Yes, but then you confessed." Lindsay didn't add the "Damn it" Noah saw in her eyes. "Trey told me you intended to before Aunt Dovey showed up. Vivienne never tells the truth unless she's cornered."

"You could say the same thing about me—I was cornered."

"That's why I asked you to walk Aunt Dovey to her car. It was the perfect exit line. I expected you to take it, but you didn't." The puzzled tilt of her head said she still couldn't figure out why. "The Noah Patrick I knew in L.A. would've trampled Aunt Dovey to beat her out the door, but you stayed. You stayed and you faced me."

"In case you haven't noticed, princess, I'm not the same Noah Patrick you knew in L.A."

"I realize that. I just don't know what to do about it yet." Lindsay sighed again. "I never expected you to be the same, Noah. I expected to never see you again."

"You aren't happy about me being here, are you?"

"My family thinks you're wonderful," Lindsay said, which was just as good as no. "They're fed up with Jolie, ready to bail on her and the theater, but they're staying to help you get your career back on track."

"They don't have to stick on my account. I'll survive."

"Ron won't hear it. Neither will Dovey or Sassy. Donnie and Lonnie won't quit on you and Frank thinks you're a hero. No one knows Vivienne better than the Varners and the Fairchilds. You can't fool them."

"But you told them different," Noah said, keeping the "Didn't you?" he wanted to add to himself. "Reminded them that I'm an actor, that my stock in trade is fooling people."

"I considered it. I was so upset that they're ready to abandon Jolie. In case you haven't guessed, abandonment is her major issue. She's done everything she can to drive us all away, but she's family and you're not. I told Uncle Donnie that as soon as the play ends you'll be on the next plane to L.A., but it didn't faze him."

"I like your uncles. They're good guys."

"So are you." Lindsay frowned. "I can't tell you how amazed I am to find a nice person buried under your colossal ego and foul mouth."

"Nice. Jesus, princess. I'm sure I've been called worse things but at the moment I can't remember what or when."

"Buck up, Patrick. Some women think nice is sexy."

"You wouldn't happen to be one of them, would you?"

"No." Lindsay looked him in the eye, got up, and went to the TV. She brought the remote back, handed it to him, and nudged his tea aside as she sat down. "I'm not interested in having an affair with you, Noah. It's nothing personal. I'm not interested in having an affair with anyone."

"Have you seen a doctor about that?"

"I'm not kidding, Noah. I'm dead serious."

"You're not dead. But you might as well be if that's how you feel."

That lit sparks in her eyes. "There's nothing wrong with

me just because I don't think sex is the be all and end all of the universe."

"It comes damn close if it's done right. Be glad to show you."

"There's so much more to a man and a woman being together." She leaned toward him with the heels of her hands braced on the table edge. "I feel sorry for you if you don't know that."

They were back in Cool Little Platitude Country. They'd last visited here on Sunday when Lindsay mouthed all that phony crap about how sorry she was he was leaving, how glad she was that he'd quit drinking."Who says I don't know?" Noah demanded.

"You had women stashed all over the *BBT* set. In makeup, in wardrobe—the script girl. You joked about it. I've got Susie in wardrobe at ten, you'd say. A long lunch with Carol from publicity. Cindy in makeup at two. I'd hardly call those meaningful relationships."

"Maybe they were for me. And for Susie and Carol and Cindy, too." Noah sat up and swung his feet to the floor. He expected Lindsay to shy away but she stayed put knee to knee with him. "Where do you get off saying they weren't? How in hell do you know?"

"Most people feel lucky if they have one glorious affair in their lives, Noah. A grand passion, if you will. Some are fortunate enough to find the love of their life. I'm twice blessed. I've had both."

"And that's it? That's all you get?" Noah wanted to grab her and kiss her, smear her lipstick and her condescending smile all over her face. "One grand passion, one love of your life? And if you hit the jackpot and land them both, your sex life is over? What about a quickie? A one night stand? A fling with an old friend?"

Lindsay's eyes narrowed. "You and I were *never* friends."

"We were something, damn it." Noah pushed forward on the couch, bumping his knees against Lindsay's and slapping his hands down on the table on either side of her. She jumped and stiffened, but she didn't pull away. "I know it. I can *feel* it."

"Then why can't you remember it?"

Noah blinked and backed off an inch. Lindsay drew a breath, a shallow, careful breath so her breasts wouldn't touch his chest. She hadn't meant to end up here, she'd only meant to draw her boundaries, but here she was nose to nose with Chaos. She could feel it radiating off Noah, heat and anger, frustration and desire.

"I remember something, princess. Don't tell me I don't."

If she told him about her birthday party, that they'd slept together at his beach house, Chaos would claim her. It was already reeling her in with the memory of how he'd touched her, the taste of him. The blue of his eyes and his thick golden hair, his tanned and lean-muscled body, hot and damp against hers. She felt dizzy and light-headed, spinning out of control into the wild, beautiful Chaos that was Noah.

"You remember Sam and Jesse," Lindsay said. "All the times we kissed and groped and fondled each other like the horny little teenagers we were supposed to be."

Noah blinked again and backed off another inch, a wary gleam in his eyes, uncertainty in the tilt of his head. She breathed a little easier, felt his arms, ready to crush her against him a second ago, relax, the adrenaline surge quivering in his biceps, his forearms.

"Then why do I think there's something else?"

"You're confused, Noah." And he looked it, so bewildered that Lindsay wanted to curve her hand around his cheek to comfort him but didn't dare. "You've scrambled fantasy and reality. Sam and Jesse with you and me. That's all."

He blew a breath through his nose and fell back against the couch. Ran a hand through his hair and let his shoulders sag, his wrists fall against his thighs. "Okay, princess." He shrugged. "If you say so."

Oh, wasn't this great? She'd lied through her teeth and he believed her. Lindsay felt sick. She got to her feet, took her car keys out of one pocket, her sunglasses out of the other and slipped them on.

"I put the fruit and the veggies in the fridge and turned the soup down. It's chicken noodle. Aunt Dovey made it so it's safe." Her gray lenses made Noah look pale and washed out. He'd leaned his head back against the couch and closed his eyes. "I left my home number, the store and my cell phone on the desk. Eat and take a nap. Uncle Lonnie will be up later with the Parcheesi board."

"And all his scintillating conversation." Noah cracked a sour eye at her. "Just shoot me now."

"No whining," Lindsay chided and turned away, her heart in her mouth all the way across the dining room and the kitchen expecting Noah to call her back or come after her.

He didn't, which only made her feel guiltier. She stumbled up the steps and across the grass, blown-down branches from the hickories snapping under her feet, and jumped into her Civic. She fumbled the key in the ignition, dropped it, and groped for it under her knees.

Her fingers brushed something fuzzy, something fuzzy that moved. Lindsay yelped. Pyewacket sprang over the console into the passenger seat, twitched his bristled tail, and glared at her as if to say, *Why'd you scream and scare me?*

"Pyewacket." Lindsay clapped a hand to her throat. "Where in hell did you come from?"

The moon said his indignantly narrowed eyes. From under the seat said the gray dust clinging to his black fur. He arched and purred and stepped over the console into her lap. Lindsay smoothed her hand down his back, shook dust and cat hair off her fingers, fished for her keys and started the engine. Pyewacket wound back into the passenger seat, stretched up on the window and meowed.

"Mouse patrol, eh?" Lindsay asked and lowered the glass.

Pyewacket sprang out of the Civic and loped toward the barn in his sideways, herky-jerky, I'm-not-a-cat-I'm-a-cheetah run.

Lindsay put the car in reverse and adjusted the rearview mirror.

"I'm Vivienne Varner's daughter," she said wretchedly to her reflection. "And I'm a liar."

Chapter 18

Trey went to work with Lindsay on Saturday and cleaned the stock room. Emma dusted the window displays, wiped the shelves in all the sections, and spruced up the cash wrap. Lindsay vacuumed, tidied the offices, and cleaned the bathroom. By eleven The Bookshelf was spotless.

At two o'clock they had an author coming to do a book signing.

Emma left to grab some lunch and pick up a cookie tray at Brown's Bakery. Then it was Lindsay's turn to make a quick pass through Country Mart, which she should've done on Friday because Country Mart was closed on Sundays, but she'd been too tired and too strung out from her showdown with Noah and Chaos.

In the dairy aisle Trey wheedled five bucks out of her and made a beeline for Burger Chef. Like Lindsay was supposed to believe he was dying of hunger with Meggie Hannity flipping her ponytail right out front, but oh well.

She gave him half an hour to flirt, picked him up, and drove home. The message light was flashing on the answering machine when she let herself into the kitchen. She swung her purse onto the desk and hit play.

"Rehearsals are suspended till Monday to give our *star*—" Jolie sneered and Lindsay felt her heart wrench "—time to recuperate from his hospital stay. That's the sixth at seven P.M. Be there."

This was the first peep she'd heard out of Jolie since Wednesday. So far she was playing by the rules Lindsay had laid down. Aunt Sassy had seen Jolie on Thursday coming out of the post office with an express mail envelope. Lindsay had hit the roof about that.

"I'll bet Trey's pictures were in that package," she'd said

to Emma. "It would be so like Vivienne to ignore me and send the photos back to Jolie."

Yesterday Susan saw Jolie as she was leaving the Belle Coeur Café. No one else in the family had seen hide nor hair of her. Was she okay, Lindsay wondered, did Jolie feel like she did, that someone had cut a giant hole in her heart? No. Of course not. Jolie didn't have a heart.

Lindsay hardened hers, pushed her thumb on the delete key, and listened to the long electronic beep that erased her sister's voice.

"Stuff a sock in it, Jolie," she snapped and turned toward the fridge with the gallon of milk in her hand.

Trey stood by the table watching her, holding a paper sack full of mostly frozen foods in his arms. "Don't tell me," he said. "You and Jolie are fighting."

"We're not fighting." Lindsay didn't make him say Aunt Jolie. So far as she was concerned, he didn't have an Aunt Jolie. "We've come to a parting of the ways."

"For how long this time?"

Lindsay leaned into the fridge with the milk. *He's not a baby, he's almost sixteen,* she told herself. *Lay out the facts, tell him the truth.* She straightened, shut the fridge, and faced Trey. "This time it's forever."

"Yeah, right. You never get mad at anybody, Ma." Trey put the sack down and pulled out a quart of chocolate ice cream. "Not even me."

"You're sort of what brought Jolie and me to this." Lindsay opened the freezer and took the Ben & Jerry's from him. "Do you want me to tell you what happened?"

"Gimme the short version." Trey passed her a bag of frozen broccoli. "I've gotta tape the *Buffy* marathon that starts in twenty minutes."

"Jolie needed money to make repairs to the barn so she sold your school pictures to Vivienne." Lindsay plopped the broccoli in the freezer and gave him a pointed look. "For fifty thousand dollars."

"Jolie *swore* she wouldn't tell you!" Trey slammed a can of Minute Maid on the table. "I suppose you want the fifty she gave me."

"Why did Jolie give you fifty dollars?"

"Uh," Trey said. *I'm dead* said the wide-eyed blink he gave her. "It was only a couple of snapshots."

"You *posed* for these pictures Jolie sent Vivienne?"

"They weren't porn, Ma. Just a couple pictures of me on my dirt bike. The one Dad bought me," Trey said belligerently. "The one you won't let me ride 'cause I might skin my knee."

"You might break your neck!" Lindsay shouted. If she didn't break it for him. Her heart was starting to pound, her breath hitching in her chest. "I can't *believe* you took part in this photo op for Vivienne!"

"I don't get you. You let me keep the cards she sends and the money, but you're stroking out 'cause Jolie sent her some pictures."

"I've returned the money and there will be no more cards. No *Buffy* marathon, either."

"Ma." Trey gritted his teeth. "I told Meggie I'd tape it for her."

"Trust me. It'll be on again."

"You won't let me drive! I can't ride my dirt bike!" Trey threw his arms up. "Now I can't turn on the VCR! Can I *breathe*?"

"So long as you do it on the way to your room."

"Why don't you get a life and butt out of mine?"

"I *have* a life! Tormenting *you*!" Lindsay thundered. "Now *go*!"

"I'm going!" Trey shouted and stomped away.

Lindsay's throat clamped shut. She clutched the back of a chair and dragged air into her lungs. When Trey's bedroom door boomed shut she lurched out of the kitchen and across the family room, struggling to breathe, bumping into furniture, fumbling with the French doors. She flung them open and fell outside onto the covered deck.

The broom Trey had forgotten to put away leaned against the dove gray brick wall of the house. She grabbed it and swung at the blue and mauve flowered cushions on the redwood love seat.

She whacked the frame a few times but mostly she connected with the pads, cursing Jolie and Vivienne in her head because she didn't have breath enough to scream. Seams split, buttons popped out of tufts and rolled on the deck boards. The vise in her chest let go and she collapsed on the ruined cushions, out of breath from exhaustion rather than panic and blind-eyed fury.

Well, wasn't this grown-up, in-control behavior? Shrieking at her child, busting furniture, lying to Noah. Lindsay leaned her head back, closed her eyes, and waited for the jitters that followed the adrenaline burn off to subside. Then she put the broom away in the tall Rubbermaid deck locker and went inside. She found the *TV Guide*, the channel for the *Buffy* marathon and turned the VCR on to record.

In the kitchen she found the can of Minute Maid half-melted on the table. She tossed it in the freezer anyway and shut the door. A magnet bounced off at her feet, a Blue Delft heart that said WORLD'S GREATEST MOM. Lindsay picked it up and bit her lip.

She couldn't believe she'd yelled at Trey. She never yelled at Trey, but she wanted to storm into his room and yell at him some more. What were you *thinking* when you helped Jolie mollify Vivienne? What part of Mother from Hell don't you understand?

Lindsay sighed and stuck the magnet on the fridge. Trey had never met Vivienne, never spoken to her. Sure he'd heard the horror stories but what did they mean to him? He hadn't lived them; they were only family gossip. To Trey, Vivienne was nothing more than the Phantom Menace.

She should apologize for screeching at him like a fishwife. Like Vivienne. *Oh my God,* Lindsay realized. *Vivienne isn't sitting out in L.A. pulling all our strings—she's right here in my kitchen. After all this time, after all my careful boundary drawing, I've let Vivienne into my house just as surely as if I'd opened the door to her.*

The tea leaf reading exploded in her head. Zipped across her skull like a spear of lightning. She saw the knife in Jolie's hand, the symbol from the reading of a threat to her comfort and security, shut her eyes, and clutched her head until the image faded and the pain backed off.

Then she phoned Emma at the store.

"I'm asking this because my head feels like it's going to

blow up," Lindsay told her. "How do I clear negative energy out of my house?"

"Any idea where it's coming from?"

"I think it's Vivienne."

"Call an exorcist. That failing, burn white candles."

Lindsay lit two in every room. Vanilla scented that eased the sick pulse in her head. She told herself it was just coincidence. She told herself a lot of things while she looked through her closet for something to wear to the book signing.

She did not owe Noah the truth. She didn't owe him anything. She could be courteous and she would be professional. She'd do the play and put up with Satan's Handmaiden for the sake of his career, but that was it. No more dinner invitations. The day he left Belle Coeur she'd break out her tap shoes and do the happy dance. If he got in her face again with that asinine, we-were-something-I-know-it-I-can-feel-it crap, she'd flap ball change him right in the head.

Now that was a picture. It made her smile and eased the headache some. She blew out the candles, checked her watch, and decided she had time for a cup of tea. Normal tea steeped from a bag, no leaves swirling in the bottom to torment her. She'd just finished rinsing her cup when the doorbell rang.

"Hey, Lindsay." Uncle Ron smiled when she opened the door. "I wonder if I could borrow Trey for a while."

"How long do you have in mind? Six months? A year?"

"A couple hours. I figure I stand at least a chance of getting out of Country Mart alive if I'm accompanied by a child."

Lindsay stepped onto the porch, out from under the overhang of the roof, and waved her hand. The sun was out, the sky was blue, the front lawn almost summer-green. "But Uncle Ron. It's a beautiful day."

"Isn't it?" He squinted sourly at the sky. "I forecasted rain."

"Oh." She winced sympathetically. "Come on in."

Ron went down the hall to Trey's room. Lindsay went into the kitchen and tried to look busy till her son slouched up beside her at the sink with his hands in his pockets and a chip on his shoulder.

"Can I go with Uncle Ron or am I grounded for the rest of my life?"

"You aren't grounded." Lindsay hung the dishrag over the faucet. "I just wanted you to go away so I couldn't yell at you anymore."

"You okay, Ma? You look kinda pale."

"It's just a headache." The same one she'd had since Noah Patrick came to town. "Have Uncle Ron drop you at the store, okay? And keep an eye on him, hmmm?"

"I won't let anybody pick on him." Trey pushed off the sink, started away, and turned back. "Can I set up the VCR before I leave?"

"I already did. You might check it, make sure I did it right. I had to get out the instruction booklet."

"Thanks, Ma." Trey looped a bony-armed hug around her neck. "You're the best."

He was almost as tall as she was. He'd be taller at eighteen, maybe as tall as Mark or Uncle Donnie and Uncle Lonnie. He'd be tall and handsome and he'd be off to college. But please God, not to Berkeley. Anywhere, dear Lord, but California.

"You, too." Lindsay hugged him tight and squeezed her eyes shut.

She managed to keep back the tears that were clogging her throat until Ron's dark green Explorer turned out of her driveway. Then she slid down the wall in the foyer, wrapped her arms around her legs, leaned her forehead against her knees, and sobbed.

For Jolie because she loved her and missed her, because she was so miserably unhappy and refused to see it. Lindsay cried for herself because she was exhausted. Four panic attacks in a week were enough to fell an elephant. But mostly she cried for Trey because she'd yelled at him, because he was so precious and so fragile and she was so afraid she'd turn into Vivienne and break him.

There. She'd admitted it. Finally let the thought form in her head. Oh God. Now what? She couldn't keep sitting here on the floor crying. Her eyes were throbbing and she could only breathe through her mouth. She had to get up, fix her face, and get back to the store for the signing. Lindsay pushed off the floor and spent ten minutes in the bathroom blowing her nose, leaning on the vanity with her back to the sink.

Look at me, Lindsay, look at me, it murmured, like the mirror over Aunt Dovey's dresser had whispered to her on Sunday. Not on your life. Not till she had to put her face back together, thank you.

Lindsay was in the kitchen making an ice bag to keep her eyes from puffing up when the phone rang. Thinking it was Emma calling to tell her to get her fanny back to the store, she snatched the cordless receiver off the base without checking the caller ID.

"Whoa," Noah said. "Who has pneumonia now?"

"I have a headache," Lindsay said, appalled that her eyes filled with tears and her throat swelled at the sound of Noah's voice. "How are you feeling today?"

"Better than you sound. You're crying, aren't you?"

"No. I—" Lindsay's voice quavered and broke. So did what little control she'd managed to scrape together. "Yes! I'm crying!" she shouted. "But I'm not crying over *you*!"

"Well, who said—" Click. The connection broke in Noah's ear.

He held the phone to his nose and stared at it. Like every moron did when a beautiful woman hung up on him. Like he didn't quite get it, like somehow it was the telephone's fault.

Pyewacket roused from a nap on the chair next to Noah's at the dining room table. He'd shown up on the kitchen window ledge last night just as it was getting dark. He stretched up on his haunches on the chair seat, yawned, and gave Noah a *what-did-you-expect-dipshit* blink.

"Go back to sleep," Noah growled.

He got up, put the phone on its base inside the desk, shut the doors and sat back down in front of his script. He'd been studying his lines all day. Six hours straight and he was lucky if he could remember ten words. He wondered if a person could OD on gingko, how long he should wait before he called Lindsay again.

Why had she said she wasn't crying over him? Why would she be?

A knock sounded at the back door. Noah tipped his chair away from the table, looked through the archway into the kitchen, and saw Lindsay's kid through the window holding up two white plastic sacks from Country Mart.

"Dude," Trey said, nodding over his shoulder at the Corvette when Noah opened the door. "What happened to your car?"

"Your mom got a little pissed and belted it a couple of times."

"Yeah, right." Trey laughed. "What happened, really?"

"The squirrels dropped hickory nuts on it. When I get it back from the body shop Donnie suggested I not park it under the trees."

"You aren't going to change the color, are you?"

"I'm thinking about red. What's your opinion?"

"Yellow's my favorite color." Trey shrugged. "But it's your car."

"You like Corvettes. I remember the posters in your room."

"That's my dream car. I mean really." Trey nodded wistfully over his shoulder at the horse piss yellow Corvette. "That's it. Right there."

Jolie sold Trey's pictures, Lindsay said, and every detail of his life to Vivienne for fifty thousand dollars. If it was coincidence that she'd sent him her grandson's dream car in his favorite color, then Noah decided he was Robert Redford.

"What's in the bags, sport? You moving in?"

"I wish. It's the stuff you asked Uncle Ron to get for you. I went with him to Country Mart. My second trip today."

"C'mon in." Noah stepped back. Trey went past him and dumped the bags on the counter. "Did you see your girlfriend?"

Trey turned red around the ears. "My girlfriend?"

"The carhop across the street. What's her name?"

"Meggie." Trey's ears went up in flames. "She's not my girlfriend."

"Yeah, but you'd like her to be, wouldn't you?"

Trey shrugged and looked away. Pyewacket jumped up

on the counter and stuck his head in one of the sacks. Noah shooed him down and emptied the contents on the counter.

A bag of Doritos Nacho Cheese Chips, Lay's Sour Cream and Onion Potato Chips, Chee-tos, Oreos, and Chips Ahoy. Two chilled six-packs of Cherry Coke. Trey's eyes lit up.

"Sweet." He peeked into the second sack. "What's in here?"

"Healthy shit." Noah pitched the bags of chips through the cutout onto the dining room table. "That's for tomorrow. Today we feast."

Trey pulled a can of Coke out of its plastic collar, popped the top and drank. Noah cradled the second six-pack to his chest.

"Cherry Coke." He sighed. "I may have to have Ron's baby."

Trey snorted and spewed Coke all over the counter.

"Leave it." Noah pushed him toward the dining room. "Let's eat."

They inhaled the Doritos and the Lay's, left mostly crumbs in the Chee-tos bag, shared the Chips Ahoy and one whole row of Oreos with Pyewacket, and emptied eight cans of Cherry Coke.

Noah blew cheese dust off his script, eyed the chip and cookie debris and the can rings on the table. Already he felt the first flare of heartburn, but he didn't care. The salt and sugar binge had done the trick, taken the edge off the agitated, I'm-going-batty-cooped-up-here restlessness that had kept him awake half the night. That and the crazy dreams, faces and colors that almost but didn't quite fit together. All night long they'd rolled and tumbled and jerked through his head.

Trey rocked his chair back on two legs and belched.

"Beg my pardon," Noah said to him, "and you'll never dine at Chez Patrick again."

"I like this restaurant." Trey reached for the script and turned it toward him. "I don't know how you guys memorize all this stuff."

"Neither do I, not anymore. I seem to have lost the knack."

"I'm helping my mom learn her lines. I could help you, too."

Noah hesitated. That wasn't what he'd had in mind. He'd had Lindsay in mind. That's why he'd called her.

"I'm good at this." Trey pulled the script closer. "Here's Moira's line in Act Two, Scene Three: 'Last night you caught me at a weak moment. It won't happen again.' " Trey glanced at him. "And Cliff says—?"

Noah shrugged. "Beats me."

"Cliff says: 'You want me, Moira. I know it.' Moira says: 'I want you out of my dressing room this second.' " Trey looked up at him, his eyebrows lifting expectantly. "And Cliff says—?"

Noah said, "Uh . . . "

"Oh man, you suck. Cliff says: 'I want you, Moira. Right here, right now.' The stage direction says, Cliff drags Moira onto the daybed, kisses her, and—" Trey broke off and stared at the page.

"What?" Noah took back the script and put on his glasses. "Cliff drags Moira onto the daybed, kisses her, fondles her." *Yahoo yippy,* he thought, took off his glasses, and glanced blandly at Trey. "So?"

"Are you and my mom gonna do that stuff on stage?"

"Yeah," Noah said. Oh yeah, oh baby. He could hardly wait to do that stuff with Lindsay. Preferably off stage, but he'd settle for on, which was not a comfortable thought to have in front of her son. "We did stuff like this every day on *BBT.*"

"I know. I've seen all the episodes like a gazillion times."

"But she wasn't your mom then, was she?"

"She doesn't even look like my mom in those old shows."

"So what's the problem? You've seen her kiss guys on stage."

"No, I haven't. This is the first play she's done for Jolie."

Well. This was interesting. "I didn't know that."

"The only guy I've ever seen my mom kiss is my dad." Trey made a face at him. "Do I sound, like, weird?"

"You sound, like, normal. Like a guy who's wondering how bad his buds are gonna razz him when they see his mom on stage necking with some bozo from L.A."

"Exactly," Trey said unhappily. "What am I gonna say?"

"I'd start with 'Look, burger breath,' " Noah put a snarl in his voice, " 'That's my *mother.*' "

"Burger breath. That's good." Trey grinned and tapped the script. "Study this and we'll try it again."

While Noah concentrated on Act Two, Scene Four, Trey picked up the red leather album and settled on the bed Lindsay had made on the couch, the one he'd thrashed around on most of the night.

"Okay, Mr. DeMille." Noah turned in his chair, his elbow bent on the back. "I'm ready for my close-up."

Trey blinked at him. "Huh?"

"Never mind. Get over here."

Trey brought the album, put it down on the far end of the table, and took the script from Noah. They went through the scene twice. Trey reading Moira's part, Noah struggling to insert the right line in the right place, sweating with the effort like he'd just run a marathon.

"Could you put a little feeling into it?" Trey said. "You sound like one of those canned voices on an answering machine."

"I've got to know the line before I can feel it."

"That's not how Mom does it. She emotes all over the place."

"Well, swell. That's how she does it. This is how I do it."

"I just think if you felt the words they'd be easier to learn."

"Thank you, Steven Spielberg, but I'm not Marlon Brando."

"Who's Marlon Brando?"

"*On the Waterfront? A Streetcar Named Desire?*" Noah pushed to his feet, threw his arms out, and howled at the ceiling. "*Stel*-la! Stel-*la*!"

Trey gave him a blank look. Noah sighed and sat down. "Brando's a method actor, kid."

"What is that exactly? I asked my mom if it was hard for her to cry all the time on *BBT*. She said no because she was a method actress."

"A method actor becomes the character he's portraying. He finds an aspect of the character he can relate to and identify with. A personality trait, maybe, or a life situation.

Brando, for instance, got so into being Fletcher Christian when he made *Mutiny on the Bounty* that he married the Tahitian actress who played his squeeze in the movie."

"Really." Trey looked at him askance. "Are you a method actor?"

"Not hardly. I'm just a pretty face. Least I used to be."

"You don't look bad for an old guy." Trey reached for the album and opened it between them. " 'Course you look a lot better here."

Noah put on his glasses and leaned over the photograph Trey had his finger on. It took him a second to recognize himself standing on the beach, gazing out at the surf with his board under one arm.

Damn he looked good. Tan and lithe with sand glistening on his chest, his sun-bleached, nearly shoulder length hair a wind and water tangled mane. Nice bulge in his electric blue Speedo, too.

"Boy, those were the days," Noah said.

Trey grinned wickedly. "Got a rolled-up sock in here, don't you?"

"You wish, little man. That damn Speedo was hell. By the end of a day-long shoot I'd be so chafed I could hardly walk."

"My mom says you're a really good surfer. Good enough, she said, that you could have turned professional."

"I should have. I was always sober when I surfed." Noah stared at his twenty-something-year-old self, felt his throat tighten, and closed the album. "Only an idiot climbs on a surfboard drunk."

"Well, hey." Trey shrugged. "Maybe you aren't brain-dead after all."

"I see you took your smart-ass pill today."

Noah plucked an Oreo out of the package and threw it at him. Trey grinned, snatched it off the floor before Pyewacket grabbed it, and threw it back. Noah retaliated with a fist full of Chee-tos.

"Food fight!" Trey hollered and fired a volley of Oreos.

The kid had an arm like a rocket launcher, the cat sense enough to run for cover. The brain-dead old guy had smarts enough to put the table between him and Trey and use it like a fort.

They'd eaten most of the junk so it didn't take long to reduce their ammo supply to crumpled-up chip bags. Noah had the last one mashed into a tight ball in his fist. He reared up on his knees, fired the crushed Chee-tos bag over the table, and watched it bounce off Mrs. Doubtfire's chin as she came through the kitchen.

She batted at it, startled, glanced at the wreck of the dining room, at Trey and Noah leaping to their feet, and laughed.

"Mrs. Harrington." Noah pushed around the table. "Are you okay?"

"Lord, yes." She waved a hand, still laughing. "I see you two been having fun. No wonder you didn't hear me knock."

"My mom sent you to spy on me, didn't she?" Trey asked, swiping his thick blond bangs out of his eyes with an Oreo-caked hand.

"No, Smarty Pants. Ron sent me to shag you downstairs so he can take you back to your mother. I come by to have a cup of tea with Noah." Mrs. Doubtfire plucked a hankie out of the pocket of her dress, blue and green striped silk with a bow at the neck. "You got icing on your nose."

"Oh." Trey flushed and wiped his face. "Thanks."

" 'Fore you go anywhere, you get out the vacuum and help Noah clean up this mess. I'll tend to the kitchen."

Which was another wreck entirely, the counters Coke-sprayed and piled with the breakfast dishes. Noah felt guilty watching Mrs. Doubtfire fill the sink with suds, but she was smiling and humming so he left her to it and dug into the dining room with Trey.

The dust and crumbs started him sneezing, then coughing so hard he had to excuse himself to gag and hack up green crap in the bathroom. He thought all the junk he'd eaten might come up, too, but it didn't. He was draped over the sink, hanging on to it till he got his breath, when Trey thumped on the door and hollered, "Uncle Ron's here. Gotta go."

"Right, sport. Later."

The inhaler was on the bedside table. He'd left it there

sometime during the night. He'd slept like Goldilocks, shifting between the bed and the couch—too hard, too soft—wired from the cortisone and so agitated by the dreams that he'd barely closed his eyes. Which was just as well since he'd had to let the damn cat in and out at least a dozen times.

Noah took two hits off the inhaler, sucked the mist deep into his lungs, and felt the spasm in his chest relax, a soft buzz start in his brain. What were the chances he'd get hooked on steroids from two puffs every four hours? Probably nil, but he wasn't taking any chances. He was clean and he was staying that way.

Noah threw the inhaler away in the bathroom trash can, dusted the worst of the cookie and chip crumbs off his shirt and jeans, and headed for the dining room to have tea with Mrs. Doubtfire.

Chapter 19

MRS. DOUBTFIRE sat in the chair that faced the kitchen, holding Pyewacket in her arms and scratching his ears. The cat's chin rested on her shoulder. His eyes were closed and a purr rumbled out of his chest.

The beige berber carpet was vacuumed; the table clean and set for tea. Yellow place mats, cups and saucers with green leaves that matched a sugar bowl, a creamer, and a china pot curling steam out of its spout.

"A tea service." Noah sat down in the empty chair at the head of the table. "Where'd that come from?"

"Back of the cabinet where Joe Varner stuck it." Mrs. Doubtfire put Pyewacket down and poured the tea. "I give a tea set to everybody in the family. You take milk or sugar?"

"Straight up is fine, thanks."

"Put in a smidge of mullein. You won't taste it but it's good for the lungs. How you feeling? Don't look as peaked as you did the other night."

"I'd feel better if I could get out of this apartment. Every time I head for the door Donnie or Ron or Lonnie shows up." Noah lifted his cup and blew steam at Mrs. Doubtfire. "Funny how that is."

"Don't get your shorts in a bunch. Lindsay means well."

"I figured she was behind it." The tea was scalding. Noah put his cup down. "She pulled the same thing while I was in the hospital."

"Lindsay would like us all to think she don't give two hoots in hell what happens to you, but she does." Mrs. Doubtfire took a healthy swig of tea. *Jesus,* Noah thought. *She must have a cast-iron mouth.* "I'm not saying that means she wants to hop into bed with you."

"Gee, I wish you would. That'd perk me up."

"I'm not saying she don't, either." Mrs. Doubtfire's eyes twinkled at him. "Hard to tell with Lindsay. Drink your tea."

"I'm letting it cool. Lindsay's pretty closed up, that's for sure."

"She's repressed. Puts all her energy into raising that boy. She says Trey is all she needs, but he's just an excuse for her to stay stuck in the rut she dug with Mark. Nice fella, Mark, but b-o-o-r-*r-i-n-g*. Never did understand what Lindsay seen in him, 'cept he was steady as a rock. Thick as one too, you ask me." Mrs. Doubtfire sipped more of her tea and winked. "Which you didn't, but I thought you might be interested."

"If I didn't know better I'd say you were reading my mind."

"If I was a comedian, I'd say that's a real short story."

"Or a one-act play."

She laughed and Noah raised his cup, made sure the tea wouldn't weld his tongue to the roof of his mouth, and took a swallow.

"Leave me enough to swish 'round the bottom," Mrs. Doubtfire said, "and I'll read your leaves."

Oh yeah. He'd forgotten about the tea leaf reading. Noah left a couple mouthfuls in his cup and handed it to Mrs. Doubtfire. She held the saucer on her left palm, made three swirls to the right, and put the cup and saucer on the table.

Noah leaned on his elbows to watch the leaves in the bottom spin and settle.

"How'd you learn to do this?"

"My mama was what folks used to call a water witch. She could find water in the ground with a forked stick. She could see things in water, too. Visions and such. Sometimes she seen 'em in mirrors."

"I used to see things. In tequila, though, not water."

Mrs. Doubtfire cocked her head at him. "Why do you do that, Noah? Make jokes about your drinking?"

"I've found it's like having a really big nose. If you point it out and make fun of it, people don't seem to notice it quite as much."

"Since you don't drink anymore, why bother?"

Noah opened his mouth but nothing came out. He couldn't think of a snappy comeback. Mrs. Doubtfire leaned over his cup.

"You heard the expression cow in clover, ain't you, Noah?" She glanced up at him and smiled. "That's what you're gonna be. Up to your knees in success and good fortune. Unless you're planning to relocate to the country. It could mean that, too."

"Not in my teacup. I'm an L.A. boy. I've got smog in my lungs, which is probably why I caught pneumonia. All this damn clean air."

"Just giving you all the possibilities," Mrs. Doubtfire said and turned back to his cup. "Here behind the cow there's a mountain, an obstacle that's hidden from you and clouds gathering above it like clouds do before a storm. Whatever this obstacle is it's gonna give you some trouble if you're not careful."

"Hope the tea leaves know what it is. I sure as hell don't."

"Tea leaves don't know anything. They only show what *could* happen. The Good Lord give us all free will. What you do with your life is up to you so the future is always changeable."

"When does the future start, anyway? Five minutes from now, a nanosecond? I've always wondered."

Mrs. Doubtfire chuckled and leaned back in her chair, giving Pyewacket room to slither onto her lap. She stroked the cat with one hand, lifted the pot with the other, and refilled their cups.

"I do love a man with a sense of humor, Noah."

"I don't mean to be flip. I just find it hard to believe that my future is floating around in a teacup."

"Don't see why. How many years did you spend looking for it in the bottom of a tequila bottle?"

Mrs. Doubtfire sipped her tea, her brown eyes glimmering at him over the rim of her cup. Vivienne and Jolie had brown eyes, too, but they were sharp, beady little ferret eyes, so pale a shade they were almost yellow. Mrs. Doubtfire's eyes were a soft, deep, comforting brown. Kind of like that cow in clover, with a keen, I-don't-miss-a-trick glint.

"Did you find out what you want to know?" Noah asked.

She put her cup down and blinked at him. "Beg pardon?"

"I think this tea leaf reading was more for your sake than mine."

"Oh no, no, no. The leaves were speaking to you, not me. If I was that damn curious about what kind of fella you are I'd read your palm."

Noah smiled and held out his left hand. "Go ahead."

"You're right-handed. That's the one I want to see."

Noah gave her his right hand. Mrs. Doubtfire spread his fingers, lightly touching the pads with hers. She didn't trace the obvious lines that even Noah knew, the life line and the heart line; she simply brushed her fingertips over his palm in soft strokes that started his head buzzing.

Like it had on Saturday when he'd looked into Emma Harrington's laser-sharp brown eyes. Mrs. Doubtfire's eyes, Noah realized, which figured since she was Dovey Harrington's daughter.

"There's a break here in your life line where you got off track for a spell. 'Bout ten years it looks like." Mrs. Doubtfire glanced up at him, her eyebrows drawn together. "You come close to dying, didn't you, Noah?"

"Which time?" he said and regretted it instantly. It was a smart-ass answer and the compassion he saw in her eyes was genuine.

"Last time wasn't that long ago." Noah remembered the

dismally cold beach where Vivienne had found him half-drowned and half-frozen. Mrs. Doubtfire couldn't possibly see that in his hand. Could she? "You're fine now, back on track. A whole lot better equipped to follow the path you was meant to than you would've been if you hadn't spent all that time rolling around like a lost ball in high weeds."

"Well. It's good to know that I'm not brain-dead after all."

"Your brain was never dead, Noah, just pickled. This mound here says you got a knack for reading people, for knowing how to make 'em do what you want. But you abused it. You was selfish, like Vivian. You used folks to satisfy your own needs and desires and to hell with theirs."

Not exactly a news flash, still Noah cringed. He'd heckled Lindsay, shagged her like a dog. She'd hated it, despised it, and he hadn't cared. Hell. He'd been so in love with himself and tequila he hadn't even noticed. No wonder she'd punched him.

"That's a powerful gift to misuse, Noah. It carries a price. This little kink here—" Mrs. Doubtfire traced a line but didn't name it "—says you've paid it ten times over. See where the kink smoothes out and fades away? That means you learned your lesson."

"I took an oath when I sobered up to only use my powers for good." It was a borderline smart-ass answer, but Mrs. Doubtfire gave him a twinkling-eyed smile. "You see anything about a hidden obstacle?"

"You need to mind your health, eat right and such, but you know that." She stroked his palm again, turned his hand sideways in hers, and frowned. "You got any interest in marriage?"

"That was subtle." Noah laughed. "Why didn't you just ask me?"

"I *did* just ask you. What I'm seeing here says one wife and at least one child, but you sure don't strike me as the marrying kind."

"Why not?" Noah bristled. "What's wrong with me?"

"Well, for starters." She looked down her nose at him through the bifocals of her glasses. "Your prospects at the moment ain't exactly the best in the world, are they?"

"I don't have a pot to piss in or a window to throw it out of, but there's success and good fortune dead ahead. You just said so."

"I didn't say so. The tea leaves said so."

"What the hell? You don't believe in your own tea leaves?"

"Tea leaves is just signs and portents, Noah. Facts is facts."

"I'll give you a fact." He parked his elbow on the table between them and pointed a finger at her. "If I had a pot *or* a window I'd have Lindsay. In a flash. In a heartbeat. In a goddamn New York—" Noah snapped his mouth shut. "Damn. You are *good*."

"Thank you." Mrs. Doubtfire smiled and saluted him with her teacup. "Lindsay's got more money than Carter has little liver pills, you know. She's got plenty of pots and windows."

"But they're her pots and her windows. For Christ's sake, Vivienne bought my underwear. A man should be able to pay for his own Jockey shorts, don't you think?" Noah clapped his hand to his head. "Holy Christ. Shoot me. I sound like my old man."

"Vivian's paying you a salary, ain't she?"

"Yeah, and a bonus at the end of the run. If we make it to the end of the run, which I'm beginning to have serious doubts about."

Mrs. Doubtfire touched his script, stacked on top of the red leather album at the end of the table. "Trouble learning your lines?"

"Like you wouldn't believe, but that's not the problem. Here's the problem. My contract is with Vivienne. So is Jolie's. Probably Lindsay's, but I can't say for sure 'cause I haven't read it. I'm not sure Lindsay has, either. Anyway. My contract and Jolie's both say that if either Lindsay or I miss a performance between opening night and closing, the contract is null and void and nobody gets another dime."

"That looks plain crazy on the surface, but Vivian never does anything without a reason. If she don't care that this play succeeds—" Mrs. Doubtfire narrowed her eyes, thinking out loud "—then there's something else Vivian wants. Something else she's looking to gain from this."

"I can tell you in two words—her grandson. Not twenty minutes ago Trey told me that yellow Corvette parked out back is his dream car." Noah flipped his hand toward the back door. "That's how he phrased it. 'That's my dream car. I mean really. That's it. Right there.' "

"I know yellow is Trey's favorite color, but how did Vivian know?"

"My guess is Jolie told her when she sent Vivienne the pictures."

"What pictures?"

"The pictures of Trey that Vivienne has all over her house."

"*What?*" Mrs. Doubtfire screeched, startling Pyewacket out of her lap.

"Uh," Noah said. "I thought you knew about this."

"No, I don't know about this. How do *you* know about it?"

"I stayed with Vivienne before I came out here. I saw the pictures."

"Does Lindsay know Vivian has pictures of Trey?"

"Lindsay knows," Noah said. "I told her."

"I never been on a airplane in my life. But I'm gonna buy me a ticket and fly out to Los Angeles and smack my sister." Mrs. Doubtfire drew a breath, a long, deep one that flared her nostrils like a dragon priming itself to cremate a village. "Soon as I'm done smacking Jolene."

"It's none of my business, but I'd hold off on that if I were you."

"I've spent my life cleaning up Vivian's messes." Mrs. Doubtfire pushed to her feet. "I swore when I cleaned up the one she left when she lit outta here with Lindsay that I'd never clean up another one."

She snatched their teacups off the table and stalked into the kitchen. Noah tucked the creamer in the crook of one elbow, the sugar bowl in the other, grabbed up the teapot, and followed her.

"Poor heartbroken Joe. The little monster she made out of Jolie." Mrs. Doubtfire dumped the cups and saucers in the sink with a crash, took the pot away from him, the pitcher and the sugar bowl, slammed them down on the drain board and faced him. "No more. This time I'm gonna stop Vivian before she wrecks Trey's life like she done Jolene's."

And Lindsay's, Noah thought, but didn't say so. If Mrs. Doubtfire didn't know about the panic attacks he wasn't going to tell her.

"If you storm out to L.A. Vivienne will pull the plug on this whole deal. She's perverse enough to do it just because she can. If you smack Jolie over the pictures, she'll call Vivienne and whine and the same thing will happen. Vivienne will pull the plug. Where will that leave Jolie? Still up to her ass in debt and struggling to keep this white elephant afloat."

"Damn." Mrs. Doubtfire frowned. "I didn't think of that."

"Vivienne is absolutely convinced that she's holding all the cards, but she isn't. She dealt the best hands to Lindsay and me." Mrs. Doubtfire's eyebrows shot up. "I know that doesn't sound like a mistake Vivienne would make, but it's an easy error in judgment if you underestimate your opponents or you think they're dumb as dirt."

"Now that I can see." Mrs. Doubtfire snorted. "Vivian's always thought the rest of us was just a bunch of hicks from the sticks."

"And she thinks I'm brain-dead. Vivienne's the one who made that crack. Jolie just repeated it. I can't wait to prove her wrong."

"Tell me how you're gonna do that." Mrs. Doubtfire glared at the microwave clock, then at Noah. "Me and Lonnie got cookies to bake for the potluck supper at church tomorrow. And you'd best make it good," she warned, the scorch-a-village smolder still in her eyes. "Or the second the last batch comes out of the oven I'm going to go smack Jolene."

"I used to be just like Vivienne. I know how her mind works. She wants to get her hands on Trey, yes, but the play isn't a total toss off. She expects to get the credit for its success plus make a profit on her investment. Which is hefty, believe me. No me, no Lindsay, no play, no profit. Are you getting my drift?"

"Might be," she said slowly. "Are you talking about blackmail?"

"Extortion, coercion, giving Vivienne the shaft. Whatever you want to call it, yeah, that's what I'm talking about."

Mrs. Doubtfire clapped his face in both her hands, jerked him up on his toes, and gave him a hard, smacking kiss on the mouth.

"Noah Patrick." She grinned. "You are a genius."

"If there's a God in heaven," Noah said, his lips numb and his head ringing, "Lindsay will share your enthusiasm for my plan."

"Let's hear it. What's the plan?"

"Lindsay and I refuse to play Vivienne's game. She meets our demands or we walk. Don't ask me what the demands are. That's up to Lindsay, whatever she decides she wants when I tell her about the plan."

"When's that gonna be?"

"If I can escape the guards, the second you leave to bake cookies."

"I'll have a word with Lonnie." Mrs. Doubtfire grabbed her purse and pushed past him. "Lindsay's at the store. You get over there and start figuring out how to stick it to Vivienne. I'll hold off on the plane ticket and smacking Jolene." She stopped halfway through the door and looked back at him. "Change your shirt. You got cookie crumbs all over."

Twenty minutes later Noah was in the Corvette. Heading, he hoped to God, for Lindsay's bookstore. He'd taken a shower, put on clean underwear and socks and jeans. A blue shirt with a windowpane check, rolled-up sleeves, and a sweater so Lindsay wouldn't fuss about a chill. He'd shaved, washed and dried his hair, and brushed his teeth. If the cops found the Corvette in a week or two out of gas on some godforsaken country road, they'd at least be able to tell his mother that he was clean when he died.

The Bookshelf was on Main Street. He remembered that much. What he couldn't remember was which one of the goddamn one-way, up the hill and down the hill streets got him there. He lucked out and found Spring Street, goosed the Corvette up the long-ass hill, parked in front of McGruff's Hardware, and went inside to ask for directions.

Along the front of the store stretched a dusty and scuffed wooden counter. A cash register caged by wire racks that held all kinds of hardware thingamabobs sat in the middle. At the far end two men on stools leaned over a domino board. One of them looked up when Noah stepped inside and the bell over the door rang.

Oh shit. The man was Uncle Ezra. And he was scowling.

Then he blinked and a grin spread across his long, homely face. "Well, hey there, Noah. How you be? Heard you was real sick."

"I'm fine, Mr. Pantz, thanks." Oh crap. He was wearing the tweed jacket he'd yanked Lucille out of last Saturday. "Can you tell me how to get to Lindsay's bookstore?"

"Why, sure. It's 'bout a block past my store. I just closed up for the day. This here's Fred McGruff."

"How do." The bald, portly man on the second stool nodded. "I've whupped Ez three games straight so you can have him."

"Keep the board warm. I'll be back soon as I take care of Noah."

Ezra unwound his tall, bony frame from the stool and opened his coat. Sure enough, there was Lucille, tucked inside and secured by Velcro straps. Noah's heart shot into his throat.

"Mind if I leave Lucille under the counter?" Ezra asked. "If Sassy's at The Bookshelf and she catches me with Lucille I'm a dead man."

"You can leave her if she ain't loaded," Fred replied.

Ezra unbuckled Lucille and slid her under the counter. "Let's go, Noah. It ain't far."

Oh yes it was. It was a long damn way to L.A. where all you had to worry about was getting sunburned or your car keyed in a parking lot.

To The Bookshelf it was only a three-block walk. On the way they passed Ezra's store. He swept an arm proudly at the glass storefront. Pantz Pressers and Dry Cleaners. Somehow Noah kept a straight face.

"You need your trousers pressed you come see me," Ezra said. "I can set a crease so sharp you'll cut yourself you ain't careful."

Oh, to be in Los Angeles, Noah thought, *now that spring was here.* He'd missed the Oscar billboards and the first

Mercedes to cruise Rodeo Drive with the top down. The smog would be thickening up again now that the winter rains had passed and there'd be surfboards on the beaches. Everywhere there'd be surfboards. Oh man. What he wouldn't give to be the hell out of Missouri and back in California.

So Noah was thinking. So Noah thought until he stepped inside The Bookshelf with Ezra and saw Lindsay.

Her beauty hadn't faded one iota since yesterday, but for the first time he barely noticed it. The store was full of people, most of them clustered around a small wooden table. Lindsay was smiling and bending over a small woman with apricot hair in a motorized wheelchair. She held a cookie tray, tipped just a bit to make it easier for the little woman with the crippled hands to slip a sugar cookie off the white paper doily and into a napkin in her lap.

He'd seen the same smile on Lindsay's face yesterday when she'd hung up his jacket, in the hospital when she'd tucked the covers around him. He'd heckled her and she made him tea, lied to her and she'd made him tiramisu. He'd shagged her like a dog but she'd rescued him from the bears and invited him to dinner. She'd made him a bed on the couch and enlisted her uncles to keep a watch on him.

'Course he'd kissed her and she'd punched him. She wasn't perfect, but neither was he. She was golden and beautiful and kind. She'd protected him from her rotten bitch sister and she protected her rotten bitch sister from the world. Lindsay didn't laugh much, but he could fix that. Mrs. Doubtfire said she was repressed. He could fix that, too, and love every second of it. Love every inch of her if she'd let him.

Emma Harrington spotted him first. Noah felt her laser beam eyes on him, looked to his left and saw Mrs. Doubtfire's daughter standing at the cash register behind a glass-fronted display case. He raised his hand and waggled his fingers. Emma gave him a thin smile, arched an eyebrow at him beneath her streak of white hair, and glanced at Lindsay.

So did Noah, just as she turned away from the woman in the wheelchair and saw him through a break in the people milling between them. She blinked, surprised, then again, panicked. It wasn't I-never-expected-to-see-you-again, it was

I-never-expected-to-see-you-*here*. She glanced away, then squared her shoulders, pasted her fake I'm-in-control smile on her face, and came toward him with the cookie tray.

The crowd shifted, masking Lindsay from sight and opening a gap between Noah, the table, and an easel holding a sign that said MEET THE—that's all he could see around Frank Fairchild's broad backside. He stood talking to a tall, dark-haired guy wearing a blue blazer, jeans, and a royal blue ball cap with KC in white letters above the bill.

A cute little blond chick with curly hair sat at the table signing a book for Susan. She wore a tailored green suit and a big diamond wedding ring. Nice legs, which Noah leaned back and to the right to get a better look at under the table. She raised her head with a smile to hand the book to Susan, looked straight at him, and blinked.

The book in her hand hit the table with a thunk. "Is that him?"

Susan glanced a puzzled *Who?* over her shoulder. "Oh—hi, Noah." She smiled. "Come meet Cydney Parrish. She's a huge fan of—"

"My God! It *is* him! Oh, Gus! It's *Noah Patrick*!"

The cute little blond—Cydney Parrish, he assumed—shot to her feet and squealed his name in a shrieky, half-fainting voice Noah hadn't heard since the last time he'd stepped out of a stretch limo onto a red carpet. It was sweet balm to his spirit until someone—he thought it was Emma Harrington—snorted and guffawed behind him.

Cydney Parrish started toward him, a dazed expression on her face, and walked straight into the table. The bump almost knocked her off her high heels, but the guy in the blue blazer—her husband Gus Noah guessed, by the flash of a gold band on his left hand—caught her by the shoulders and kept her on her feet.

"It's *him*! Oh Gus, it's *him*!" The blond clutched her husband and hyperventilated into his denim shirt. "It's *Noah Patrick*!"

Anyone who hadn't heard her shriek his name the first time did the second. Noah was pretty sure dogs in the next county heard her. A ripple of laughter went through the crowd. Cydney Parrish went stiff as a board, her face buried in her husband's chest.

"Don't tell me," she said in a no-really-*don't* tone of voice. "He's angry. I've embarrassed him. He's not saying anything."

"Well, since you're obviously already taken," Noah said. " 'I want to be the father of your children' seems a little pointless."

Frank and everyone standing nearby laughed. Cydney's husband grinned. She gripped his lapels, drew her shoulders straight, and turned toward Noah, her almond shaped eyes huge in her small face.

"How do you do, Mr. Patrick. My name is Cydney Parrish." She put her right hand out, her fingers and her voice trembling just a little. "Cydney Parrish Munroe. This is my husband Gus."

"Nice to meet you, Cydney Parrish Munroe." Noah clasped her hand, watched the barely there blush on her face deepen to an oh-my-God-he's-touching-me-he's-actually-touching-me shade of hot pink.

Emma Harrington could snort and guffaw till she turned blue and choked. His bashed in, stomped on, and left for dead ego needed this.

"You, too, Gus." Noah tried to take his hand back but Cydney had her fingers clamped around it like a vice. She was a tiny little thing. So petite she made him feel like a six-footer, but she was strong as an ox.

"C'mon, babe." Gus Munroe took hold of his wife's hand and winked at Noah. "Let go before you cut off the circulation."

"Oh! So*rry*!" She snatched her hand back and clasped it, quivering, to her throat. "This is such a huge *thrilll* for me! I love you *sooo* much! I *dooo*! You're my favorite TV actor of *alll* time! I *loove BBT*! I *loove* Sam! You're *sooo* wonderful! *Sooo* talented!"

In books people gushed. In real life, not unless they sprang a leak, but *gush* was the only word Noah could think of for the breathy, be-still-my-heart tumble bubbling out of Cydney Parrish. He hoped Emma Harrington was getting every word of it.

"You were so *gor*-geous in those skimpy little swim trunks. Those are my favorite episodes, the ones on the beach with you and Lindsay. You were *sooo* perfect, *sooo* beautiful together. Jesse and Sam." She sighed and gazed at him starry-eyed. "Fifteen forever and forever in love."

Lindsay. Where was the heck was she? She ought to be in on this. Noah glanced over his shoulder, didn't see her in the crowd clustered around the table, and turned back to Cydney Parrish.

"Are you sure you don't want me to be the father of your children?"

She laughed and flushed to the roots of her hair. Gus Monroe grinned again and cupped his hands around her shoulders.

"You'll forgive my wife. She gets a little starstruck."

"Oh, this is nothing." Cydney waved a hand. "You should've seen me when I realized Lindsay West is Lindsay *Varner*. *The* Lindsay Varner. Now that was—*Lindsay*!" Cydney shrieked again and leaped out of her husband's grasp. "There you are!"

Noah turned and saw Lindsay, stuck in the crowd with her cookie tray, trying to push her way forward. She did not look happy. For the second their eyes met, she looked annoyed. Then she saw Cydney diving at her and her face cleared, her fake smile sliding into place like a mask.

"Why didn't you *tell* me Noah was coming?" Cydney took the cookie tray from Lindsay and shoved it at Emma, who had come out from behind the cash register. "Susan said he was here to be in a play with you, but she didn't say he was going to be here *today*! With a little preparation I could've made a lot bigger fool out of myself."

She was grinning and laughing at herself, pulled Lindsay forward, and planted her beside Noah. He gave her a winsome, sorry-'bout-this smile. She arched an oh-sure-you-are eyebrow but the edges of her phony smile softened just a bit.

"Would it be okay," Cydney asked, "if I take your picture?"

"Fine with me," Noah said, and started to loop his arm around Lindsay.

Started to and stopped. It was habit as much as a desire to touch her. No matter how pissed they were at each other on

BBT—and he had a sudden, clear memory of the two of them being pissed at each other *a lot*—they always smiled, always touched. Always put aside whatever was between them to look as gooey-eyed as Sam and Jesse for the camera.

"Of course." Lindsay smiled, and inched closer to him.

"I *knew* I brought my camera for a reason!" Cydney clapped her hands and scurried around the table. She snatched a black leather bag with a zillion zippered pockets off the floor and grinned at them. "I was a professional photographer in my former life. These will be great pictures if I can stop shaking. Would you like copies?"

"That would be lovely," Lindsay said. "Thank you so much."

"Great!" Cydney pulled a camera out of the bag and started ripping open zippers. "I just need a lens, then I'll be ready."

"If I put my arm around you," Noah asked Lindsay in a low voice, "will you belt me?"

"If you don't," she murmured, "I think Cydney will belt you."

"Then I'm putting my arm around you," Noah said, and did.

"I'm warning you." Lindsay slid her arm around his waist. "If you pull that stupid turn your head and kiss me on the cheek at the last second trick I will deck you."

"No problem, princess. I said I wouldn't heckle you. I meant it."

Noah pulled Lindsay close and felt a wait-a-minute-we've-done-this-before jolt. Made it look good for the camera, yeah, but the warmth of Lindsay's skin, the curve of her hip against him . . . his brain might be dead, but Noah could've sworn his body remembered something.

Cydney took about six shots and thanked them profusely. Then she put her camera away and went back to signing books.

"That was good of you," Gus Munroe said to Noah and Lindsay. "Cydney really is a huge *BBT* fan. She owns all six seasons on DVD."

"Wow." Noah whistled. "I didn't know we were on DVD."

"Don't get too excited." Emma Harrington came up beside him. "*Scooby-Doo* is on DVD."

Noah turned on one foot and scowled at her. Emma smiled and offered him the tray. "Cookie?"

Chapter 20

CYDNEY PARRISH MUNROE and her husband Gus invited Noah and Lindsay to dinner. Cydney wouldn't take no for an answer.

"I owe you," she said to Lindsay, "for turning the lovely book signing you arranged for me into a *BBT* fan convention."

"Now that's funny." Noah laughed. "Like anybody who watched our show would band together like a bunch of Star Trekkers."

"We did," Cydney blurted, then added swiftly, "I mean, *they* did. I still belong to the fan club so I get the newsletters."

She flushed and ducked away to collect her camera, her purse, and her husband. Noah looked at Lindsay.

"*Betwixt and Be Teen* conventions?" he said.

She shrugged. "Takes all kinds."

Noah thought about it and smiled. "It's kind of sweet, isn't it?"

Lindsay frowned. "You're feverish again, aren't you?"

"I meant in a gag-puke sort of way."

"This is your first full day out of the hospital." Lindsay laid a hand on his arm. "Are you sure you're feeling up to an evening out?"

"Whoa," Noah said. "That sign went by fast."

"Sign?" Lindsay blinked. "What sign?"

"Never mind." He meant the sign that said WELCOME TO COOL LITTLE PLATITUDE COUNTRY. "What I'm feeling up to is charming Cydney. If the fans in the clubs are nuts enough to hold conventions, they're nuts enough to fly, drive, or kayak out here to the backwater of nowhere to see the play."

"I'm sure Jolie has already thought of that. But if she hasn't . . ." Lindsay's voice trailed off in a sigh. "Trey is with Uncle Ron. I'll call and see if he can stay with the uncles this evening."

She headed for the back of the store, frowning like she'd just been invited to dine with Hannibal Lecter. Noah watched her, felt a buzz up the back of his neck, and glanced at the glass display case.

Emma Harrington leaned on her elbows next to the cash register, a pair of half-glasses on a gold chain folded against the front of her aquamarine sweater. The fluorescent tubes inside the case shimmered on her streak of white hair. A real stunner, Emma Harrington. Noah had the feeling he was seeing Mrs. Doubtfire as she'd looked as a young woman.

The store was mostly empty of customers. A few lingered by the signing table chatting with Cydney and Gus. Noah walked over to Emma and folded his arms on the edge of the display case.

"I'll take that cookie now, please."

Emma picked one up wrapped in a napkin and gave it to him.

"Oatmeal. My favorite." He took a bite and chewed. "Why am I not surprised that you know that?"

"It was a lucky guess. You're full of surprises, Noah."

"If I'd known about the book signing, I wouldn't have crashed it."

"I didn't mean that. This was the best signing we've ever had. And great PR for the play. Nice job. Congratulations."

Emma Harrington smiled. A genuinely warm smile. Noah would've sworn she didn't like him. He was so surprised he almost choked on his cookie, chewed carefully, and swallowed the last mouthful.

"Too bad," he said, "that Satan's Handmaiden will profit from it."

"I think it's hilarious that you call Jolie that, but don't underestimate her. And do *not* turn your back on her."

"Your mother told me the same thing."

"Have you had tea with Mama yet?"

"This afternoon. Just before I came here."

"Good. Take a cookie for the road." Emma handed him another one. "I've got to close the store and here comes Lindsay."

Noah turned away from the display case a full five seconds before Lindsay came through the doorway from the back. He felt another buzz up his neck and glanced at Emma Harrington.

She smiled at him. "I'm just full of lucky guesses today."

It was all arranged. The uncles would hang on to Trey and Lindsay would drive, following Cydney and Gus Munroe to Columbia, the closest big town, where they knew a great steak house.

After his junk food binge the thought of dead cow made Noah nauseous. He had a salad and grilled shrimp, declined to join Gus in a beer, and drank ice tea. Lindsay had a vegetable plate.

"Are you two vegetarian?" Cydney asked, an eager gleam in the smile she aimed first at Noah, then at Lindsay.

"We two?" Lindsay blinked, startled. "We're not a *two*." She swung her head toward Noah, an *are-we* glint in her eyes.

"Nope. No two over here," he agreed. "Just a one and a one."

"You are *sooo* funny." Cydney laughed delightedly then hunched forward on her elbows. "Tell me, Noah. In episode one hundred and fifty, 'It's my Beach Party and I'll Wipe-Out if I Want To,' why did you change the color of your surfboard? Why did you go from red to blue?"

Noah hadn't a crapping clue. He glanced at Lindsay but she was no help, just gave him a gee-I'd-love-to-know lift of one eyebrow.

" 'Cause I broke the red one," he ad-libbed. "Caught a twenty foot wave the wrong way and the sucker cracked right down the middle."

"See? I knew it was that simple." Cydney knuckled Gus in the arm. "There's this discussion on the *BBT* message boards. Some people think you went from red to blue as a tribute to Lindsay. A secret yet open declaration of love. The lunatic fringe in the club is absolutely convinced you two had this huge, giant thing for each other going on in real life."

Lindsay burst out laughing. Noah laughed with her, though he didn't think it was funny. He thought Cydney had said what his body remembered but his brain couldn't. Until the head rush hit him. Five Cherry Cokes, two cups of hot tea strong enough to strip varnish off a table, his third glass of ice tea sitting next to his plate. Too much caffeine. That's all it was.

"Fooled you." Noah grinned at Cydney, then Lindsay. "Who was it, princess? The TV critic who said that together we couldn't act our way out of a paper sack?"

He and Lindsay and Gus laughed. Cydney looked disappointed, then drew a small green photo album out of her purse.

"Emma says you have a fifteen-year-old son." She waved the album at Lindsay. "Ours is two and a half. Want to see?"

"Absolutely. I just happen to have a few pictures of Trey." She smiled and took her wallet out of her purse. "Ladies' room?"

"Great idea. Then we can *ooh* and *ahh* all we want."

Noah rose and held Lindsay's chair. Gus did the same for Cydney. He watched his wife walk away, then grinned at Noah.

"Make no mistake." Gus cocked his thumb at Cydney's back. "She's one of the chief lunatics on the fringe of the *BBT* fan club."

Noah laughed. "I picked up on that."

"You're very kind to come out this evening." Gus sat down. "And very patient to put up with Cydney's gushing and grilling."

"She's a lot of fun. I'm enjoying myself," Noah said, surprised to realize that he meant it. "Lindsay told me on the way here that you're Angus Munroe the mystery writer. I've read your books. They're good."

"Thanks." Gus smiled. "I appreciate it."

He wrote about a seedy, down on his luck private detective named Max Stone. Very popular among seedy, down on their luck drunks.

"If I'd known I'd have bought your latest and had you sign it."

"Don't give it a thought. I enjoy watching Cydney shine."

Noah liked Gus Munroe. Angus Munroe was a big damn deal. A lot bigger deal than Noah Patrick had ever been, yet Gus seemed perfectly content to sit back and let Cydney be the star, the center of attention. Noah remembered and squirmed at all the times he'd pushed Lindsay away from a camera or beat her to a microphone. One by one he kept finding all kinds of reasons why she'd punched him.

Lindsay, Cydney, and Gus had chocolate cake covered in hot fudge sauce with their coffee. Noah a dish of sherbet and water. Lots of water to flush the caffeine out of his system.

When the check came Gus flipped out his American Express gold card. It bothered Noah, made him think about the millions he'd made and pissed away on tequila and Christ knew what. No wonder he was stuck in Missouri wearing underwear Vivienne Varner had paid for.

He tried to be gracious, thanked Gus for a great evening and shook his hand. In the parking lot he let Cydney kiss him on the cheek.

"I'm putting the word out on the *BBT* message boards that you and Lindsay are back together." She beamed a where-you-belong smile at the two of them. "I hope the Belle Coeur theater has lots of seats."

"Oh it does," Lindsay said quickly. "Lots and lots." She dug in her purse, came up with a business card and gave it to Cydney. "Here's the theater's Web site address and the toll-free ticket line."

"Great! Opening night is May twenty-fourth, right?"

"Yes. Saturday night. That's Memorial Day weekend. Belle Coeur puts on quite a show. Fireworks displays and the Riverfront opens. Wonderful craft shops there and the steamboats will be running."

"Oooh. Shopping." Cydney grinned at Gus. "Guess where we're going to be on Memorial Day weekend?"

"I never doubted it." Gus laughed, draped an arm around her shoulders, and pulled her close.

Noah wanted to put his fist through something. Or his head.

His beach house looked like it belonged in Bosnia, not Malibu, when the sheriff's department came to evict him. The walls full of holes, carpet ripped away from the baseboards, the sink in one of the bathrooms broken on the floor. He had no idea how he'd torn a sink out of the wall, but he knew he'd done it in a drunken rage. A rage that always followed a sudden, crushing depression like this one.

Lindsay and Cydney chatted a bit more, then said good night. Noah got into the Civic and belted himself in. Lindsay started the engine and looked at him slouched beside her, the beautiful curve of her face outlined in the glow of the dash lights. He turned his head away.

"Noah?" Lindsay said. "Are you all right?"

The pissy little "Fine" he wanted to grit through his teeth wouldn't fool her. She wasn't an idiot. He was the idiot.

"No. I'm not all right."

"Are you sick?" She put her foot on the brake, the Civic halfway out of its parking spot. "Do you need a doctor?"

"No, Lindsay. I don't need a doctor. I need you to just drive, okay?"

"If you're sick, feeling feverish, the hospital is just a block—"

"You're not gonna back off, are you?" Noah pushed up in the seat and scowled at her. "You're gonna keep at me till I tell you."

"I'm trying to help you," she snapped. "Tell me what?"

"If you must know, I had Ron buy me a boatload of junk food today. He sent Trey up with it. We ate ourselves sick. If I don't get an Alka-Seltzer pretty damn quick I'm gonna be buying new carpet for your car."

Lindsay's smile gleamed in the half-dark. "Will Tums work?"

Thank Jesus she believed the lie. "And maybe some gum, too."

Lindsay found a Quik-Trip, bought him a roll of Tums and a pack of Wrigley's Peppermint. Noah put his seat back and shut his eyes. He chewed Tums he didn't need, folded two sticks of gum into his mouth. Lindsay left him alone till she turned the Civic onto Main Street.

"Where's your car?" she asked, stopping in front of The Bookshelf.

"In front of the hardware store. I walked over with Ezra."

"Oh." She reached for the gearshift. "I'll drive you."

"No!" Noah jumped out of the Civic, leaned inside to grab his sweater off the back of the passenger seat, and smiled at Lindsay's puzzled expression. "I'm getting a headache. The air will do me good. Thanks for driving. G'night."

He tied the sweater over his shoulders by the arms and struck off down the sidewalk. He stopped when he heard a car door slam.

"Noah," Lindsay called to him. "You're going the wrong way."

He turned around and saw her standing in the street next to her car. A couple feet past the front bumper stood a black iron lamppost with a white glass globe. The light it cast glinted on the Civic's metallic blue hood and hung a misty halo around her golden head.

"I got turned around. Things look different in the dark."

"You don't have a headache, do you?" Lindsay drew her powder blue cardigan around her, stepped up on the sidewalk, and tipped her head at him. "I'll bet there's nothing wrong with your stomach, either."

No, but there was plenty wrong with the rest of him. Noah sighed.

"Just leave it, princess. Okay? I'll be fine."

"When you get to the corner, turn left."

"Will do. G'night, Lindsay."

She folded her arms. "Good night, Noah."

He struck off again, this time going the right way. He'd glimpsed the time on the Civic's dash clock. Nine-oh-seven and Main Street looked like a ghost town. No traffic, no cars parked along the scrubbed-clean curbs. All the stores were closed, their awnings rolled up.

He stopped for a second in front of the Belle Coeur Café. A whiskey barrel of tiny flowers sat by the door, their fragrance cloying on the cool night air. Noah almost gagged. He looked through the window at booths and a lunch counter, shiny stools on tall chrome poles, glanced behind him at the long line of neatly spaced lampposts, neatly pruned trees and saw Lindsay getting into her car.

Thank Jesus. He didn't know how much longer he could hold it together. Noah wheeled around the corner onto another picture-perfect block of storefronts and spotless sidewalks. *Mayberry R.F.D.* What the hell made him think he could function here, survive here?

He hurried on, scraping his nails through his hair, popping the gum in his mouth. It was tasteless. He spat it out like a bullet into the gutter and walked faster. Didn't help. Neither did deep breaths.

Okay. This was not good. He stopped in the middle of the sidewalk, his hands shaking. He had tears in his eyes, stuck to his lashes, blurring his vision, a huge lump of them like a fist in his throat.

He swept his sleeve across his eyes and saw the Corvette parked a half a block away. Right where he'd left it in front of McGruff's Hardware, shimmering like a Day-Glo banana under a black iron lamppost.

What the hell? Why not? It worked for Lindsay.

Noah broke into a run. The Horse Piss Mobile was headed for the body shop, anyway, bright and early Monday morning. He raced up to the Corvette, his right fist drawn back to punch out the passenger window. His knuckles were no more than an inch from the glass when he caught a glimpse of his reflection in the side mirror.

The face he saw wasn't his. It was the messed-up, scared shitless kid he'd once been, raging through his house breaking things because his life was spiraling out of control and he didn't know how to stop it. If he put his hand through this window he'd be that sorry-ass, spoiled rotten little dick again. He'd sooner be dead.

Noah flung his hands out, spread them on the roof of the Corvette. He could hardly breathe his throat was so parched from running, so raw with tears. His head roared, his heart thundered. He was juiced on adrenaline, his muscles gorged with it, ready to rip a sink out of the wall.

Or roll this ugly, here-little-boy-come-to-Gramma carrot on a string on its side in the middle of the street. He could do it. He could feel it. He'd never been sober in the rage before. It was freaky, scary, knowing he could tear the sunroof off the Corvette with his bare hands.

He wouldn't. But he had to get rid of the adrenaline that had been dripping into his system all week like the IV in the hospital. That hadn't helped, landing flat on his ass with pneumonia. Drip. The drugs and the inhaler. Drop. Jolie and the contract. Drip. Lindsay's keep-away attitude. Drop. Ezra and Lucille. Drip.

Christ. No wonder he felt like the Incredible Hulk, about to burst out of his clothes and chew through the Corvette.

He settled for kicking the right front tire. Once. Twice. The third time so hard he popped off the wheel cover. Noah stood back a step, watching it spin on its rim on the sidewalk, flung his hands on the roof of the car again, and hung his head between his arms.

"You have panic attacks, too," Lindsay said quietly.

Noah raised his head. She stood about ten feet away from him, a blurry, smeary shape through the tears in his eyes.

"This isn't a panic attack. It's a blind-eyed fucking rage." Noah dragged his sleeve across his eyes. "Go away, princess. I hurt people when I'm like this. I don't want to hurt you."

He'd wiped the tears on his shirt so he could see her face half-lit by the lamppost. Her drawn together eyebrows, the sympathetic moue her mouth made as she took a step toward him. Noah's breath hitched.

"I mean it, Lindsay. Get the hell out of here."

She ignored him, came up beside him and laid her hand on his cheek. "I'm so sorry for everything that's happened to you."

"Don't waste your sympathy. I did it to myself."

"We all do. You're no different. You're a good man, Noah."

"Oh yeah. I'm great." He gave a snort of laughter, rolled away from her and leaned against the Corvette's right front fender, spread his feet apart on the curb. "And now I'm getting maudlin." Noah sighed, his throat aching. "I wish you'd go away."

"You didn't go away when I had a panic attack."

"Only because I was too sick to crawl out of the room."

"You gave me a paper bag." Lindsay stepped off the curb

and in between his legs. Noah's heart jumped when she slipped her arms around his waist and laid her head on his shoulder. "I'm here, Noah. You can hold on to me."

He crushed her against him, buried his face in the curve of her neck. How did she know? How many times he'd thought when this shit got a grip on him, that if he just had somebody to hold on to he'd be okay? Noah breathed Lindsay's perfume, almost tasted it on his tongue. He couldn't remember the last time anyone but his mother had held him, just held him for the sake of comfort and human contact.

The lump in his throat exploded. He clung to Lindsay and wept. She held him and rocked him from side to side, rubbing circles between his shoulder blades with her hands. Every rotten thing he'd done in his life spilled out of him onto Lindsay's shoulder. Everything he'd had and lost, the people he'd hurt, all the stupid shit he'd done to himself.

He cried till he couldn't cry anymore, then raised his head and tipped it back to look at the sky. His lashes were so wet the stars looked like fuzzy little cotton balls. Till he blinked and they leaped into focus, huge, giant, brilliant white against the black sky.

"I should've beaten the hell out of the Corvette." He drew a shaky breath and yanked the sweater off his neck, scrubbed the tears off his face, and tossed it on the hood of the car. "That's what I meant to do."

"Why?" Lindsay frowned. "Did something happen at dinner?"

"Oh no." He touched a fingertip to the wet spot he'd left on her shoulder. "I just thought if you happened to follow me I'd burst into tears and impress the hell out of you with my male sensitivity."

"The body does what it needs to take care of itself, Noah." Lindsay stepped out from between his legs. He moved over and she hiked herself up on the fender beside him. "Sometimes whether we like it or not."

"Are you talking about my crying jag or your panic attacks?"

She smiled at him sideways, ruefully. "Both."

"Maybe we can find a shrink who'll give us a two-for-one discount."

Lindsay laughed and pushed her shoulder against his, laid her left palm on the back of his right hand and tucked her fingers through his.

"We're a fine pair, aren't we, Patrick?"

Noah pushed back and smiled. "I thought we weren't a *we*."

"The body is very wise, but most of the time we ignore it," Lindsay said. *Yeah,* Noah thought, *like you just ignored what I said.* "We tell it to shut up and do what we want." She let go of his fingers, looped her arm through his, and leaned against him. "We'd all be healthier, mentally as well as physically, if we'd just learn to listen to our bodies."

Noah could hear his, loud and clear. The kick in his pulse at the warm, soft press of Lindsay's body against his, the stir of an erection.

"You sound like your Aunt Dovey," he said to her.

Ramp it down, he told his libido. *We are not jumping Lindsay's bones.* He tipped his head up again to look at the stars. He couldn't get over how big they looked out here. The only stars he'd paid any attention to in L.A. were the wrong kind, the ones with two legs.

"Why did you follow me?"

Lindsay leaned away from him, turned her head toward him.

"Why didn't you beat the hell out of the Corvette?" she asked, looking him right in the eye as she ignored his question.

"I decided I've broken enough things in my life."

"Good choice." Lindsay put a barely there kiss on his mouth. Noah made a face. "That wasn't a kiss."

She laughed, slid off the car and got between his knees again, laid her hands on his shoulders, and kneaded his drawn-tight muscles. Noah put his hands on her waist, holding her a safe distance away from the throb behind the zipper of his jeans.

"You could use a massage," Lindsay said.

"I could use a lobotomy." Noah rolled his head, groaning

as his neck muscles loosened. "And a statement signed in blood that you'll never tell anyone you saw me like this."

"I wouldn't call this a rage, Noah." Lindsay's hands stilled on his shoulders. "I think you're depressed."

"That's what the body does with anger you don't vent. It buries it and makes depression out of it. That's what the shrinks in rehab said—I don't express my anger appropriately. I blow stuff off till I explode. Then I do things like punch directors and get myself fired."

"What did the psychiatrists do to help you? To treat this?"

"Not much, since I was indigent. Meditation, behavior modification. When I had a few bucks I tried biofeedback and karate to learn some self-discipline. Nothing worked for long. Primarily because I was drinking like a fish. That only made it worse."

"But you're sober now." Noah looked for the *"Aren't you?"* he used to hear from his parents, but didn't see it in Lindsay's eyes. "What happened to bring this on?"

She was persistent. Evasive, but persistent. What would he sound like if he reeled off the reasons? Waa-haa-haa. No thanks. He'd already cried like a baby. Noah shrugged. "Don't know."

"Tell me this." Lindsay rubbed his shoulders again, digging a little, coaxing him with her touch. "How long have you been alone?"

Another lump of tears swelled and started his throat aching.

"Some days it seems like every second of my life."

Lindsay wrapped him in another hug. Noah kept his hands on her waist, kept her away from the jackhammer pulse in his groin. She wasn't trying to inflame him. She was just being kind, trying to comfort him. God, wasn't this depressing? Good thing he already felt like jumping off a bridge. All he wanted was to be inside her, to feel her gentle, soothing spirit fill the cracks in his soul, and she couldn't care less.

He'd had plenty of bed partners but never a lover, not a single woman who gave a genuine damn about him as a fellow member of the human race. Until now, until Lindsay, and she had zero interest in his body, such as it was these days. Served him right.

"You know what we're doing here, don't you?" he asked Lindsay.

"Let me think." She drew away, her arms in a loose loop around his neck. "Practicing psychiatry without license?"

Noah laughed. "Maybe we could get on *Oprah* with this."

"Or *Dr. Phil*," Lindsay said. They both laughed, then Lindsay smiled. "Would you like to come to Sunday dinner tomorrow?"

"I'd love to come." Noah said. *Inside you,* he thought, *first chance I get.* "But I'll pass, thanks. I made this bed. Time I learn to sleep in it."

"You don't have to learn tomorrow, do you?"

"Tomorrow's as good a day as any."

Lindsay lowered her arms and took a step away from him. "This isn't a pity invitation, if that's what you're thinking."

"I wasn't. Look, princess. I didn't intend to end the day sobbing all over you. I came by the store to talk to you about Vivienne."

"Oh?" Lindsay took another step back. "You're trying to make me cry now, is that it?"

"This came to me while I was having tea with your Aunt Dovey. It sounds nuts, but if you think about the way Vivienne wrote the contracts—"

Tires squealed, a long, whoa-hoss screech of rubber on pavement. Noah pushed off the Corvette and turned toward the sound half a second before a small red convertible with the top down came roaring around the corner from Main Street. The front end jerked and the car leapt forward, the transmission squealing as the driver shoved it out of first and into second with hardly a pause to clutch between gears.

The car came ripping up the street going way too fast for the stop sign at the far end of the block. Close to fifty, Noah figured, as it flew by with Trey in the passenger seat and Meggie the carhop behind the wheel. They were both laughing, their heads thrown back—from the G-force, Noah figured—totally absorbed in each other and the high old time they were having. Neither one of them saw him nor Lindsay standing on the sidewalk in front of McGruff's Hardware until the little red rocket—a Mazda Miata, Noah thought—shot past. He thought he saw Trey's head turn toward the Corvette then, and his eyes fly open.

"That's my son!" Lindsay whirled after the speeding red bullet.

Noah swung around with her, hoping to God Meggie had brains enough if she'd seen them not to slam on the brakes. She did. The Miata slowed, the transmission squealing as she downshifted. The red convertible hovered for a second at the stop sign, the reverse lights flashing on, then off before it zipped around the corner in a hard right turn.

"Give me your keys." Lindsay spun toward him, her hand out, her face pale in the glow of the lamppost. "I'm going after them."

"I'm pretty sure Trey saw us." Noah took his time reaching into his pocket. "He's your kid and you can do what you want, but I'd give 'em a minute to go around the block and cook up a story."

"Look at that intersection." Lindsay pointed at the storefronts straight across the street from the stop sign. "If Meggie hadn't gotten that car stopped they could have gone right through those windows."

"Could have, yeah, but they didn't." Noah took Lindsay by the arms. He wasn't surprised that she was trembling. Her face had gone a shade whiter. "That means you still got a shot at him."

"This isn't funny," she snapped. "What if they don't come back?"

"Where are they gonna go? Trey knows he's busted. He's a good kid, Lindsay." *A smart-ass,* Noah thought, *but basically a good kid.* "Give him a chance to prove it to you."

She bit her lip and looked away. "All right." She bent her wrist to look at her watch. "I'll give them three minutes."

The Miata was back in two, purring sedately around the corner, and easing to a stop behind the Corvette. Trey and Meggie got out and shut the doors. She was still in her carhop uniform, khaki shorts and green T-shirt. Trey had on jeans and a nylon St. Louis Rams football jersey. They came around the car, stepped up on the curb, and linked hands.

Lindsay didn't like that. She didn't frown but her eyes narrowed.

Noah leaned back against the Corvette, crossed his arms and his ankles, and turned his head away. He was dying to watch, but Trey had enough trouble facing the minefield between his mother and Meggie. He didn't need an audience.

"Careful, princess," Noah murmured under his breath. "If your baby boy is old enough to have a girlfriend, he's way past being told to get out of the street."

Chapter 21

"WHERE'S UNCLE RON?" Lindsay asked, amazed that she sounded so calm with the image of Trey and Meggie crashing through the plate glass window of Peterson's Insurance Agency reeling through her brain.

"He's at Burger Chef with Donnie and Lonnie," Trey said, keeping a wary eye on her and his fingers solidly linked with Meggie's. "We got hungry so we came into town for a burger."

"So how is it that you're with Meggie?"

"Ron said it was okay if she showed me her mom's new car."

No wonder he hadn't howled about being baby-sat. He'd known he stood a much better chance of conning his uncles into bringing him into town when Meggie got off work than he'd ever have talking her into it.

"Meggie?" Lindsay tucked her hands in her folded arms to keep from grabbing her cute little ponytail and shaking her silly. "Did your mother say it was okay for you to hot-rod her new car through town?"

"I'm sorry, Mrs. West. I hit the gas too hard." *Oh sure,* Lindsay thought. *I must look as stupid as Meggie thinks I am if she expects me to believe that.* "If you feel like you need to tell my mom I understand."

"That's good, because I *am* going to tell her."

"It was an accident, Ma. Meggie didn't mean to hit the gas." Trey notched his chin up in defiance, defending Meggie, tightening his grip on her hand. "Can't you give anybody a break?"

I'll give you a break—right in the arm. Lindsay could hear the words in her head in Vivienne's voice. She was so angry, so frightened by what could have happened she could hardly think.

"By the grace of God it wasn't an accident, but it *could* have been! That's not a toy!" Lindsay flung a shaky hand at Pat Hannity's jazzy red sports car. "That's a thousand pounds of metal wrapped around an engine! If you can't control it you've got no business driving it!"

The shrill in her voice echoed in the empty street. A wide-eyed Meggie scuttled back a step, dragging Trey with her. He blinked at Lindsay, then he grinned. *My son is an idiot,* she thought. *I'm screaming at him like a banshee and he's grinning.*

So was Noah. Lindsay could just see him from the corner of her eye. He'd given up his I'm-not-here slouch against the Corvette, lowered the hand he'd cupped over his mouth and grinned at her. He was an idiot, too. They were both idiots.

"You said we had nothing to worry about." Meggie spun toward Trey on one tiny little foot. "You said your mom doesn't yell at people."

"She doesn't," Trey said to her, still grinning. "But isn't it cool?"

"Cool!" Meggie and Lindsay both screeched at him, then Meggie burst into tears. Lindsay bit her lip. "Oh Meggie, honey." She went to her and put an arm around her. "I'm sorry."

"It's okay. You just startled me." Meggie turned into Lindsay's shoulder and wailed, *"But my mom is gonna kill me!"*

"Ma. C'mon." Trey pleaded over Meggie's head. "Do you have to tell Mrs. Hannity?"

"Yes, I do. Meggie needs to learn how to drive a sports car without endangering herself and her passengers."

Meggie wailed again. Lindsay patted her and sighed. Her right shoulder was already wet; now her left one would be, too. She glanced at Noah, leaning against the Corvette with his arms folded smiling at her. Not a single trace of tears showed on his face, damn him. Her eyes still felt like burned-out sockets from the crying jag she'd had earlier.

Meggie was sobbing now and Trey was scowling and looking sullen. Lindsay guessed a pack of their friends were waiting for them at Burger Chef. What was the point in whizzing around in a hot car if there was no one to see you and envy you?

"Meggie," Lindsay said, loud enough to override her tears. "Can I trust you to drive home without any more reckless foolishness?"

The girl stopped crying, raised her red eyes and red nose. "Y-yes."

"And tell your mother about this before I call her tomorrow?"

"Y-y-yes," Meggie stammered on the verge of another wail.

She shot Trey a teary, help-me look. He wheeled away from her on one foot, powerless, impotent, and took a furious swipe at his hair.

It was only three blocks to Burger Chef. If she didn't let Trey go with Meggie she'd be just like Vivienne, clamping a choke chain around his neck, keeping him at heel, penned and caged till he found a way to break free and did something really stupid and dangerous. The thought scared Lindsay half to death; Meggie scared her the rest of the way. She was a nice girl—Lindsay knew Pat Hannity too well to doubt it—and yet she was Chaos. The unknown, the uncontrollable. Lindsay's worst nightmare in her trim little shorts.

"How about Trey?" she asked Meggie. "Can I trust you to drive him back to Burger Chef without putting him through the windshield?"

Trey spun around, so surprised he almost fell over. Meggie shot him a dazzling smile, then turned soberly back to Lindsay.

"Yes, Mrs. West. I'll drive slowly and carefully. I promise."

"All right. You can go say good night to your friends. I'm sure they're waiting for you." Lindsay eyed Meggie first, then Trey. They both ducked her gaze. Yep. Just as she'd thought. "I'll be there shortly to pick you up, Trey. And Meggie. I will call your mother tomorrow."

"Yes, Mrs. West. I'll tell her." Meggie caught Trey's hand and gave him a hurry-up-before-she-changes-her-mind tug toward the car.

"We'll go straight back, Ma," he said over his shoulder. "Honest."

Lindsay watched them fasten their seat belts. The little red sports car crept up the street like Aunt Dovey was at the wheel. At the sign Meggie made a full stop, put on the blinker, and made a putt-putt right turn that would take them back to Burger Chef.

"Take a bow, princess." Noah applauded. "Well done."

"That was *not* well done! I yelled at my son in front of Meggie! I yelled at her, too! Another woman's child!" Lindsay turned on Noah, still angry and shaking. "That's the second time today I've yelled at Trey! Stood in his face and shrieked at him like a fishwife!"

"Now you're yelling at me." Noah grinned. "But you're not having a panic attack. You aren't even thinking about having one, are you?"

"*No!* I'm *not*! But I—" Lindsay blinked, raised a hand to her throat and drew a deep, unrestricted breath. No hitch in her chest, no clamp on her windpipe. "I can breathe. And I don't want to hit anything."

"Ta-da!" Noah swept his arms apart. "Success."

"But I wanted to." Lindsay closed her eyes and rubbed the bridge of her nose where the week-old headache pounded. "I wanted to smack Trey and shake Meggie till her teeth rattled."

"Yeah, but you didn't. Give yourself points for that."

She heard Noah push off the Corvette, the creak of its springs and the scrape of his shoes on the sidewalk. Lindsay rubbed her forehead, opened her eyes, and saw him standing in front of her. Not close enough to infringe on her space, but near enough to make her heart skip.

"The fact that I wanted to is what scares me, Noah."

"Is that why you keep a lid on all your feelings? You're afraid you'll turn into some monster mommy and pop Trey when he scares the crap out of you and then gives you lip about it? That's what he did—copped an attitude. Shit. I wanted to smack him and he's not my kid."

"That's what Vivienne would've done." And did, more than once, but Lindsay didn't say it. "That's why those impulses when I get them scare me to death."

"Oh princess." Noah laughed, cupped her elbows, and let his hands slide down her arms. Shivers trailed behind his fingers, settled in her wrists, and made her pulse jump as he caught her hands and held them. "You couldn't be any less like Vivienne. Now Jolie." He raised his eyebrows. "There's no doubting the gene pool that spawned her, but you." He shook his head. "I think Vivienne found you in the cabbage patch."

"She didn't. Trust me. I'm her daughter. Sometimes I can feel her inside me, clawing to get out. I have awful thoughts, terrible thoughts." *And I lie,* Lindsay added to herself. *I lied to you.* "If I keep a lid on myself, that's why. One Vivienne in the world is one Vivienne too many."

"So you have panic attacks instead. That doesn't seem very bright."

"I haven't had a panic attack since Mark died, but in the last week I've had four. My life was so neatly arranged, so perfectly in order." Lindsay built a row of air blocks with her hands in the space between her and Noah. "Now it's all gone to hell and it's all because of Vivienne."

"I can help you with Vivienne," Noah said. "If you're interested."

The gleam in his eyes said he could help her with a lot more. Like the slow burn that was smoldering inside her and had been since she'd put her arms around him to comfort him. It was Chaos, that gleam, and oh it was tempting. So was Noah, but he always had been. Thank God she wasn't an eighteen-year-old idiot anymore. Thank God she could control herself.

"So long as you know," Lindsay said. "I draw the line at murder."

"We're aren't going to kill Vivienne. We're going to beat her at her own game."

"Scheming, lying, cheating, and manipulating? I could get up for that, so long as we don't break any laws. How do we do it?"

"I should probably read your contract first, make sure I know what I'm talking about."

Just because she couldn't see tears in his eyes didn't mean Noah was okay. Her panic attacks were a hangnail compared to the despair he called rage. She'd never seen a grown man cry before, not like Noah had, clinging to her and shaking. She was still reeling from it—that and nearly seeing Trey put through a plate glass window—yet she felt calm inside and at least semi in control.

"My contract is at home," Lindsay said. "If you want to read it, you'll have to come to dinner tomorrow."

"That's good, princess." Noah pointed a finger at her. "You're thinking down the right back alley."

"The right back alley? What on earth—" Lindsay's breath caught. "*Blackmail*? Do you mean we're going to *blackmail* Vivienne?"

"If the Good Lord is willing and the creek don't rise." Noah grinned at her. "I heard Donnie say that the other day."

"Noah," Lindsay said firmly. "Blackmail isn't legal."

"Then call it coercion."

"I don't think that's legal, either."

"Christ, princess. Do you want Vivienne off your back or not?"

"Yes, I want her off my back, but I will *not* stoop to her level."

"Vivienne didn't stoop to anything. She just dangled the right carrot to make you and me and Jolie do what she wanted, which was sign the contracts. If yours says the same thing mine does and Jolie's does, all we're going to do is hang her with her own agreement."

"But how—" Lindsay started, then held up her hand. "Never mind. If what you're saying is possible, even remotely feasible, then this can't wait till tomorrow." She pulled her keys out of her pocket and pushed past Noah toward the Corvette. "Follow me home."

"I've been waiting my whole life to hear you say that."

It wasn't exactly what he'd said to her at her birthday party. When she'd slow danced him into a dark corner of the ballroom Vivienne had rented at the Roosevelt Hotel and planted a wet-mouthed kiss on him. He'd said, "I've been waiting six years for you to do that," but it was close enough to give Lindsay a rush of déjà vu. And an *uh-oh* shiver up the back of her neck as she turned around and looked at Noah.

"Sorry, princess." He winced at her. "Old habit."

"You're forgiven," Lindsay said. *Whew,* she thought. "Now get over here and take me to get my car."

Noah tamped the wheel cover on the Corvette's right front tire, drove her to The Bookshelf to pick up the Civic, then followed her to Burger Chef. Meggie and the little red death bomb were nowhere in sight. Trey leaned against Uncle Ron's Explorer. She waved to her uncles sitting inside the truck sipping milkshakes.

Pyewacket sprang out of the driver's side window and got into the Civic with Trey. He slithered between the seats, hopped into the back window, and curled himself in a ball to watch behind the car. Trey glanced in the side mirror as Lindsay pulled out onto Spring Street.

"Why is Noah behind us? He can't find the barn from here?"

"He's coming home with us. He and I need to talk about the play."

"So you're not gonna kill me till tomorrow."

"No. Tomorrow I'm going to teach you to drive safely and responsibly." Lindsay glanced sideways at his thunderstruck expression. "Once you've learned, if I ever see or hear of you driving the way Meggie drove tonight, then I *will* kill you."

"Thanks, Ma!" Trey launched himself over the console and hooked an awkward hug around her neck.

Lindsay remembered when he was small, how he'd come up beside her reading chair, loop his arms around her, and press a kiss to her cheek. She blinked away tears and pushed him back in his seat.

"That's rule number one," she said firmly. "Don't mug the driver."

Trey laughed and bounced around to fasten his seat belt. "How about the Corvette? Can Noah teach me to drive it?"

Lindsay's gaze lifted to the rearview mirror. Between Pyewacket's ears she saw the Horse Piss Mobile stop behind the Civic at the intersection of Spring Street and 152. Letting Noah teach Trey to drive the Corvette wasn't keeping him an outsider. She wasn't sure when that plan had gone by the wayside. Somewhere between watching Noah throw a hedge apple and his confession that he'd lied about the car keys.

"I suppose." Lindsay made a left onto 152, checked the mirror, and made sure the Corvette was following. "But I say when and where."

"Sweet," Trey said and rubbed his hands together.

The gleeful look on his face and the flash she had in her mirror of Noah behind the wheel of the Corvette made Lindsay's stomach drop. *This time last week,* she thought, as she steered the Civic through the short jog 152 made onto Ridge Road. *Only seven days ago I was in charge of my life and my child. How did I lose control so fast?*

The motion sensitive light mounted on the eaves blinked on when she wheeled the Civic around the corner of the house and pushed the door opener clipped to her visor. Trey jumped out of his seat before the car rolled to a stop in the garage. Pyewacket shot out of the car behind him and through the cat door into the house.

Lindsay switched off the engine, got out of the Civic, and watched Trey dance excitedly from foot to foot while Noah parked the Corvette in the drive and swung out from behind the wheel.

"Dude! Guess what?" He caught the edge of Noah's door and pushed it wide open. "Ma said you can teach me to drive the Corvette!"

Noah stretched to his feet and shot Lindsay a what's-up-with-this look. She stood beside the Civic, the headache between her eyes pulsing in the glare of the bright light on the garage door opener.

"If you can't beat 'em," she said, "might as well join 'em."

"You're the boss." He shrugged, then said to Trey, "Cool, slick."

"It's beyond cool!" Trey flung his arms around Noah's neck, then wheeled into the garage. Lindsay had just a glimpse of Noah's startled expression before Trey plowed into her. "You're the absolute best, Ma!"

He smacked a kiss on her cheek that left her ears ringing and dove into the house. Noah shut the driver's door on the Corvette and scowled.

"This car has got to go," he said. "Your son told me this afternoon that this hunk of ugly yellow plastic and fiberglass is his dream car. 'That's it, right there,' he said. 'That's my dream car.' "

"You said Vivienne knew the right carrot to dangle." Lindsay sighed and swung her purse out of the car. "Come on in. I'll get my contract."

Chaos, she'd always thought, was like a vampire. It couldn't come in unless you invited it, but here she was, through no fault of her own, neck deep in Chaos. So why the heck not invite Noah Patrick, the Crown Prince of Chaos, into her kitchen?

But that's as far as he'd go. "I'm fine here," he said when she suggested he wait in the living room. Lindsay expected he'd sit down at the table while she fetched the contract but he was still leaning against the counter next to the fridge when she came back.

"Please. Sit down." She laid the contract on the table and pulled out one of the Windsor back chairs. "Can I get you a glass of milk?"

"I wouldn't mind a glass of water. Can I take this outside?" Noah picked up the contract and nodded at the hallway that led to Trey's bedroom. "I don't think you-know-who should hear us discuss this."

"Good point." Lindsay crossed the family room and flipped on the outside lights, unlatched and opened the doors. "I'll be out in a minute."

"Don't rush." Noah stepped past her onto the covered deck. "It'll take me a few minutes to read this."

Lindsay shut the French doors, looked through them, and watched Noah sit down with her contract on the chaise she'd beaten the crap out of that morning. Did he seem uncomfortable in her house or was it her imagination? She drew a breath and smelled the candles she'd burned earlier. Was he allergic? Vampires hated garlic. Did Chaos hate vanilla?

Did she sound like an idiot? Lindsay made a face at her reflection in the glass and went into the kitchen. She took off her sweater and hung it on a chair. She didn't have any lemons, so she sliced a lime and put the wedges in a small bowl. She was filling Grandmother Fairchild's cut glass pitcher with ice when Trey came into the kitchen in the navy sweat pants and white T-shirt he slept in.

Shaving cream smeared his left earlobe. He shaved at least three times a day in hopes it would help his beard grow. His hair was stuck to the back of his neck from one of his thirty-second showers. Lindsay ruffled his hair, on top where it was already half-dry, lifting the wheat blond strands away from the small, round patch of black hair that grew underneath near his crown. It was a birthmark, Aunt Dovey thought, like the white streak in Emma's hair, only in reverse.

"Don't forget to dry your hair before you go to bed," Lindsay said.

"Right, Ma." Trey ducked away from her hand, plucked a lime wedge from the bowl, and bit it between his teeth. "Guess I need to brush more often, huh?"

Lindsay's heart clutched. If Meggie hadn't stopped the car in time Trey might not be here, standing next to her acting goofy. She pushed the image of shattered glass out of her head and laughed, a sob catching in her throat. Trey spat out the lime and tossed it in the sink.

"Where's Noah?"

"Out on the deck reading."

"Ma, listen." Trey followed her as she shut the freezer and carried the pitcher from the fridge to the sink. "I saw Noah this afternoon when I was with Uncle Ron. He's having a tough time learning his lines."

"He is?" Lindsay turned on the faucet and glanced at Trey, leaning on his elbows on the edge of the white porcelain sink beside her. "Why?"

"Booze kills a lot of brain cells."

"Who told you that?"

"Noah. I think it would be easier if you helped him. You know, if you guys sort of learned your lines together."

"Oh, do you?" Lindsay raised an eyebrow at Trey. *And why does it matter to you,* she wondered, *whether or not Noah learns his lines?*

"That's what rehearsing is, isn't it? Learning your lines and stuff?"

"Yes, that's what it is." Lindsay turned off the water and lifted the pitcher out of the sink onto the tray where she'd already put glasses and the bowl of lime wedges. "I'll ask Noah if he needs a hand."

"Cool." Trey grinned. "Let me get that for you."

He lifted the tray and headed for the deck. Lindsay followed him, batting at the moths bumping against the coach lights mounted on the brick wall of the house as she stepped outside. Spears of light jeweled through the faceted globes and shot stabs of pain through her head.

"I'm hitting the sack." Trey slid the tray onto the table next to Noah. "Ma's gonna teach me to drive safely and responsibly tomorrow."

"Great." Noah laid the contract facedown on the cushion Lindsay had split with the broom. "Maybe she'll teach me, too." Trey laughed and Noah held his hand out palm up. "Later slick."

" 'Night Noah." Trey gave him a hand slap, turned toward Lindsay, and kissed her. "Love you, Ma. Don't forget to wake me up for church."

"I won't. Love you, too, son. Good night."

When the French doors shut behind Trey, Noah grinned at her. "What a perfect little angel."

"Isn't he though?" Lindsay swung away from the laser beam of light shooting from the coach lamp above Noah's head through the back of her skull. "Would you turn the lights off for me? I'm breaking out the citronella candles. They'll get rid of the moths."

And Chaos, Lindsay wondered. *Would they get rid of Chaos, too?*

Noah leaned into the house and flipped the switch. The lights went out and Lindsay sighed, the darkness easing the pain in her head. She opened the Rubbermaid locker, took out a box of kitchen matches, the candles in their net covered cups, and put them on the picnic table.

When Noah stepped onto the deck and shut the French doors, she lit a candle. He didn't vanish in a puff of smoke, just walked across the deck and stood beside her. Damn. Citronella candles didn't work; she'd have to get rid of Chaos on her own. She'd taken the first step with Meggie—now for Vivienne.

"So how does my contract compare with yours and Jolie's?"

"It's identical. You've got the same clause, the one that says that if either one of us misses a performance the contract is null and void and all bets are off. That's the one we need to hang Vivienne."

Lindsay lit another candle and handed it to Noah with the first one. "How do we do that?"

"We tell her the show won't go on until she meets your demands."

"I didn't know I had any demands."

"Now's the time to think of some. Where do you want these?"

"Over there, please." Lindsay nodded. Noah carried the candles to the back rail, the one that overlooked the pool, and set them down about six feet apart. "What are your demands, Noah?"

"I don't have any." He faced her and leaned against the rail, his arms and his ankles crossed, the candles flickering on either side of him. "Vivienne cut me a nice deal. A grand a week salary and a hundred thousand dollar bonus at the end of the run."

"She certainly made it impossible for you to say no."

"She did the same thing to Jolie."

Lindsay snatched the last two candles off the table, the wicks she'd just lit flaring as she spun on Noah. "Are you defending Jolie?"

"No, no, no." He waved a quick hand. "I'm just saying."

Lindsay realized she was holding the candles like she meant to throw them. She put one down on the picnic table, the other one next to the tray and poured two glasses of water. Tossed a couple lime wedges in one and carried them across the deck to the back rail.

"Thanks." Noah held the glass with lime, took a long swallow, and set it aside on the rail. "You're the only one who's not getting anything out of this deal. I know that now 'cause I've read your contract."

Lindsay leaned on her elbows and wrapped her hands around her glass. "All I wanted was to help Jolie."

"Yeah, and look where that got you." Noah turned to face the rail and leaned on it beside her.

His elbow brushed hers, lightly, accidentally; still a shiver went through Lindsay. A small one, just enough to tremble the ice in her glass and make her sharply aware of Noah standing beside her.

The candles were a really bad idea. When your eyes couldn't see your other senses kicked into high gear to help out. Lindsay had learned that stumbling around the darkened wings of the Belle Coeur Theatre.

Her nose told her Noah smelled good, like almond-scented soap and shampoo. The brush of his sleeve against her bare forearm—why oh why had she taken off her sweater—said his shirt was brushed cotton, that underneath it was a lot of warm skin and firm muscle.

Lindsay remembered the scald she'd felt when his fingers wrapped over hers on the front door of the theater, the handful of his chest hair she'd grabbed in the hospital. She could almost feel it in her fingertips, would've sworn she could hear him breathing, his heart beating, that she could taste lime on her tongue, her senses were so heightened.

"Why did Vivienne write the contracts this way?" Lindsay felt herself swaying toward Noah and stepped away. "A clause that gives you and me all the power doesn't seem like a mistake she'd make."

"Your Aunt Dovey said the same thing. That's when this came to me, while she was reading my tea leaves." Noah drank from his glass, put it down, and nudged toward her on his elbow, closing the gap she'd put between them. "I told her it's an easy error in judgment to make if you underestimate your opponents or you think they're too dumb to live."

"Vivienne does think she's smarter than everyone else, but that almost seems too easy." Lindsay put her glass on the rail and edged away from Noah again. "What if she wrote the clause that way deliberately?"

"I'm sure she did. Vivienne loves threats and intimidation."

"Don't I know it," Lindsay said, recalling all the times and all the ways Vivienne had browbeaten her.

Noah shifted his weight on one foot and half-turned to look at her. His hip brushed hers like it had in the store when he'd put his arm around her for the photograph. The lights and the crowd had helped her ride out the sizzle of that contact. But now it was just the two of them, their heads together conspiring to defeat Vivienne and the sizzle was spreading, amplified by the darkness, becoming a slow, heated flush of he's-a-man-and-I'm-a-woman awareness.

"So let's hear it, princess," Noah said. "What do you want?"

I want you to hold me, Lindsay thought. *I want you to tell me I don't have to be afraid, that Vivienne can't hurt Trey, that I'm nothing like her, that I'm a good mother and everything will be all right.*

"I want Vivienne to leave my son alone."

"Then that's your demand."

"What on earth makes you think she'll just go away?"

"If we tell her we won't put one foot on the stage of the Belle Coeur Theatre until she does, what choice does she have?"

"She could fire you and demand her money back from Jolie."

"She won't. She's got too much invested in this play. She expects to make a hefty profit and reap accolades if it's a hit. Kudos are just as important to Vivienne as money. She won't pull the plug."

"But what if she does? What happens to you and Jolie?"

"I'll survive. So will Satan's Handmaiden. She'll probably lose the theater, but that was gonna happen before Vivienne bailed her out."

Everyone in the family knew that. Everyone in Belle Coeur knew it, too, that without a giant hit or a miracle the theater was going down for the count. It didn't surprise Lindsay that Noah had figured it out.

"How will you survive?" she asked him. "Tell me that."

"That's not your problem, Lindsay. Let me worry about that."

"I'm not worried," she lied. "I'm just curious."

"If I was in L.A. right now, there'd be surfboards everywhere, all over the beaches." Noah hunkered over the rail on his folded arms and gazed at the pool, still covered for the winter and scattered with leaves that had blown through the fence. "I've got a few grand, thanks to Vivienne. I could start a school, teach surfing. I'm good at that." Noah turned his head and looked at her, the candle behind her dancing flames in his eyes. "I don't drink when I surf. I don't even want to."

"What about acting? What about your career?"

"What career?" He gave a short, bitter laugh. "I got lucky, princess. Plucked off the beach and plunked down in the middle of a show that would've been a hit no matter who they'd cast to play Sam. It was a once-in-a-lifetime shot and I blew it."

Noah drank the last of his water, shook an ice cube into his mouth, and crunched. A breeze stirred, scurrying leaves across the polyurethane cover on the pool. The candles flickered; so did something in Noah's eyes.

"What about now?" Lindsay asked. "Do you want to drink now?"

"Right now? This minute?" He swallowed the ice and sighed. "When I was drinking all the time, this would be one of the bad nights. If I knew where you kept the booze I'd be tempted, but I wouldn't." Noah turned his head toward her, his eyes a little too bright in the glow of the candles. "One drink. That's all I have to avoid. Taking one drink."

"And if your great plan to hang Vivienne with her own rope blows up in our faces? No thank you." Lindsay snatched Noah's water glass out of his hand and wheeled toward the table by the chaise to refill it. "I don't want the death of the Belle Coeur Theatre and your only chance to get back into acting on my conscience."

"That's not gonna happen." Noah followed her across the deck. "I know how Vivienne's mind works, princess. Trust me."

"I do trust you, but you aren't clairvoyant." Lindsay turned to face him, his glass in one hand, the pitcher in the other. "You have no more idea than the man in the moon what Vivienne might do. Neither do I."

"I know that no matter what she does I won't run for the tequila."

"This season is Jolie's last chance to pull the theater out of the red. Our play could do it. That isn't my risk to take."

Noah scowled. "You're afraid of Vivienne, aren't you?"

"You bet I am. With damn good reason." She filled his glass and put the pitcher back on the table, her hand shaking so badly the ice cubes that hadn't melted rattled in the glass. "I've got a bad feeling about this." Lindsay sounded like Emma and didn't care. "A really *bad* feeling that if we call Vivienne's bluff we'll be playing right into her hands."

"Put the glass down before you drop it." Noah took it away from her and put it on the table. "Look at you. Vivienne's trying to shanghai your kid and you're pouring me a glass of water. If I wanted one, I'd get it myself but no, you have to rush to the rescue 'cause Christ knows I could die of dehydration if I don't get a glass of water in the next five seconds."

"I was *not*," Lindsay snapped, "rushing to the rescue."

"You do it all the time, charge in to save people. You did it when I was in the hospital. This afternoon, for crissake, your Aunt Dovey had to call off the uncles so I could get out of the apartment. You've protected Jolie your whole damn life. God knows she needs it 'cause otherwise somebody might smother her in the middle of the night, but what I want to know is this." Noah gripped her arms. "Who protects you?"

"I protect myself," Lindsay said between her teeth.

"No, you don't. You're too damn busy protecting everybody else. That's how Trey ended up in Vivienne's crosshairs. You didn't see it coming 'cause you were up to your ears in trying to save me from myself and save Jolie from being lynched by the rest of your family." Noah tightened his grip on her, almost but didn't quite shake her. "I'm offering you a way out. A chance to stick it to Vivienne. Why won't you take it?"

"You're offering me a *possible* way out," Lindsay countered. "And you're taking a huge *gamble* that Vivienne won't turn on you and Jolie. I can't ask my sister to jeopardize the theater and you to risk your career for Trey and me. I'll find another way to get rid of Vivienne."

"Okay. Fine." Noah let go of her and flung up his hands. "Thanks for letting me cry on your shoulder. Good night."

Chapter 22

NOAH LET GO of her so suddenly that Lindsay stumbled. Swept past her so quickly she barely had time to spin around and say, "Wait a minute," before the French doors banged shut in her face.

"Oh, I don't *think* so," she said, and went after him. Saying thanks for letting him cry on her shoulder did *not* give him the right to slam *her* door in *her* face.

Noah beat her across the kitchen, jerked open the door to the garage and punched the wall switch to bring up the overhead. The light on the door opener winked on as Lindsay chased him down the step, almost running to catch up with him.

"Would you wait a minute?"

"I'm not angry." Noah stalked past the Civic. "I'm just leaving."

"I'd like to talk to you."

"What about?" He spun to face her, so abruptly Lindsay had to back up or bump into him. She stumbled against the Civic, put her hand out, and caught herself on the trunk lid, her pulse leaping at the simmer of temper and Chaos in Noah's eyes. "Trey told me you're having trouble learning your lines."

Noah snorted. "Steven Spielberg Junior to the rescue."

"He thought if we rehearsed together it might help."

"Spielberg Junior thinks if I feel the lines I'll be able to learn them easier. He says that's the way you do it, emote all over the place."

"That's how I've always done it. It's the only way I know."

"Great. Then let's get started." Noah spread his hands on the trunk lid on either side of her, pinned her against the car, and kissed her. A hard, angry kiss that left the imprint of his mouth throbbing against her teeth. "Sixteen. That's how many times Cliff kisses Moira. I counted. If we're gonna learn lines, then we're gonna learn everything. Every word, every kiss, every grope. Think you can handle that?"

"Don't be ridiculous," Lindsay said. Her insides were quaking but her voice was steady. "You're behaving like I've never kissed you before."

"You haven't kissed me. Jesse kissed Sam a bunch of times, but Lindsay Varner never kissed Noah Patrick." He leaned closer, so close she could feel his breath on her mouth, hers catching in her throat. "Unless there's something you'd like to tell me."

"There's nothing to tell. Trying to twist what I say won't change it."

"If you keep saying that I might start believing it." Noah pushed off the Civic and wheeled toward the Corvette. "But I wouldn't count on it."

The motion sensitive light on the corner of the eaves blinked on as he flung open the driver's door. Lindsay was so angry she was shaking. So livid that Noah had trapped her against her *own* car in her *own* garage that she had to clench her fists to keep from screaming.

"Don't worry, Patrick. I learned long ago not to count on you."

Noah slammed the door and spun away from the Corvette. "What did I do to you? Why did you punch me?"

"I told you why I punched you. Because you kissed me."

"That nothing little peck? Bullshit." He threw his keys through the open window and stepped away from the car. "I think you lied when you said you never expected to see me again. I think you hoped to Christ you'd never see me. Why? Just tell me."

"You said it didn't matter, that you wouldn't remember anyway."

"I changed my mind. I want to know. I *have* to know." He started toward her and stopped, his fingers flexing at his sides. "You're driving me crazy, Lindsay. One minute you're the Ice Princess, the next you're pouring your heart out, telling me all this shit about Vivienne and Jolie, then boom—you're the Ice Princess again and it's back off, buddy."

"Ice Princess?" Lindsay repeated. "Is that what you mean when you call me princess? *Ice Princess?*"

Noah snorted. "Like you didn't know."

"No, I—I didn't." Lindsay wilted against the Civic. She'd thought he meant it as a compliment. How stupid could she be? "You bastard," she said, so stung she felt tears in her eyes. "You know better."

"How would I know better? C'mon, princess." Noah gave her a come on, let-me-have-it wag of his fingers. "Tell me. How would I know?"

If he hadn't called her princess—*Ice Princess!*—Lindsay might've been able to slam the lid on the fury she could feel bubbling up inside her. But that blew the lid off like a geyser.

"Don't you *ever* call me that again!" she shouted, her voice echoing in the garage. "And don't tell *me* you can't remember! You just want to hear me say it so you can gloat! So you can hound and torment me and heckle me to death! Well, forget it, Patrick! You can go to hell!"

Lindsay wheeled off the Civic, cut her Scarlett O'Hara flounce a little short, and bumped into the fender. She pushed off the car and stormed toward the kitchen rubbing her hip, made it up the step, and closed her hand on the doorknob before Noah's voice stopped her.

"We made love, didn't we? That's it, isn't it?"

The light on the door opener clicked off. Lindsay could've left it off, could've slammed into the kitchen and brought the overhead down on Noah, but that would be running away. She'd been running from Chaos all her life yet here she was, cornered by it in her own garage. If she didn't turn around and face it in the light—face Noah and tell him the truth—Chaos would only keep running her to ground.

Lindsay tapped the wall switch. Once to activate the timer and bring the light on; again to stop the door.

"We did not make love." She turned on the step and looked at Noah standing just inside the garage. "We had sex the night of my eighteenth birthday. It was awful. I was petrified, scared to death that Vivienne had followed me, that she'd burst into your house and drag me away. You were so drunk you could barely stand. That's why you don't remember."

"Jesus." Noah swept a hand through his hair and looked at the garage floor. He drew a breath, blew it out in a gust, and raised just his eyes to her face. "Well. At least now I know why you hate me."

"Oh, Noah." Lindsay sat down on the step, so weary all of a sudden her bones throbbed. "I don't hate you. I tried, believe me, but even when things were at their worst with Vivienne and I wanted to choke you on the set, you could always make me laugh."

"Oh Christ," he said in a strangled voice. "Don't tell me I made you laugh in bed."

"No." Lindsay laughed, surprised that she could and it didn't hurt.

Noah blew out another breath, walked up the driver's side of the Civic and leaned against the left front headlight. "Did I make you cry?"

"In bed? No." Lindsay shook her head and cupped her hands around her knees. "I left when you fell asleep and came back around noon the next day. You answered the door with a naked blond wrapped around you. 'Princess. Babe,' you said to me. 'Go chill by the pool. When Jilly and I are done it'll be your turn.' "

Noah made a noise in his throat and shut his eyes. "Was I drunk?"

"Of course you were. You were always drunk."

Noah blew out another breath and opened his eyes. "You don't know how glad I am that I can't remember this. I hope you belted me."

"Oh I did. Right in the nose." Lindsay sat up straight

on the step, squared her shoulders, and lifted her chin. "I knocked you and Jilly the Jiggle Queen right on your naked butts."

"I'll bet that was a picture." Noah smiled. "Good for you." He gave her a thumbs-up and sighed. "I know sorry doesn't cut it, but that's all I can say, Lindsay. I'm sorry. Sorrier than you'll ever know."

"I'm sorry I lied to you. I should've told you the truth. I should've told you yesterday. I don't know why I didn't. I just—" Lindsay raised her hand and let it fall. "Choked."

"I can understand that. It wasn't exactly the finest hour for either one of us, was it?" Noah pushed off the Civic. "Scoot over."

Lindsay did and he sat beside her. It was a narrow step so he kept one foot on the floor, still a match flared where his hip touched hers.

"What did you do after you knocked me on my ass?"

"Called Emma. She finagled me a plane ticket." Lindsay focused on what she was saying rather than the press of Noah's hip against hers and the flush spreading through her. "When Vivienne left for the office I called a cab to take me to LAX. I got on a plane with just my purse and came home. Mark picked me up in St. Louis and we eloped."

Noah nodded. "Smart choice."

"Safe choice," Lindsay said. "I always make the safe choice."

Noah turned his head toward her. "Always?"

He was close enough to kiss her if he wanted to. *If I let him,* Lindsay thought, and felt her heart skip. "So far."

The bulb inside the door opener clicked off, pitching them into darkness. Till the backwash from the outside floodlight spilled into the garage and Lindsay blinked. Noah was still sitting beside her on the step. The jerk she'd known in L.A. would've jumped her in the dark.

"You know what I think?" Noah lifted her left hand and laced his fingers through hers. "I think you should keep on making safe choices."

He raised her hand to his mouth, pressed a quick, fervent kiss to her knuckles, and stood up. When he tried to loosen his fingers Lindsay tightened hers and let Noah pull her off the step. On her way up she hit the wall switch and turned on the lights. Noah blinked in the sudden glare as he turned to face her and said, "What?"

"You aren't going to run for the tequila bottle, are you?"

"After what you just told me? After hearing what tequila cost me?" Noah stared at her, incredulous. "My one and only chance to ensnare you while you were young and naïve and make you my sex slave for life?"

Lindsay laughed. "So can I take that as a no?"

"You can take that as a *hell* no."

Lindsay heard a bump behind her; she glanced over her shoulder and frowned at the shadows she could see flickering in the crack of light between the kitchen door and the floor. Noah let go of her hand, raised one foot on the step to reach past her, and gave the door a quick inward shove. It hit something with a thump. Something that yelped, "Ow!"

It was Trey Lindsay saw when Noah pushed the door open all the way. Her angelic son was hopping on his right foot and holding his left.

"You broke my toe!" he howled at Noah.

"I'm rusty," Noah said. "I used to be able to crack my sister Phyllis in the nose when she peeped through my bedroom door."

"I wasn't peeping," Trey said indignantly. "I was eavesdropping."

"Oh, well. That makes all the difference."

"I thought you'd gone to bed." Lindsay frowned at Trey.

"I did." He put his left foot down and winced. Pyewacket wound around his ankles and meowed. "Then I heard you yelling at Noah and got up to alert the media."

"Very funny. Go to bed."

"I'm going. Soon as I make an ice bag for my *broken toe*." Trey glared at Noah and limped into the doorway. "Thanks for helping this ingrate, Ma." He laid his hand on her shoulder and looked at Noah. "See? I told you the lines would be easier to learn if you felt them."

"Lemme try this door thing again," Noah said. "Couple more shots and I'll bet I can nail you with the knob smack between the eyes."

"Ha, ha," Trey said but he grinned and kissed Lindsay's cheek. " 'Night, Ma. See you, Noah."

"Go, Pye." Lindsay shooed the cat after Trey and shut the door.

"Okay. He's your kid," Noah said. "Does he really think he heard us sitting out here running lines in the dark?"

"He was covering his butt 'cause he got caught." Lindsay smacked the kitchen door with the side of her fist. "This is insulated steel. To hear anything clearly Trey would've had to listen through the cat door. If he'd pushed it open even a teensy bit we would've heard it."

On cue Pyewacket slithered through the flap and jumped over Noah's foot. The hinge at the top creaked like a frog with a sore throat.

"See?" Lindsay smiled at Noah. "It squeaks."

"Trey said he heard you yell at me."

"Maybe. If his bedroom window is open, but that's all he heard."

"If you say so." Noah swung away from the step and scowled. "If that damn cat's in my car there's gonna be trouble."

Lindsay followed him outside and called Pye while Noah searched the Corvette. Beyond the reach of the floodlight it was black as pitch. She couldn't see Pyewacket, but she could almost feel him crouched in the tall grass past the edge of the drive laughing at them.

"I've got to stop leaving these goddamn windows down." Noah slammed the driver's door and stuck his head inside the 'Vette. "If you're hiding under the seat you'd better stay there! I'm not getting up twenty-five times in the middle of the night to let your sorry ass out!"

"Big talk," Lindsay said, leaning on the left front fender.

Noah pulled his head out of the car. "I mean it," he said to her, then poked his head through the window again. "Hey, you! I *mean* it!"

"You don't just let Pye out, do you? You sit up and wait for him."

"Why go to bed?" Noah backed out of the 'Vette and turned to face her. "I just have to get up again when he wants in."

"Noah Patrick." Lindsay laughed. "Friend to animals and children."

His gaze lifted past her and settled on the house. "I hope to hell Trey didn't hear what you said to me."

"He didn't. He was ad-libbing. Trust me. I know my son."

"I don't mind that he knows I was a drunk." Noah didn't frown but his face changed. Or maybe it was just the harsh glare of the floodlight that made his jaw look like it had sagged and his eyes like they were hollow. "But I'd just as soon he didn't know I was a sleaze, too."

"That was a long time ago," Lindsay said. "That's not who you are now. I don't think it ever was. Not really."

"If I ask you nice and say please will you do me a favor?" Noah said and she nodded. "Don't invite me here anymore."

Lindsay bristled and shoved herself off the Corvette. "Why not?"

"Being here makes me want things I've got no business wanting. Things I could've had if I hadn't fucked up my life. Things I didn't even know I wanted till I saw you and Trey. In this house, in this place." Noah gave an amused, almost amazed shake of his head. "This funky, weird-ass little town that I'm beginning to wish was someplace on the coast of California instead of the middle of crapping nowhere Missouri."

"Oh, Noah." Lindsay sighed and took a step toward him.

"Do *not* come over here and hug me." He flung a hand up and backed away from her. "I'm only human, for Christ's sake."

"Well so am I," she shot back. "I'm not made of ice and I do *not* float around with a loopy, I'm-happy-oh-so-happy smile on my face thinking my life is perfect."

Noah cocked his head at her. "Who said you do?"

"Satan's Handmaiden," Lindsay said, annoyed that the cheap shot Jolie had taken at her on Easter at Aunt Dovey's house had stuck in her craw. "She says I'm too damn dumb to realize that I'm miserable."

"That's the pot calling the kettle black."

"Is it? I don't have panic attacks for the hell of it."

"Jolie loves to mess with people's heads, Lindsay. She tried it with me. Don't you buy into her bullshit."

"Maybe it isn't bullshit."

"Maybe it is and you're just tired."

"Could be." Lindsay sighed and rubbed her forehead. "Or maybe it's this headache." The dull, smack-in-the-middle-of-her-forehead thud was back and now it had a half-sick-to-her-stomach edge to it. "I've had it for a week and Tylenol isn't helping."

"Sounds like you could use a massage, too."

"My cousin, Jo Beth? Who gave you the back rub in the hospital?" Lindsay lowered her hand and looked at Noah. "She's a massage therapist. Maybe she'll give us a two for one discount."

"Till we find a shrink who will? I'll take it."

Noah's grin fell a watt shy of its usual hey-baby-here-I-am dazzle, but at least the hollow-eyed sag she'd seen in his face was gone.

"Will you be all right?" she asked him.

"Someday. Maybe." He got into the Corvette, fired up the engine, and smiled at her. "Good Lord willing and the creek don't rise."

"In the middle of crapping nowhere Missouri it's pronounced *crik*."

"*Crik.*" Noah saluted. "Got it. G'night, princess."

Lindsay let that slide and backed away from the car. "Good night."

She stood in the drive till the neon yellow Corvette faded into the dark and all she could see were its red taillights. She realized then that she was shivering, rubbed her arms, and turned toward the house.

Pyewacket sprang out of the grass at her feet, curled his tail around his paws, and said, "Meow." Which in cat speak probably meant something like, *Hey! How'd you like that one? Pretty good, huh?*

"Come on, you wicked cat," she said to him. "Let's go to bed."

Lindsay took a shower first, a long hot one to chase away the shivers. Then she put on flannel pajamas and brushed her teeth. She could still feel the imprint of Noah's mouth on hers and a warm little pulse where his hip had pressed against hers on the step.

Pyewacket was already asleep on her bed, stretched out and snoring on the folded back bedspread, his black fur gleaming like ebony in the glow of her reading lamp. Lindsay drew her knees up under the sheet and blanket and opened the book she'd started last night. She'd barely read five pages when the words started jumping on the page. So did her nerves, jumping and twitching in places they hadn't in years.

Damn Noah. She'd been perfectly happy with Mel Gibson and her vibrator. Lindsay slapped the book shut and tossed it aside. She didn't feel shivery anymore. She felt hot and achy and restless. She got out of bed and made a cup of tea, sat with it at the desk in the kitchen and thought about calling Emma, Queen of the Night Owls. She picked up the phone but she dialed Noah's number.

"If you won't come here," Lindsay said when he answered, "I'll come there and we'll work on lines. What time's good for you?"

"Can't sleep, huh?" He sounded like he'd been trying, his voice burred and deeper than usual. "Me, either."

"I didn't tell you about my birthday to make you feel bad." When Noah didn't say anything, Lindsay sighed. "Okay. Maybe I wanted you to feel bad just a little bit."

"That's more like it. Did you find the shitbag cat?"

"He's sound asleep and snoring on my bed."

"Lucky cat," Noah said and Lindsay's stomach fluttered. "What time's good for you?"

"There's a potluck at church tomorrow evening. If the Hannitys are going and Pat's willing, I'll let Trey tag along with Meggie. So—five-ish?"

"That'll work. See you then."

Lindsay put the phone down. Well. That wasn't hard. Dangerous, potentially insane, but pretty darn easy. She'd heard Noah's voice. That's all she'd wanted, to hear his voice and know he was okay. It was possibly the biggest lie she'd ever told herself.

Lindsay poured her tea down the drain—the last thing she needed was caffeine—and went to bed. She twitched and moaned, finally gave up and reached for her vibrator. It did not do the trick. What she wanted inside her was Noah.

Obviously, she'd lost her mind. Or blown out all her brain cells yelling at Trey.

She finally fell asleep, still twitching but no longer moaning. The next thing she knew Trey was shaking her awake.

"Ma. C'mon. Your alarm's been going off for an hour."

Lindsay slapped a hand on the radio, pushed up on her elbow, swept her hair out of her eyes, and peered at the clock face.

"Eight-fifteen!" She shot out of bed. "Get dressed! We're late!"

"We could skip church," Trey said hopefully.

"No, we can't." Lindsay stumbled and bumped into the bed on her way to the bathroom. "This is my Sunday to work in the nursery."

"Rats," Trey muttered, but he was up and moving toward his room.

Lindsay barely had time for a cup of microwave coffee and Trey a bowl of cereal, but they made it to church and slid into a pew out of breath five minutes before the nine o'clock service. The headache was back, pulsing between her eyes with every beat of her heart.

It was still there when she made her way to the nursery before Sunday school started. But fortunately—and blessedly—Jo Beth was working the nursery, too. Once they had the two- and three-year-olds settled with graham crackers and milk she turned to her pale, waifish blond cousin and planted her index finger in the middle of her forehead.

"I have the headache from you know where right here. What can you do for me?"

"Pray," Jo Beth said, then grinned. "I'm kidding. Sit down."

Lindsay sat in a straight-backed chair, keeping her Mother Eye on the toddlers while Jo Beth massaged her forehead and her temples and her neck, removed the clip she'd barely had time to scoop her hair into, and scrubbed her scalp with her magic fingers.

"I'd lose this." Jo Beth handed the clip to Lindsay. "Any better?"

"Not really, Jo. It's still there. Right in the middle."

"I'll take another crack at it Tuesday. Come by the shop

when you close The Bookshelf. If it gets any worse before then, I'd talk to Emma."

"Oh, Jo. I don't want to hear that. Especially in church."

"God bestows all kinds of gifts, Lindsay." Jo Beth wiggled her fingers. "He gave me these. He gave Emma, mmm, certain sensitivities."

"How 'bout my sinuses?" Lindsay pressed her fingers to the sides of her nose. "Did you check my sinuses?"

"Your sinuses are fine. Your neck's tight. Your ears crunched a little, but not much. This," Jo Beth touched a fingertip to her forehead, "is out of my territory."

Lindsay felt a tingle and a shiver up her neck. White candles she could handle. The rest of Emma's territory scared the bejesus out of her.

Aunt Sassy came through the nursery door to relieve her, late as usual, but in time to help Lindsay break up a baptism by milk. On Sundays she wore a skirt with her leotard, lime green jersey knit today over pineapple yellow.

"I been asking around," she said to Lindsay in a low voice. "Nobody's seen Jolene since I seen her Thursday coming out of the post office with that package. Wonder what was in it?"

"Who knows?" Lindsay said and shrugged.

Trey's pictures, she was sure, but she was keeping her lip zipped. Only Emma and Noah knew about the photos. She could trust Emma to keep quiet and who would Noah tell?

After the eleven o'clock service, Lindsay went looking for Trey. She found him strolling around the baseball field behind the church with Meggie. Pat Hannity watched them from the shade beneath the budded out lavender red bud trees lining the parking lot.

"Meggie told me what happened last night," Pat said. "Little Miss Mary Margaret is on her way to driving school. She doesn't get behind the wheel of anything but her ten speed until she completes the course."

"Did she tell you I yelled at her? I feel bad about that."

"Oh, don't." Pat gave her a forget-it wave. "It's not the first time she's been yelled at and I'm sure it won't be the last."

Getting rid of her panic attacks couldn't be as easy as

Noah suggested—yelling at anybody and everybody whenever she felt like it. That's what Vivienne did, which meant Lindsay wouldn't. She'd find another way, even if she had to ask Aunt Dovey to read her tea leaves.

"They look cute together, don't they?" Pat nodded at Trey and Meggie bumping shoulders as they rounded third base. "Thank God they aren't eighteen."

"I wish that was a guarantee," Lindsay said with a sigh.

"I'm an RN." Pat grinned. "I've scared Meggie spitless with horror stories about sexually transmitted diseases."

"You're a wonderful mother, Pat," Lindsay said, and they laughed.

In the car on their way home she told Trey she was dropping him at the Hannitys at four-thirty. He turned his head and looked at her.

"You aren't going to the potluck?"

"No. I'm going to help Noah learn his lines." When Trey didn't say anything, Lindsay glanced at him. "It was your idea."

"Do you like Noah, Ma?"

"Of course I like him."

"You could've fooled me. You never talked about him. When I asked you questions about him you wouldn't answer."

Please don't ask me now, Lindsay prayed. *I'm winging it here, son. I haven't a clue what I'm doing.* Maybe because it was Sunday God was merciful. Trey turned on the radio, just in time to hear Uncle Ron's taped voice giving today's forecast.

"We'll have showers in the morning. Thunderstorms, possibly severe, later this afternoon, with a high around sixty."

It was seventy-five if it was a degree, the sun so bright Lindsay had her sunglasses on and the visor down. She and Trey exchanged a sympathetic wince and said "*Oooh.*" He turned off the radio and pulled his seat belt all the way out so he could turn sideways to face her.

"But do you *like* like Noah? Do you want to date him?"

Lindsay arched an eyebrow at him. "Ex*cuse* me, young man?"

"Well." Trey gave her a bold stare. "You grill me about everything."

"I'm your mother. Besides. People my age don't exactly date."

"I know. I've seen the soaps." He grinned when she shot him a startled look. "I tape them and watch them after school."

"No wonder you're flunking geometry."

"I'm not flunking. That was just my ploy to get Meggie to notice me. She's a whiz at figuring out angles."

"Apparently," Lindsay gave him a stern frown, "so are you."

"I asked Meggie to the spring dance. She said yes. Can I take her? Will you drive us?" Trey notched his chin up belligerently. "Or do I have to tell her you won't let me out of the backyard till I'm eighteen?"

You're too young, Lindsay wanted to say, but that dog wouldn't hunt. She'd been married at eighteen and a mother three months shy of her nineteenth birthday. "I thought you'd get your driver's license before you got a girlfriend."

"That's life, Ma. It throws you curves." *He calls it curves,* Lindsay thought, *I call it Chaos.* "So can I take Meggie to the dance or not?"

Lindsay made the turn onto Ridge Road and glanced at her son. He looked so handsome, so eager that it made her throat ache. *Don't be in such a rush to get your heart broken,* she wanted to tell him, but she knew he wouldn't listen, knew it wouldn't make any difference.

"Yes." Lindsay sighed. "You can take Meggie to the dance."

"Sweet, Ma. Thanks. Can I call her when we get home?"

She smiled at him and nodded. "Sure."

When she pulled the Civic into the garage Trey flew into the house, grabbed the phone, and dashed for his room. If she had any sense at all, Lindsay thought, she'd call Noah and tell him she wasn't coming. Last night facing Chaos had seemed like a great idea, but it was 12:30 according to the microwave. Only four and a half hours till she had to face Chaos again—by her own choice, in its own lair.

That wasn't a safe choice. The safe choice was stay home

and put fresh batteries in the vibrator, but Lindsay didn't want safe. She wanted Noah. She wasn't a child anymore. She was a grown woman. She understood what the tingles and twitches in her body meant and what Noah could do—oh so much better than her vibrator—to make them go away.

She'd told him the body is very wise. She'd learned that in therapy; that the body does what it needs to take care of itself. Hers was telling her that it wanted the real thing, that it was sick and tired of her brain telling it to shut up, that it wanted to yell at people and stop having panic attacks.

Go ahead. Sleep with Noah, said a voice in Lindsay's head while she peeled potatoes. *Get him out of your system once and for all. Meet Chaos head on, face it on its own terms, and put it on the canvas.*

Was this her body talking, her brain, or the two of them in cahoots? Would sleeping with Noah really get him out of her blood or was that a rationalization? Would it defeat Chaos or was she just as bad as Aunt Sassy, who said her favorite dance was the horizontal tango?

It wasn't like Noah could break her heart; her heart wasn't involved. Well. Not much. It ached for him when she remembered how he'd cried in her arms. If a fling with an old friend helped him feel better about himself, convinced him that he deserved better things to happen to him now that he was sober, that was a good thing.

Wasn't it? She wasn't trying to justify an act of insanity, was she? Lindsay couldn't decide. And before she knew it, it was four-thirty. Time to pack up the au gratin potatoes she'd made in the Pyrex carrier and deliver them with Trey to the Hannitys. He fidgeted all the way—so he hardly noticed that she did, too—checked his hair and his teeth in the rearview mirror every five seconds. He had his door open the instant she turned into the Hannitys' driveway, the Pyrex carrier in his hand and a grin on his face as he hopped out of the car.

"Have fun, Ma. Don't do anything they wouldn't do on the soaps."

Lindsay waited in the drive till Pat's husband Terry opened

the door for Trey and waved at her. She smiled and waved back. Meggie's father ought to keep Trey's jets cooled.

Hers were so revved by nerves and anticipation—Would Noah make a move on her? Would she make a move on Noah?—that her hands were shaking on the wheel by the time she got to the barn.

It was habit to look for Jolie's truck, but Lindsay didn't see it in the main lot or by the workroom, which was unusual. Satan's Handmaiden rarely took a day off. Neither did Vivienne. Like mother like daughter, in oh so many ways.

Lindsay parked the Civic between the hickory trees next to Noah's shattered Corvette. She hoped he was planning to have the body shop change the color. She'd love to see it go back to Vivienne painted a shocking shade of lavender or puce.

Lindsay got out of the Civic with her script tucked in the curve of her elbow, her purse over her shoulder. Pyewacket popped out from under the passenger seat and shot through the open door.

"Pye!" she shouted, wheeling after him. "Come back here!"

He was already gone, a little black blur rocketing around the corner of the barn. Oh well. Lindsay locked the car and walked across the grass toward the apartment.

She thought the kitchen light was on, but she could only see the top half of the windows below the railing around the stairwell. She went down the steps, opened the storm door and held it with her shoulder, rapped on the window in the inside door and stood waiting with her pulse thudding and her stomach quivering for Noah to answer.

The kitchen light was definitely on. Still she thought she was seeing things when she glimpsed Noah coming out of the bathroom. He couldn't possibly be wearing gray coveralls. Why would he be? But he was, Lindsay saw, when he pulled the door open. Gray coveralls like Uncle Donnie and Uncle Lonnie wore because they were too afraid of Jolie's temper not to wear them, with NOAH stitched in red on a white oval sewn on above the pocket.

"Hi." He smiled. "Either you're early or I'm running late. I'm just washing up. Come on in."

Chapter 23

LINDSAY WENT THROUGH the door like a rocket, threw her purse one way and her script the other. She heard them land, her purse with a clunk, the script with a splat, but didn't look to see where. She didn't care. She was so furious she could hardly stand up straight.

"What are you *doing* in that coverall?" Lindsay demanded, though she could guess by the sawdust sprinkling the hair on his arms.

"I'm sawing boards for Donnie." Noah frowned at her, his head tipped to one side. "I'm helping him build the Murphy bed."

"This is Jolie's doing!" Lindsay grabbed the front of Noah's coverall and yanked. The snaps gave way and ripped open to his waist. "Take this damn thing off!"

"Whoa. Lindsay." Noah caught her wrists against his chest. His bare-beneath-the-coverall, hairy, and very warm chest. "It's okay."

"It's *not* okay!" She jerked her hands back. "This is an insult!"

"That's how Jolie meant it." Noah shrugged the coverall over his shoulders and fastened the top three snaps. "But she did me a favor."

"This is not a favor, Noah! This is a slap in the face!"

"Your uncles are great guys. They're teaching me things. I can't remember shit but I can turn on a big-ass saw and cut a board."

"You aren't supposed to be cutting boards!" Lindsay shouted. "You're supposed to be learning your lines! You're an actor, Noah!"

"There are TV critics who'd still give you an argument about that."

"Take this *off*!" Lindsay grabbed his lapels and wrenched her hands apart. The coverall split all the way to the crotch, all the way to the bulge in Noah's Jockeys. He clamped his hands around her wrists and backed her up against the sink. "What is your problem with this?"

"It's demeaning and degrading!" Lindsay fought to free her hands but couldn't. "Jolie did this to make you feel like gum stuck to the bottom of her shoe! Why don't *you* have a problem with this?"

"If you don't stop trying to rip my clothes off—" Noah pressed himself against her "—you're gonna have a problem you don't want to handle."

He meant the erection she felt throbbing against her. Lindsay notched up her chin and pushed her pelvis at him. "You think I can't handle it? I'm not a child anymore, Noah. I'm a woman."

"Don't start this, Lindsay," he warned. "I'll finish it."

"If you don't finish it I will," she said, and kissed him. An open-mouthed kiss that made him groan and loosened his grip on her wrists. Lindsay snaked her arms around him, her hands inside his Jockeys. Noah broke the kiss and caught her face in his hands.

"You better mean this," he said, a pulse leaping in his throat.

"Throw me on your bed and find out how much I mean it."

Noah swung her off the floor, wheeled through the bathroom with her, and tossed her onto the bed. Lindsay bounced up on her elbows and popped the snap on her jeans. Noah yanked them off her legs, ripped off his coverall, and sprang onto the bed. Lindsay hooked an elbow around his neck and pulled his mouth over hers, struggling to open her blouse and push up her bra so she could feel his chest hair against her nipples.

Noah tore off his Jockeys and her panties, touched her, and drove inside her, raking his mouth over hers, thrusting until Lindsay exploded, bit his shoulder, and clutched him against her. Noah collapsed on top of her, his heart thudding hard against her breastbone.

It felt wonderful, glorious, the weight of him on top of her, the pulse of his spent erection inside her. Lindsay sighed, rubbed her breasts against his chest, and purred in his ear. Noah made a noise like a moan, shoved up on one elbow, and slapped a hand over his eyes.

"That's one for the record books. Whattaya think? Sixty seconds?"

"It was perfect." Lindsay ran her tongue up Noah's sideburn and felt him shiver. "Just what I wanted. Exactly what I needed."

"A blink of an eye quickie? Great. Glad I could help."

"How about a fling with an old friend, then?"

Noah lowered his hand. "Did you come here to seduce me?"

"No. I came to rekindle my grand passion."

"Me?" Noah blinked. "You mean *me*?"

He looked so startled Lindsay laughed and felt him stir. He pushed inside her, a slow wow-whattaya-know grin spreading across his face.

"I don't know how you can say that but I needed to hear it."

I know, Lindsay thought, but didn't say it. She kissed his chin, felt whiskers scrape her lips, and folded her arms around his neck.

"I can do better." Noah's breath on her collarbone raised a shiver.

Lindsay caught his earlobe in her teeth. "Prove it."

He started with her breasts, tugging her blouse and her bra over her head, rubbing her nipples with his thumbs till they ached, then sucking them, rolling his tongue around them, nipping with his teeth. Lindsay closed her eyes and clutched his shoulders. She didn't dare clutch his hair for fear she'd yank it out by the roots.

Oh it was bliss, mindless, wondrous bliss. Her neglected nerves stopped twitching and started humming, then singing as Noah's hands and mouth moved lower, caressing her stomach, between her legs. Oh to hell with changing the batteries in the vibrator. When she got home she'd throw the damn thing away.

Noah was rock hard and huge when he came inside her again, bent her head back with the weight of his body and sank a long, deep kiss into her mouth. She let him have that one then turned her head away. The taste of him made her heart swell and her heart had no place in this bed. There was only room for her body and Noah's.

He took his time, his slow, sweet time stroking her. Lindsay arched up to meet him, lifting her shoulder blades off the bed so he could reach her breasts and suckle while he pumped inside her.

The build to climax seeped like liquid fire from her breasts to her belly, then flared like a just-struck match with one hard, final stroke that would've pushed her off the bed if she hadn't grabbed Noah's shoulders and hung on while the shudders rocked her. Lindsay collapsed and he sprawled on top of her, his breath raw and ragged in her ear, her legs tangled with his, sweaty and itchy with sawdust.

She could smell it on Noah's skin. He was so proud that he'd cut those boards for Donnie. Noah Patrick. Friend to children and animals—and now a carpenter. Lindsay smiled and stroked the sweat-slick back of his neck. He kissed her jaw and pushed, still half hard inside her.

"Give me a hand job and I'll be ready to go again."

"Down boy." Lindsay laughed. "You've proven yourself."

Noah popped up on one elbow. "So that was better?"

"It was wonderful." And it was. So glorious Lindsay's heart was starting to swell again. "You were wonderful."

"Jesus, I sound needy." He bumped his forehead against hers. "I'm not. It's just been a *loong* time and Christ knows I owe you one."

"Oh, you owe me more than one, Patrick."

He pushed up on his arm again. "How many we talking here?"

"I don't know." Lindsay slid her hands down his back and cupped his buttocks, squeezed, and felt him rise inside her. "I haven't decided."

"You're clutching my best feature, you know."

"I don't recall your tush being your best feature."

Noah grinned. "I'm not talking about my tush."

"Well, what—" Lindsay blinked, then she got it. She laughed and felt Noah slip out of her.

"Uh-oh." He started to roll off her. "I'm making you laugh in bed."

"No, no, stay." She caught him by the hips, spread her legs wider and settled him between them. "You feel very nice right here."

He felt like he belonged there, snug in the V of her thighs. Noah braced his weight on his knees and slid his fingers into her hair.

"I'll remember this. Every second for the rest of my life I'll remember." He stroked his thumbs across her forehead, tracing the arch of her eyebrows. "That isn't why you did this, is it?"

"So you'd have something to remember? No." Lindsay touched her fingertip to his chin. "I did it so we'd both have something wonderful to remember about being together."

"You're too good, Lindsay." Noah curved his hands around her face, framing it on the pillow. "And so gorgeous it hurts to look at you."

Noah kissed her and she let him, let her lips melt and blend with his, let the last hurt, angry memory of her birthday fade from her head. Oh yes, this was a good thing. Such a good thing for both of them. When he left to go back to L.A. she could wave him good-bye with a smile.

"Oh God you can kiss," Lindsay said with a sigh when he let go of her mouth. "You always could. You used to melt my knees on the set."

Noah grinned. "Anything you'd like me to melt at this moment?"

"How about every square inch of me?"

"I can do that," he said, and slid down her body to her feet.

"I didn't mean literally." Lindsay raised her head to look at him, gasping as he touched his lips to the tip of her left big toe.

"Oh I did." Noah ran his tongue up the arch of her foot.

"Mmm." Lindsay sighed and let her head fall back on the pillow.

By the time Noah got to her knees her head was thrashing

on the pillow and she had the corners of it crushed in her fists. Lush, nonstop shivers coursed ahead of the barely there brush of his lips up her thighs, the dart of his tongue, the nip of his teeth. When he nuzzled her curls she caught him by the ears and stopped him.

"Oh God, no," she moaned. "I'll blow apart."

"Go ahead," Noah murmured. "I'll catch you."

And he did when he dove his tongue into her and the climax ripped through her. He pushed up and slid into her, hooked her knees around his waist, wrapped her in his arms and let her buck and scream and claw at his shoulders. When she could, Lindsay opened her eyes and blinked at Noah. He was blinking at her and he was trembling.

"Did I faint?" she asked him.

"I think we both did." He settled on top of her on his knees and his elbows and scraped back his wet-with-sweat hair. "In an hour or so I should be able to get up and turn the shower on for you."

"Uhhh," Lindsay groaned. "Don't make me move."

"You've got to, gorgeous." Noah wiped the tip of his tongue between his thumb and index finger. "You've got sawdust in your navel."

"Oh, yuck!" Lindsay gave him a shove. "Let me up!"

Noah rolled off her laughing. Lindsay sat up on the side of the bed and stuck her tongue out at him over her shoulder.

"Bring that over here," he said, and made a lunge for her.

She laughed and dashed into the bathroom, shut the doors but didn't lock them in case Noah decided to join her in the shower. He didn't, he gave her her privacy, which she appreciated. Lindsay washed her hair with the almond shampoo that had filled her senses last night and used Noah's dryer. She wrapped herself in a towel and opened the door, blinking in the dusk gathering beyond the windows. The lamp was on, there were fresh sheets on the bed but no sign of Noah.

"Noah?" She spun around and yelped when he leaned through the bathroom door behind her and smacked her on the fanny.

"Gotcha." He grinned and slapped the door shut between them.

No. He wouldn't get her. This wasn't love. This was a fling with an old friend, a sexual release for both of them. And that was fine. It was perfect. That's all it ever had been, really, but she'd been too young and miserable and confused in L.A. to differentiate between love and lust.

Thank God Jilly the Jiggle Queen had been at Noah's house when she'd come back with her suitcases in the car, ready to break her engagement to Mark and run away with him. If Noah had been alone he might've laughed at her, gotten angry. Or jumped in the car with her and driven them to a wedding chapel in Vegas. Eek.

"Thank you, Jilly." Lindsay sat down weak-kneed on the side of the bed. "Wherever you are."

If she hadn't married Mark she wouldn't have Trey. If she hadn't had Trey she would've gone insane when Mark died. Oh yes, this was perfect. Just the way it should be. She had the memory of Mark—the love of her life—tucked forever in her heart, his son to bring her joy, and six weeks of mind-blowing sex ahead with Noah Patrick, the most gorgeous and grandest passion she was sure any woman had ever had.

She didn't realize she had tears in her eyes till she raised her head when Noah came out of the bathroom and one slid down her cheek.

"Lindsay." He dropped on his knees in front of her, naked, and curved a hand around her face. "What's wrong?"

"Nothing." She laughed. "I'm just happy."

He tipped his head sideways and pursed his lips. "You sure?"

"I may not be able to walk tomorrow, but other than that I'm fine."

That pleased him; his chest puffed out. Lindsay glanced at the clock radio beside the bed. It was 8:25.

"Ooh," she said. "Trey's supposed to be home at nine."

"Do you have to be there? He's fifteen."

"I don't have to be there, no, but I want to be."

"Got it." Noah nodded and pushed off the floor, went to the chair by the dresser, and brought her folded clothes back to her.

"Thanks. I wondered what happened to these."

Lindsay took off the towel, slid the straps of her bra over her arms, and reached behind her. Noah's hands were already there. He fumbled a little but he managed to get the hooks through the eyes. When she reached for her panties he snatched them away from her.

"Can I keep these?" He grinned. "I'm starting a new collection."

"Start someplace else." Lindsay slipped into her blouse, took her panties and stood up to put them on. Noah caught the waistband from behind and tugged it over her hips, letting his fingers trail over her skin.

"You're making this hard on purpose, aren't you?"

"I think turnabout is fair play, don't you?"

Lindsay buttoned her blouse and glanced at Noah, leaning back on his hands with a grin on his face. "You really should cover that," she said and flipped her towel over his erection.

He laughed, stood up, and knotted the towel over his hip while she shimmied into her jeans, zipped them, snapped them, and blinked at her bare feet. "Any idea where my shoes are?"

"Under the bed, I'll bet," Noah said, and went down on all fours.

He didn't remember tucking the red leather album between the bed frame and the table when he'd finished looking at it last night. Until he straightened on the far side of the bed with Lindsay's right navy blue slide and saw her on her knees lifting the album onto the quilted forest green coverlet. She opened the cover to the photograph of her as Little Miss Firecracker. Noah expected her to scream and hurl the album at his head. She didn't. She looked up at him and blinked puzzledly.

"Is this the book Trey loaned you?"

"Uh, yeah. I thought it might help me remember."

"Vivienne sent me this." Lindsay turned the page and wrinkled her nose at the Spanish dancer in the black mantilla. "I threw it away."

"Trey told me. He fished it out of the Dumpster."

Lindsay shook her head and frowned. "Why, for God's sake?"

"Maybe he was curious." Noah pushed to his feet, rounded the bed with her shoe, and sat down next to the album. "Maybe he was proud of you. Maybe you should give that some thought before you kill him."

"I'm not going to kill him. I'm just amazed that he has any interest in this." Lindsay swung onto the bed beside him, spread the album open between them, and turned to the picture of Sam with Jesse in her cheerleader uniform. "This is our first *TV Guide* cover. Do you remember?"

"I remember we were photographed sitting down so you didn't look taller." Noah shrugged. "That's all."

"You were obnoxious on the shoot. As usual."

Noah heaved a sigh. "Was I ever not obnoxious?"

"Maybe twice in six years." She slid him a wink to let him know she was teasing, turned the page, and laid her finger on a photo of the two of them. "This is my eighteenth birthday party. You were my escort."

Noah had to squint to make out the façade of the Roosevelt Hotel. He stood behind Lindsay on a red carpet with his arms around her waist. Her hands were on his wrists, her head tipped back against his shoulder. He wore a tux, she a dark blue strapless knockout of a gown.

"Let me try something." Noah pulled her to her feet and tossed the album on the bed. When he stepped behind her and looped his arms around her waist, Lindsay laid her hands on his wrists and tipped her head back against his left shoulder just as she had for the photo.

"Did we dance?" Noah nuzzled her ear and felt her shiver. She swirled her fingertips on the backs of his hands and sighed. "All night."

"Fast or slow?" He lifted her hand and twirled her around. Lindsay slipped into his arms and breathed against his mouth, "Slow."

Noah slid his hands in her back pockets, pulled her tight against him, and rolled her hips against his hard-on. "Like this?"

"Um, no. More like this." Lindsay tugged his left hand

out of her pocket, slapped her right palm in his, and backed up about a foot. "Vivienne was chaperone."

Noah laughed, tucked their entwined fingers against his chest and slow danced her around the bedroom. Much as he wanted to be horizontal with her, it was nice to smell his shampoo in her hair, to feel the warm silk of her cheek against his bare shoulder.

"How'd we give Mommie Dearest the slip?"

"When the network bigwigs came in Vivienne forgot about me. I maneuvered you into a dark corner and planted a big wet one on you. Next thing I knew we were in your Ferrari headed for the beach."

"I had a *Ferrari*? Oh, man. What color?"

"Fire engine red with tan, hand-stitched, tucked and rolled leather interior. I was only in it that once but it was gorgeous."

"I was only in you that once, wasn't I?"

"No-*ah*." Lindsay pulled away from him, shocked but laughing.

"I'm just asking." He pressed her cheek to his shoulder again and kept dancing. "How'd you get home?"

"I wasn't smart enough not to go to bed with you, but I did have brains enough to call a cab when you passed out." Noah felt her flinch, heard her suck air between her teeth. "Sorry."

"Don't be." He rubbed his lips in her hair. "Keep talking."

"That's about it, really." Lindsay sighed. "You know the rest."

"Then tell me about my Ferrari."

"Boys and toys." She laughed, turned out of his arms and plopped on the bed, flipped a few pages in the album, and tapped another photo. "Right there. That's your Ferrari."

Lindsay pushed herself off the bed, her feet into her slides, and sidestepped Noah as he sat down and bent over the picture. It was him, all right, barefoot with his jeans unsnapped and his arms folded over a perfect six-pack. He swore to God that he'd do his crunches first thing in the morning. If he could get through them without hacking up a lung.

The sleek red fender he leaned on definitely belonged to a Ferrari. Noah frowned and flipped back two pages. There was the photo of him on the beach with his board. He heard Lindsay in the kitchen and got up, went through the bathroom, and leaned in the doorway. She stood at the counter trying to smooth out her crumpled script.

"Why are there pictures of me all by myself in your album?"

"They must have something to do with *BBT*. Publicity stills, interview photos." She shrugged. "You just don't remember."

"Probably," Noah said but he thought it was odd. "Why did Vivienne send you the album?"

"She always sends me something on my birthday. Last year it was the album and a note that said, 'I think it's time you looked at this.' "

"That's cryptic."

"That's Vivienne." Lindsay picked up her script and swung her purse over her shoulder. "We *will* work on lines. The good news is Jolie won't expect you to have all yours memorized tomorrow night."

"Piss on her if she does," Noah said, and sneezed.

Lindsay frowned, came to stand in front of him, and laid her hand on his chest. Noah's heartbeat quickened beneath her palm.

"You're cold. You need to put some clothes on, make yourself a cup of green tea, and go to bed and get warm."

"I'd rather run around half naked flashing you." He grinned and leaned to kiss her. Lindsay turned her head away. Noah scowled. "Why are you doing Julia Roberts in *Pretty Woman*? Why won't you kiss me?"

"You have a dangerous mouth, Patrick, and I need to leave." She raised a so-there eyebrow and brushed his cheek with her lips.

"Wait a minute. I'll put my pants on and walk you to your car."

"I want you in bed as soon as possible." Lindsay opened the door and slid him a flirty smile. "How about tomorrow night after rehearsal?"

"Oh baby, I'm there."

Lindsay made a face. "I'm not a baby, Noah."

"You don't want me to call you princess."

"Can you can come up with a princess that doesn't involve ice?"

"Oh can I." Noah sidled up to her. "Princess of my Prick."

"No-*ah,*" she said, no shocked little laugh this time but a not-funny snap in her eyes and her voice.

"This isn't heckling. This is smutty sex talk to make you hot." He curved his hand around her face. "You're mine. I can do that."

Noah started to kiss her. A flash lit Lindsay's eyes and he checked himself. Then she smiled and covered his hand with hers.

"Okay." She pressed a kiss to his palm. "Just warn me."

"Warn you." Noah stepped away from her. "Will do."

"Oh. I should warn you." Lindsay stopped halfway through the door. "Pyewacket stowed away in my car. Do not get up to let him in."

"He bangs on the door until I do."

"He's a cat, Noah. Ignore him. He'll go away. See you tomorrow."

She turned away and shut the door. When Noah flipped on the outside light, she shot him a smile, hurried up the steps and across the yard to her car. He watched the headlights come on, the Civic back away from the Corvette, lifted his hand when Lindsay tapped the horn.

"Idiot!" Noah spread his hands on either side of the window, watched her car roll away down the road, and thought about bashing his head against the glass. "Stupid, dipshit idiot!"

You're mine. That's what the flash was in her eyes—The hell I am, pal. I'll fuck your brains out but belong to you? Not in this lifetime.

It was his own damn fault. If he hadn't screwed up their lifetime in L.A.—oh no. Christ no. He wasn't going there. Noah wheeled into the bathroom and jerked off in the shower, roared like a mad bull, and punched the wall. He broke six tiles and cut his knuckles, stood with water running down his face, ceramic shards on his feet, and stared at the blood dripping down the drain like the stabbing scene in *Psycho*.

"You dickhead." Noah laughed, blubbering water and a few tears under the spray, turned it off, and ripped open the shower curtain. He wiped steam off the mirror, leaned his hands on the sink—the right one throbbing across his sliced-open knuckles—and stared at his face. "You fucked up big time in L.A. You apologized to Lindsay. That's all you can do. Let it go. Move on. Don't fuck up again."

He took hydrogen peroxide and a box of Barney the Dinosaur Band-Aids out of the medicine cabinet. Somebody had a sense of humor. Noah shut the cabinet and held his bloody knuckles up to the mirror.

"One more thing. Take better care of this hand. If things don't work out with Lindsay, Mr. Johnson is going to need it."

Chapter 24

"YOU *SLIPPED*?" Donnie stood in the bathtub peering at the cracked and broken tiles on the shower wall. "With what? Your head?"

Noah held up his hand, made a fist that showed off his purple Barney the Dinosaur Band-Aids. "With this."

"That Lonnie." Donnie grinned over his shoulder. "What a kidder."

"I'm laughing," Noah deadpanned.

"Why you want to learn how to do this? Can't see what knowing how to replace ceramic tile is gonna do for an actor."

"I broke the tiles. I should fix the tiles."

"Be easier to put down a rubber mat 'case you slip again."

"I won't slip again." Good Lord willing and the crik don't rise.

"All right." Donnie sighed. "Let's get started."

He spread a drop cloth on the floor and opened a toolbox the size of a footlocker. Took out a hammer, a chisel, a cordless handheld tool he called a grinder. A tube of caulk, and from a plastic bag the dozen new tiles they'd bought at McGruff's Hardware after Donnie followed him in his pickup truck to deliver the Corvette to the body shop.

Donnie slid a pair of bug-eyed safety glasses over his bifocals and tossed a pair to Noah. "Goggles."

Noah put them on. "Goggles."

"Mask." Donnie snapped one over his mouth by its elastic straps.

"Mask," Noah said, giving the straps on his a snap, too.

"Gloves." Donnie tugged on thick denim work gloves.

"Gloves." Noah put on the pair Donnie gave him, held his hands up like a surgeon, and stepped into the tub. "Ready, doctor."

Donnie handed him the hammer and chisel. "Go for it."

Pyewacket sat in the doorway between the bathroom and the bedroom watching. When Noah fired up the grinder to smooth out the old grout, he shot under the bed. He turned off the grinder and pulled the mask away from his mouth.

"Where can I get one of these?"

He'd let the cat in around ten, out at eleven, back in at one. He'd been up anyway struggling with his lines. Reading and repeating them, reading and repeating them with his eyes wide open. When he shut them all he could see were Lindsay's gorgeous round breasts, her shell-pink nipples gorged red and wet from his tongue and his teeth.

"What you want with a Dremel hand tool?" Donnie asked.

"Watch." Noah nodded at Pyewacket creeping back into the bathroom, his fur and his tail bristled. He pressed the trigger, the grinder whirred and the cat dove under the bed again. "I figure this should keep him away from the back door in the middle of the night."

"Buy some earplugs," Donnie laughed. "Be cheaper."

Two hours later Noah had grout dust in his hair, in his

teeth, and up his nose in spite of the mask, and six brand new tiles stuck to the wall in a neat perfect line. What a high. The best he'd had since last night when he'd made Lindsay come three times in a row.

"Good work." Donnie clapped him on the back. "You can keep the Dremel if you want. I'll know where it is if I need it."

"You are a prince among men."

Once the tools were put away and the mess cleaned up, Donnie washed in the kitchen, Noah in the bathroom. He scrubbed his hands and face, brushed his teeth, and blew his nose and went outside after Donnie. Pyewacket sprawled in the grass snapping at flies. When Noah came through the door he got up and trotted away with his tail in the air.

Donnie sat on the stairwell steps with a can of Cherry Coke in one hand, a lit cigarette in the other. Noah leaned against the cement block wall and drew a deep, smoke-filled breath that made his mouth water.

"Want one?" Donnie asked.

"No thanks." Noah fanned his right hand and the waft from the cigarette toward his face. "Just blow it my way."

Donnie stretched off the step to hand him a Cherry Coke. Noah wiped sweat off the can on the front of his coverall and popped the top.

"Lindsay had a shit fit when she saw me in this getup."

"She hates 'em, for sure. Calls 'em an emblem of servitude. Says Jolie makes me and Lonnie wear 'em so we'll look like the hired help."

"That's not the case for you and Boo but I *am* the hired help."

Employed, earning money. Oh that was sweet. Nowhere near as sweet as Lindsay's—Noah clunked himself between the eyes with the Coke can and the image of her spread thighs splintered and broke.

"When'd you see Lindsay?" Donnie asked.

"Last night. She came over to help me learn my lines."

"Seen her car when me and Lonnie drove by on our way home after the potluck at church." Donnie dragged on his cigarette, squinting at him through the smoke. "Didn't see any lights, though."

"That's because Lindsay and I were making mad passionate love."

Donnie laughed till he choked on his cigarette. The hard-on stirred by just saying mad passionate love shriveled in Noah's Jockeys.

"You and Lonnie." Donnie rose off the step, grinned, and ground out his cigarette. "Coupla kidders. Feel up to tackling the bed?"

Noah sighed. "Not anymore." Donnie roared with laughter. "Oh—you mean the Murphy bed. Sure."

Note to self, Noah thought as he followed Donnie through the apartment and downstairs to the workroom. *Keep the lights on.*

He and Donnie measured and cut the last of the boards for the Murphy bed frame and laid it out on the floor the way it was supposed to go together. The big doors stood open to let in the sun and a breeze that raised swirls of sawdust for Pyewacket to chase across the concrete floor.

When they stopped for lunch the cat followed them outside, sat between them on the cement block retaining wall way opposite the trash Dumpster, and watched every bite Noah took.

"Fat chance, furball." He chewed a mouthful of his second roast beef piled on an onion bun sandwich. "Go catch a bird."

Pyewacket narrowed his eyes. Donnie tossed some scraps into the grass and the cat sprang after them.

Besides the sandwiches, Lonnie had put up—which Noah took to mean *prepared*—a relish tray with veggies, pickles, and cheese cubes, and slabs of apple pie left over from the potluck. Lonnie was out on the tractor planting, plowing, or pillaging. Something with a *P*.

When Pyewacket finished the beef, Noah tossed him a broccoli floret just for grins. Damn cat ate it, then two radishes and a kosher dill spear.

"Glad I don't clean your litter box," he said.

It was nice out here with his shades on and the sun warming his face. His heels drumming the wall, the breeze hissing through the trees that swept down the bluff to the silver ribbon of the Missouri River curving away between steep limestone cliffs.

Donnie lit a cigarette, exhaled in Noah's direction, and belched.

"If we had a campfire and a couple of unopened Budweisers," Noah said, "we could film a beer commercial. Make a couple bucks."

"Our brother Joe done one of those," Donnie said. "He's up on the bandstand singing and playing guitar with five other guys from Nashville everybody thought drunk themselves dead years ago."

"I listened to one of his CDs the other day." Noah had found it on the shelves above the fireplace. "He's pretty damn good."

"He's awful damn good. Tragedy is he can't get up the guts to walk out on a stage 'less he's three sheets to the wind."

"Does he come around here much?"

"Now and then. Jolene don't even talk to him. Lindsay's a mite better. She'll take him out, buy him a meal."

"Kind to drunks." Noah winked, keeping up the lights-off joke. "I like that in a woman."

"Wish Lindsay wasn't so repressed. That's what Lonnie says she is. Think he heard it from Dovey." Donnie took another drag on his cigarette and blew smoke through his nose. "Too bad you was jokin' 'bout the mad passionate love. That'd loosen her springs."

"Donnie." Noah turned toward him with a bottle of Evian that Lonnie had packed with lunch. "I'm basically indigent, you know."

"Yeah. So what? I don't want you to marry her."

Noah slapped the bottle down between them. "Why not?"

" 'Cause you're basically indigent."

He flipped his cigarette in the gravel at the base of the wall, picked up the wicker lunch hamper, and strolled into the barn. Noah grabbed the Evian and wheeled after him. He raised a finger and opened his mouth, shut it, and smacked the bottle on the workbench, the flat of his hand next to it, and drummed his fingers.

"What's all the wooden cussin' about?"

Noah turned toward the saw table and Donnie. "The what?"

"The bangin' and slammin' you're doin' over there. Jolene does it constant. Drives me buggy." Donnie scowled. "What's your beef?"

"I'm just a little tired." Noah held up his pinched-together thumb and index finger. "Of you people telling me what a lousy prospect I am as a husband. It's wearing thin."

"I didn't say one word 'bout you bein' anybody's husband. I said why didn't you loosen Lindsay's springs." Donnie picked up a rag and wiped off the saw. " 'Less o' course you ain't interested in that."

"I'll tell you what I'm interested in." Noah flung himself at Donnie, his hands spread on the saw table. "I'm interested in—"

Donnie glanced up at him, blinking mildly through his bifocals. Noah snapped his mouth shut.

You bet Lonnie had gotten it from Dovey that Lindsay was repressed. She'd told him the same thing over the tea leaves. She'd seen a wife and at least one child in his palm reading but he didn't strike her as the marrying kind. Donnie said he could loosen Lindsay's springs but he couldn't marry her 'cause he was basically indigent.

Oh these people were good. Masters of reverse psychology.

"I'm interested in finishing up here," Noah said. "So I can study my lines before rehearsal tonight."

"Let's do up the cross pieces then and call it a day."

Noah measured each one twice—measure twice, cut once—like Donnie taught him. Lindsay's uncle ran them through the saw, shooting hell-where'd-I-screw-up glances at Noah that he pretended not to see.

"Shower down here in the dressing room," Donnie told him when they finished. "Them tiles need to set up least a day."

Noah shed his coverall in the bedroom, wrapped himself in a towel, grabbed another one, his shampoo and soap, and wandered through the labyrinth backstage till he found the dressing rooms. Two private ones side by side and two more communal rooms joined by a nice big bathroom with a couple chairs against the wall, three sinks, and a spotless shower stall behind pebbled glass doors.

He rarely sang in the shower but he stood under the spray scrubbing his scalp and belting out Bobby Darin's old '50s hit "Splish Splash." He could measure and cut boards and lay ceramic tile. He'd loosened Lindsay's springs but good and he was one up on her Uncle Donnie.

All in all it was a damn fine day—till he opened the fogged up shower door and saw Jolie sitting in one of the chairs by the sink. She had on a peach T-shirt, faded bib overalls, and black canvas high-tops.

"Get the hell out of here," Noah said.

"You're on my turf." Jolie threw him a towel. He caught it and tied it around his waist. "Thanks to you Lindsay isn't speaking to me."

"My work here is done. Mount up, Tonto."

"Listen, smart ass." Jolie shot across the floor and stabbed a finger in his chest. Noah clamped her wrist, felt her pulse hammering beneath his fingers, but she held her ground. "You keep your mouth shut."

"Or what? What are you gonna do? Tell everybody in town that I was a drunk? I think I've already beaten you to that."

"No one in my family will talk to me." Jolie was so livid her eyes were yellow. "What lie did you tell them?"

"I don't lie, kid. I told Lindsay and your Aunt Dovey about the pictures you sent Vivienne. I didn't say a word to anybody else."

"Liar! When they see me on the street they walk the other way!"

"Well hell. You treat them like dirt and talk to them like they're dogs. I'd say you're lucky they haven't come after you with torches."

"I'm warning you. This is *my* play, *my* script. I'm the director. You do as I fucking tell you and keep your mouth shut. I don't want to hear any more 'everybody's a hero, everybody wins in the end' suggestions."

"Everybody loves a winner. Which is why nobody likes you."

Jolie's other hand came up to slap him. Noah grabbed it.

"I'm not your problem. I'm not the reason your family won't speak to you. Your pissed off, I'll-screw-you-before-you-get-a-chance-to-screw-me attitude is the problem. That's the reason people turn the other way."

"Where'd you learn that?" Jolie sneered. "Panhandling on Hollywood Boulevard?"

"I didn't learn it. That's why I ended up panhandling." Noah pushed her away. "You need a better role model, Vivienne Junior."

He swept his second towel off the chair and made for the dressing room. Halfway through the doorway he remembered his shampoo, turned to go back for it, and saw the plastic bottle sailing toward his head. Noah ducked, heard it bounce off the carpet behind him and the door between the bathroom and the dressing room next door slam with a crack.

He was too surprised to be angry. He just stood there for a second listening to the echo of the door slam. Then he laughed.

"Well, I'll be damned. The little bitch is a coward."

Lucky for Jolie the bottle didn't break. He liked this shampoo.

She'd given up her key to the apartment but he hadn't locked the door. He gave it a push open with his foot and stepped cautiously into the living room. He wasn't sure what he expected or what he thought Jolie would've had time to do—but he sure didn't expect to find Lindsay naked in his bed at quarter past three in the afternoon. She lay on her side facing the bathroom, her head propped on her hand, her golden hair spilling through her fingers, the sheet just barely covering her nipples.

"Princess." Noah stood in the bathroom doorway, breathless at how beautiful she was, an erection rising under his towel.

"I guess you're glad to see me." A flush he thought was arousal not embarrassment pinked her throat. "Have you been flashing people?"

"Just Jolie." She thought he was kidding so she laughed. She'd closed the blinds on the windows around the bed; he locked and put the chains on both doors. Noah undid the towel, pitched it toward the bed, and let her take a good look. "I guess this is what you came for."

"Mmm-*hmm.*" Lindsay rolled over and threw back the sheet.

She didn't want him, she wanted his cock. It was a start.

Noah went to the bed, got on his knees between hers, almost but didn't quite put himself inside her. She'd rolled her head back, ready to clutch him and pull him on top of her. She blinked and looked at him.

"What are you doing?"

"This is a test of the emergency willpower system," he said. "If you can't get through the day without it, princess, you got it bad."

"I've always had it bad." The give-it-to-me-now glaze in her eyes clouded. "And I always felt so guilty. Mark was so wonderful, such a great guy. I loved him so much. But then, there you were and—"

"Yeah, yeah, I know. He was the love of your life," Noah growled. "I'm just the grand passion and ne'er the twain shall meet."

A frown creased Lindsay's forehead. "I didn't mean it that way."

"I know. Ignore me. I'm just horrified that Jolie saw me naked."

She laughed. Noah went up on his hands and drove all the way into her, withdrew and drove again. Long, single strokes that rolled her head back and dug her nails into his hips. Holy God, she was coming already. He could feel the clamp of her muscles, the spasms starting. He managed two more thrusts before she locked around him and pulled him into a climax so staggering he thought he'd blacked out.

Till it passed and he felt her legs sliding down the backs of his thighs, flutters deep inside her that were making him hard again. He pushed into her and she moaned, arched her head back, and lifted her hips, rolling and clutching him and grinding hard against him.

"Jesus, princess." He rose on his hands. "You're gonna kill me."

"You'll die happy. I promise." Lindsay grabbed handfuls

of his hair, yanked his head down, and plunged her tongue into his mouth.

Lights exploded in his head, in his brain. Starbursts he could feel popping like firecrackers. He couldn't pump fast enough, she couldn't plunge her tongue deep enough. It was a double fuck, a numbing head-ringing orgasm that blew all his fuses and left him quivering on top of her.

"Oh please, my queen. No more. I beg you."

She laughed and purred and writhed under him, trailed her nails up his back, cupped his face in her hands and gazed at him starry-eyed, her eyelashes dazzling as jewels.

"You," she breathed against his lips, "are a stunning lover."

"I was today." Noah groaned. "Don't count on tomorrow."

He rolled off her on his back, his arms and legs flung out, his heart banging, the blood still roaring in his ears. He expected Lindsay to hop out of bed, but she slid on top of him, pulled half the sheet over them, sighed, and curled his chest hair around her fingers.

Noah doubled a pillow under his head so he could look at her. "I can't believe you came here in the middle of the day and jumped me."

"I can't, either." She popped up on one elbow and grinned at him. "It wasn't a safe choice at all, was it?"

"Pretty reckless, gorgeous. Do you know what you're doing?"

"Yes." She folded her hands on his chest and propped her chin on them. "I'm having a fling with an old friend."

"Then if you aren't on the pill I need to buy some rubbers."

"I'm not on the pill." Lindsay slapped a hand over her eyes. "And I didn't even think about condoms."

"I'm disease free, believe me. Vivienne had me checked for everything under the shining sun. Toenail fungus, for God's sake."

"Noah. I apologize." She peeked at him between her fingers. "I should have thought of condoms."

"Why? Do you have a dick?" He pushed her head back on his chest where the sleek curve of her cheek felt like a little chip of heaven. He'd heard Donnie use that phrase, too. "It's not like we planned this."

"I feel like Jesse the twerp," Lindsay said. Noah stroked his fingers through her hair and felt her sigh. "Don't beat yourself up, princess."

"I never had to worry about birth control. Mark's sperm count was so low we were told it was a miracle we conceived Trey."

Okay. That was twice she'd mentioned Mark. Once more and he was gonna have to pout.

"I don't think we have to sweat it. I drank so much tequila my sperm are probably still drunk. So blotto they wouldn't know what to do with an egg if one tripped 'em and beat 'em to the floor."

"Drunken sperm." Lindsay pushed up on her elbow, laughing. "Can't you just see all those wiggly, squiggly little things?" She rolled her eyes and her head on her neck. "Reeling around, staggering, falling down snoring all over my womb."

She crossed her eyes, rolled her head one last time, and let it fall with a thunk on his breastbone. Noah laughed, laced his fingers through her hair, and lifted her face between his palms.

"Were you always funny and I just don't remember?"

"I'm no Lucille Ball but I have my moments. Emma says I'm the perfect straight man."

"Then I'll just call you Ethel Mertz."

Lindsay laughed. Her eyes were shining, her nipples tightening, the laughter quivering her belly making him stir.

"If my mouth is dangerous," he said. "Your tongue is lethal."

"Glad you like it." She flicked her tongue across his right nipple. "My vibrator and I have a good time with *The Joy of Sex*."

"Get out." Noah laughed. "The Ice Princess has a vibrator."

"I'm a widow and this is a small town." Lindsay bent her head and swirled her tongue around his left nipple. Noah jumped and stiffened, caught her face, and cupped it. "Uh-unh, princess. Drugstore first."

"Drugstore later." She slid her tongue into his mouth and made him moan, went back to his nipples and licked, rubbed her lips down his torso, darted her tongue into his navel, nuzzled lower and took him in her mouth, sucked him once, and looked up at him. "Is this okay?"

"Oh God, yes. Oh Christ, please."

She wrapped her hand around his shaft, ran her tongue around the head. Noah kept his eyes open, swept the golden curtain of her hair back from her face with shaking fingers so he could watch her blow him. What he could see through the flashes going off in his head, what he could focus on beyond the bliss of her tongue swirling him in her mouth.

She made a noise in her throat, cupped his balls and caressed them, her eyelids quivering, her nostrils flaring. Noah brushed her cheek and felt her shiver. Her lashes fluttered open and she saw him watching her. The corners of her mouth curved and she purred. She was enjoying this. Loving it, thank Jesus, praise God, just as much as he was.

"Lindsay, baby," he murmured. "If you don't suck I'll never come."

She let go of him and raised her head. "Aren't you enjoying this?" She closed him in her hand, teasing him with her thumb. "I am."

Noah reached the towel off the floor beside the bed and tossed it to her. "Once I come you can wipe me off and hop on."

"Oooh." Her lashes jumped and her eyes lit. "Promise?"

"Promise," he said, wishing to God she'd kiss him on the mouth.

She lowered her head and went to work like a Hoover, plunged him into an orgasm he thought to Christ was going to give him an aneurysm. She wiped him gently with the towel, pressed tender, delicate kisses all the way up his shaft, climbed on top of him and spread her hips, put him inside her and moaned so deep in her throat he could feel it.

"Oh Noah." She spread her palms on his chest, her eyes fluttering open to look at him. "You are sooo much better than my vibrator."

"And you don't have to change my batteries."

"Mmm," she said, and smiled.

Noah curved his hands around her hips and started her rocking. When she had the rhythm and her nails dug into his chest, he cupped her breasts in his hands to hold her up, to help her lift and thrust. When her head tipped back and her breath caught, he pushed up on his hands and buried his face between her breasts. She bent like a bow and clutched him, closed her teeth on his left earlobe and nearly shattered the drum with her scream.

Noah muffled most of it with his mouth. When hers went slack and her arms limp, he laid her down, trembling, tucked a pillow under her head, covered her, and stretched out beside her, his hands folded under his head, so proud of himself he wanted to get up and dance.

"Heaven," Lindsay sang. So softly, her voice so breathy Noah thought he could hear her heart beating in it. "I'm in heaven."

He turned his head toward her and she smiled. A glassy, loopy smile, her hair a tumbled mass of gold on the pillow. He rolled up one arm to kiss her. She faked a huge yawn.

Still no kissing. Fucking like rabbits, but no kissing. Noah blew out a breath and lay down beside her again.

"Where'd you tell Emma you were going when you left so early?"

"I told her we were going to work on our lines before rehearsal."

And what did Emma Harrington, she of the lucky guesses, make of that story? He didn't know what to make of it when Lindsay scooted off the pillow onto his chest. Maybe she was cold. He wanted to put his arm around her, but didn't, just let her settle and tug the sheet over them.

"Trey is staying after school with Meggie," she said with a sigh, "to help decorate the gym for the spring dance."

"There's a real Sam and Jesse thing for you."

"I said he could take her to the dance. 'Course he'd already asked her and she'd already said yes. I'm driving them Saturday night."

"I'll go along. We'll double date." She raised her head, blinked at him, and burst out laughing. "Why is that funny?"

"Trey would be sooo mortified if I showed up at that dance."

"Who says we're going to the dance? We're going to wait in the car."

"Oh? And what are we going to do while we wait?"

Noah put his right index finger through the circle he made of his left thumb and middle finger. He didn't realize he'd lost his Band-Aids, that they'd come off in the shower, till Lindsay caught his hand and frowned at his sliced but starting to scab knuckles.

"What did you do to yourself?"

"I slipped in the shower and broke a couple tiles on the wall."

Lindsay arched an eyebrow. "You *slipped* and broke the tiles?"

"Okay. I got pissed and punched the wall and broke them."

"No-*ah*." She tsked at him, a yeah-right twinkle in her eyes.

"I replaced them this morning, but no shower till the grout dries."

"That's fine. I'll take a bird bath in the sink."

He wanted to grab her, keep her in this bed forever, but he let her go, watched her gather her clothes and pad into the bathroom, her hips swaying above those long, scrumptious legs of hers. When the door clicked shut he grabbed the pillow and pressed it over his face.

She promised he'd die happy but she lied. He'd die in L.A., far away from her, alone and miserable unless his Pac-Man memory kicked in the second his plane lifted off the ground in St. Louis and started chewing holes in this tape. He wanted to chew through the pillow. All he'd ever wanted in a woman was a good fuck. Now that's all he was to Lindsay.

Jesus, life was cruel. No wonder he'd turned to drink.

Hold on. Noah threw the pillow off the bed and stared at the ceiling. It could be worse. She liked him. He made her laugh. She was totally, utterly, and completely in love with his cock. How hard could it be to make her fall in love with the rest of him? Like he had a clue what love was, but if this wasn't it he didn't want to know about it. Ever.

Okay. He had a plan. Noah sprang out of bed and paced. Make Lindsay fall in love with him and marry her. If he cried on her shoulder maybe she'd say yes out of sheer pity. Marry her and—

Noah stopped beside the bed. Marry her and what? Support her on his salary from Vivienne and the end-of-the-run bonus until he got himself established? Established doing what? He swung around and paced the other way. Acting? That boat was a *long* way from shore. Sweeping up for Jolie? Helping Lonnie do things that start with *P* on a tractor?

And when his money ran out, then what? Live off hers? Oh yeah. He could see that lasting about a nanosecond. Supporting a man was the kind of thing a woman did for the love of her life, not her grand passion.

He wasn't permanent, he was a fling. He was sex and laughs. Saint Mark had beaten him to the Tower of the Evil Queen and rescued the beautiful princess. He'd boinked her and fallen out of the window drunk.

When Lindsay came out of the bathroom he was dressed and back in his right mind. He caught her around the waist and danced her into the kitchen, bent her backward in a death spiral dip that left her laughing, her hair swinging against the floor and her eyes shining.

"What are you doing, Patrick?"

"Rehearsing." He growled and nipped her throat, felt her breath catch and the pulse under his lips quicken. "I've got to dance you around the stage in a couple hours."

"I don't remember a dip in the script."

"You don't remember it because it isn't there." Noah grinned. "I'm suggesting we add one and drive Jolie nuts."

"Oooh," Lindsay breathed. "I like the way you think."

"Follow my lead, princess. I'll have Satan's Handmaiden foaming at the mouth in twenty minutes flat."

Chapter 25

THE DIP didn't faze Jolie. It came late, right at the end of the play, and by then they were all exhausted. Blocking was hell, figuring out who would stand where, sit where, turn how, move when, marking each character's movements with strips of different colored tape on the stage floor. It was entirely possible that Jolie was just too tired to notice.

Then again . . . maybe the twitch in her right cheek did start jumping just a teensy bit more. The tic appeared in the third scene of Act Two when Noah moved the floor lamp *again*. Lindsay was on his side and even she wanted to smack him.

"Was it my imagination," Emma said to her Tuesday morning while she opened the PC and Lindsay counted the base fund. "Or was Noah doing everything he could think of last night to piss off Jolie?"

"It wasn't your imagination," Lindsay said. "Noah and Jolie got into it yesterday. She caught him in the shower in the dressing room."

Emma's eyes widened. "Naked in the shower?"

"So he said." But that's all he'd said.

"That's what Jolie needs to sell tickets for."

Oh, Em. If you only knew. Lindsay closed her eyes, saw Noah sprawled naked beside her, and felt her stomach quiver.

She had to blink four times to get rid of the image. She could not walk around today like she had yesterday. It was dangerous. She'd damn near fallen off the ladder that ran on a track around the perimeter of the store when a flash of Noah popped into her head. Wrapped in a towel and hard against her belly while they'd danced around the bedroom. She'd blown at least a dozen transactions on the register when he popped into her head again, gorgeously naked, fondling her breasts.

She'd left work before she hurt herself and went straight to Noah, straight to the most glorious afternoon of her life. She wouldn't mind doing it again, but today the plan was pizza for lunch with Emma and comparing the notes they'd made in their scripts last night.

It was Noah's suggestion, made when Jolie announced that Darcy's consulting job was going to keep her in Denver through the run of the play so Emma was stepping into the role of Roxy. It was a responsible, you can count on me to show up and know my lines suggestion. It would be productive and fun, still Lindsay felt a twinge of disappointment.

Till Noah came through the door of The Bookshelf at twenty past twelve carrying a pizza box and her heart flipped at the sight of him. Oh God he was handsome. More handsome now than he'd been on *BBT*. He'd been almost too beautiful then, but now he was perfect.

And he was her lover. The word shot a thrill through Lindsay.

She stepped away from the magazine rack and craned her head out the front window. "Where's Uncle Donnie's truck?"

"At the hardware store." Noah shut the door, the sleigh bells clanging above his head. "It's the only place in this town I can find without getting lost. From there I have to ask directions and walk."

"Noah. It's simple. From the barn you just go to one-fifty-two, turn—"

"Don't confuse me. It's balled up, I know, but it gets me where I want to go. Like today, with this." He swept the pizza box toward her with a flourish. "Half pepperoni and half tomato and olive."

"Thick crust?" Emma piped up from the cashwrap. "Extra cheese?"

"Yes, ma'am." Noah leaned past Lindsay and grinned at her.

"Then haul those three pounds I don't need on my hips back to the break room," Emma said. "I'm starving."

So was Lindsay, to touch Noah, to feel him touch her. She had it bad, all right, but her headache was gone. She'd risen from Noah's bed Sunday night pain-free for the first time in a week. Sure beat Tylenol.

Emma knew to pull two cans of Pepsi out of the fridge—one for her, one for Lindsay—and a bottle of Evian for Noah. If she *knew* they'd spent yesterday afternoon in bed, she was keeping mum. Emma could do that, unlike Darcy. Aunt Sassy wasn't too bad, but Darcy? Forget it.

Emma and Noah polished off the tomato and olive. Lindsay was too keyed up to eat, her senses so tuned to Noah it was silly. Every time he moved, spoke, so much as flicked an eyelash her pulse jumped. It was utterly idiotic. She was behaving like Jesse the twerp and she didn't care.

They made it halfway through the second scene of the first act, reading each other's notes about who was supposed to be where and doing what when the sleigh bells clanged and Emma said, "I'll go."

She rose from her chair licking cheese from her fingers. That's when they heard the war whoop.

"Wilburta and her grandchildren," Lindsay said. Redheaded, four-year-old twins, a prissy six-year-old girl and her eight-year-old brother who thought the comic book spinner was a toy. "I'll go with you."

"No, stay." Emma sighed. "Just come if you hear me scream."

She left the break room and shut the door to the front of the store. Lindsay's fingers shot across the table and met Noah's halfway. His cut knuckles were covered with purple Barney the Dinosaur Band-Aids.

"Where did you get those?" she laughed.

"A gag gift from Lonnie. I'll replace them this afternoon when I drive to Columbia to buy condoms. Donnie thought that was best."

"Donnie thought *what* was best?" Lindsay's heart nearly stopped. "Buying new Band-Aids or buying condoms?"

"Both. He's tired of Lonnie laughing every time he looks at my hand. Yesterday he suggested that I loosen your springs."

"Loosen my—*what*? Uncle Donnie?"

"Lonnie got it from Dovey that you're repressed. He told

Donnie. I don't think they mean sexually, but hey." Noah shrugged. "I'm from L.A."

"How did you and Donnie get from my springs to condoms?"

"He and Lonnie didn't see any lights Sunday night when they drove home from the pot luck. When he asked me about it, I told Donnie you and I were making mad passionate love. He laughed."

"If he thought you were kidding, how did you get to the condoms?"

"He said Lonnie's sniggering was driving him nuts and why didn't I buy different Band-Aids. I said I was thinking about it. He said why didn't I think about it in Columbia. I could buy whatever I damn pleased in the drugstore there and no one in Belle Coeur would be the wiser."

Lindsay could hear Donnie say it just that way. It astounded her, but she could hear him say it. "And he told you I'm repressed?"

"No, Lonnie told him you're repressed. Dovey told me."

"Dovey!" Lindsay shrieked. She didn't mean to, but she was pretty sure the giant thump she heard muffled it from Emma. "When did Aunt Dovey tell you I'm repressed?"

"When she read my tea leaves. Then she read my palm and asked me if I had any interest in marriage." Noah sat back in his chair and folded his arms. "I gotta tell you, princess. I was offended."

"I don't blame you. What a thing to ask. What a thing to say."

"Tell me about it. Then Donnie started in on how I could loosen your springs but I couldn't marry you because I'm basically indigent."

"That's ridiculous! You're acting again. You're earning money."

"Technically no." Noah held up a finger. "I'm not acting again yet. I am earning a few bucks, but that's not the point. The point is I thought you should know that your family is divided into two schools. One thinks I should marry you. The other thinks I should just loosen your springs."

"*You* should marry *me*." Lindsay stared at Noah, so

stunned she could hardly think. "*You* should loosen *my* springs."

"Cheeky bunch, aren't they? Coming to me with this when they should be coming to you. Hell. You could line 'em all out in five seconds."

"Oh could I? What do you suggest I tell them?"

"How about mind your own business? You know what's going on, I know what's going on, and we're the only two who need to know. That's why I'm driving to Columbia this afternoon. So it won't be all over Belle Coeur ten minutes after I walk out of Murphy's Drugs with a box of Band-Aids and a case of condoms that we're sleeping together."

"When you say it like that," Lindsay snapped, "you make it sound like I'm ashamed of you."

"I know you're not, princess, but somebody could think so. Or somebody could think I'm ashamed of you. Like your Uncle Ezra. He might feel compelled to ask Lucille to have a little chat with me."

"Ohhh," Lindsay said. "I didn't think about Uncle Ez."

"I admit I didn't think about him, either." Noah shrugged. "Not while you were giving me the deep throat blow job."

"*No-ah!*" She said his name in two sharp syllables, just as something else went bang up front. "I am not repressed, but there are children out there wrecking our store."

"You're not as repressed as you were, but you've got a ways to go. So do I and I'll probably get lost so I need to give myself time to find my way back before rehearsal." Noah stood up, spread his hands on the table and leaned toward her. "Warning. Smutty sex talk. Want to come?"

"*No-ah.*" She made two syllables of his name again. Two breathy, caught in her throat, oh-God-*yes* syllables. "I can't leave Emma with the aftermath of Wilburta's grandchildren."

Something big crashed in the front of the store. Lindsay pushed out of her chair and Noah wheeled toward the door.

"What was that?" he asked.

"Probably the comic book spinner," she said.

It was, Lindsay saw, when she and Noah hurried up front. The black metal rack lay on its side like a felled tree; the carpet around it littered with comics. Emma leaned her back against the door.

"Are they gone?" she asked.

"Yes," Lindsay said. "The coast is clear."

"That Tyler Allen." Emma sighed and blew the white streak in her hair out of her eyes. "Makes me glad I don't have children."

Noah hauled the spinner off the floor and put it back on its stand.

"Need a hand with these?" He nodded at the spilled comics.

"No, thanks." Lindsay smiled. "We can manage."

He headed for the break room to collect his script. Lindsay wanted to go with him, wanted to feel his arms around her, his body against hers. She wanted to go to Columbia with him to buy condoms and help him open the package. Were these the thoughts of a repressed woman?

When Noah left and the comics were picked up and tucked back in their pockets, Lindsay headed for the reference section and pulled a dictionary off the shelf. Emma was behind the counter muttering and wiping sticky fingerprints off the top of the glass display case.

"Let me read you something, Em." Lindsay said, carrying the dictionary toward her. " 'To keep under control, check or suppress desires, feelings, actions, tears, et cetera.' " She put the book down in a clean spot on the display case. "Does that sound like anybody you know?"

"Yes," Emma said. "It sounds like you."

"Hell." Lindsay slapped her hand on the glass case. It stuck. She peeled it away and made a face at a glop of cherry sucker on her palm.

Emma gave her a Windex wipe. "That's the definition of what?"

Lindsay scrubbed her hand and frowned. "Repressed."

"I can't blame this one on Darcy. She's in Denver. Who blabbed?"

Lindsay blinked at her, startled. "You've heard this?"

"I hear it from Mama every time you come up in the conversation."

"Jeez, Em." Lindsay jammed her hands on her hips. "When were you going to tell me that the whole damn family thinks I'm repressed?"

"If I'd said to you, 'Lindsay. The whole damn family

thinks you're repressed,' what do you suppose you would have said?"

Lindsay wiped up the cherry sucker smear and thought about it.

"I don't suppose I would've said anything." She folded her elbows on the glass case. "I think I would've had a panic attack, because that's what repressed people do. Isn't it?"

"Bing." Emma flicked her index finger off her thumb like she was striking a bell. "Who told you that you're repressed?"

"Noah. He heard it from Aunt Dovey and Uncle Donnie."

"Mmm." She folded her elbows and leaned down almost nose to nose with Lindsay. "So are you going to let him loosen your springs?"

"Em-ma!" she snapped, her arms flooding with gooseflesh.

"Oh, calm down. I didn't read your mind. I eavesdropped."

"That's appalling!" Lindsay screeched and then she laughed. "Why am I laughing? This isn't funny. I'm losing my mind."

"You aren't losing your mind. You aren't repressing for once. You're releasing." Emma straightened and drew in a deep breath, lifting her arms and filling her lungs. "Out with the bad thoughts, in with the good."

"It's not that easy, Em. I can't go around laughing inappropriately and yelling at people just so I don't have panic attacks."

"You don't have to yell *at* anybody. Just yell and blow the lid off." Emma caught her hands in hers and squeezed them gently. "Chaos is fun, Lindsay. It's exciting. Chaos makes it worth getting out of bed in the morning just to see what's going to happen today."

Lindsay could feel the Chaos in Emma, the tingle of it in her fingertips. It danced in her dark eyes and it laughed in Lindsay's head. She heard it as clearly as she'd heard Mark's plane stutter and stall, a giggly little two-step with flute accompaniment.

"You can control Chaos, Em. I can't." Lindsay's throat swelled and filled her eyes with tears. "It took Mark from me."

"Oh honey, no." Emma curved her hand around her

cheek. "Chaos didn't take Mark. A bad piston in the engine took Mark."

"But I *heard* it, Em!" The tears burst out of Lindsay in a sob. "I never told you, but I heard the engine sputter! I heard it stall!"

"Oh Lindsay." Emma shot out of the cashwrap and pulled her into her arms. "If you couldn't tell me you should've told Mama."

"I was too frightened." Lindsay cried and clung to Emma, like Noah had clung to her. "I know better. I've heard you say it and Aunt Dovey say it a million times, and still I thought I'd made it happen."

"You didn't make it happen and neither did Chaos."

"I know that," Lindsay sobbed. "But I had to blame somebody."

"Lindsay." Emma lifted her face from her shoulder and cradled it in her hands. "Chaos isn't a somebody. You know what it is."

"Oh God, Em, please." She sucked back a sob and wiped her eyes with her fingers. "Don't say the *M* word."

"It isn't magic, you dunce." Emma made a face. "It's everything. Everything there is in the universe. It's you and me and Mama and Aunt Sassy. It's Trey and the uncles. Uncle Frank and Aunt Muriel, Susan and Darcy. It's Noah. It's Jolie and Vivienne, God help us. All our atoms are connected to each other. And to the moon and the stars, to the trees and the sun, and they're all zipping around, from Belle Coeur to Jupiter, from your house to mine, to L.A. and back."

"Have you been reading Stephen Hawking again?" Lindsay asked and Emma laughed. "I don't mind the dancing, but I hate the flutes."

"Do you hear them?" Emma held her at arm's length. "Really?"

"Oh yes." She sniffled and sighed. "Especially around Noah."

"You should see it when you two are in the same room."

"See it?" Lindsay reached over the display case and plucked a tissue out of the Kleenex box next to the register. "See what?"

"The colors." Emma swooped her hand through the air

like a paper airplane. "Curling around the two of you like ribbons of light."

"Okay, Em. That's enough." Lindsay put her hands up. "You are now beginning to freak me out."

"But Lindsay. It will be so *good* for the play. Not everyone can hear the flutes and see the colors, yet they respond to them. Why do you think *BBT* was such a hit? Why do you think it still is?" Emma grabbed her hand and towed her toward the back of the store. "You have to see this."

The PC in Emma's office had a DSL hookup. She pushed Lindsay into her chair, shook the mouse to clear the screen saver, and there it was. The Official *Betwixt and Be Teen* Fan Web site.

Beneath the graphic across the top was a photo of her and Noah on the beach. He was in swim trunks lying on his board in the sand. She in a hot pink bikini on his back, her arms around his neck, both of them grinning and gripping the front end of the surfboard. The blue one Cydney Munroe had asked Noah about at dinner Saturday night.

This was Tuesday. In three days hundreds of emails with titles like *"Yippee! They're Back!" "Noah in the Flesh!" "Where the H*ll Is Belle Coeur Missouri?"* had been posted. The fans of the show were checking air fares, rental car rates from Kansas City and St. Louis, planning caravans from all over the country.

Lindsay read posts and iced her tear-swollen eyes. She heard the sleigh bells now and then and Emma talking to customers. She popped into the office, said, "Now check out the theater Web site. Darcy did an update last night," and left to answer the phone up front. When Emma came back, Lindsay looked up from the monitor and blinked.

"I can't believe it. The first three weeks are already sold out."

"Behold," Emma said. "The power of the Internet."

"Jolie knows about the ticket sales, doesn't she?"

"Sure. Darcy told her when she talked to her before rehearsal, to tell her she was stuck in Denver. Darce called me late last night."

"Maybe the ticket sales are the reason Jolie didn't kill Noah."

"That would be my guess. That was Jo Beth on the phone. She has a cancellation. She can take you now for your massage."

Lindsay glanced at the clock on the computer monitor. "It's only one-thirty. I can't bail on you two days in a row."

"Yes, you can. I say you can."

"All right. I'll go, but I'll come back."

"I don't want you to come back. I want you to go home and think about telling Mama what you told me."

"There's no point driving home, Em. Rehearsal tonight and I have to pick Trey up at school before that, after his chess tournament."

"I'll grab him and take him for a burger. We'll meet up at the barn."

Maybe she could meet up with Noah before rehearsal. Maybe he'd be back from Columbia by the time Jo Beth finished with her.

"No," Lindsay said firmly. One day, fine. Two in a row could become a hard-to-break habit. "It's too much."

"You cover for me during tax season. Say yes and go."

Lindsay went. Not like a rocket, but close, to Jo Beth's cute little shop on Spring and into her magic hands, hoping she'd have a chance to deliver herself into Noah's magic hands before rehearsal.

She felt loose and limber when Jo Beth finished with her and so aroused from lying naked on Jo's table for an hour thinking about lying naked with Noah that her heart was banging between her breasts. She sat in the Civic with the windows down, her hair lifting in a breeze, took out her cell phone to call Noah, stared at it a minute, then tossed it into the seat and drove to the barn. He'd either be there or he wouldn't.

He was there. He opened the backdoor with his half-glasses on, a grin on his face and a bulge in his jeans. Lindsay slipped through the door, leaned against it to shut it, slid her hands in his back pockets and pulled him against her. She parted her lips to kiss him, but he turned his head away and nuzzled her ear.

"I'm going to owe Emma a boatload of chocolate for

this." Lindsay slid her tongue in his ear, felt him shiver and a jump behind his zipper.

"I'll chip in." Noah backed away from her and cupped his hands around her breasts. "Go see what I have for you in the bedroom."

He had condoms. About a zillion boxes laid out on the bed. Colored ones, ribbed ones, flavored ones. Lindsay picked up one of the boxes, turned toward him as he came through the bathroom door.

"Key lime pie?" she laughed.

"I thought you might like to go tropical." He cupped her breasts, found her nipples with his thumbs. Lindsay tipped her head to kiss him but again he turned his head. She frowned. "You don't want to kiss me?"

"I didn't start the no kissing stuff, pretty woman."

"That was a bad idea," Lindsay admitted. "And it doesn't work. It doesn't make me want you less. It only makes me want you more."

"Then I may never kiss you again. On the mouth anyway."

"Tough guy, huh? I dare you not to kiss me."

"A dare." Noah's eyes lit. "I haven't had one of those in years."

"So. Are you on?"

"I will be as soon as you take your clothes off."

"He or she who kisses first on the mouth loses."

"That's you, so you might as well kiss me and tell me what I win."

"You are not going to win."

"Yes, I am. You're putty in my hands." Noah slid his right hand between her legs. Warning flares of imminent orgasm shot through Lindsay. She wanted to moan but steeled herself and cupped his bulge. "I can make putty out of this in a heartbeat, pal."

"The hell you can." Noah popped the snap on his jeans and ripped the zipper. "Get your slacks and your panties off."

Lindsay peeled off her sweater, unfastened the front catch of her bra, raised her arms to stretch and bare her breasts, and watched Noah's nostrils flare. When she cupped her breasts in her hands his eyes glazed.

"Jesus," he said, his voice raw. "You play dirty."

"I want to win."

"No way, gorgeous." Noah dropped his pants and kicked them away. Lindsay didn't dare look. "You are going down."

"That was my plan." She tore open the key lime condom with her teeth, slid it over Noah like a banana skin, and took him in her mouth.

He closed his hands in her hair, let her suck twice, then lifted her onto the bed. She helped him peel off her slacks and panties, opened her legs and held her arms up to him. He slid on top of her, his fingers inside her, and rolled her toward him on her side.

Another batch of flares went off in her head but she beat them back and wrapped her fingers around Noah, stroked him while he teased her. She was doing fine, holding her own, till he bent his head and sucked her left breast into his mouth. When he closed his teeth on the nipple the orgasm hit her like a thunderbolt.

Noah felt it, how could he not with his fingers inside her, rasped, "Oh Jesus, princess," in her ear and rolled her on her back, spread her legs and got between them and drove into her.

Lindsay hooked her legs around his waist, taking him as deep as she could for two blinding, white-hot thrusts till he came as hard as she did, his head thrown back, muffling a roar between his gritted teeth. He fell forward on his hands, spent, his palms spread on either side of her head. Lindsay cupped Noah's face and gazed up at him, sucking air through his flared nostrils, her fingers trembling on his jaw.

"I give," she said, just as he said, "I give," and their mouths dove together in a long, long kiss that melted and molded them together.

Noah raised his head to take a breath and then he kissed her again. Lindsay kissed him back, savoring the shape and the taste of his lips. He was still inside her, growing hard. She groped on the bed for another condom, ripped open the foil and had it ready when he pulled out so she could change him and slide him back inside her.

It was sweet and it was slow this time, a long, languid kiss of their mouths and their bodies. Closer to magic than anything Lindsay had ever felt in her life; the orgasm he gave her a caress, a bloom of lavender pleasure wrapped in soft pink bliss and sealed with a kiss.

The colors, Lindsay thought. *Oh my, there they are.* They faded when she sighed and Noah drew a deep, shuddery breath. He settled on top of her, his weight on his arms and his knees and kissed her temple.

"This is the best sex I've ever had in my life," he murmured in her ear. " 'Course it's the only sex I can remember having in my life."

Lindsay laughed and kissed him and darted her tongue in his mouth. Noah groaned and slid his fingers in her hair. His breathing quickened but when she rolled her hips he slipped out of her.

"I think you broke my spring," he said, and she laughed again.

Noah reached for a pillow and tucked it under their heads, caught the corners of the green coverlet and pulled it around them. Lindsay smiled at him across the pillow. He smiled back and stroked her hip.

"You smell like eucalyptus. You had a massage."

"I made an appointment for you with Jo tomorrow at four."

"How do I get to her shop from the hardware store?"

"Just come to The Bookshelf and I'll get you there."

"How was the key lime pie?"

"Awful. Did you buy cherry?"

"I bought every flavor known to man. How about strawberry-mango? Or mandarin-orange kiwi?"

"Sounds like *you* were in a tropical state of mind."

"I was thinking about L.A. About the beach." Noah turned on his back, bent his arm under his head and grinned at her. "I could've damn near bought a surfboard with what I spent on condoms."

"You won't regret the investment." Lindsay rolled up on her elbows and kissed him. "I promise."

That wasn't what she wanted to say. She'd wanted to say "Would you *rather* have bought a surfboard?" but it was snippy and petulant and didn't belong in pillow talk between two old friends having a fling.

"I'm going to open the pool Saturday." She laid her fingers on his chest and stroked. "Why don't you come swim? No surf, but it's water."

"We've had this conversation." Noah frowned. "I even said please."

She ran a nail around his nipple. "You could see me in a bikini."

"Big whoop. I can see you naked."

"When I *let* you see me naked."

"Is this gonna end up in another dare?"

"If you don't say yes, maybe."

"Lindsay. Leave it." Noah turned on his side and curved his hand around her face. "You said you wanted a fling. I'm fine with that. I'll give you a fling. Just don't torment me, okay?"

He brushed his thumb across her cheekbone, went into the bathroom, and came back with two towels. He sat down on the side of the bed and gave one to Lindsay as she scooted up beside him.

"I just want you to come swim with me," she said.

"I'll swim with you, princess." Noah wiped off the massage oil she'd rubbed into his chest hair with her breasts. "But not in your pool."

"The farm ponds are too muddy."

"Gee. Tough break. Too bad."

"I think you're being silly. It's only a pool."

"Jesus Christ." Noah flung the towel over his head and pressed it to his face, yanked it away and turned sideways on the bed to look at her. "My house is the only thing I remember. It had a pool four crapping times the size of yours and beyond that the Pacific Ocean. Big, blue, spectacular. I don't think I was born. I think I was spawned. That's how much the ocean means to me. I could step out of my bedroom into the surf. There were days when that's all that kept my head together and it's gone. I fucked it up and I pissed it away and it's gone."

"Oh," Lindsay said softly, amazed that she could push her voice past the ache in her throat. "It's not just a pool for you. It's a symbol."

"This I can handle." Noah made a sweep with one hand.

"This isn't my room. This isn't even my bed. This place isn't mine. It's never going to be mine." He cupped her cheek and smiled. "And neither are you."

Lindsay reared up on her knees and crushed him to her, laid her cheek against his hair, felt his arms close around her and sucked back tears. Her heart was thundering; she imagined Noah could feel it between her breasts. She dropped on her knees and kissed him, a hard, fierce kiss, then gripped his face in her hands.

"It was a beautiful house, Noah. White carpet, teak woodwork. All glass across the back. You could see the ocean from every room." He smiled, a soft *oh yeah* smile Lindsay thought would break her heart. "I want you to have it back. Your house, your career. All of it. I want that for you and you can have it. You can, Noah. You *can*."

She went up on her knees again and kissed him, lifting his face in her hands. He groaned and reached for her breasts. Lindsay curved her hands over his, grazed his fingertips across her nipples. She let him lick twice then sat back on her heels, gripping his fingers in hers to keep her hands off his erection. His face was flushed, his eyes glazed.

"My spring isn't broke anymore."

"Your spring isn't the problem." Lindsay gave him a finger-flip on the forehead. "Your brain is the problem. Where's your script?"

"Ow." Noah stuck his lip out. "That hurt."

Lindsay pecked a kiss between his eyes. "That's the last kiss you get *anywhere* until you know all your lines in Act One."

"Well, fuck. Shoot me now and be done with it."

"And none of this." Lindsay stuck her right index finger through the circle she made of her left thumb and middle finger. "Till you know your lines in Act Two."

"Well, in that case." Noah gave the towel an indignant flip over his erection. "I hope you enjoyed your little fling because it's over."

"When you know your lines in Act Three—" Lindsay pursed her lips and puffed a tiny breath across his mouth. "When you know *all* your lines, I will blow you from here to Cincinnati and back."

"Christ Jesus in heaven," Noah said. "Where's my script?"

Chapter 26

INCENTIVE. That's all Noah needed. The right incentive.

It was better than calling it blackmail. Which of course it was, but that was too close to Vivienne's modus operandi for comfort, so Lindsay chose to call it incentive. And it worked.

Noah spent mornings building the Murphy bed with Donnie and afternoons at The Bookshelf working on his lines with her. When she wasn't on the phone or waiting on customers, he followed her around the store with his script while she stocked or alphabetized.

Emma coached. Pyewacket lay on the PC and yawned.

Rehearsals were dicey. Noah tended to panic when he stumbled on a line or lost his place in the script, which Jolie allowed them to use for the first week. Fortunately most of his scenes were with Lindsay. She was there to toss him a word or a gesture that helped him recover.

"Damn this is tough," he said to her. "No camera. No do-overs."

"You'll get the hang of it," she assured him. "It's not that hard."

"Do *not*." Noah scowled. "Say that word in my presence."

When they closed the store he took out the trash and vacuumed. When the UPS guy came, he unloaded all the books.

"Handy to have around, isn't he?" Lindsay said to Emma.

"Yeah, and not bad to look at, either." She grinned.

On Saturday morning Lindsay opened the store. When Emma came in at two she went home to meet the pool guy. At five she dropped Trey at Jo Beth's on her way to the barn. She'd made the arrangements on Tuesday before she'd come up with her brilliant incentive plan for Noah. If only he'd learned his lines, Trey wouldn't be the only West sleeping over tonight.

That made her sigh, and then yawn, a huge, jaw-cracking yawn. She was so exhausted from lying awake wanting Noah, so bleary-eyed from learning his lines, too, that the inside of her skull felt sore.

She was sure all Noah needed was a shot of confidence. If he could get the first act down the rest would be a snap. She was certain of it, positive. But just in case she'd be ready to bail him out if he froze up on opening night. She'd never tell him. The last thing he needed was doubt from her. He had enough of his own.

Since Tuesday they'd taken to calling each other at bedtime. She'd been wary at first, thinking Noah was trying to lure her into phone sex, but they were short conversations, like he just wanted to hear her voice.

Last night he'd said to her: "Have dinner with me. I'll cook."

Picturing Noah in the kitchen naked was one thing. Picturing him in the kitchen cooking was frankly scary.

The Corvette was a nice surprise. It sat beneath the hickory trees no longer horse piss yellow but a glistening shade of marina blue. When she knocked on the back door, Noah answered in jeans and a navy blazer with a white dishtowel folded over his forearm.

"Bonsoir, Madame." He bowed. "Welcome to Chez Patrick."

He offered his elbow and led her into the dining room.

She recognized Aunt Dovey's lace tablecloth and her candlesticks. Crystal with teardrops and lit white tapers casting a soft glow on the most incredible meal Lindsay had ever seen. She clapped a hand over her mouth, let Noah seat her, and spread a cloth napkin in her lap.

"For the appetite of Madame," he said, sounding uncannily like Peter Sellers as Inspector Clouseau. "We have the chocolate sampler."

A lettuce bed arranged with artistically sliced Hershey bars, plain and almond, Dove Bars, Mounds, Milky Way, Snickers, and 3 Musketeers.

"For the first course, we have the chocolate mousse soup. Perfectly chilled." Noah kissed his fingertips. "For the main course, Madame will nibble with her succulent pink lips on the strawberries dipped in dark chocolate. And for dessert—" He swooped Aunt Muriel's lidded silver serving dish in front of her. "—the *pièce de résistance.*"

With a flourish he swept the cover off a life-size chocolate penis.

Lindsay screamed, slapped her hands to her burning cheeks, and howled with laughter. Noah stayed in character, a wounded, befuddled French waiter, till she fell out of the chair on her hands and knees.

"Oops. Princess overboard." He put down the dish, hauled her to her feet, and held her up by her elbows. "Are you okay?

"I'm almost afraid to ask, but *where* did you get that thing?"

"I'm telling you," Noah grinned, "Lonnie can get anything."

"Lonnie!" She shrieked and laughed till she cried. Noah held on to her till she could breathe on her own.

"Thank God you're a good sport."

"That's the funniest thing I've ever seen," Lindsay said. "I don't think I even care that half my family knows about it."

"Lonnie's the only one who knows about *it.* Though I imagine he told Donnie. I just borrowed dishes and stuff from your aunts."

"Well." Lindsay wiped tears off her cheeks. "Shall we eat?"

Noah seated her again and took the chair on her left.

"Why the chocolate smorgasbord?" she asked.

Noah bit into a strawberry and licked chocolate off his lip. "I'm told women rely on it heavily to cure a bad case of gotta-have-it-but-can't."

"I don't want to know which one of my cousins told you that."

They laughed, ate the strawberries, and shared a bowl of mousse soup. Noah put the appetizer tray on the coffee table between them after they cleared the table and settled on the couch with their scripts.

His hand was in the tray more than hers. He kept licking chocolate off his bottom lip. Like every five seconds. Just to tease her, Lindsay was certain, just to tantalize her. She ignored him.

"Yech. That's it. That's triggering my gag reflex." Noah made a face, pitched a half-eaten Snickers on a napkin. "I don't know why you women think this shit works. It isn't doing a damn thing for me."

Lindsay bit into a Dove bar, stretched her right foot toward Noah and tickled his knee. "You've got the wrong hormones, big guy."

"I'll show you big." He grabbed her ankle and gave her a yank. Planted her foot in his crotch—his hard, throbbing crotch—and sighed.

Lindsay snatched her foot away. "What do you think you're doing?"

Noah frowned. "I thought I was getting off."

"There's a delicate phrase. You aren't getting off with my help." Lindsay tapped a pencil against her script. "Till you know your lines."

"I'll be crippled before then." He pointed at his distended zipper. "Do you know how difficult it is to walk around with one of these?"

"Learn your lines." Lindsay tapped her pencil. "Or get a crutch."

"Just give me your foot. Your hand would be better, but I'll settle."

"No-ah." Lindsay evaded the grab he made for her and tucked her feet under her. "What did I say?"

"You said you wouldn't kiss me, screw me, or blow me till I know my lines. C'mon, princess," he wheedled, rubbing his knuckles on her knee. "All I want you to do is touch it."

"I am not going to touch it."

"Would you look at it? Maybe that would get me off."

"No!" Lindsay said, so flushed and damp she was having trouble keeping her voice firm. "I will not look at it."

"Why the hell not? You've been ogling it in the store for the last three days when you think I'm not paying attention."

"Please, Noah. You're making this extremely hard for me."

He closed his eyes. "I asked you not to use that word."

Lindsay tossed her script on the table and took his face in her hands. He opened his eyes, almost but didn't quite stick out his lip.

"You're doing so well. You've already got the first scene and you're *sooo* close on the second. If you concentrate we can get two tonight and move on to three tomorrow. I'll have all day to devote to this."

"All I can think about is you," Noah said, his voice deeper than usual, his eyes a darker shade of blue. "How beautiful you are. How much you love having me inside you. Jesus, that's a high."

"Don't think about me. Think about Moira. *Be Cliff. Think about Moira.*" Lindsay gave his head a little shake. "Call me Moira if you have to. I'll call you Cliff if it'll help."

"Might work." Noah pursed his lips. "Keep talking, Moira."

"You love me, Cliff. You've always loved me. We went from nowhere to the top of the world together. We struggled, we starved. We fell in love. We became huge stars on Broadway. You were unfaithful. I cast you out, but you can't forget me. All these years you've regretted your mistakes. You'd do anything to turn back the clock and finally your chance comes. A revival of our show, a chance to win me. What can you do? How will you convince me that you're worthy of my trust and my love?"

They blinked at each other for a second. Then Noah said, "Whoa. Sound like anybody you know?"

"In places." Lindsay let go of his face and rubbed the gooseflesh on her arms. "Except you didn't break my heart."

"Did I break your—" Noah caught himself. "Sorry. Let me rephrase that. Were you a virgin?"

"Thank you," Lindsay said primly. "No. I wasn't a virgin."

"It wasn't that I couldn't forget you. I couldn't remember you."

"In L.A. I didn't trust you any farther than I could see you."

Noah tipped his head at her. "What about now, princess?"

"I don't sleep with someone I don't trust, Noah." Lindsay slid her hands into his. "You're sober. You're kind to animals and children. You're a whole new you."

"Yeah." He laughed. "Yeah I am." He said it thoughtfully, pressed her palms together between his and smiled. "I think I might be okay, princess. No matter what happens with the play."

"You can saw boards!" Lindsay grinned and flung her arms out above her head. "The sky's the limit!"

"If I can learn these goddamn lines." Noah sighed, picked up his script and his glasses, and frowned at her. "Where do you suppose Satan's Handmaiden came up with the idea for this play?"

"Lately I've been trying *not* to think about how Jolie's mind works." Lindsay retreated to her corner of the couch and opened her script. "Okay. Cliff and Moira are in her dressing room. Moira says. 'I want you out of my dressing room this second.' Cliff says—"

"Can I watch you eat dessert?"

"No!" Lindsay thundered at him, laughing.

She was still laughing on the drive home. She hummed in the shower, smiled while she creamed her face, sighed as she settled in bed with her book. When the phone rang it was Noah.

"What did you do with dessert?" he asked.

"I wrapped it in foil and half a roll of freezer paper, wrote SUMMER SAUSAGE on the Ziploc bag, and stuffed it in the bottom of the freezer."

Noah laughed, then sighed. "Wish you were here." She hadn't told him Trey was spending the night with Denny; it was too cruel.

"Learn your lines," she said in a singsong voice.

"Yeah, yeah. The more I wonder how Satan's Handmaiden came up with the idea for this play the more it bugs me."

"Boy meets girl, boy loses girl, boy wins girl back is the oldest plot in the book, Noah. Stop wondering."

"So I'll see you and Trey about one tomorrow, right?"

"Yes. We'll stop for a sandwich after church."

"No, don't. I'll take us out to eat someplace."

Lindsay warned Trey about the Corvette on their way to the barn. He got out of the Civic and walked around the now blue car. She heard the back door slam, glanced up, and saw Noah coming toward them.

"So what do you think, sport?" he asked.

Trey came around the front end of the Corvette and cocked his head at Noah. "Why'd you paint it the same color as my mom's eyes?"

"What?" Lindsay pushed off the Civic and wheeled toward Noah. He stopped next to her and peered at her face. "Well. What d'you know. Guess I did. I just liked the color."

"It's okay." Trey shrugged. "I just like yellow better."

"It glowed in the dark, kid. I'm telling you. Even with the bedroom blinds shut I had to wear my shades to sleep."

"Yeah, right." Trey rolled his eyes but he grinned.

Nothing would do but they had to go to lunch in the Corvette. It was a tight squeeze, but Trey managed to wedge himself onto the tiny rear deck between the bucket seats. They zipped out of Belle Coeur with the sunroof open and a Beach Boys CD in the player. Noah and Lindsay sang along to "409" and "Fun, Fun, Fun." Trey hammed it up car dancing the Swim and the Mashed Potato.

They ate at Mrs. A's, a country style restaurant on Route 10. Chicken fried steak, mashed potatoes, green beans, and cinnamon rolls.

"Where'd you get the Beach Boys CD?" Trey asked him around a mouthful of apple cobbler à la mode.

"I found it in the trunk. In a bag with a bunch more CDs."

"Okay. Let's try this. *Why* are you listening to it?"

"A little respect, please. That's the music of my heritage. Sand and surf bunnies and boards with so much wax on 'em you slide off."

Just to torment Trey, Noah punched up Neil Diamond's "Sweet Caroline" and "Cherry Baby" on the way back to Belle Coeur. To the barn and Noah's apartment to rehearse.

"Okay, you two." Trey dragged the coffee table away from the couch, sat on Noah's script, and opened Lindsay's to Act One, Scene One. "Show me what you got."

"Oh jeez." Noah said. "Spielberg Junior."

Lindsay helped him move the rest of the furniture to approximate the stage arrangement, took her mark, and gave Noah his first line. "Well, well. *Clifford*. Still up to the same old tricks, I see."

"Wait a minute, Moira. This isn't what you think. I can explain."

And away they went with Trey feeding the lines spoken by the other characters. The first scene was flawless, the second pretty darn good. Three was pretty rocky, still Lindsay was so pleased for Noah and so proud of him she gave him a high five.

"Not bad," Spielberg Junior said, his lips pursed. "But I'd like to see the third scene again."

"How about sixteen?" Noah said. "Would you like to see sixteen?"

"Ma," Trey said. "Don't let him hurt me."

They ran through the third scene twice more, took a break, then repeated the entire first act. Even Noah was jazzed when they finished and he'd only flubbed a handful of lines.

"You worked on the third scene after I left last night, didn't you?"

"It's a lot easier to concentrate when you aren't hopping up every five minutes to let a pain in the ass cat in and out."

Pyewacket came to work with Emma Monday morning, jumped up on the display case and rubbed noses with Lindsay. "Did you have a nice weekend?" She stroked a hand down his back. "I did."

"Wait till you see." Emma's eyes glowed with excitement. "Darce called. She had to update again last night. The theater Web site took so many hits over the weekend the server went down."

"I'm dying to see," Lindsay said. "But let's wait for Noah."

When he came in with his script about one, Emma dragged him back to her office with Lindsay. The counter on the bottom of the theater Web site had jumped almost twenty thousand since Tuesday. Four and a half weeks of *Return Engagement*'s run were sold out.

"Yow." Noah grinned. "We may be looking at an extended run."

Six more weeks of *Return Engagement*. Six more weeks of Noah doing things to her they hadn't even thought of in *The Joy of Sex*.

"I think I can handle that." Lindsay smiled at him.

"You ain't seen nothin' yet." Emma clicked the mouse and showed Noah *The Official Betwixt and Be Teen* Fan Web site.

He gave a shout of laughter at the photo of the two of them on the surfboard and dropped into Emma's chair. The message boards amazed him. Lindsay leaned over his shoulder to show him how to use the mouse, felt the sizzle, the tiny leap of Chaos between them.

Noah turned his head a fraction, almost but didn't quite nuzzle her neck, his nostrils flaring as he inhaled her perfume. Emma looked the other way. If she didn't see it, Lindsay was sure she sensed it.

The *Where the H*ll is Belle Coeur Missouri*? post made Noah roar with laughter. "I've been wondering that myself," he said to Lindsay.

Noah in the Flesh made him grin and his eyes light up. She got such a kick out of watching him browse the messages, laughing and cracking jokes. He leaned back in Emma's chair and looked up at her.

"Jesus, princess. We're bigger than The Grateful Dead."

It was a great ego-builder, just the shot of confidence he needed. He sailed through Act One at rehearsal that evening. Never flubbed a line, never missed a cue. Noah Patrick strode the boards of the Belle Coeur Theatre like he'd been born in a costume trunk.

It was a wondrous thing to watch. Lindsay felt a leap in the Chaos meter and she wasn't the only one. Uncle Frank and Uncle Ron beamed, Aunt Sassy and Susan, who'd taken Emma's job as stage manager, were flushed and starry-eyed.

Lindsay could almost see the nimbus of Chaos shimmering around Emma—and the ugly black storm cloud brewing above Jolie's head.

She sat in the front of the house, about ten rows back from the center stage, her leather portfolio open in her lap, her script on top of it. A tight, twisted, pinched up little ball of teeth-gnashing fury.

"We're making progress." She slapped her portfolio and her script shut and shot to her feet. "Act Two tomorrow night. Seven o'clock."

She pushed her way out of the empty row and stalked up the aisle.

"I think she expected Noah to fail," Lindsay said to Emma from the corner of her mouth. "I think she was hoping he would."

"Of course she was. Then she'd have a reason to scream at him. It wouldn't be so obvious that she hates his guts." Emma nodded at Noah, standing with Uncle Frank in the space the Murphy bed would occupy. "Did he ever tell you what he and Jolie argued about last week?"

"No. He just said it was the same shit, different day."

Noah looked around at Emma's laugh, saw Lindsay and smiled. A hot-eyed, you-owe-me smile that made her pulse jump.

Uncle Lonnie was prop manager. She helped him and Susan place the props for the start of Act Two, swung her purse over her shoulder and tucked her script in the curve of her elbow. She felt a prickle up the back of her neck and turned around. Uncle Frank was still bending Noah's ear. He slid her a wait-for-me-I'll-be-there glance. Lindsay nodded and headed for the Civic.

She'd parked in the main parking lot tonight, took her keys out of her purse as she walked up the aisle, out of the auditorium and into the lobby. She was halfway to the hat check room when Jolie called to her.

"Lindsay." The sound of her name on her baby sister's lips made her heart catch, her steps falter. "Lindsay. Wait a minute."

She ignored her and kept walking, heard Jolie's footsteps pounding down the stairs from the landing. *Go away,* she thought. *Just go away.*

"Damn it, Lindsay!" Jolie barked. "I said *wait a minute!*"

Lindsay whipped around, so suddenly Jolie blinked and backpedaled. "I told you not to talk to me. I told you not to come near me."

"Here. These are yours." Jolie thrust an express mail envelope at her. "Trey's pictures. Vivienne sent them to me."

"That figures." She grabbed the envelope and spun on her heel.

"You're fucking Noah, aren't you?"

The blast of Chaos almost bent Lindsay's knees. Wild, furious colors exploded in her head. Red so deep it was almost purple, green swirled with black. This was the Chaos that terrified her. Jolie seethed with it; she always had. Lindsay realized now that she could see it. She had no idea why she could see it, she only knew that she could—and that it wouldn't be wise to leave such anger behind her unchallenged, snapping at her with razor teeth. She drew a breath and turned around.

"Is that what this is, Jolie? You want to be in Noah's bed?"

"Oh please." She made a face, stuck her finger in her mouth, but her gaze jumped away and a flush started up her throat.

"That's exactly what it is. That's why you kept a key to the apartment, why you were in his bedroom Easter morning. That's why you followed him into the shower. Just so you could see him naked."

"You had him in L.A. When you two were on *BBT*," Jolie shot back, her face scarlet, her eyes blazing. "Why shouldn't I have him now?"

"Emma told me this is why you hate me. You think Vivienne should've taken you to L.A., made you the star. You think my career should've been yours, that everything I have should be yours. I can't change any of that, Jolie, but if you want Noah—" Lindsay made a sweep of her arm. "Take your best shot with my blessing."

She turned away shaking inside, her face hot, her hands cold. She hadn't lied. She hadn't denied and she wouldn't. She'd simply evaded.

"Everybody in town knows you're in the sack with him," Jolie jeered at her. "The whole world knows. It's all over the *BBT* Web site."

"Oh *please*. That old story's been on there forever." Lindsay turned to face Jolie. She'd put six or so feet between them so the lash of Chaos wasn't quite so overpowering.

"The lunatic fringe in the club," she said, repeating what Gus Munroe told Noah, "has *always* thought Noah and I had a thing going off camera. If that's where you got your information—"

"Vivian told me. She knows all about you and Noah."

"Vivienne is a liar." Which was true, but apparently she was also a damn good guesser. "She'd claim black is white if it suited her purpose."

"How do you think I came up with *Return Engagement*?" Malice lit Jolie's eyes. "She paid me an extra fifty grand above everything else to write it exactly the way she wanted it."

"I hope you said thank you. It's a damn good play, but it's fiction." That was also the truth. "Boy meets girl is the oldest plot on earth."

That was it. She'd said enough. Lindsay wheeled away from Jolie, pushed through the doors and into the warm spring night that took some of the chill out of her. She'd intended to wait here for Noah, but scotched that plan. She jumped in the Civic and drove around to the apartment, raced across the grass, almost fell down the steps, and used the key Noah had given her, the one Jolie had left on the dining room table, to let herself into the kitchen.

She drank a glass of water to take the ache out of her throat, made a cup of tea in the microwave to calm down. She burned herself, she was shaking so badly.

"Princess. Did I miss the signal?" Noah came through the living room door, shut it, and put on the chain. "I was looking all over for—"

He was halfway across the dining room when Lindsay hit him like a thunderbolt, threw her arms around his neck and clung to him.

"Whoa, honey." Noah held her, rubbed his hands on her back. "You're shivering. What the hell happened?"

"Listen. Just listen and let me tell you." She told him as quickly as she could, quoting her confrontation with Jolie word for word, watched something dark and dangerous leap in his eyes. "I'm not ashamed of you." She held Noah's face between her hands, the heat in his skin finally warming her fingers. "I did not lie about us. I simply evaded."

"If it's all over town your little bitch sister put it out there."

"I know that. It could just be a lie. That's the thing with Jolie, you're never sure, but I have to think about Trey."

"That's a given. What do you want to do? Just tell me."

"I don't know." Lindsay backed up a step, caught Noah's hands, and held them tight. "I just don't want Trey to hear rumors about us."

"Okay. How about this? We keep evading. Both of us. We laugh it off, say yeah, yeah, go check out the Urban Legends Web site. Our mad passionate love affair is on the top ten list."

"That's good." Lindsay laughed; surprised that she could, not at all surprised that it had a hysterical edge. "I think it might work."

"You can't come here anymore." Noah turned her by the elbow toward the back door. "You need to get the hell out of here right now."

"Wait." Lindsay lifted her arm out of his hand. "I owe you a kiss."

Noah pushed her against the wall, spread his hands on either side of her face. Almost but didn't quite press his body against hers, still Lindsay could feel the heat, the Chaos sizzling between them.

"I don't how you're gonna pay me off for Act Two," he said.

"I'll think of something," she promised and kissed him.

Colors spun in Lindsay's head. So gorgeous she couldn't name them. She could only feel them in the taste of Noah's mouth. Hot, frantic cinnamon, soft, lingering citrus. He pressed his thumb to the corner of her mouth, broke away from her, and sucked a breath.

"Kiss me like that again and I'll rent a billboard, tell the world."

Lindsay raised her eyebrows. "There's an idea."

"A really lousy one. The first person who hassles Trey I will deck." He took her elbow again. "C'mon, princess. I'm just your old platonic pal walking you to your car."

Chapter 27

THE REPORTER *People* magazine sent to Belle Coeur loved Noah's comment about the Urban Legends Web site. She laughed till her cute little blond head rolled on her neck like a bobble head doll. She was putty in Noah's hands. Lindsay knew the feeling.

She'd called The Bookshelf on Tuesday. A staff Internet reporter noticed the buzz on the *BBT* site and gave her a heads-up. She wanted to bring a photographer to Belle Coeur and interview her and Noah. Lindsay made the arrangements, hung up the phone, and went to meet Noah for lunch on a bench in the middle of the town square park.

"If she's bringing a photographer," he said, "I better get a facial."

"If it's a slow news week she's hoping for the cover story." Lindsay looked at the ham sandwich in her lap, wrapped it up, and put it back in the basket Uncle Lonnie had packed. "She wants beach pictures."

"You told her Missouri only has muddy ponds, didn't you?"

"I told her I have a pool. She said that would work."

Lindsay glanced sideways at Noah. He'd stopped chewing and sat scowling at her over his sandwich.

"It's for the play, Noah. And your career."

"Shit." He sighed and took a swig of Evian. "When's she coming?"

"Thursday, day after tomorrow."

A car horn tooted. Lindsay turned her head and waved at a young, pretty brunette cruising past in a red SUV packed with kids.

"Mary Lou Hanley's daughter Carol," she said to Noah.

"Nice and friendly." He nodded. "How many is that?"

"Three cars, four pickups, Carol's SUV. And five pedestrians."

"No screams of 'Fornicators!' and no thrown tomatoes. I'd say Jolie was lying through her teeth. But we'll still play it safe."

It was Thursday and they were still playing it safe, sitting on opposite ends of the couch in her living room watching the cute little head of the cute little reporter from *People* roll around on her neck. Her name was Morgandy, a combination of Morgan and Brittany. She looked to be all of twelve. She'd loved *BBT* when she was in elementary school. Lindsay was doing her best not to despise her. Morgandy was doing her best to keep her eyes off Noah's crotch.

He was still a sight to behold in a pair of swim trunks. Cute little boxer-style blue ones with green palm trees she'd bought in Columbia when she and Emma went shopping. He'd put them on in the guestroom, looked at himself in the full-length mirror, at Lindsay sitting on the foot of the bed in the bikini she'd bought, and slammed into the bathroom.

"What was that about?" she asked him when he came out.

"You in that damn bikini. I had to put on a jock strap."

The photographer hollered through the French doors that he was set up and ready for them. Trey did a cannonball into the deep end. Yesterday he'd whooped it up because he was getting a day off school for this. Last night after rehearsal he'd been short and snippy, but this morning he seemed fine. Teenage boys.

Noah stood on the side of the pool, his hair lifting in the wind, hands on his hips, shades on his nose. For a second Lindsay thought he might wheel back into the house, then he tossed his shades onto a chaise and dove in, his body a perfect arc that barely rippled the surface. She smiled and for some idiotic reason felt tears on her lashes.

This wasn't what she'd had in mind when she'd asked Noah to come swim with her. She'd been thinking skinny dip in the dark, but it was fun horsing around with him and Trey in the pool while the photographer took photos. Flashing smiles at the camera, dunking each other, hanging off the float, slapping a volleyball around.

Noah dry in swim trunks was one thing. Noah wet in swim trunks was a slow burn to meltdown. He stood on the side of the pool with the volleyball, laughing while he waited for Trey to surface so he could bean him. The hair on his head slicked back, the hair on his chest glistening; the rivulets of water sliding down his body delineating his sleek muscles and the even-with-a-jock-strap bulge in his trunks. Lindsay's nipples were hard and Morgandy's eyes were glassy.

This was the easy part, looking good for the camera. The interview worried her. Unlike the citizens of Belle Coeur, who may or may not know that she was sleeping with Noah, the whole world knew about his crash and burn. Of course Morgandy asked. It was her job. She was a *BBT* fan and therefore sympathetic, but she asked. Lest Noah accuse her of rushing to the rescue, Lindsay kept her mouth shut.

"I'm an alcoholic but I'm not a drunk. Not anymore," Noah told her. "I've been sober for two years and I plan to stay that way."

"Are you following a program? Are you in therapy?"

"My program is don't pick up the bottle. Therapy? Yeah. I probably will when I can afford it. In the meantime, I'm sawing boards for the sets." He held his hands up and grinned. "And I've still got all my digits."

The kid reporter laughed. She laughed harder when he told her about getting his ass stuck to the Dumpster his first day in Belle Coeur, so he told her about the Murphy bed. About Pyewacket weaving in and out of the ropes while he and Donnie were stringing them through the pulleys, getting lassoed around the belly and hauled off the floor yowling.

"Wish we'd been here to see that." She shared a laugh with her photographer. "Sounds more like a guillotine than a Murphy bed."

"It's a great little piece of engineering. Lindsay's uncle designed it and built it. C'mon." Noah stood up. "I'll show it to you."

The kid reporter tipped her head at him. "Where is it?"

"At the theater. You want to see the theater, don't you?"

"Yes. We're due to meet Jolene Varner there at two o'clock."

"Great." Noah clapped his hands together. "Then we have time for a tour of Belle Coeur. And lunch. May I suggest a barbecued pork tenderloin sandwich and a blueberry milkshake?"

"*What?*" The kid reporter said it with a laugh—Lindsay with a what-the-hell-are-you-doing snap in her voice as she shot to her feet.

"A local delicacy." Noah ignored Lindsay, lifted the kid reporter out of her chair and nodded at the grinning camera guy. "Grab your gear, pal. We'll get dressed and move this party down the road."

"Take your time," the kid reporter said. "We'll wait here."

"Great." Noah caught Lindsay's elbow. "Right with you."

Two steps inside the house she wrenched away from him, shut the French doors, and wheeled on him. "What are you doing?"

"Call the uncles, tell them we're coming. Do *not* call Jolie."

"Like I would." Lindsay snorted. "What are you up to?"

"Lindsay." Noah cupped her shoulders. "You know how it works in L.A. The last thing you want to do is look like you need a job. I don't want to look like I need a job."

"But why the tour of Belle Coeur?"

"Why not?" Noah shrugged. "It'll be fun."

And he'd have pictures to help him remember this place and this time in his life. He couldn't imagine forgetting his first glimpse of Lindsay when he came down the stairs from Jolie's office or Ezra coming after him with Lucille, but he'd have photos just in case. The photographer would shoot everything; photographers always did. If he didn't offer the negatives Noah would talk him out of them. Maybe he'd buy an album.

"All right," Lindsay said. "Your clothes are in the guestroom."

Noah dried off and dressed, jeans and a blue polo, put on his shoes and rummaged in the drawers in the bathroom vanity till he found a hair dryer. He used it and put it away. He'd forgotten a brush and did the best he could with his hands to make his hair look like something.

He didn't realize the bathroom connected to Trey's bedroom till the kid slouched into the second doorway, a sober expression on his face.

"Hey, sport. What's up?"

"Are you boinking my mother?"

Noah had him pinned against the wall, an arm across his throat before he knew what he was doing. Trey's eyes were huge, a startled, angry glitter in them. Noah lifted his arm but kept him nailed to the wall.

"Am I *what?*"

"That's the right word, isn't it?"

"The right word for what?"

"Sex. Screwing. Fu—"

"Watch it, smart mouth. We're talking about your *mother*."

"I know we are! Why do you think I'm asking?"

He had tears in his eyes. Noah let him off the wall. Trey wrenched himself straight and stood toe to toe with him glaring.

"Did you make this up? Or did somebody say something to you?"

"Jolie told me. I figured she ought to know."

"Anybody else whisper in your ear?" Trey shook his head. "Don't you think that's odd? In a town this small?"

"You didn't answer my question."

"I'm not going to answer it. I'm an adult. You're a kid. My sex life is none of your business. Same with your mother and you damn well know it. You asked me 'cause you knew better than to ask her."

Trey flushed and looked away. "I thought I could trap you."

"Now you know you can't. I'm sorry about the wall."

"Why did Jolie say that to me, about you and my mom?"

"She's not a happy camper, kid. And if she ain't happy, ain't nobody gonna be happy."

"That's what Uncle Ron says."

"Smart guy. I'd listen to him. Are we okay here? You and me?"

"Yeah, we're okay." Trey shrugged. "Are you gonna tell my mom?"

"No. This is just between us guys. Want to ride with me?"

Trey's eyes lit up. "Can I drive the 'Vette?"

"Not today. We've got places to go and things to do."

First they ate an early lunch at Burger Chef, at one of the metal picnic tables under the canopy out front. The kid reporter liked the tenderloin so much she hardly noticed he didn't eat his, but Lindsay did.

She noticed the gleam of Chaos in Noah's eyes, too, and felt her stomach sink. Oh God. What was he up to? *Really?*

From Burger Chef he led them to McGruff's Hardware. Morgandy thought it was hysterical that it was Noah's point of reference for finding his way around town. He had his photo taken with Fred McGruff and his beat-up old backgammon board. Lindsay had no idea why.

Next stop Pantz Pressers and a photo op with Uncle Ezra. Lindsay had a fit about Lucille being in the picture, but Noah insisted. He stood beside Uncle Ez, the two of them cradling Lucille between them. It was too weird for words.

At the Belle Coeur Academy of Performing Arts, Noah tugged Aunt Sassy into an impromptu soft-shoe. Lindsay had forgotten Noah could dance. He wasn't Fred Astaire, but he wasn't bad. Aunt Sassy swooned when he spun her into a tango. She pinched him on the ass when he dipped her. Noah kissed her. Lindsay had no idea what he was doing.

The lightbulb came on in her head when they stopped in The Belle Coeur Café and Noah glanced at the clock on the wall above the lunch counter. *He's trying to beat Jolie to the barn,* she realized. To steal her thunder, to cut her out of the interview. What a wicked thing to do. Just the kind of thing Satan's Handmaiden would do. Lindsay couldn't think of anyone who deserved it more.

Noah spied Susan having lunch with Uncle Frank and Aunt Muriel, hopped into their booth, and waved at the photographer, whose name Lindsay found out was Jim. He took pictures of everyone in the café, of Mary Lou selling Noah a nosegay of daisies for Morgandy, and last of all Emma and Aunt Dovey—neither of whom looked surprised to see them—when they swept into The Bookshelf.

Pyewacket was there so they scooped him up, piled into the cars, and headed for the barn. Uncle Donnie had the big doors open when they pulled in and parked. He and Lonnie stood grinning in their coveralls.

Noah showed Morgandy and Jim the table saws, the uncles' amazing array of tools, how they stored the scenery flats, how they built them. He had his picture taken with Donnie and Lonnie. Morgandy wanted one of Noah on top of the Dumpster. Then he led them up to the stage, dragging Uncle Donnie along to show off his creation.

The Murphy bed was in place, its shape eerily like that of a guillotine on the dimly lit stage till Noah brought up the lights and the shiver racing up Lindsay's back vanished. When Donnie worked the pulleys and dropped the bed out of the scenery wall, Pyewacket hopped onto the mattress, curled into a ball in the middle of it, and went to sleep.

"Noah. Lindsay," Jim the photographer said with a grin. "Get up there with the cat and let's get a little sex into this."

"Oh Christ I wish we could," Noah muttered, as they laid down facing each other, hands on their heads, with Pyewacket between them.

"Jolie will be furious that she missed all this," Lindsay murmured to him, smiling for the camera. "I could just kiss you."

"Good luck to her if she tries to blacken our names after today."

"That's not the only reason you did this. You gave people who never get a chance at it a shot at the limelight."

"Well." Noah shrugged. "That, too."

"You're a good man, Noah Patrick." Lindsay puckered up so it looked staged for the camera and leaned toward him. "Kiss me."

"That's great," Jim the photographer said. "Give her a buss, Noah."

"I'll force myself." He grinned and met her halfway over Pyewacket's pointed black ears.

There wasn't much Chaos in the kiss, just the tiniest spark, but a blast of it hit Lindsay when the auditorium doors swung open and Jolie blew through them like a dark, ugly wind. "Oh yippee," Noah muttered. "Spawn of Satan."

"Spawn of Satan? When'd you come up with that?"

"This morning while I was changing."

For once Jolie looked the part of Creative Director of the Belle Coeur Theatre. A green pantsuit and shoes with heels, her hair done up in a loose chignon. She did not look happy to see them on her stage nearly an hour earlier than they were supposed to be here.

"*Hel-lo* there." Jolie put on a gushy smile as she came up the stage steps. "I'm Jolene Varner. You're early. I wasn't expecting you till two."

"Nice to meet you." Morgandy shook her hand. "Actually, we're just finishing. We had the most amazing tour of this wonderful little town."

"Well, how nice. Step this way—" Jolie made a one-armed sweep "—and I'll give you a tour of the Belle Coeur Theatre."

"We've already had a tour, thanks. Courtesy of Noah."

He was on his feet, elbows resting on the back of the prop wing chair when Jolie's gaze, loaded with livid Chaos, zapped him like a laser. Noah grinned and gave her a jaunty little salute.

"Great to meet you, really." Morgandy shook Jolie's hand again. "Thanks for letting us shoot here."

Jolie blinked. "You're leaving?"

"We're finished. Might as well get an early start back to St. Louis."

Noah's grin widened. He swept a hand over his mouth and ducked his head. Lindsay turned her back on Jolie, thunderstruck and seething, and said under her breath to Noah, "Mission accomplished."

He wagged his eyebrows. "I love it when a plan comes together."

"Just a suggestion. But I think you've done enough for one day."

Noah hadn't even started, but he didn't tell Lindsay that.

He thought he was never going to get her out of the barn, but finally she and Trey were in the Civic, the kid reporter and Jim in their rental car, and he and the uncles were waving them good-bye.

"One question, fellas." Noah faced Donnie and Lonnie. "Will you miss Jolie if I break her neck?"

"Nope." Donnie glanced at his brother. " 'Bout you, Lonnie?"

He grinned and gave Noah a thumbs-up.

Jolie was still on the stage, sitting in the wing chair staring at the floor in a daze. She raised her head when she heard his footsteps on the stairs, blinked and a spark leapt in her eyes.

"You brought them here early on purpose. You meant to cut me out of this, didn't you?"

"Damn skippy betcha I did. Better get used to it. Henceforth, I plan to treat you exactly the way you treat me and everybody else."

"You—" Jolie seethed at him "—are a fucking sonofabitch."

"Takes one to know one, kid. We had this conversation the day I got here. I thought you and I understood each other. You don't screw with me and I don't screw with you."

Jolie sucked a breath and narrowed her eyes. "I should fire you."

"Go ahead. Throw my ass and the only chance you have to save this place right out the front door with it."

"You don't think I will, do you?"

"I don't care what you do to me. Take your best shot." Noah flung his hands on the arms of the wing chair, pinning Jolie narrow-eyed and furious against the back. "Take another shot at Lindsay's kid, your own nephew, and I'll show you what I do to people who *really* piss me off."

Jolie slapped him hard enough to make his ear ring. He just smiled and walked off the stage whistling. He didn't realize she'd cut him with one of her poison thorn fingernails till he was in the Corvette on his way to Lindsay's house and he felt a trickle of blood.

"Look. A dueling scar." He showed his cheek to Lindsay when she opened the front door. "Where's Trey?"

"He's in the pool."

"Is he likely to come in on us?" Noah saw the pulse in Lindsay's throat leap.

"I don't think so. Oh, I hope not."

He stepped inside, leaned her against the wall, and kissed

her. Oh Christ her mouth was heaven, the feel of her arms around his neck, the brush of her fingertips. The press of her body against his, the swell of her breasts. He broke the kiss while he could, before it got out of hand, before he never stopped kissing her and to hell with who saw them.

"I thought you weren't coming here anymore," Lindsay said when he stepped away from her. "I don't mind, I was just wondering."

"Oh what the hell." Noah shrugged and grinned. "You lured me into your pool. I might as well throw caution to the winds."

"Let me have a look at that cheek, then I'll lure you into the pool again." Lindsay led him into the bathroom, sat him on the toilet and dabbed hydrogen peroxide on his cut. "Any marks on Jolie?"

"I wouldn't hit her. I might choke her but I wouldn't hit her."

"I wish you'd stop poking sticks at Jolie, Noah."

"She deserves it. Besides, it's fun. You aren't afraid of her?"

"Oh no, but she's chock full of Chaos. It's so wild and out of control in Jolie." Lindsay eyed him soberly. "You should be careful."

"What the hell is Chaos?"

"I'll tell you when you aren't jumping around like a live wire."

"I'm jazzed from today. Aren't you?" He stood up and put his hands on her shoulders. "I haven't been that *on* for that long since—" He broke off and grinned at her. "Well. Obviously *I* can't remember."

"Go swim." Lindsay laughed. "It'll take the edge off."

He swam in her pool every day for the rest of the week. Lindsay gave him a key to the gate in the fence so he'd have access. Oh, it was nice to come home after a hard day slinging books to find a gorgeous, wet, half-naked man sprawled and snoring in a chaise on her deck with his script damp and wrinkled in his lap and his glasses on his nose.

He was busting his ass, as Noah phrased it, to learn his lines. When she wasn't helping him at The Bookshelf or on the phone late at night he studied them on his own. When he nailed Act Two at rehearsal tears of pride and want filled Lindsay's eyes. It was hell to stand at the French doors watching him sleep on her deck, aching to slide into the chaise with him, feel his sun-warmed skin and his mouth on hers.

They were still being careful and Noah, thank heaven, wasn't antagonizing Jolie. He bugged her at rehearsals, irritated her every chance he got, but there were no more confrontations like the one in the shower and the slap that drew blood.

So far. The closer they got to opening night the shorter Jolie's fuse burned. When Morgandy called to tell Lindsay the photo of her and Noah kissing over Pyewacket's head on the Murphy bed made the cover, her heart flipped with excitement; then sank with dread imagining the hissy fit Jolie would throw if she wasn't even quoted in the article.

She was, but only in passing. "We're thrilled here at the Belle Coeur Theatre to be the venue for the reunion of these two great stars."

Emma made a face at Lindsay over the brand spanking new issue of *People* delivered by their magazine vendor barely twenty minutes ago.

"Wonder how she got that out without choking."

"Oh God," Lindsay groaned. "It doesn't even say she's my sister."

"You've got the same last name. It says Belle Coeur is your hometown. People will figure it out. And it might not be a bad thing that no one knows you're related to Satan's Handmaiden."

"Spawn of Satan," Lindsay said. "That's Noah's new name for her. There's no mention of Vivienne, either. Wonder how that will go over?"

"She's mentioned." Emma pointed. "Right here in the we of 'we're thrilled at the Belle Coeur Theatre.' We all know who *that* we is."

"Thank God Jolie's in St. Louis and Kansas City till Thursday," Lindsay sighed. She was making a PR sweep, buying radio time, placing print ads. "We've got three days to batten the hatches."

"Lindsay. You're choking. Don't block Chaos, let it flow."

"Right." She closed her eyes, focused on the colors it was becoming easier to see in her head every day, inhaled through her nose, and blew out through her mouth. "Breathe it in, transform it, let it go."

"Atta girl." Emma clapped her on the back.

Lindsay was letting Emma teach her things about Chaos, simple things that didn't freak her out. Like how to breathe it and release it so it didn't bottle up inside her and cause a panic attack.

"Oh, looky girls! Looky!" Aunt Sassy burst into the store, the sleigh bells clanging. She was hopping up and down, her eyes shining, almost popping, a copy of *People* waving. "I'm dancing in a magazine! Folks all over the country's gonna see me doin' the tango with Noah!"

"Aunt Sassy!" Lindsay and Emma cried together. "You're a star!"

"Woohoo!" She put her arms over her head and boogied.

Lindsay and Emma sprang out from the behind the counter and joined Aunt Sassy, caught her hands and danced with her, all the steps she'd taught them from the time they could toddle. Aunt Dovey came in, clapped her hands at all the hip-bumping going on, and joined right in.

It was an all day party. Everyone in Belle Coeur found their way to The Bookshelf to admire their photographs, to goggle at their tiny little town in the pages of *People* magazine. Emma ran for donuts. At lunch they ordered so many barbecued pork tenderloin sandwiches, blueberry milk shakes, and onion rings that the Williams family, who owned and ran Burger Chef, had to close down for the day and join the party.

Oh it was Chaos, beautiful, happy Chaos, merry pink and sunburst yellow, spooling in ribbons over the heads and through the hearts of everyone who came through the door. Lindsay could see it, caught her breath at the wonder of it, felt her heart swell and nearly burst when Noah came in carrying Pyewacket.

The crowd engulfed him, cheered him, lauded him and thumped him on the back, passed him around and hoisted him up on the cashwrap. Everyone wanted his autograph on the cover.

"Get Lindsay up here," he said. "I won't sign unless she does."

He'd come in with Uncle Donnie and Uncle Lonnie. Donnie lifted her up beside him with a plunk that bumped her shoulder against his.

"Hi, gorgeous," he said in her ear and handed her a ballpoint from the pen cup on the counter behind them. "Get ready for writer's cramp."

Mary Lou Hanley tiptoed in nervously with an arm full of eye-popping pink gladiola. Aunt Sassy met her at the door, pointing at the tiny little picture of her face in the window of her shop, taken when they'd crossed the street to The Bookshelf. Lindsay remembered Jim wheeling on the curb to shoot it. Mary Lou blinked and gave a startled whoop. Aunt Sassy gave her a grin and hip-bump. They laughed and they hugged.

At three-thirty the bus from the high school stopped at the curb. Trey and his classmates piled out, Meggie and the rest of the cheerleading squad shaking their red and white pom-poms.

"Oh Christ," Noah said to her. "It's Sam and Jesse in the flesh."

They kept the store open late so everyone who worked nine to five could join the celebration. About six, Lindsay went outside with Aunt Dovey and sat for a few minutes on the lawn chairs Donnie brought as the sun set and the maple trees hissed softly in a breeze off the river.

"Can you hear it, Lindsay? The music in the trees and the wind?"

"You mean the flutes, Aunt Dovey?"

"It's not just flutes. It's a whole orchestra. One day you'll hear it."

"I heard Mark's plane the night he died." Lindsay drew a breath. Breathed, transformed, released. "I heard it sputter and I heard it stall."

"I've wondered, way you act sometimes." Dovey gave her hand a gentle squeeze. "You didn't cause it. You didn't think that?"

Lindsay didn't answer, just nodded.

"Chaos doesn't cause things, child, and neither do you. Chaos just is, there's no bad or good. Our Dear Lord made Chaos and he made all of us. We're here by His grace and we're here on His time. When He wants us back, we go. It's just that damn simple. No harm or hurt to it."

Lindsay felt tears in her eyes till the breeze lifted, the trees sang. Then her tears were gone. "I won't cry about Mark anymore."

"No reason you should. He's where he's supposed to be. So are you. So am I." Dovey slid her a grin and a wink. "So's Noah, by the way."

Lindsay laughed. "I wondered when you'd get to him."

"Question is when are you gonna get to him?"

Soon as we close the store, she decided. Trey had gone home with Jo Beth and Denny and Tiffany. He could stay till ten, Jo said, so the only problem was where. The maple trees knew. Lindsay heard them and smiled, gave them each a pat on her way back inside. She found Noah in the crowd and tugged him into the cooking section.

"Where's the Corvette?"

"Where do you think?" He grinned. "At the hardware store."

"Be in it at eight o'clock. When I drive by, follow me."

"To the ends of the earth, gorgeous."

Dutiful, beautiful man. He did exactly as he was told. Lindsay led him out of town, past the barn and onto the farm roads past where he and Trey had gotten lost. Down a tractor path to the farthest reach of the fields, a rolling stretch of tree-lined pasture glistening with moonlight.

Lindsay was out of the Civic in a flash, caught Noah in her arms as he stretched out of the Corvette, and pulled his mouth over hers. Her momentum made him stumble, but he caught her, lifted her, and sat her on the fender, pushed between her knees and pressed against her. He was so hard she moaned and sucked his tongue into her mouth.

He broke free of her mouth and caught her face in his hands. "There's a condom in my back pocket," he said, his voice raw. "But just one."

"That'll work." Lindsay hopped off the car.

Noah ripped off his shirt. She peeled off her slacks, then her panties, took the condom from Noah and tore it open while he dropped his jeans and his Jockeys. He threw his shirt on the fender and lifted her onto it. She rolled the condom over him and raised her arms around his neck. He gripped her hips and drove into her. He kissed her, rubbed his lips across hers, and set her off like a match.

"Oh Jesus. You're coming." Noah sucked a ragged breath, flung his hands on the hood of the car. "Oh Christ, so am I."

Lindsay wrapped around him and sucked his tongue into her mouth. Hooked her knees around him and let him thrust till he tore his mouth away from hers, flung his hands on the hood, pumped her one last time, then caught her in his arms and gasped for air.

"That's for Act Two," she purred in his ear, and kissed him.

Chapter 28

THE CAMPGROUND and RV Park covered six acres on Route 10, the southernmost boundary of Belle Coeur. On Tuesday, the day after the *People* article appeared, two campers and two SUVs pulling pop-up campers with Missouri license plates rolled in.

It was a little unusual for this third week of May, two weeks prior to schools across the state setting their captives free for the summer. On Wednesday a Winnebago from Wisconsin and an Air Stream from Indiana came to town. All full of women. No kids, no hubbies, just women.

That was very unusual. Sheriff Chub Allen drove out Route 10 to have a little chat with the new arrivals. He filed an official report in his office, an unofficial one at McGruff's Hardware.

Aunt Muriel happened to be there purchasing a new

battery for her red scooter. She came by The Bookshelf to tell Lindsay and Emma.

"A lovely group of ladies, according to Chub," she said. "Members of your fan club, Lindsay. Yours and Noah's. They're here to see the play and see Belle Coeur. They read about it in that nice magazine story."

"Aunt Muriel," Lindsay said. "The play doesn't open for two weeks. Why are they here so early?"

"Oh yes, I remember now. Chub said something about a meeting."

That afternoon six members of the *BBT* fan club came into The Bookshelf. They were very nice, as delighted to meet Emma as they were Lindsay. They talked about *BBT*, they asked for Lindsay's autograph. They talked about children and husbands and they bought books.

While Emma rang up their purchases they asked oh so casually where in town Noah was staying. That's when Lindsay saw the needle on the Chaos meter leap into the danger zone. Without that warning flash of hot, passionate, pulsing pink she might've missed the gleam in their eyes, might have remembered too late that *fan* was short for *fanatic*.

"I'm sorry, but I can't tell you." Lindsay smiled. "It's theater policy to protect the privacy of our visiting celebrities."

Oh yes, yes, of course. They understood. Would she tell Noah how much they were looking forward to seeing him in the play? No one said the word *dying* but it glittered in their eyes. Would she let him know that if he'd like to join them for dinner some evening he could just give a ring.

They left cards with cell phone numbers, pager numbers, email addresses. Lindsay saw them to the door, slammed it so hard the sleigh bells hit the floor, and lunged for the phone. Emma was already punching Noah's cell phone number and tossing her the receiver over the counter.

Lindsay glanced at her watch. It was two-thirty. Noah should be at her house swimming his daily fifty bazillion laps.

"Hi, gorgeous." His voice sounded groggy. "Glad you called. I fell asleep in this killer lounge chair of yours. I can't stay awake in it."

"Don't ask questions, Noah. Just do as I say. Go in the house. Lock the doors. Close all the blinds. Do not—"

Lindsay heard a thump somewhere beyond the phone. "Hang on, princess. Something just hit your fence."

"No!" Lindsay shouted. "Noah! Do *not* go near the fence!"

She heard a clunk like he'd put the phone down, another thump, then a scream. A horrible clunk on the line, like maybe he'd dropped the phone, then a bang, a slam, and a chorus of muffled squeals.

"Mayday, princess!" Noah shouted. "Mayday!"

That's all he said, then the connection broke.

"Call 911." Lindsay pitched the phone to Emma and raced for her office, her purse, and her car keys. "Tell Chub my house is under attack!"

Technically, Lindsay thought, *you'd call it a siege.* There were three women on her front porch and a ladder thrown up against the twelve-foot privacy fence around the pool. She climbed it, looked over the top, and saw six women on her deck tapping on the French doors.

"Noah!" They called in wheedling voices. "We know you're in there. We saw you run into the house."

Fury hit her, then the absurdity of what she was seeing. Four attractive, nicely dressed, perfectly normal looking women reduced to trespassing by want of a man. Lindsay could relate.

"Hi, ladies!" she called. "I'm Lindsay Varner! Can I help you?"

"Oh, Miss Varner!" A plump little blond gushed, appalled, as her friends jumped away from the French doors like scalded cats. "We had no idea this is your home! We saw Noah's car in the drive, the blue Corvette from the *People* magazine article. We thought he was staying here."

"He just swims here. Would you come out of my backyard now?"

"Oh! Of course! Oh, Miss Varner! We're so sorry!"

Lindsay climbed down and met them as they came double time through the unlocked gate. "Why did you bring a ladder?" she asked.

"We're so sorry, Miss Varner." The plump blond flushed

to her dyed roots. "We just intended to peek a little. Till Martha realized the gate was open and then—oh goodness. We just lost our heads."

So had she over Noah. A looong time ago.

"You poor things," she said and meant it. All four of them looked utterly mortified. "Why don't we pretend this never happened?"

"Oh Miss Varner. You're so kind. Thank you so much."

They swooped her into a tearful group hug that lasted till Lindsay heard a pop and a crackle followed by Chub Allen's amplified voice.

"PUT DOWN THE BINOCULARS AND STEP AWAY FROM THE HOUSE. NO, NO, MA'AM—DON'T PUT UP YOUR HANDS. JUST PUT DOWN THE BINOCULARS."

"That's the sheriff," Lindsay said. "I suppose we should go have a word with him."

It was a stern word, a firm word about the penalties for trespassing that sent the *BBT* ladies scurrying to their cars with promises it would never happen again. When they drove away, Chub burst out laughing, so hard Lindsay had to help him into his squad car. He promised he'd call her as soon as he could talk about this and keep a straight face.

"What d'you mean the Sheriff *left*?" Noah demanded, outraged. "I was almost *assaulted*!"

Lindsay got down on the floor and lifted the lace dust ruffle so she could see him better, hiding under her bed beside Pyewacket.

"You were almost assaulted by four women, Noah."

"Christ! Ow!" He whacked his elbow on the frame as he slapped a hand over his eyes. "I used to have wet dreams about four at once. I must've been out of my mind. It's terrifying."

"They didn't intend to assault you. It was all Martha's fault."

Noah spread his fingers. "Who's Martha?"

"The one who realized the gate was open. That's when they lost their heads and charged you."

Noah blinked at her. Then he smacked his hand on the floor, buried his nose in the carpet, and laughed till he sneezed.

"Oh Jesus." He raised his head and rubbed his nose. "How stupid do I look hiding under your bed?"

"Pretty damned," Lindsay said gently.

"See?" He glared at Pyewacket. "I told you this was a dumb idea."

"Uh, Ma?" Trey said. "Who're you talking to?"

"It's me." Noah elbowed his way out from under the bed. "I was assaulted—well, almost assaulted—by four women."

Trey grinned. "Lucky devil."

"Yeah?" Noah stood up, still in his swim trunks, and brushed dust and lint out of his chest hair. "Wait till it happens to you."

The phone rang. Lindsay answered it in the kitchen.

"Lindsay, hi. It's Uncle Ron. Is Noah there?"

"Yes. Do you want to speak to him?"

"I want you to keep him there. The barn is surrounded."

"Surrounded?" Lindsay repeated. "Surrounded by what?"

"Women," Uncle Ron said. "Fifty or sixty. They're waiting to see Noah. We've got the doors locked, Donnie told them rehearsals are closed, but they're still out there."

"Oh my gosh, Uncle Ron. What are you going to do?"

"Join them for dinner. They're tailgating in the parking lot."

The cast of *Return Engagement* assembled to rehearse in Lindsay's living room at 7 P.M. Susan was in charge in Jolie's absence; she made the decision. Aunt Sassy offered, but Lindsay made the coffee and defrosted a Pepperidge Farm Coconut Cake in the microwave.

She could hear Noah's voice in the living room. It sounded good, it resonated, plucked a string in her heart. She wasn't sure she'd ever want to *know* things the way Emma did, but standing in her kitchen Lindsay *knew* she could get used to hearing Noah's voice in her house.

There was no reason she couldn't for the time he'd be here in Belle Coeur, before he went back to L.A. and resumed his acting career. She could make him not want to go, make him want to stay. Lindsay knew she could, but she knew she wouldn't, no matter how much she wanted to hear his voice in her house every day for the rest of her life.

Noah needed to go back, to make it in L.A. just to prove to himself that he could. She knew he could and she *knew* he would. The article in *People*, the droves of *BBT* fans showing up in Belle Coeur said he was a hot property again. The big boys in Hollywood would realize it and pick up the phone. Soon. Lindsay *knew* that and for once it didn't spook her. For once it made her smile, though she had tears in her eyes.

When they finished at ten-thirty, Uncle Ezra stood up and laid a hand on Noah's shoulder. "Don't you fret, son. Me and Lucille'll git you back safe to your place tonight."

And they did. Noah told Lindsay when he called her at bedtime.

"No women anywhere in sight. They'd gone back to their campers. I felt kind of sorry for old Ezra. Nutty as a fruit-cake, but a nice guy."

On Wednesday a caravan of campers and mobile homes rolled into the Campground and RV Park. By high noon there were close to three hundred vehicles and a thousand women in residence. By two there was a hot air balloon filling and rising behind the cement block showers.

Lindsay and Noah lay on their stomachs on the top of a bluff above the camp, taking turns watching the balloon through a pair of binoculars Chub had confiscated at her house yesterday.

"I'm feeling a yen for camouflage paint." Noah peered through the glasses. "I can't see what's on the side of the balloon. Your turn."

Lindsay took the binoculars and a look. "I think it's a face."

"Let's forget it for a while." Noah sat up with his back to the balloon, his arms looped around his knees. "Vivienne called."

"I'm not surprised." Lindsay sat up beside him. "I'm sure she's seen this week's issue of *People* magazine by now."

"She wants me to come to L.A." Noah turned his head and looked at her. "I'm up for a part. Can you believe it?"

"Noah!" Lindsay went up on her knees and threw her arms around him. He caught her around the waist, his face buried in the front of her T-shirt. She could feel his breath hot between her breasts, her nipples harden, and rocked back on her heels. "Already! How exciting!"

"A really small part on some sitcom, but it's better than nothing."

"It's a beginning." Lindsay caught his hands, held them in hers tight against her knees. "I'm so happy for you."

"Vivienne wants me in L.A. Sunday. See the producer and the casting director Monday. Shoot Tuesday, maybe half a day Wednesday, be back here on Thursday two days before we open."

"That will work." Lindsay touched his face. "Are you excited?"

"You mean when I'm not petrified?" He blew out a breath. "How can I learn my lines without you?"

How can I do anything without you? That's what Noah wanted to say. Christ. He couldn't get through a day without seeing her, touching her, at least talking to her. She was worse than tequila.

"It's a small part." Lindsay patted his cheek. "Fax me the lines. We can do it on the phone."

"No we can't." Noah turned toward her, drew her between his legs, and put his hands on her waist. "Not as well as we can do it here."

"I wouldn't recommend it." She kissed his nose, crawled out from between his legs, and picked up the binoculars. "It's chigger season."

"What's a chigger?"

"Microscopic bugs. Worse than mosquitoes." Lindsay trained the glasses on the balloon and adjusted them. "They live in the grass."

Noah jumped up and brushed off his jeans.

"Oh my God." Lindsay gasped and shot to her feet. "Take a look."

She handed him the binoculars. Noah looked through them, then flung them away like they'd burned his hand. *"That's my face!"*

"Wonder how much you could get for that on eBay?"

"What are they gonna do with a hot air balloon with my face on it?"

"Do believe they mean to sell tickets," Chub Allen said.

Lindsay and Noah turned and saw the sheriff huffing and puffing up the steep path to the top of the bluff behind them. He plucked a folded pink sheet of paper out of his uniform pocket.

"Found this," he said, "stuck to a tree on Main Street."

BBT FANS!!
WIN A HOT AIR BALLOON RIDE WITH NOAH!!
A TWO-HOUR FLIGHT FILLED WITH FUN AND ROMANCE!!
TICKETS $5.00 EACH—
DISCOUNTS AVAILABLE FOR WHOLE ROLL PURCHASES!!
VISA, MASTERCARD, AND AMERICAN EXPRESS ACCEPTED
CONTACT CLUB PRESIDENT, VIRGIE KEYHART

"Raffles are illegal in the State of Missouri," Chub said. "But I'm afraid to go down there and tell 'em. Might start a riot."

"I remember the name Keyhart," Lindsay said. "The president was in The Bookshelf yesterday with five of her friends."

Noah looked at her. "Did I agree to this and I don't remember?"

"The president was very eager to find you. I'll bet this is why."

"Got a call from two TV stations in St. Louis and one in Kansas City. Camera crews and reporters oughta be here any old time," Chub said. "Looks like we got us a media circus on our hands."

"Looks like *we've* got—" Lindsay said to Noah with a grin that drew a small, shell-shocked smile from him "—a hit play on our hands."

The TV crews were due at The Bookshelf at three-thirty.

The store was swamped with customers, most of them *BBT* fans hoping for a Noah Sighting, but they were buying. Aunt Dovey was there to lend a hand. Emma was frazzled, her white streak doing a flyaway thing over her forehead, but her dark eyes danced with excitement.

"I tried to call you," she said to Lindsay, pulling the

door to the front of the store shut behind her. "Where were you?"

"Spying on the enemy. I had my cell phone, Em, but I've never seen so many satellite dishes in my life. Some of those RVs have bigger and better receivers than I do on my house."

"Where's Noah? Is he okay? Did they capture him?"

"He's in my office. The coast is still clear out back. The advance scouts have yet to discover the alley."

"That won't last. You'd better get him out of here."

"Where am I going to take him?"

"Brace yourself." Emma held her shoulders. "Chub deputized Uncle Ezra to help with crowd control. He and Lucille and Uncle Frank are standing guard at your house. I'll send the TV crews out there."

"Thank God Uncle Frank is there." Lindsay held up a finger, started to turn away. "I'll call you when we get there."

Emma caught her arm, drew her back. "Isn't this fun?"

"It's a blast," Lindsay laughed. "I can't eat, I can't sleep, I'm having so much fun. Where has Chaos been all my life?"

"Right here." Emma touched a fingertip to her nose, smiled at her. "You have to let Noah go back to L.A. You do know that."

"He's on his way," Lindsay said. Her heart clutched but she told Emma about the call from Vivienne. "Is that wonderful?"

"It's great!" Emma gave her a push. "Go while you still can."

Three sawhorses blocked the lip of Lindsay's driveway. Uncle Ezra leaned against the middle one, cradling Lucille in his arms. The badge glittering on the lapel of his tweed shooting jacket was the scariest thing Lindsay had seen since—No. It *was* the scariest thing she'd ever seen.

"My man! Ez!" Noah lowered the window and stuck out his hand.

Uncle Ezra shook it. "Afternoon, Noah. When I move the sawhorses, Lindsay, you scoot on through and I'll put 'em right back."

"Thank you, Uncle Ez. It's good of you to help."

"Glad to." He beamed and turned toward the sawhorses.

The Corvette was in her garage for safekeeping. Uncle Frank was in the kitchen making a pot of tea.

"It's chamomile," he said. "Dovey suggested it to keep Ezra calm."

"You checked his pockets for shells, didn't you?"

" 'Course I did. Don't worry, Lindsay. He's been just fine since I convinced him we really don't need to dig a moat around the fence."

She told Uncle Frank about the TV crews and went to clean up. Noah was in the guestroom. He'd packed a suitcase this morning when she picked him up, just in case.

Lindsay paused outside the door. He was already in the shower. She could hear the drumbeat of the spray, feel it in her nipples. Wouldn't it be glorious to slip under the spray with him? Soap his back, let him soap her breasts? She sighed and went on down the hall.

The hot air balloon with Noah's face swung on its guy wires on the six o'clock newscast out of St. Louis. Trey blinked at it. Then he burst out laughing. He laughed till he fell off the leather couch in the family room and rolled on the carpet howling.

"Does he have these fits often?" Noah grinned at Trey.

"Shhh." Lindsay pushed the volume up on the remote control.

"Welcome to Belle Coeur, Missouri." The perky Morgandy clone who had interviewed her and Noah flashed her smile at the camera. "The new Mecca of *Betwixt and Be Teen* fandom. Nearly a thousand women have come here from across the country to worship at the shrine of Noah Patrick, star of the megahit television series.

"These faithful—" She turned, swept an arm over a long shot of the Campground and RV Camp behind her "—have made *Betwixt and Be Teen* the most popular syndicated series in television history."

From the Campground and the balloon the report shifted to Noah, about a three minute snippet of this afternoon's interview.

"Wait a minute." Noah snatched the remote from her, frowned, and flipped the channel. "Where are you?"

"I'm not the story. You are." Lindsay laughed at him. "This is wonderful! Jolie will love it!"

Aunt Sassy came for dinner; Susan, too, with Aunt Muriel. Aunt Dovey came with Emma to watch the rehearsal. Uncle Donnie came with Uncle Ron and Uncle Lonnie to help spell Uncle Ezra at the barricade.

"There's safety in numbers," Uncle Ron said. "Chub said he should have his extra guys in place by tomorrow night so rehearsals can move back to the barn."

"Good," Lindsay said. "That should make Jolie happy."

"I wouldn't count on it," Susan said to her in the kitchen while they were making coffee. "Jolie called me today from Kansas City. She's livid that all this is going on while she's not here."

"Then why doesn't she come back?" Lindsay slapped her hands on the edge of the sink, lifted her right one. "Look at all the free publicity we're getting. Why pay for more?"

"She's afraid of being cut out and humiliated again," Susan said. "The article in *People* really stung. She didn't say so, but I know Jolie."

Lindsay woke up exhausted the next morning. Too much excitement, she thought, and likely more ahead. She went to work to schmooze with the *BBT* fans, leaving Noah in Uncle Frank's capable hands. She arranged a lunch with Virgie Keyhart, the fan club president, and broke it to her gently about raffles in the State of Missouri and Noah's fear of heights.

"A fear of heights," she said dubiously. "That's not in his bio."

"It's an old age onset sort of thing," Lindsay said straight-faced.

That evening, she saw black storm clouds spinning around Jolie's head when she stepped into the theater for rehearsal with Noah and Trey swinging down the aisle ahead of her. She wished she'd left Trey at home, but he'd wanted to come to see how Chub and his men had cordoned off the barn.

Jolie wasn't sitting in her usual seat ten rows back from the front of the house. She was on the stage, striding the stage, the Chaos in her a tight, furious ball just waiting to be flung like a fist.

Aunt Sassy, Uncle Lonnie, and Susan were all frowning, clustered together near the orchestra pit on the auditorium floor. Uh-oh.

"She kicked us off the stage," Susan muttered to Lindsay as she tucked her purse into a seat in the third. "She's loaded for bear."

"If it gets ugly," Lindsay whispered, "get Trey out of here."

"Will do," Susan promised.

The rest of Jolie's cast was on stage with her. Uncle Ron, Uncle Frank, and Emma. She had her head down but lifted her eyes and met Lindsay's as she came up the steps to the stage with Noah.

Careful. Lindsay almost jumped out of her skin. She could hear Emma's voice in her head as clearly as if she'd spoken. *Do not let Noah antagonize Jolie tonight.*

"Here they are, everyone. *Our stars.*" Jolie spread her hands. "Two dazzling orbs of talent that light our way, illuminate our path through the darkness of artistic interpretation."

"The shit's deep in here," Noah said. "Everybody bring hip boots?"

Everyone laughed. Even Jolie but there was a glint in her eyes.

"Marks!" Jolie slapped her hand against her thigh only because she didn't have a riding crop. "Begin!"

Within ten minutes, Lindsay wished she had a riding crop. Jolie jumped on the tiniest flub, shrieking at her cast in a voice far above High C. Noah watched her with a muscle leaping in his jaw.

"Don't," Lindsay hissed. "She wants you to say something."

Jolie left her and Noah alone. Uncle Ron she ragged mercilessly. He yelled right back at her, which only made it worse. She screeched.

"All right, young lady! That's enough!" Aunt Sassy stormed onto the stage in a zebra stripe leotard, her redheaded temper flashing in her eyes. "You didn't learn to abuse your performers this way from me!"

"Get off my stage!" Jolie whirled on her. "You're fired!"

Aunt Sassy blinked, then she laughed. "You can't fire me."

"Oh yes, I can. I'm the director. On this stage I'm God."

"Then Lord save the world." Aunt Sassy put her hands on her hips. "You're a snippy, sniping, pissy little bitch, Jolene Varner."

"Takes one to call one, Aunt Sassy."

"Stop it, Jolie," Uncle Frank warned her. "Right this second."

Jolie spun on him. "You learn your lines, old man!"

"Hey!" Noah shouted, stepping toward her. Lindsay made a grab for him but he shook her off. "Jolie Almighty!"

Jolie wheeled toward him. "Back on your mark!"

"When you're through with your tantrum, let me know." Noah pitched his script at her feet. "Then maybe we can get some work done."

"I *said*!" Jolie thundered. "Back on your mark!"

"Blow me," Noah said, and turned to walk off the stage.

"Get back here!" Jolie roared at him.

Noah flipped his middle finger at her.

A second before Jolie snatched the prop book, a slim, hardcover volume of *Sonnets from the Portuguese*, off the drum table, Lindsay saw the leap in Chaos. A vivid scarlet splash like a solar flare.

"Noah!" she cried. "Look out!"

The book was already flying, streaming a trail of red Chaos. It hit Noah in the back of the head. Blood spurted through his fingers as he clutched his skull and wheeled around, staggering a little.

"Good one, Vivienne Junior." He laughed at Jolie, blinking like he was having trouble focusing. "I didn't think you had it in you."

Jolie stared at him, stricken and horrified. Aunt Sassy slapped her.

Lindsay vaulted the pulled out Murphy bed to reach Noah. She slid her arm around his waist, saw the speckles of blood on the collar of his blue polo shirt. He reeled away from her but Emma was there to steady him and help Lindsay sit him down on the side of the Murphy bed.

"You and your mother warned me." He squinted at Emma. "You both told me not to turn my back on Jolie."

Everyone else had already turned away from Jolie. She stood by the drum table, the print of Aunt Sassy's palm livid on her cheek.

"Put your hand down, Noah," Lindsay said. "Let me have a look."

"Ow!" He shot her a glare, tried to duck away from her probing fingers, but Emma was there to hold his head steady. "That hurts!"

"Oh, stop. It was a book in the head, not a brick," Lindsay snapped in her Mother Voice. "I need to see this."

The bloody split in his scalp, yes. The black streak in Noah's hair, underneath near the crown, exactly like the one in Trey's hair, was the last thing she needed to see. Her fingers froze on Noah's scalp. Emma saw it, too, as she helped Lindsay spread Noah's hair.

"Hospital," Emma said, all but slapping Noah's hair down.

"Ow!" he howled. "Watch it, Nurse Ratchet!"

"Hospital," Lindsay agreed, her voice shaking, her hands like ice.

Dear God, she prayed. *Let me be seeing things.* The streak was bad enough, but her heart wrenched between her ribs when she stepped to Noah's right side to help Emma steady him and she saw Trey.

Her son stood next to the Murphy bed, wide-eyed and pale faced, staring at the back of Noah's head.

Chapter 29

"CHRIST." Noah groaned. "My head hurts."

He heard a rustle beside the bed, cracked an eye, and saw the brunette nurse from his last visit to the Belle Coeur Community Hospital bending over the rail to pull the sheet and blanket over his chest.

"Three stitches and a mild concussion will give you a headache every time." She smiled. "Be glad it wasn't a brick."

"Felt like one." That's what Lindsay had said. It was a book, not a brick. "Why do I have to stay here?"

"You don't." She waved toward the door. "I'm sure every one of the two hundred women in our parking lot would love to kiss your boo-boo. They might tear you limb from limb, but you're free to leave."

"Oh yeah." Noah closed his eyes. "I forgot about them."

Everything up to Jolie Almighty, Spawn of Satan beaning him with the book was clear as a bell in his head. Everything since was blurry and starting to jumble. Christ. He swallowed a lump of panic. Losing more of his memory was the last thing he needed.

He needed Lindsay to kiss his boo-boo. "Where's Lindsay?"

"Downstairs talking to our security people. She'll be here." The nurse patted him on the shoulder.

What was this woman's name? She was the mother of Trey's girlfriend. He'd signed an autograph for her. What the hell had he written?

"Pat." Noah blurted. "Your kid's a brat."

"I beg your pardon?" she snapped.

"Your name is Pat." He opened his eyes, checked her name tag to make sure, and grinned. "Pat. Your kid's a brat. That's how I remember things. I make up little rhymes."

"Oh." She laughed, put the call button where he could

reach it, pulled the string on the light and dimmed it. "Better?"

"Some." Noah closed his eyes. "Thanks."

"If you need anything, give us a buzz."

He needed Lindsay. Needed to hear her say it was a book, not a brick. Calm down. You'll remember. He'd believe it if Lindsay said it.

Noah turned his head on the pillow, felt the rasp of the bandage on the back of his head like sandpaper across his teeth. Bad idea. He raised his head to turn it and lie flat on the pillow, faceup like he was dead.

Be glad it was a book. A brick might've killed him. Oh goody. Happy thoughts. Just what he needed. Where the hell was Lindsay?

When the door creaked, he put his tongue between his teeth before he turned his head and saw Trey hanging just inside the room, one hand on the door like he wasn't sure he should come in. Or if he wanted to.

"Just the smart aleck kid I wanted to see. Do me a favor?"

"Maybe." Trey stood half in shadow, half in the light from the hallway. It made Noah's eyes blur to look at him. "What is it?"

"The keys to the 'Vette are in my pocket, in that crack in the wall they call a closet. Hang on to them for me, would you? I've gotta go to L.A. this weekend. Vivienne called. I'm up for a part."

"Are you coming back?"

"Did somebody hit you in the head, too? You know all those lines I've been learning, for the play that opens next weekend?"

"I just *asked*," Trey snapped at him.

"If I don't get the part I'll be back on the next plane. If I do I'll be back on Wednesday. Thursday at the latest."

"Why d'you want me to keep the keys? I can't drive the Corvette."

"Your mother can drive it. I thought maybe if you asked her nice she'd help you practice backing it up and down the driveway."

Trey stepped into the room and let the door shut, walked

up to the bed, and stood staring at him. Noah blinked to clear his eyes. The kid looked pale, like he'd been sweating.

"Are you okay, sport? You don't look too good."

"What's that streak of black hair in the back of your head?"

"Some kooky thing that runs in the family. My dad has one, too."

"So do I," Trey said. "Like yours. Exactly like yours."

What was wrong with this kid? He looked like he'd been crying.

"Least it's not a skunk stripe like Emma."

"Did you know about it? Did you know that I have a black streak in my hair identical to yours?"

"No, I didn't know. Why would I know? I'm not your father."

But Trey thought he was. Noah realized it a nanosecond after he said it—the kid thought he was his father. Holy Christ.

Trey grabbed the bed rail, leaned over it, and said in his face, "You'd better not be my father." Then he wheeled out of the room.

Noah didn't try to stop him, didn't call him back. He couldn't move, couldn't even blink. His tongue was stuck to the roof of his mouth.

He couldn't be Trey's father. It wasn't possible. Noah closed his eyes and did the math. It made his head throb but he did it and realized with a sick wrench in his gut that yes, it was possible. Trey said the black streak in his hair was exactly like his. Noah's father called it the zebra stripe. It ran in the Patrick family. The black streak in his hair was exactly like the one in *his* father's hair. Christ Almighty.

He didn't even go to why Lindsay hadn't told him. He knew damn good and well why and he didn't blame her. He did wonder why she hadn't told him since they'd become lovers, but then he realized why—Trey. Lindsay wouldn't risk fucking up Trey's head or Trey's life for him. Noah didn't blame her for that, either. He was proud of her in fact, so proud he felt his throat swell and his eyes fill with tears.

One trickled from the corner of his right eye when Lindsay laid her palm on his forehead, when he realized he knew her touch even with his eyes closed. He blinked and looked at her, leaning on one arm over the bed rail, a frown on her face. Trey's face.

"Why are you crying, Noah?"

"Trey was here. He wanted to know why he has a black streak in his hair that's identical to the one in my hair."

Lindsay's hand jerked on his temple. "What did you tell him?"

"I told him I wasn't his father. He said I'd better not be."

"Oh God." She bent her elbows on the bed rail and covered her face, made a noise like a sob, and folded into the chair beside his bed.

"Tell me, Lindsay," Noah said. "Is he mine?"

Her head shot up, a fierce blaze in her eyes. "He's *mine.*"

"Hang on, Mama bear. I'm not going to take your cub. I just want to know." Noah couldn't say *if I have a son.* "Am I Trey's father?"

"I've slept with two men in my life. You and Mark." She sounded tired, looked exhausted. "One of you is Trey's father. That's all I know."

"How could you *not* know which one of us got you pregnant?"

"I thought I knew. I thought it was Mark. Until tonight, until I saw the black streak in your head, and yes, it *is* identical to the black streak in Trey's hair. Till then I thought I'd given birth to my husband's child."

"So. To cut to the chase all three of us got the shock of our lives."

We're all in the same boat. All three of us. One of us doesn't have to get out. That's what Noah wanted to hear Lindsay say, felt his heart start to pound waiting for her to say it.

"Yes." That's all she said. She stood up, let her hands fall against the front of her pleated khaki trousers. "I have to find Trey and talk to him. I thought Susan had taken him home. Are you okay?"

"Oh, I'm peachy. I've got three stitches in my head. The first audition I've had in fuck knows when in four days.

Maybe I've got a son, too, but you don't know. Doesn't look to me like you much care, either."

"Trey is a child, Noah." The blaze leaped in her eyes again but it was banked. "I don't know if he's Mark's, I don't know if he's yours, but he's mine. He's confused and angry and far more important at the moment than anything you're feeling or anything I'm feeling."

Lindsay spun on her heel and stalked out of Noah's room. She wasn't surprised that he didn't call her back. She was glad and she was grief-stricken. For herself, for Noah, but mostly for Trey. Why had he gone to see Noah? Why hadn't he come to her? Where was he?

"Trey's in his room," Uncle Frank told her when she called home on her cell phone. "Want to speak to him?"

"No." Lindsay sighed, relieved. "I'll be there shortly."

She made it in ten minutes and went straight to Trey's room. She hadn't the first clue what she was going to say to him till she opened his bedroom door, saw him lying on his bed in his T-shirt and sweatpants, staring at the ceiling with his hands folded under his head. Lindsay stepped into the room, shut the door, and leaned against it.

"I had no idea that your dad might not be your father until tonight, Trey. But he'll always be your dad no matter who your father is. You're my child no matter who else's you may be and I love you."

"Why don't you know who my father is, Ma?" Trey's voice shook.

Oh God. What a question to hear from your own child.

"I know how this must look to you." *How I must look to you,* she thought. Lindsay went to the bed and sat beside her son. "I was only eighteen. Only two years older than you are now. I was miserable, so unhappy in L.A. I hated being on TV. I thought Noah cared for me. I realized—after—that he didn't. I loved your dad and he loved me. I came straight home and we were married. That's why I'm not sure."

"I talked to Noah. I asked him about the black streak. He says it runs in his family. Doesn't that mean he's my father?"

Of course it did. It tore a hole in Lindsay's heart to hear Trey say what she couldn't bring herself to face.

"Yes. It probably does. We can find for sure and I think we should. If Noah is your father, that could change your medical profile."

"You mean DNA tests, right? Aren't those expensive?"

"We can afford it. If you want to know, we'll do it."

Trey turned his head and looked at her. "Don't you want to know?"

If she knew, things would change between her and Noah. They had already. They'd change again if she knew for sure, if he knew for sure that Trey was his son. That was the thing about knowledge. It changed things. For better sometimes, for worse others, but always irrevocably.

"I want to know how you got to the hospital."

"On my dirt bike. I snuck it out of the garage."

"How did you get past Uncle Ezra?"

"I went overland."

"In the dark?" Lindsay's heart almost stopped. "Why did you do such a crazy, dangerous thing?"

"I needed to know about this hair thing."

"Why did you go to Noah? Why didn't you come to me?"

"I was pissed at him 'cause I thought he knew." Trey pushed off the pillow, sat up, and glared at her. "I thought you did, too. I thought I was the only one who didn't. I thought you'd been lying to me my whole life."

"I understand why you felt that way, but I've never lied to you. I never will. I'm telling you the truth right now so far as I know it."

"Yeah, I know, Ma. I wasn't thinking real straight." He flopped back on his pillow and sighed. "I told Noah he'd better not be my father. If he is I probably shouldn't have said that, huh?"

"I'm sure he realizes you were upset."

"I like Noah. I was pissed at him, but I like him. I'm not sure how I'll feel about him if I find out he's my father."

"That's the thing about knowledge." Lindsay smoothed Trey's hair out of his face, felt a brush of whisker stubble on his cheek. "It changes things. You can't ever go back to knowing less than you did."

"Yeah well, this not knowing crap bites. I want the tests."

"I'll talk to Noah. He'll have to agree to give samples."

"He will, won't he?"

"I'm sure he will." Lindsay was positive because she'd kill him if he didn't. "The tests may take time. It could be a few weeks."

"That's okay. I can wait."

She stayed with Trey till he was almost asleep, then she checked on Uncle Frank and Uncle Ezra, sound asleep in the guestrooms, and went to the kitchen for a cup of tea. Emma was there with a pot of Earl Gray and a pan of brownies.

"Uncle Frank let me in," she said. "I couldn't sleep so I baked."

"Chocolate. Thank God." Lindsay ate two brownies and drank a cup of tea, remembered telling Noah he had the wrong hormones for chocolate and felt tears in her eyes. "Chaos is change, isn't it?"

"Chaos isn't any one thing, Lindsay. It's everything."

"But it changes things, doesn't it?"

"You aren't trying to blame Chaos for this, are you?"

"I'm trying not to blame myself, Em, for being such a naïve little dimwit that it never dawned on me I'd gotten pregnant with Noah."

"You still don't know. I admit, the black streak kind of nails it, but you can't be positive unless you do DNA tests."

"Trey wants them. Noah will whether he likes it or not."

At nine-thirty Friday morning Lindsay marched into the Belle Coeur Community Hospital. She wore slacks, a sweater, and her Mother Face. She was not prepared to take no for an answer. She was prepared to ask Pat Hannity what samples were needed for a DNA test. If Noah refused to give them, she was prepared to take them out of his hide.

Pat was at the nurse's station when she stepped off the elevator. She closed the chart she was writing in and smiled. "Hi, Lindsay."

"Morning." Lindsay pointed her thumb over her shoulder. "Where did Noah's two hundred closest friends go to? I didn't see a single Winnebago in the parking lot."

"Simple." Pat grinned. "When he left, they left."

Lindsay blinked, startled. "Noah's gone?"

"He checked himself out half an hour ago and left with Chub."

Lindsay thanked Pat, got on the elevator, went back to the Civic, and called Chub on her cell phone.

"Drove him out to your place to pick up his car," the sheriff told her. "Said he had a plane to catch in St. Louis."

"I must've just missed him." Lindsay couldn't believe it. If she'd taken five more minutes to drink her coffee.

"Said he was going anyway on Sunday. Thought it might calm things down around here if he went a bit earlier. Mighty considerate."

"Yes. Wasn't it?" Lindsay said, and disconnected.

She sat in the Civic, stunned. Then her heart leaped. Maybe he was waiting for her, drinking coffee and eating brownies with Uncle Frank at the kitchen table. She punched her number with shaking fingers.

"He just left," Uncle Frank told her. "Not ten minutes ago."

Noah hadn't waited for her. That hurt. She could call his cell phone but if he'd wanted to talk to her he would've waited. Or called her. She could try to catch him on I-70 but if he drove the Corvette the way he'd driven his Ferrari she and her little Civic hadn't a prayer.

This was not the way she'd planned to let Noah go. She'd planned another overnight for Trey and a skinny-dip in her pool, planned to show Noah how to stay awake in that killer lounge chair of hers. She'd planned to drive him to St. Louis to catch his plane, to be there to pick him up when he came back, but she hadn't told him. If she had would it have changed things? Would he still have left like this, without a word?

He'd be back, but things had changed. They'd change again by Thursday. She didn't know how, she just knew they would.

That merry little prankster Chaos would see to it.

Chapter 30

THE ONLY PERSON Noah called before he left was Vivienne.

"Change my flight. I'm on my way," he said. "If I can find the fucking airport I'll be in St. Louis by nine your time."

"Problem?" Vivienne said. He could hear her puffing a cigarette.

"Change the flight. Get me a car. Have your ass in Malibu."

He punched off the cell phone and focused on driving. Wouldn't do to cream himself on a bridge abutment till he'd killed Vivienne Varner.

He found the airport. Thank God it was right off I-70. He slept all the way to L.A. It was sleep or let the headache he'd had since Vivienne Junior beaned him blow the top of his head off.

In L.A. he bumped and dodged his way through the terminal looking for a limo driver holding a sign that said PATRICK, though he thought DICKHEAD would probably be more apt.

Because he hadn't seen him in ten years, it took Noah a minute to recognize his father, Noah Patrick Senior, working his way toward him through the crowd doing a similar where-is-he head bob.

Noah stopped, clenching the duffel he'd packed in Belle Coeur, and waited for his father to see him. Only took a couple seconds. Wasn't difficult to recognize the face you saw in the mirror every morning when you shaved it. That's how much he looked like his old man.

Old man. Jesus. Now he was somebody's old man.

His father raised a hand to him. Noah raised one to him. They walked up to each other and stopped. He had at least two inches on his father. He figured Trey would have damn near a foot on him by the time he stopped growing. He took after his mother's family.

"Noah." His father offered his hand.

"Sir." He shook his father's hand and felt the tremble in it, saw his chin start to quiver. Noah put his duffel down and said, "Dad."

His father, who wouldn't say prick if he had a hard-on, lost it right in the middle of the terminal. He threw his arms around his son and wept, but what the hell. So did Noah.

Noah Senior had left his Cadillac in the valet lot, called for it in his State Supreme Court Justice voice, and drove him to Malibu. On the way he told Noah he'd tracked him down through the kid reporter from *People*. He'd called The Bookshelf this morning and talked to Lindsay. They'd had a nice chat. Lindsay told him he was on his way to L.A.

"Sounds like she's still a pretty little thing," his father said.

"Oh, she is," Noah said. And she's the mother of your grandson.

"You'll come for dinner tonight, won't you?"

Noah turned his head, surprised. "Am I welcome?"

The old man's chin started again. "Your mother has missed you."

"Will Phyllis be there?"

"No. Your sister lives in San Francisco now."

"Great. Then I'll come," Noah said, and his father laughed.

"I'll pick you up at six."

"Actually. If you wouldn't mind waiting, this won't take long."

"All right." He looked surprised but he didn't ask, just parked the Cadillac in front of the black iron gate that barred Vivienne's driveway.

Noah pushed the intercom, said, "It's me," when Vivienne answered, and shoved through the gate when it buzzed.

She was in the living room, sitting in a chair that cost half as much as his father's Cadillac. Unlike Jolie she didn't flick so much as an eyelash when he spread his hands on the arms and leaned into her face.

"Why didn't you just tell me that Trey is my son?"

"I wasn't sure. I'm still not sure, but obviously you are."

"Trey has a black streak in his hair. So do I, so does my old man. Three little black streaks all in a row. Yeah, I'm sure he's my son."

"I think we should have DNA tests. I'll arrange it."

"The hell you will. You'll leave my son and Lindsay's son the fuck alone. You couldn't get him any other way, could you? Jolie was no help so you dragged me into it. You thought I'd be so damn grateful that I'd do anything for you, even help you take Trey away from Lindsay."

"I don't want to take him from her. I just want to see him."

"That ain't gonna happen. You're done. So am I. I quit. I quit the play and I quit your little plan for Trey. Don't even try to tell me you don't have one, that you just want to see him. I know you, Vivienne."

She turned her head, narrowed her eyes. "What is this?"

"It's a stick-up. How's it feel to be on the other end of the shaft?"

"What do you want?"

"I want you to know that I'm on to you. Lindsay wants you off the planet. She's got a call in to NASA."

"I'll sue you for breach of contract."

"I've been sued by the IRS, Vivienne. You don't scare me."

He was scaring her though. He could see tiny yellow flickers in her eyes. Jolie's whiskey-colored eyes did the same thing, turned yellow when she was freaked. God, this was fun, but it was time to back off.

"That's it. That's all I have to say, except thanks for the lift to L.A."

Noah pushed off the chair and wheeled out of the room. Vivienne followed him into the long hall that led to the sunlit tile foyer.

"You can't walk out on the audition. It's all arranged."

Noah reached the front door and turned around. "What part of *you're finished arranging things* didn't you understand?"

"I'm your agent, Noah."

"Not anymore. You're fired."

He slammed the door behind him, walked down the driveway, and slid into his father's Cadillac. "Pacific Palisades here we come."

Noah Senior called ahead on his car phone. Noah's mother was in the driveway, pacing in white capris and a melon colored tank top, her blond hair butched around tiny ears pierced with diamond studs. She had to look at him first, hold his face in her hands like Lindsay, then she kissed him on the mouth.

Over and over till she had him weeping. Her eyes were filled with tears but she never shed one. Tough little cookie. Mary Katherine Patrick for the defense struck terror in the hearts of prosecutors in L.A. County. She didn't embrace him till she fed him, then she caught him at the kitchen sink. Noah wrapped her in his arms, laid his cheek on the top of her head. Used to be the other way around when he was ten.

His parents took him out on the boat, sailed him to Catalina and back, and got him sunburned. The sizzle on his skin felt great. While he changed for dinner he checked messages—five total, all from Vivienne.

Noah smiled, glanced up at the tap on the door.

"Brought you a tie." His father stepped into the room, handed him a bit of silk that probably cost two hundred bucks—and a check.

"Why is this made out to me? Why does it have all these zeros?"

"Syndication money from *BBT*. Some years ago you gave me your power of attorney. I paid all your debts and I've been investing for you."

Noah couldn't count all the zeros without his eyes blurring. He wiped his lashes and looked at his father. "How did you know you'd ever be able to give this to me?"

"I didn't know," his father said. "But I kept hoping."

Noah returned Vivienne's call Saturday morning after Noah Senior killed him on the squash court.

"What the fuck do you want?" she demanded.

"Well. Since you ask so nicely. I want Vivienne Junior's ass out of Belle Coeur before she's burned at the stake or I break her neck."

"I've already given Jolie a considerable sum of money."

"She doesn't want money. She wants her mommy. Go figure."

Noah hung up and drove his mother to the spa. He had a massage while she had her facial and her nails done, then she took him to lunch. That evening they took in a play. *Bell, Book, and Candle.*

Where was Pyewacket tonight? Who was letting him in and out fifty times? Who was feeding him? Was anybody checking his tail for burrs? If you didn't, you'd find a bed full with your bare feet. He had a lump in his throat. Jesus, he missed that stupid cat. Christ he missed Lindsay so much he could hardly breathe.

Vivienne called during Sunday brunch at the club. Noah left the table, went out on the terrace that overlooked the golf course.

"I can't do a thing about Jolie till the end of the run."

"My French toast is getting cold." Noah hung up.

He was on the tennis court after a round of bridge, having a heart attack while his father hopped up and down at the net waiting to take him three sets straight when she called back.

"All right. Jolie's leaving for New York first thing tomorrow."

"Just ahead of the posse, I'm sure."

"Now what are you prepared to do for me?"

"Not one fucking thing."

His mother leaned out of the judge's chair. The tennis court was the only place she could overrule Noah Senior. She raised an eyebrow above her Armani shades and said, "Language."

"I was talking to Vivienne Varner."

"I'll allow it." She nodded and turned back to the net.

He was in the locker room toweling off after a shower when his cell phone rang. He swiped it off the bench and said, "Yes, Vivienne?"

"Jolie called. She's backed out. She refuses to leave."

"Convince her it's in her best interest."

"What do you want me to do? Drag her bodily out of Belle Coeur?"

"If that's what it takes."

"I'll be lynched if I show my face in that town."

"Worst case scenario, we'll have a double hanging."

"I'll try again," Vivienne said between her teeth. "What else?"

"The Corvette. Sign it over to me."

"Done. You'll do the play?"

"I'll do the play, but I'm not sure Lindsay will."

Vivienne let out a shriek in the range of dog whistles. Noah hung up and laughed. When Vivienne called back her voice was shaking.

"Will I *ever* be allowed to see my grandson?"

"That's up to Lindsay. She's the Mama Bear."

"You have no influence, no input? He's your son."

"Christ, Vivienne. At this point I'm just the sperm donor."

Noah Senior swung away from his locker, his eyebrows shooting up into his hairline.

"I'll call you back." Noah hung up and faced his father. "You have a grandson in Missouri. The blond kid in the *People* article. The one jumping into the pool. He's my son. Mine and Lindsay's."

Noah Senior sat down on the bench and blinked. His mother sat down on the couch and blinked when he told her. It was the first time in his life he'd ever seen her speechless. Then her nostrils flared.

"You had an affair with Lindsay. She was a child, Noah."

"She was eighteen, Mother. I slept with her once."

"What about now? Are you sleeping with her now?"

"I'm in love with her." Noah smiled. "I think she likes me."

"My God." His mother gasped. "Vivienne Varner is my grandson's grandmother."

"True. But Lindsay is his mother. Trey's a great kid. I'd like to bring him to see you and Dad if Lindsay will allow it."

"That's all right, dear. We'll meet him on opening night." His mother smiled. "Your father and I have third row seats."

After dinner his father gave him the keys to the Cadillac. Noah drove to the beach, got there as the sun was setting, peeled down to his trunks, and raced into the surf. He was drying off when Vivienne called.

"Christ on a stick, Jolie's a stubborn little bitch. If you'll agree to the audition, I'll go back to Belle Coeur with you."

"Lindsay gets five minutes alone in a room with you. She needs to say thanks for fucking up her life."

"I don't see it that way."

"Lindsay does. That's all I care about."

"*Then* can I see my grandson?"

"No promises. It's still up to Lindsay."

He waited till Monday night to call Lindsay, counting the minutes till it was 10:30. Bedtime in Belle Coeur. He stretched out on the bed in the guestroom, half-hard, nerves jumping, punched her number.

"Hi, gorgeous," he said when she answered. "I got the part."

"No-*ah*." She sighed his name, made two breathy syllables out of it like she did when he licked her nipples. "Congratulations. I'm so happy for you. How many lines is it?"

"Three words. They're doing a send-up of old TV shows. I get to be me—well, Sam—run into the shot in trunks with a surfboard, yell, 'Surf's up, dudes!' and run off again like I'm diving into a wave."

Lindsay laughed. She sounded giddy, like maybe she was glad to hear his voice. Then her breath caught. "Surely not in a Speedo."

"Oh yeah. I hope to Christ I don't humiliate myself."

"I hope you don't hurt yourself. When do you shoot?"

"Wednesday. I'll be back Thursday. I'm bringing Vivienne with me."

"*What?*" He heard her rip the covers back, roll up on the side of the bed. "Are you insane? I don't want her here! No one wants her here!"

"Jolie does," he said, and Lindsay moaned.

"Oh God, Noah. What are you doing? Do you have any idea?"

"Belle Coeur ain't big enough for me and the Spawn of Satan. One of us has got to go. Jolie wants to, but she doesn't have the guts. She'll go with Vivienne. You know she will. Vivienne is what she wants."

"And what does Vivienne get?" Lindsay's voice turned frosty. "What did you promise her? A visit with her grandson?"

"Vivienne gets you and me in the play. Anything else is up to you."

"You're putting me in a very bad position here, Noah. Trey is intensely curious about Vivienne. I don't like this."

"Let him satisfy his curiosity. He's a smart kid. He'll see through Vivienne. And you need to let her have it. Rip into her. Tell her how you feel. Get her off your back, out of your head once and for all."

He heard Lindsay sigh, settle back on the bed. "I'll think about it."

"How's Spawn of Satan been at rehearsal?"

"She hasn't been at rehearsal. She's been banned, barred by her own cast," Lindsay said proudly. "Susan took over. Trey's helping her."

"I'll bet Spielberg Junior's a terror."

"Oh, he's having a great time lording it over the grown-ups." He heard the smile in her voice, then the pause. "We have a child, Noah."

"It's starting to sink in, isn't it? Are you gonna be okay with this? I mean, that Trey is mine and not Mark's?"

"Yes. I've been thinking about it. I've decided that as low as Mark's sperm count was, you gave him a blessing. Without you, Mark might never have known the joy of having a child, having a son."

"Jesus," Noah said, his arms prickling with gooseflesh. "How do you think of this stuff?"

"I have the hormones for it. Are you staying with Vivienne?"

"Brace yourself. I'm at my parents' house. My mother invited me to dinner three days ago and I'm still here."

"Noah. That's wonderful. Your father called The Bookshelf."

"He told me. He said you sounded like you were still a pretty little thing." Lindsay laughed. Noah closed his eyes, felt it in his chest. "Christ I miss you. You wouldn't like to get me off over the phone, would you?"

"*No,*" she snapped primly. It was one of the things he loved about her, how prissy she could be one second, the hottest mama on the planet the next. "I miss you, too. I'll show you how much on Thursday."

"I can't wait that long. Gimme a hint. Just a clue."

"No. You are not tricking me into phone sex."

"Warn the family Vivienne's coming, but don't tell Jolie. And let her in to the rehearsal Thursday night."

"Noah. Trey would like to know for certain who his father is. Will you agree to DNA tests?"

"I can't believe you had to ask me that. Of course I will."

"May I tell him? Or would you like to?" Progress. She was including him in a decision about Trey.

"Your call. You're the Mama Bear."

"I'll see you Thursday, Papa Bear. Good night."

Papa Bear. Noah's heart flipped. She'd called him Papa Bear.

He jumped off the bed, did a little I'm-bad dance, put on his trunks, raced down to the pool, did a cannonball into the deep end. He swam laps till his mother came outside to see if he'd drowned.

He was so focused on Lindsay, on seeing her and his son again that he aced the shoot. Three words with a surfboard wasn't Shakespeare but he stayed loose and had fun. Hammed it up but good, did a dead-on parody of himself as Sam, surfer dude and coolest guy in school, just so he could be done with it and get back to Belle Coeur.

He drew applause, a few slaps from the crew, a squeeze on the ass from the casting director who said she'd keep him in mind, and he was free. He took his parents out to dinner because now he could afford to, repacked his duffel eight times, and lay awake all night picturing what Lindsay would do to show him how much she missed him.

Noah Senior drove him to LAX Thursday morning. He embraced him, didn't weep but he teared up. "Your mother and I. I can't tell you what this means to us, to see you like this, to know that you're going to be all right now. That's all we ever wanted for you."

Noah put his arms around his father and kissed him.

He met Vivienne in the VIP lounge. On the first-class flight to St. Louis, he sipped Evian and she knocked back Bloody Marys. How appropriate. Noah asked her how she'd figured out Trey was his son.

"No one saw Lindsay leave the party with you, but you disappeared about the same time she did. She came home at three in the morning, distraught and defiant. She refused to tell me where she'd been. I slapped her, sent her to her room. When I came home from the office the next day she was gone. The cab driver who'd picked her up at your house had gone to San Diego so it took me a while to find him. By then I'd heard Lindsay was six months pregnant." Vivienne shrugged. "I did the math."

"Seems mighty damn thin to me."

"I'm a woman. I'm a mother. We have a sense for these things."

The right hormones, Noah thought, glad he had the wrong ones.

Vivienne refused to drive to Belle Coeur with him in the Corvette. She had a limo waiting. Noah followed the long black stretch east on I-70, then north to Belle Coeur. He imagined Vivienne slugged a few more Bloody Marys on the way. Her eyes were yellow all the way from L.A.

At just past one o'clock, the limo purred up to the curb in front of The Bookshelf. Noah yanked on the Corvette's emergency brake, totally pissed that a goddamn stranger could find this place and he couldn't.

Lindsay stepped outside onto the sidewalk in a marina blue knee-length skirt and sweater set. She kept her arms loose at her sides, her shoulders straight, lifted her chin. She knew who was in the limo. Noah got out of the Corvette, stepped up onto the walk to stand beside her.

The tinted glass on the limo's passenger window slid down like Darth Vader's visor. Vivienne gazed at her oldest daughter.

"*Hel*-lo, Lindsay," she said.

"Hel-*lo*, Vivienne," Lindsay replied.

It was a real Jerry v. Newman moment, straight out of *Seinfeld*.

"I'll be just a minute," Lindsay said to Noah.

She stepped off the curb and into the limo, sliding into it with a graceful, blood-thumping stretch of her long, shapely oh-baby-wrap-'em-around-me legs and shut the door in his face. Noah went inside.

"Is she in the limo with Vivienne?" Emma asked.

"She's in the limo with Vivienne," Noah said.

"Oh goddess," Emma breathed. "Get back out there."

Noah went, a heartbeat before Lindsay rose out of the limo, her eyes blazing, her face flushed, but her smile serene. The window slid down behind her and he saw Vivienne's eyes, big and yellow as lemons.

"Rehearsal at 7 P.M. sharp," Noah said to her. "Don't be late."

Vivienne blinked. "What am I supposed to do for six hours?"

"Why don't you sit in the town square," Noah suggested, "and let people stone you?"

"Kiss my ass," Vivienne said. "Driver, take me to—" She gave the guy behind the wheel an address, the window slid up, and the limo swung away from the curb like an aircraft carrier.

Noah turned to Lindsay. "Where's she going?"

"That was Aunt Dovey's address." Lindsay grinned.

"Oh, to be a bloodsucking leech in Vivienne's pocket." He reached for Lindsay. She jumped away and put up her hands. "No. I don't want you to touch me till I'm naked."

"Christ Jesus in heaven, princess," Noah said, his voice strangled.

"Follow me home."

He beat her there by two minutes. No sawhorses across the drive and no sign of Ezra and Lucille. He paced stiff-legged outside the garage doors, followed Lindsay's Civic through the one that lifted when she pulled in, opened her door, grabbed her elbow, and pulled her out of the car. He towed her behind him, laughing, up the step into the kitchen, hit the button to bring down the overhead as he swept her past it, through the house, down the hall, pushed her ahead of him into her bedroom.

"Get naked," he said, and tore off his shirt.

She was out of her skirt, her sweater set, her bra, and her panties in the flash it took him to shed his jeans and his Jockeys, stood in front of him beside the bed, already flushed, her nipples swelling.

"Now." Lindsay stepped toward him. "Touch me, Noah."

She slipped her arms around his neck. He wrapped his around her waist, pressed the tortured hard-on he'd had all day against her warm soft belly, and shuddered.

"Oh God, Lindsay, lie down. I'm ready to come." He started to swing her toward the bed then froze, his hands on her hips. "Christ. What am I doing? I don't have a condom."

"I don't care, Noah." Lindsay took his face in her hands. "I intended to send you off to L.A. with my very best wishes. I did not intend to send you with my heart, but it jumped in your suitcase. I want it back. I want yours, too. I'll take good care of it." Her voice started to quaver, her eyes filled with tears. "If you can't stay in Belle Coeur, I understand. I'll go to L.A. with you. I'll go anywhere. I love you so much it *hurts*." Her voice broke on a little whimper. She bumped her forehead against his, sucked a shuddery breath, lifted her head, and clutched his face hard enough to break his jaw. "Marry me. Don't think about it, just do it. Put a ring on my finger. You won't regret it. I promise."

"You stole my lines," Noah said.

She laughed, she cried, she kissed him. Drew him onto the bed, laid him on his side, arched a hip over his pelvis and somehow took him inside her. His eyes crossed and he groaned. He couldn't move. He'd break something if he tried. Christ Jesus it was bliss just to lie there, joined with her, pulsing inside her.

"Is this from *The Joy of Sex*?" Noah asked raggedly.

"Mmmhmm." She kissed him, eyes shining. "Like it?"

"Oh, mama," he moaned.

"Noah. I want babies."

"Spread your legs." He panted. "Let's get started."

They finished before Trey came home from school, late because he had a chess tournament. They made the bed together, got dressed together, brewed a pot of tea, and sat down at the kitchen table to drink it.

"Okay. I gotta know," Noah said. "What did you say to Vivienne?"

"I told her she wasn't in charge anymore. I told her I was. I told her she was on probation, that she had to make things right with Jolie first, before I'd even consider allowing her to see Trey. What do you think?"

"I couldn't have done it better." Noah kissed her, heard footsteps, and looked behind him. Trey stood in the doorway. "Hey, sport."

He put his books on the counter and said, "Hi."

He didn't look thrilled to see him. Noah rose and faced his son.

"I was wrong the other night. I am your father. I don't want to be your dad. You had a dad. He must've been a helluva guy because your mother loved him. I love your mother. I didn't when you happened but I do now. I want to marry her. Is that okay with you?"

"Did you ask her to marry you? What did she say?"

"Actually, she asked me. No. She told me I had to marry her."

"Get out." Trey's eyes widened, swung toward Lindsay. *"Ma."*

Noah turned on one foot to look at her. Her face was pink, but she was smiling, her eyes still shining. "Does that shock you, Trey?"

"Nah. I saw it coming." He shrugged, then he grinned. "I watch the soaps, remember."

They watched the clock, left early for rehearsal so they'd be sure to beat Vivienne to the barn. Spawn of Satan was on stage but she was very subdued. Noah expected her to turn her back on him when he climbed the steps with Lindsay and moved to his mark for Act One, Scene One, but she came right up to him and looked him in the eye.

"The book in the head was way out of line. I like the work you've done. Here—" She swept a hand across the stage "—and helping Uncle Donnie build the Murphy bed. I didn't think you could do it. I didn't think you would.

I'm surprised and frankly a little pissed, but hey." Jolie shrugged. "You did it."

" 'Scuse me?" Noah cupped his ear. "Did you say something?"

"Goddamn it," Jolie growled. "I apologize."

"Lindsay?" Noah turned to her. "Did you hear something?"

She blinked innocently. "Not a thing."

"All *right.*" Jolie sucked back her temper, her eyes turning yellow and said between gritted teeth, "I apologize to all of you."

"And I apologize to you, Jolie." Vivienne's throaty, one-Pall-Mall-too-many voice floated up to the stage from the dark auditorium.

Jolie spun around. When Vivienne stepped forward into the pool of light spilling over the lip of the stage, Jolie's eyes flew wide open.

"Vivian," she said. "What are you doing here?"

"You won't leave, so I came to get you. It's your turn."

"My turn to *what*?" Jolie lashed at her. "Be a TV star like Lindsay? That'll never happen. I've got your face."

"You have my drive and my tenacity, too. Plus you can write and direct. You're very gifted. Why are you still in this backwater burg?"

"*You left me here!*" Jolie cried. "You took Lindsay and you left me!"

"I apologize for that but I can't change it. I offered you New York and you refused. Do you want Hollywood? London? I can open doors in any city you want. Pick one and let's go. I have a limo waiting."

"I don't trust you. Why should I go with you?"

"Because it's what you've been waiting for. I realized it when you turned down New York. You wanted me to prove myself. You wanted me to come for you. All right. Here I am. Let's go. This is a one-time offer. I won't make it again. Stay or leave. Now or never."

Jolie hesitated, staring at Vivienne, her fists opening and closing.

"What if she won't go?" Lindsay whispered, reaching for Noah's hand.

"Don't worry, princess." He squeezed her fingers. "She's going."

She took her sweet time. Noah was starting to worry when Jolie finally tossed her script in the wing chair.

"Don't you dare screw me again, Vivian. I'll hunt you down, so help me I will." Jolie wheeled toward Susan. "Can you handle this?"

"Sure thing, you bet," Susan said quickly. "Good luck, Jolie."

Jolie swept a glance over her cast and a bittersweet smile that couldn't hide the excitement in her eyes. "You'll be great, fabulous. A smash. I just know it. Break a leg."

The house lights came up as Jolie marched offstage. Noah turned his head and winked at Trey, working the high dollar light board just inside the stage left wing. His son grinned at him.

Vivienne backed away from the steps as Jolie swept past her. She flipped Noah a salute, he snapped one back, then Vivienne wheeled behind Jolie up the aisle toward the lobby. When the auditorium doors bumped shut behind them, Noah let out a breath.

"There they go," he said. "Back to the Dark Side."

"Whew," Frank sighed. "That was awful close to Plan B."

"Plan B?" Lindsay blinked at Noah. "What's Plan B?"

"I made some calls while you were in the shower. Frank had the rope, Ron the gag. Vivienne a purse full of money to buy off the driver."

They shared a laugh and a kiss, the entire cast gave Noah high fives, then they got down to work. After rehearsal, he tucked Lindsay and Trey in the Civic and sent them home. He took a shower and flopped on the bed in Joe Varner's apartment, tired but happy.

He was almost asleep when he felt a weight on his chest, opened his eyes, and saw Pyewacket curling up to go to sleep. He rubbed noses with Noah, closed his eyes and started to purr.

Noah didn't see the cat again till opening night, when he hopped onto the Murphy bed in the second scene of Act Two. Right in the middle of the first big clinch between Cliff and Moira.

"Get your own, buddy," Noah ad-libbed. "This one's mine."

The audience laughed. When he tore his shirt off at the end of Act Three the ladies from the *BBT* Fan Club swooned and wolf whistled. He blushed all the way to his balls. They got a standing ovation and six curtain calls.

Lindsay thought his full body blush was hysterical. She laughed so hard at the after-party he thought was going to have to give her CPR, but she recovered. Damn it. His parents hugged and kissed her, met Trey, and stood gazing at him, agog with delight. He was a sport about it, slid up to Noah at the punch bowl later and said out of the side of his mouth, "Are they gonna stare at me like this every time they see me?"

"Nah," Noah said. "You're just new. It'll wear off."

They closed the show for two weeks in the middle of August so he could marry Lindsay on Saturday the sixteenth. She thought she might already be pregnant. That made Noah weak in the knees. So did the sight of his son in a tuxedo, standing in front him with his tongue screwed in the corner of his mouth as he struggled to pin his father's boutonniere on the lapel of his tux.

"I appreciate you doing this," Noah said, his throat so tight he could hardly speak. "It means a lot to your mother."

"No big." Trey stepped back from the crooked rose and shrugged. Then he grinned. "I'd be a real little shit if I couldn't stand up for my old man when he marries my mother, wouldn't I?"

The ceremony began at two o'clock in Mrs. Doubtfire's living room.

Lindsay wore an ivory knee-length dress. Silk. Oh Christ what it did for her figure. She knew it, too. Her smile said so. Emma was her matron of honor; Susan and Emma's sister Darcy her bridesmaids. Trey was Noah's best man, Frank and Ron his groomsmen.

Uncle Donnie and Uncle Lonnie gave Lindsay away. When the minister asked, "Who gives this woman to be married to this man?" Lonnie pressed a kiss on her cheek and said, "We do."

The reception was a barbecue in the backyard. There was dancing on the deck. Je-*sus* Lindsay could dance. She had his pulse pounding in his crotch in a nanosecond. When Noah took Aunt Sassy out for a spin, he kissed her on the mouth. "Thank you," he said. "From the bottom of my heart, thank you."

Noah danced with his mother and Morgandy, the kid reporter from *People,* Lindsay with Jim the photographer. Noah danced with Cyndey Parrish Munroe, gave her a dip that made her swoon. He saved the death spiral dip for Lindsay, made her breath catch and her eyes shine.

"Lindsay Evelyn Varner West Patrick." Noah drew her to her feet and tugged her tight against him. "Got a nice ring to it."

She wiggled her gold band. "I like this one better."

"Whattaya know." Noah raised his left hand. "Got one just like it."

That was the photo that made the cover of *People*.

At five o'clock they hopped in the Corvette and took off on their honeymoon, a road trip to the Rock and Roll Hall of Fame. They stopped at a motel every two hundred miles so Lindsay could blow him to Cincinnati and back.

Epilogue

Los Angeles, California
5 Years Later

NOAH WAS TEACHING Trey to surf. He sucked. That gene hadn't made the jump, but the kid was trying.

"Damn it!" Trey tossed his board in the sand, threw himself on the king-size beach towel next to Noah's and sat fuming with his elbows jammed over his raised knees. "Why do I keep falling off?"

"You think you're going to fall off." Noah rubbed a

towel over his face, used it to swipe his hair out of his eyes. "So you fall off."

"I do not think I'm going to fall off!" Trey raised his arms, made a swoop off his knees with the heels of his hands. "The damn board has so much wax on it I slide off!"

"Trey." Noah laid a hand on his shoulder. "The waxed side goes in the water."

"The side with the little fins?" Trey deadpanned. "I knew that."

Noah laughed and gave him a push in the head. Trey fell over on his right arm grinning, plucked his shades off the towel and put them on, leaned back on his elbows, and crossed his ankles.

Christ he was a good-looking kid. The image of Lindsay, heavy on the testosterone. He had Noah's chest hair and Noah's voice since it had changed. Mary Katherine often mistook Trey for Noah on the phone.

Trey and Meggie had broken up two weeks ago, just before they'd left Belle Coeur. A month shy of Trey's scheduled departure for his last year at Berkeley. He'd seen through Vivienne in five minutes flat when Lindsay had finally relented and let her see Trey on his seventeenth birthday. Even so, he wasn't allowed to be in California, the same state as Vivienne, on his own. This year their early departure couldn't be helped. Noah's fifth movie in three years started filming in ten days.

Meggie wanted Trey to stay with the uncles and stay with her till Labor Day. Lindsay did *not* want Trey to stay in Belle Coeur without them but she was afraid to tell him he couldn't. He was twenty years old, after all. She'd been terrified that if Trey stayed behind, Trey and Meggie would well-you-know the minute they left town. Noah didn't tell her he was pretty damn sure Trey and Meggie had already well-you-know about a billion times.

He kept his son supplied with condoms, warned him that if he ever told his mother *he* was the supplier he'd have to choke him. He also told Trey that if he *ever* failed to use one to protect Meggie he'd better be a man about it and take care of her or he'd choke him for that, too.

Noah put his shades on and leaned back on his elbows

next to his son. Trey's crossed ankles stretched about three inches past his.

"Where's Ma and Emma?" Trey asked.

"In the toilet, would be my guess," Noah said.

"Every time we come out here to surf they're in the can."

"It's a girl thing, sport. Get used to it."

"It's a pregnant girl thing." Trey slid his shades down his nose. "When are you guys gonna stop?"

"It's not me." Noah lifted his shades and looked at him. "It's your mother. I'm putty in her hands."

"Oh, right." Trey laughed. "This from Mr. Always Use a Condom."

"Your mother loves babies. I love your mother. I'm stuck between a rock and a hard place here. You talk to her."

"Oh right, and get decked. She'd have a shit fit if she knew you and I talked about this kind of stuff."

Noah lifted his shades again. "Language."

"Here they come," Trey said with a nod.

Lindsay and Emma. His wife and his daughter. Watching them stroll hand in hand through the surf curling gently up the beach now that the big boys had died down for the day took Noah's breath away. God, they were gorgeous. Lindsay, eight months pregnant. A floppy hat on her head, her free hand pressed to her belly, a print sarong wrapped over her swimsuit. Emma in her little red maillot and her cloud of dark, almost ebony hair. She had Noah's deep blue eyes and his mouth, Lindsay's chin and her cheekbones. The tiny white strands in the front of her hair had been there since the day she was born. What else could they name her but Emma?

"Ma looks tired." Trey hopped off the towel. "I'll get Em."

"I'll get your mother." Noah pushed to his feet and went with him.

Lindsay smiled when she saw them, her eyes lighting first on Noah, then on Trey. Little Em squealed with glee when her big brother dove at her, swooped her up, and swung her on his shoulders. Noah pressed his hands to Lindsay's abdomen and kissed her.

"Think you've had enough beach for one day, Mama Bear."

"Oh Noah." Lindsay lifted his hands from the watermelon it looked like she'd swallowed to her breasts, her nipples peaked and hard inside her maternity bra. "Oh God, these hormones. I want you so much."

She wanted him all the time, even more when she was pregnant. Just the sight of Noah trotting toward her, golden from the sun with sand glistening in his chest hair, was enough to swamp her with lust.

"Not in front of the children, princess." Noah grinned, massaged her breasts gently, and made her sigh. "Besides, the baby doesn't like it."

Emma hadn't minded Noah being inside her, but this baby hated it. He'd punch her in the ribs, kick her in the kidneys. While she lay panting from a stunning orgasm and wincing at the baby's displeasure, Noah would kiss and nuzzle her swollen belly, rub and caress till the baby settled. "Calm down, little sport," he'd murmur to her navel. "This is what put you there. Relax and enjoy the ride."

God, how she loved this man. Her husband, her lover, the father of her children. All her children. The DNA tests confirmed that Noah was Trey's father. He'd never tried to be his dad, just his pal. Now and then Trey would slip and call him Dad. Noah never made a big deal of it. He let it pass, let it slide, but Lindsay could tell by the sheen that came into his eyes how much it meant to him.

Giving her Noah to give her Trey, dear Mark to help her raise him while Noah couldn't, then giving Noah back to her to love her and give her Emma and this baby, was the best and most beautiful trick Chaos had ever played on her.

"Warning, Papa Bear," Lindsay said. "I think I'm going to look like a whale after this one."

"Don't worry, gorgeous." Noah kissed her. "I'll work it off you."

"Promise?" Lindsay felt her stomach flutter, the baby kick. "Even if I'm a blob of baby fat?"

"You won't be for long." He laughed and grinned. "Promise."

Emma helped Trey roll up the towels, take down the umbrella Lindsay sat under, fold up the beach chairs. Noah pitched in and they hauled the gear up the beach toward the conversion van he'd bought. It had a nice wide berth in the back for Lindsay, room for the boards, room for Emma's toys. Looked like a cavalry maneuver when they came here to surf. It would be worse when the baby came. Noah was thinking about buying a trailer for all the crap he'd have to haul.

"Daddy?" Emma piped up when they were halfway to Malibu. "Can I surf when we get home?"

"Ask Mommy," Noah said. "She's the boss."

"Mommy?" Emma popped her head around her seat. "Can I surf when we get home?"

"Yes, Em. If Daddy feels like it."

"Daddy. Do you feel like it?"

"You bet, sugarpuss."

"Mommy. Will you watch me surf?"

"Yes, Emma, sweetie." Lindsay yawned. "I'll watch you surf."

The check Noah Senior gave him when he'd flown to L.A. to kill Vivienne paid for a big chunk of their house in Malibu. Lindsay sold her condo in Telluride to cover the rest. The house had white carpet and teak woodwork, glass all across the back. Noah could see the ocean from every room. It wasn't his house, the one he remembered, but Lindsay had done her best to copy it.

Emma fell asleep but woke up when Noah opened the garage door. Donnie's big old pickup with Missouri plates sat next to Noah's Corvette, a 1956 classic, black with white slashes on the sides. The blue-as-Lindsay's-eyes Corvette lived in Belle Coeur. Noah had given it to Trey on his sixteenth birthday and had bought himself another one. Ferrari red. He'd put flame decals on the side that made Lindsay laugh.

Since Trey had opted not to stay in Belle Coeur, Donnie and Lonnie had driven out for a visit. The uncles loved the stretch of beach behind the house. The places where he and Trey went to surf—or Noah went to surf and Trey went to fall off his board—where the breakers roared toward shore like bulls in rut scared the piss out of them. They stayed home and played pinochle.

Lonnie had dinner ready. Coq au vin and crème brûlée, Lindsay's favorites. Pyewacket was curled on one of the kitchen barstools. Lindsay scratched his ears, gave Lonnie a kiss on the cheek, and burst into tears. Lonnie shot Noah a distressed look.

"It's okay, Lon," Noah told him. "It's just hormones."

On their honeymoon Lindsay had explained Chaos to him. Noah thought it was bullshit, but it seemed to mean something to her. 'Nother one of those things you had to have the right hormones for.

No such luck that Emma would forget about surfing. "Come on, Daddy. Come on. Come on, Mommy. Come on." She grabbed their hands and towed them toward the pool.

Noah eased Lindsay into a chaise and kissed her. "Okay?"

"Fine." She puffed out a breath, slipped on her shades, and stuffed her hat on her head. "You may have to get a crane to pull me up."

"When you've had enough, say so." He kissed her again.

Lindsay had his heart and his soul, Emma his spirit and his love of the water. Lindsay wouldn't let him take her out in the surf on a board yet, but surfing in the pool Emma loved. She stood bright-eyed on the edge with her floaties on her upper arms while he pitched one of his boards in the water and straddled it, lifted her onto it between his knees and paddled her around.

"Mommy, look!" Emma flung her arms out, feet spread, knees bent, hips just so like she'd seen Noah do a thousand times. "I'm surfing!"

Lindsay slid her shades down her nose, tipped up the brim of her hat, and applauded. "Yea! Mommy's beautiful little surfer girl!"

Oh Christ. There was an image. His baby daughter, grown-up and gorgeous in a bikini. With Lindsay's genes she'd be a stunner. She'd leave tongues hanging in her wake. Maybe Ezra would loan him Lucille.

Uncle Lonnie came to get Emma for her nap. Her eyes lit when he clapped his hands and held them out to her. Noah paddled her to the side, Lonnie lifted her onto his shoulders, and away they went. Noah pulled himself out off the pool and picked up a towel. Mama Bear was sound asleep in her chaise. God how he loved her.

Noah kissed her awake. Lindsay curved her hands around the wet back of his neck and smiled. "C'mon, Moby. You need a nap, too."

"That's a nice name." Lindsay grunted as he pulled her up.

"You're the one who said you look like a whale."

Lindsay's eyes flashed. "Don't start with me, Noah."

Hormones. Jesus. He coaxed her into their bedroom and laid her on the bed, put a pillow under her knees while he opened the doors to the deck that led down to the beach. The roll and *whoosh* of the surf seeped into the room and Lindsay sighed. Worked every time.

Noah sat down at her feet and rubbed her puffy ankles. Jo Beth had shown him a few tricks that usually made Lindsay purr. Today they made her snore. He grinned, laughed softly, and kept rubbing.

Emma had not been happy when Lindsay told her she was pregnant, that Daddy had put another baby in her tummy. His own eyes had flashed at Noah from his daughter's face as she'd spun on him.

"Why, Daddy?" She flung a hand at Lindsay's only slightly poofy belly. "Why'd you do that?" Then she burst into sobbing, wailing, heart-rending tears. "You said I was your baby!"

Noah had fallen on his knees in front of her, stricken. Lindsay cocked a "See? You spoil her" eyebrow at him. He'd pulled Emma into his arms, felt her tears on his shoulder. Christ. What had he been thinking to let Lindsay lure him inside her without a condom? Having glorious, mind-blowing sex with his gorgeous wife, getting her pregnant, watching her belly swell. God that turned him on. He'd had no idea it would break his daughter's heart.

He shot Lindsay a "Help me" look. She waved her hands in front of her and backed away shaking her head, an unh-huh-pal-you-made-this-mess-you-clean-it-up glint in her eyes. He finally got Emma calmed down enough to listen to him.

"Here's the deal, sugarpuss. This baby is a boy. His name

is, uh—" He looked at Lindsay again. They hadn't decided yet. She turned her back on him. "His name is Whosits."

"Whosits?" Emma giggled. "That's a silly name."

"That's just his name while he's in Mommy's tummy. I put my ear to Mommy's tummy and he told me to tell you that he was coming here—" oh, bad choice of words "—to be your brother."

"I've got a brother." Emma glared. "I don't want another one."

"But you need another one, sugarpuss. When Trey graduates and gets a job he won't be around all the time, so Whosits is stepping in to take over for Trey. He told me to tell you that he'll be littler than you for a while, but that pretty soon he'll be big and strong. He'll have muscles like Daddy—" Lindsay rolled her eyes. "—and he'll be your pal and your buddy and if anybody tries to take your toys he'll hit 'em in the eye."

Lindsay was glaring at him. Noah could feel it but he was working without a net here. Emma tipped her head at him, calculating.

"Will Whosits hit anybody I want in the eye?"

"You'll need a really good reason."

"Mommy." Emma spun toward Lindsay. "Can I talk to the baby?"

"Sure, sweetie." Lindsay sat in a chair, drew Emma between her knees. Emma bent her head and yelled at Lindsay's tummy. "Hey you! Whosits! You better hit anybody I want in the eye right when I say or I'll punch you in your head!"

Then she'd flounced away to her room, her nose in the air. Noah grabbed Lindsay to keep her from falling on the floor laughing.

"Well," he said. "She seems to have the whole brother-sister dynamic thing down."

The sister-sister dynamic between Lindsay and Jolie hadn't changed one iota. Jolie was in L.A. with Vivienne, but they rarely saw her when they were out here. She was far too busy writing scripts and directing for HBO. At the moment Spawn of Satan was in Belle Coeur, supervising the season for Lindsay and Noah. They were holding the barn in trust for Trey. His major was Theater Arts and he wanted the Belle Coeur Theatre.

"Noah," Lindsay said sleepily. "I want to have another baby."

"That's good to hear since you're about to give birth to one."

"I mean another baby after this one."

"Jesus, princess." Noah looked at her over his shoulder. "How much to-do you think your ankles can take?"

"*No-ah.*" Lindsay pushed up on her elbows and glared at him over the mound of her belly. "I told you I wanted babies. You said spread your legs and let's get started."

"You were naked. I'd agree to anything when you're naked."

"We can afford it, Noah."

"We can afford the Taj Mahal but it'd be a helluva commute."

"This is the best time of my life, Noah." Lindsay's bottom lip quavered. "I love being pregnant. I love giving you babies."

"Princess. C'mon." He put her foot down, turned around on the edge of the bed to face her. "I'd like to kick these brats out of here someday and spend the rest of my life making love to you without worrying that I'm knocking you up again."

"Brats. Oh yes. The brats." Lindsay looked down her nose at him, one eyebrow arched. "Precious little sugar-puss. You're worse with Trey. You drop him at Berkeley and you cry all the way home. Don't tell me you don't. I find tear-stained Kleenex stuffed in the glove box."

"Christ, Lindsay. I'll be forty-four. How much longer do you think I'll be able to get it up?"

"Oh *please*," she said disgustedly. "We'll have to break it off to close the lid on the coffin."

"Okay. All right. You win." Noah gave up. "I'll give you one more baby. But you tell Emma somebody else put it in there."

Since Lonnie cooked, he and Trey cleaned up the kitchen and loaded the dishwasher. Then Noah went upstairs and leaned a shoulder on the wall outside Emma's room.

He listened to Lindsay read Emma her bedtime story. *Big Al,* about the biggest, ugliest fish in the ocean. Emma patted Lindsay's tummy, rubbed circles, and talked to Whosits. She told him they had his room ready, that she'd helped Mommy buy Pampers and toys. Some of those toys she really liked so he'd better not cry when she played with them.

When Lindsay told her good night and kissed her, it was his turn. Emma's eyes lit when he came through the door. She sat up and flung her arms out. "Daddy!"

Noah went to his knees next to her bed and kissed her. Emma fell back on the pillow dragging him with her, her arms around his neck.

"Daddy. Mommy says I'm going to preschool here in Cafilornia while you're making up your movie."

"That's the plan, sugarpuss. Mommy's taking you to visit your new school tomorrow. Did she tell you?"

"Will you take me to my school every day?"

"Sure will, sugarpuss. On my way to making up my movie."

"And will you kiss me good-bye?"

Noah wagged his eyebrows. "Mmmhmm."

"Daddy." Emma giggled, then eyed him soberly, put her little hands on his face like her mother did when she wanted his attention or she wanted him in bed. "Will you do me something?"

"Anything." Noah buried his face in her tummy, breathed the scent of her skin and felt his heart swell. Then he raised his head and grinned. "What, sugarpuss?"

"When you kiss me at my school and you tell me good-bye don't call me sugarpuss. I'm not a baby, Daddy. Mommy says Whosits is the baby now and that I'm a big school girl."

"Oh Papa Bear." Lindsay pressed a sympathetic kiss to his mouth when he came out of Emma's room. The brush of her huge belly made him stir. "No more sugarpuss."

"Ow." Noah put a hand over his heart. "You could've warned me."

Lindsay shrugged. "It just came up."

"So did something else." Noah took her hand and let her feel.

"Dad-dy." Lindsay purred in her throat. "Come with me. I'll kiss that and make it all better."

She did, too, wondrously and magically. Then she fell asleep. Noah tucked Lindsay in, gave her and Whosits a kiss and checked on Emma. Donnie and Lonnie were passed out snoring in front of the TV in the family room. Trey went out to hang with some of his Berkeley buds.

Noah pulled on a sweater, rolled up his pant legs, slipped out through the bedroom and sat on the beach in the moonlight, knees up, arms looped around them, listening to the surf. This was his chill-out time, just him and the ocean at the end of the day. It wasn't the Pacific that kept him sane anymore; it was Lindsay and the kids. Trey and Emma, the baby boy who was due any day, and now, Christ help him, one more. Noah was pretty sure he could get up for it.

Seven years he'd been sober. He never thought about tequila, couldn't even remember what it tasted like.

Noah wrote his name in the sand with his index finger. When the surf washed it away he got up and went inside, took off his clothes, and slipped into bed naked. He spooned around Lindsay and felt her sigh, the baby kick beneath his palm. Noah smiled and fell asleep with his wife and his second-born son cradled in his arms.

Author's Note

When I was a young and foolish writer I swore there were two things I would never write a book about—a cowboy and a secret baby. Especially a secret baby. Why? Because it's never truly a complete secret and how could you ever make it one?

Most writers are smart enough not to say things like this. Our brains are programmed to play "What if?" To take the impossible and make it happen. I came up with the secret part okay, but then I got stuck on how to reveal it.

Till I remembered the jet-black streak of hair in our oldest son Christopher's otherwise perfectly blond head. Underneath, near the crown. Just like Trey's. So thank you, Chris. Thank you, son.

While I'm at it, I should thank my husband Michael, the funniest man in the known universe. I've been stealing this guy's jokes for years. (Keep 'em coming, honey. I've got another book to write.)

Our youngest son, Paul, can't find his way out of a walk-in closet. Just like Noah. So thank you, Paul, and I'm sorry Dad and I cursed you with the initials PMS. We were young and not into acronyms.

Thanks to Nancy Haddock, Cynthia Tady, and Ruth Scofield Schmidt, for reading along as I wrote *Return Engagement* and telling me where I zigged when I should've zagged. To Leslie Russell for reading the finished manuscript. To Dovie Jacoby for inspiring Lindsay's Aunt Dovey. Special thanks to my editor, Charlotte Herscher, fellow cat lover. A chin scratch and a tummy rub to every feline I've ever known for Pyewacket.

Oh, boy. Now I can hardly wait for the cowboy to show up.